off the record

D0460503

Books by Elizabeth White

Fair Game

Fireworks

Prairie Christmas

Sweet Delights

The Texas Gatekeepers

1 | *Under Cover of Darkness*

2 | *Sounds of Silence*

3 | *On Wings of Deliverance*

off the record

elizabeth white

ZONDERVAN.com/
AUTHORTRACKER
follow your favorite authors

Off the Record
Copyright © 2007 by Elizabeth White

Requests for information should be addressed to:

Zondervan, *Grand Rapids, Michigan 49530*

Library of Congress Cataloging-in-Publication Data

White, Elizabeth.
    Off the record / Elizabeth White.
       p. cm.
    ISBN-10: 0-310-27304-8
    ISBN-13: 978-0-310-27304-2
    1. Women judges—Alabama—Fiction. 2. Reporters and reporting—Fiction.
    3. Political campaigns—Fiction. 4. Political fiction. I. Title.
    PS3623.H574O34 2007
    813'.6—dc22

                                                   2007013708

Published in association with the literary agency of Alive Communications, Inc., 7680 Goddard Street, Suite 200, Colorado Springs, CO 80920.

Interior design by Melissa Elenbaas

Printed in the United States of America

07 08 09 10 11 12 13 • 10 9 8 7 6 5 4 3 2 1

*For Tammy, who has been there
since the beginning.*

Acknowledgments

One of my favorite parts of the publication process is giving credit where credit is due. I'll start with the night at El Chico when my husband, Scott, and my son, Ryan, helped me brainstorm the initial story. Thanks, guys! I also wish to thank my growing list of prayer warriors who prayed me through the writing of this story. You know who you are. And I deeply appreciate my extended family who supports me with emails, phone calls, and prayer. I love you.

I'm grateful for my agent, Beth Jusino, who connected me and *Off the Record* with the fine folks at Zondervan. My editors, Leslie Peterson and Becky Shingledecker, have been a joy to work with. As always, *mi amigo* Tammy Thompson provided a sounding board for plot ideas and character development — and of course a lot of the lawyer stuff.

Research for this book was fun and educational. Retired political campaign strategist Ed Ewing granted me access to his vast experience and resources, introducing me to a variety of knowledgeable and talented people. I spent a cold February day in our Alabama state capital, Montgomery, firing question after question about the election process, which Ed answered with generosity and great good humor. He is a gifted writer and storyteller in his own right, and a true man of God. The Angel Food outreach of his church, Frazier Memorial Methodist in Montgomery (with a little inspiration from my own church in Mobile), is the prototype for Gilly's PBJ ministry. My thanks also go to Ed's longtime friend, Mary Edge Horton, who granted us a private tour of the Alabama Judicial Building. The tour included a fascinating lesson in the history and daily operation of Alabama's court system.

I'd like to express my appreciation to Mobile attorneys Andy and Linda Clausen—talented lawyers, good neighbors, great friends—who answered legal questions related to the story. Also, my writer-buddy Donna Harris assisted with details related to a journalist's career. Sheila Morgan, a new friend who lives part-time in NYC, did some legwork to make sure my hero's apartment wound up in an appropriate place. Thanks, Sheila. Hats off as well to Shelley Brigman, historian of the famed Boll Weevil Monument in Enterprise, Alabama, who tracked down the bug's weight for me. Not everybody has such an interesting a job.

Last but not least, I'd like to thank Mobile Judge Rosemary DeJuan Chambers, who graciously allowed me to sit in her courtroom last summer, observing. Judge Chambers is a woman of compassion and common sense, as well as a gifted mediator and a dedicated public servant. I was honored that over lunch she answered my questions with intelligence and sensitivy. No confidences were broken, but I came away with a great respect for the responsibility of the judicial branch of our government.

The Boll Weevil Monument of Enterprise is very real. In fact, there are two of them—the original is in the museum, and a replica stands in the town plaza. For more information on Alabama curiosities, check out www.al.com/alabamiana/index. ssf?wacky.html.

The Water Street Mission is based on several ministries currently serving the homeless in downtown Mobile. Wings of Life and the Salvation Army are two I know of that do a great job. Donations are welcome. Check them out on the web at: www. americanfamilyfunds.com/dovefoundation/index.php and www. redshield.org/us/al/mobile/.

Zuzu's Fish Shack came out of my imagination, but there's plenty of good seafood and music on the Mobile Causeway. You haven't lived until you've had gumbo with a side of garlic cheese grits!

There really is an Alabama Chicken and Egg Festival in Moulton (northern Alabama), as well as a Peanut Festival in Dothan (southern Alabama). Haven't been to either yet, but they're on my list of events to take in soon. Bluegrass concerts are a popular form of entertainment in our state, and there are several good festivals going on in the summer. Y'all come!

One final note: when this story was first conceived, Alabama had yet to elect a female supreme court chief justice (though there have been highly qualified women serving as associate justices). Interestingly, just as I was finishing the manuscript, Judge Sue Bell Cobb was elected as our first female chief justice, making history.

chapter 1

Early November

Laurel Kincade, surrounded by reporters in the rotunda of the Alabama Judicial Building, suddenly understood her great-great grandmother's propensity to shoot Yankee invaders on sight and ask questions later.

How was she supposed to remember the most important speech of her life with *him* hulking in their midst like a Great Dane infiltrating a pack of Jack Russell terriers?

Okay, so Coleman Davis McGaughan IV—having burst upon this mortal coil some thirty years earlier in a Tupelo, Mississippi, delivery room—couldn't technically be called a Yankee. And if the threadbare khakis were anything to go by, Cole had somehow mislaid his family carpetbag full of filthy lucre. One might also note that under the tweed sport coat hugging those defensive-end shoulders, there was no place to hide a gun.

Still. He'd spent the last two years in New York City (never mind how Laurel knew that) and marched onto her turf toting notepad and Bic pen. This, in her experience, could be infinitely more dangerous than a gun.

As a southern woman, hyperbole was her birthright. *Yankee invader.*

Outwardly as cool as the Italian marble beneath her feet, Laurel looked up at the white dome soaring overhead. *God, please give me strength.* The weight of the occasion, its historic significance, mashed her insides to pudding. She wasn't the first woman to declare candidacy for Alabama Supreme Court chief justice, but she could be the first one to win.

Unless Cole was here to make trouble.

Behind the crowd of supporters gathered for Laurel's campaign launch, a few reporters from Alabama's backbone papers — the *Montgomery Advertiser*, the *Birmingham News*, the *Mobile Register*, the *Huntsville Times* — as well as the wire services, stood in a circumspect clump, shuffling cameras, PDAs, and recorders. Cole was the only one she recognized from out-of-state.

Laurel checked her watch. It was almost time for her speech. She adjusted the tail of her navy pinstripe suit jacket, though it already hung with razor military precision. People expected a judge to look sober, so she bought designer suits in the Boutique at Stein Mart, where she could get a good fit for ... okay, face it, her *statuesque* figure.

Which was one reason the six-foot-four Neanderthal had managed to pull her under.

Ignore him, sister, Renata would say. Not worth a wasted brain cell. Her best friend and campaign manager, standing over by the entrance to the law library with Laurel's family, caught her glancing at the dark-haired giant at the back of the press pack. Though Laurel and Renata went all the way back to a dorm room at Spring Hill College, after graduation they'd gone their separate ways, and Laurel had always kept to herself what happened with Cole.

Therefore, Renata's brown eyes widened, not in recognition, but because Cole still had that inexplicable something. Charisma.

Never pretty-boy handsome, he had a way of tucking his chin, brows knit over eyes like raw magnesium. A ragged white scar, new since the last time she'd seen him, cut into his upper lip and veered upward across his left cheekbone. And he still had a gladiator stance that dared men to take him on and women to try to tame him.

Renata raised her eyebrows at Laurel and fanned her face. Then, with a little smirk, she tapped her watch.

Debate team training took over. Gathering herself, Laurel took a breath, released it, and stepped up to the mike. "I'd like to thank everyone for coming out to support me today. My decision to run for chief justice wasn't made lightly, though many will be surprised to learn that it's been in my plans since I was young."

The irony wasn't lost on her. Some would claim that, as the youngest woman ever to run for supreme court, she didn't have enough judicial experience to handle the job. But she'd worked and planned and kept her nose firmly to the grindstone to get here. Smart voters would recognize that youth and femininity didn't equate to stupidity.

She glanced at Cole, fumbled for her notes, and remembered she'd left them in the hotel room. Her photographic memory had blanked as if erased by acid.

Don't look at him again. Cold sweat ran between her breasts. She looked down at her hands gripping the edges of the lectern.

A camera flashed. She looked up and found a cameraman standing next to Cole lowering a big zoom lens. He elbowed Cole and stepped back.

Blinking against red and yellow spots, she lifted her chin.

In return, Cole raised his pen: a silent toast—or more likely a challenge. *Go ahead, baby, let's see what you're made of.*

She jerked her gaze off him and looked at her grandfather, who smiled his pride and encouragement. The next line of her speech clicked back into place. "I'm honored to come from a family with a rich tradition of public service, beginning with my grandparents and continuing with my parents. They have supported me, encouraged me, taught me, and presented me with incomparable examples of hard work, faith, and personal integrity.

"These are the values that have undergirded the laws of our country and our state from their inception, and these are the values that will guide me as I seek this critical judicial post."

Once she got rolling, the words flowed. She'd practiced. She'd prayed. Didn't matter what Cole was up to. God was in charge of this whole thing.

She hoped.

"Judge Kincade looks nervous," said Matt Hogan with unnecessary relish.

"Nervous? I don't think she looks particularly nervous." Cole surreptitiously stepped in front of Hogan's camera. Laurel might be famous for nerves of steel, but she was definitely distracted. He'd known it might not be a good idea to show up like this without warning.

"You said you could get an interview with her." Hogan lowered the camera, more interested in excavating Laurel's checkered past than taking her picture. "Have you arranged it yet?"

"I just flew in this morning. Give me time."

"We don't have time to waste." Hogan's whisper took on an aggrieved tone. "I've been here a week and haven't found out diddly about any dirty little skeleton in her closet—at least nothing we can document."

"Have you considered the possibility that she might be as clean as she claims to be?" The question had to be asked.

Hogan gave him a yeah-right look. "We're talking southern politics here."

Cole sighed. "Point taken. Now shut up so I can take notes." He leaned away from the column behind him to stare at Laurel. Half the copper-laced mahogany hair was twisted in a complicated knot on top of her head, with the rest swirling in fiery waves past her shoulders. She'd always worn it that way, and he wondered if she knew how telling it was—softness and passion under that tightly controlled persona.

He forced his pen across the paper as he listened.

Neutral umpire on any dispute to come before her court.

He couldn't help remembering the last time they were in the same room. She'd told him not to color her world until Jesus came back—at which time he'd undoubtedly be bound for that place of weeping, wailing, and gnashing of teeth anyway.

Editor of Law Review, *clerk for Eleventh Circuit Court of Appeals, youngest partner in firm history, state attorney general's staff, well-rounded lawyer with extensive experience in the state court system.*

She'd gained a little weight, filled out into womanly curves that catapulted images across his brain like Rockettes in a Christmas Eve show. *Oh, Lord, help me out here.*

Would interpret the law, not legislate it; loved the judicial process and promised to bring experience, leadership, and integrity to Alabama's highest court.

Hogan and his buddy Field would crucify her if they found out the truth.

He felt a sharp jab in his ribcage and looked down.

Hogan was peering at Cole's notepad. "You writing an article or drawing her portrait?"

Cole looked down, realized he'd been sketching instead of taking notes, and flipped to a clean page. "Go over there and listen in on her family. The old man with the cane—that's her grandfather, Judge Gillian. The middle-aged couple are her parents."

Hogan perked up, a hound on a scent. "I'll meet you back here after the speech."

Cole was left alone to take notes like a good boy.

Laurel would make a fine justice. She'd been the only one of her law school friends with a lick of common sense—as if he'd cared about her brain back then. The evening he met her at a university picnic, she'd been sitting at the edge of the group, a fine queenly decorum in the turned-up corners of that lush mouth. He couldn't quit staring at it—beautiful and unglossed in the natural deep rose that came from her high Scots coloring. Then she'd spiked his guns with her humor, and he'd felt like a kid slammed in the gut with a volleyball. The fact that he could still remember that moment was a measure of its impact, considering his brain had been half pickled with a six-pack of Budweiser.

"I thank you all for coming out today." Laurel beamed her warm smile, and the cameras took advantage of it. Flashes went off everywhere. "I look forward to the upcoming campaign with great excitement and anticipation."

An enthusiastic cheer erupted. As the applause faded, several reporters vied for her attention. Laurel good-naturedly ignored them.

Until Cole stuck his hand in the air. "Excuse me, Ms. Kincade! Judge Kincade, I'm sorry. I have a couple of questions."

Laurel froze in the act of removing the mike attached to her lapel. Her beautiful, elegant head turned his way. "I'm sorry, I wasn't planning to—"

"I won't keep you long." He let his voice slide into the familiar southern cadence he'd worked hard to eradicate. Charm, his stock in trade. "I'm from the *Daily Journal* in New York."

One fine line creased Laurel's milky brow. "You may call my campaign manager and request an appointment." Her smile gave him a private warning.

"I promise, just a couple of questions."

A young black woman in long, complicated braids and a designer suit, who seemed to function as some kind of personal assistant, stepped close to Laurel. "Sure, we can take just one or two," she said.

Laurel gave her a "thanks a lot" glare, then grabbed the lectern and swallowed. "All right."

They stared at one another for a long moment. Somebody in the crowd coughed.

He cleared his throat. "All right, then. Your grandfather, Judge Gillian, was involved in the Ten Commandments issue back in 2004—when the Alabama chief justice was impeached for refusing to remove the monument from this very building. Tell us how that will affect your interpretation of the Constitution regarding religion."

Laurel's grip on the lectern relaxed. "My grandfather, as much as I love and respect him, will not be seated behind this bench. My decisions have always been my own and are solely based on Alabama law." She smiled faintly. "They always will be."

"Um, that's good." He jerked his gaze away from Laurel and cased her family.

Judge Gillian didn't seem to recognize him. Silver head poised like a hawk, the old man proudly watched his granddaughter handle this unexpected inquisition. Laurel's parents, Dodge and Frances Kincade, were lined up in front of the library, in solidarity with several other people Cole had never seen.

There was so much he hadn't had time to learn about Laurel.

He glanced at Hogan, who was making circular "keep going" motions. But Cole didn't want to antagonize Laurel.

"You said two questions. Do you have another?" Laurel was back in control, smiling and confident, ready to walk off with her family and supporters.

"Yes. Yes, I do." His voice jackknifed off the marble of the rotunda. "Actually I have several more questions, Judge Kincade. Would you like to have dinner with me tonight?"

"One has to admire that young man's nerve." Her grandfather, affectionately nicknamed "Fafa," handed Laurel a tray and waited for her to collect her silverware. "Quite the bold tactician."

The Commerce Café, located in the Center for Commerce a few blocks down from the Judicial Building, was nothing fancy but was quite the weekday place to see and be seen. Laurel often had lunch here when in Montgomery on business trips.

She snatched a container of coleslaw at random from the salad array. Her hand still shook so hard that the bowl rattled against the tray. "I can't believe he asked me out in front of all those people."

Actually she could believe it. It was just like Cole to go for what he wanted without concern for the consequences. What was completely out of character was the fact that he'd let his interview go with just the one question—well, technically two, if you counted the dinner invitation. When she'd stared at him, openmouthed and speechless, he'd backed off, lips curved, leaving her to face a barrage of laughter.

Pretending to find the humor in the situation, she'd smiled and removed the microphone with a dry, "I think I'm going to recuse myself."

But Fafa's patent curiosity wasn't any laughing matter. Avoiding his gaze, she moved to the entrée kiosk. "Catfish, please," she told the server. Most of the world's ills would be cured if all its bottom-feeding scavengers were fried to a crisp and served with hushpuppies.

If she weren't such a big chicken, she'd have taken Cole on right there in the rotunda; tried to find out what he was doing down here. Instead she'd ducked out, letting Renata and Fafa carry her off for a celebratory lunch with the family.

They clustered around a table by the window looking out on downtown Montgomery. Daddy had already taken off his suit coat and loosened his tie—"left-wing Communist inventions," he always called them with a wink, ignoring the fact that Communists had gone out of style with stirrup pants and shoulder pads.

Her father got up and pulled out Laurel's chair as she approached the table. "Here's our woman of the hour. Appetite come back yet?"

"More or less." She never could get food down before a big speech. And this had been one of the biggest of her life. She sat down and opened her napkin. "Where's Mom?"

"I think she went to powder her nose." Daddy gave her a searching look. "What's the matter? You knocked their socks off, little girl. You're a shoo-in."

"Daddy. The media thinks I'm a spoiled, ultraconservative rich girl with too many political antecedents and not enough experience. Didn't you hear that question from—" She stopped. She shouldn't have brought up Cole.

Sure enough, Renata, seated across from her, joined the fray. "You mean the dinner invitation? I don't know what's the matter with you, Laurel. You should've jumped on it. Jumped on him." She laughed. "Whichever came first."

Laurel frowned. "Renata—"

"You are so prissy." Renata sighed. "But he sure was cute, in a Russell Crowe kind of way."

Fafa bent an indulgent smile on Renata. "You've got the right idea, sugar. Best way to handle the press is to give them the old soft soap. Let 'em think you're rattled, and they'll hound you to kingdom come." He picked up his tea glass and jiggled the ice. "Which is why I sent your mama back over to the Judicial Building."

The gargoyle of impending doom that had crouched on Laurel's shoulder since meeting Cole's hot silver-gray eyes suddenly swooped down and took a chunk out of her stomach. "Fafa, what have you done?"

"Honey, a New York paper wants an interview, and we need all the name recognition we can get. Your mama lived in NYC for three years. She'll know how to talk to him." Fafa sipped his tea, then dabbed his white mustache with a napkin. "She can give him your statistics and background and sell you like a Prada handbag."

At one time Laurel might have objected to the auction block terminology. At the moment she was more worried about what Cole might say to her mother. She pleated her napkin. By the world's standards she hadn't done anything so terrible; besides, it had happened a long time ago. The problem was she'd very publicly set herself above the world's standards—back in law school days and certainly in her recent career as a public servant.

Laurel Josephine Kincade—family values candidate.

She pushed away from the table. "I've got to go talk to him."

Renata's smile leaped out. "I knew it."

"Stay and finish your lunch." Daddy patted her hand. "I'm sure he'll call your office later—"

"I'm not hungry." She picked up the plate of cooling catfish. Too bad to waste it. Too bad about a lot of things.

Leaving the uneaten food on the conveyor belt, she pushed through the café door and stopped in the deserted lobby. Tracking down her mother would be easy enough. She fumbled for her cell phone, then hesitated.

Seeing Cole like this—out of the blue after all these years— was shocking. She'd thought to never lay eyes on him again, had managed to put all that behind her and move on. Okay, maybe she hadn't committed to another relationship since then, but at least she'd tried. Several times. One day there was going to be some-body who would measure up to that staggering infatuation she'd encountered and lost with Cole.

One thing was clear from the jellified state of her knees. She wasn't ready to confront him. She needed time to get her head together first. Talk to the Lord. There might not be an immediate solution to her problem, but he would bring her through some-how. Look how far she'd come. Look what she was on the verge of accomplishing.

"Laurel! Sweetie, what are you doing out here by yourself?"

Laurel jerked around. Her mother was coming up the stairs from outside. "Mom! I was just about to call—"

As if in slow motion, she caught sight of the figure ascending behind her mother. Cole, in tow like a trained bear on a chain. The impulse to dive under the nearest sofa translated into smoothing her skirt.

"Look who I brought to lunch!" Hooking an arm through Cole's, Mom charged across the lobby, Linda Pritcher sandals clicking against the tile.

Laurel thought of her junior year of high school when her par-ents had arranged for the pastor's son to invite her to the prom. They'd paid for the tickets and rented his tux, and she wouldn't be surprised to discover they'd bought her corsage too. Some things never changed.

"How are you?" she managed, then smiled at her mother. "Daddy and the others are waiting for us inside the cafeteria."

"In a minute, darlin'." Her mother's southern-belle charm lay in almost visible droplets on her still dewy skin. "I want you to meet Cole McGaughan. It turns out he's not really from New York after all. He grew up over in Tupelo, just like Elvis—" Mom actu-ally giggled—"and graduated from Ole Miss not too long after you were there in law school. Isn't that a coincidence?"

"Yes, ma'am, it's downright amazing." Laurel met Cole's eyes again. Dense piercing gray, they burned her straight through.

Then his voice rumbled, deeper than she'd remembered, shaking her. "You've been mighty kind, Mrs. Frances, but I wonder if I could have a little time alone with Judge Kincade." An infinitesimal wink appeared to delight Laurel's mother.

Mom pretended to think. "I don't see a problem with that."

"No!" Laurel nearly shouted. "I mean—we could do an interview some other time." Some other time when her family was nowhere around. Judging by her mother's demeanor, so far Cole hadn't brought up past indiscretions. Likely he was waiting to get Laurel alone and then dump the whole load.

And what did you say to the man who'd taken your virginity as if it were a free sucker at the bank?

c h a p t e r   2

Laurel looked like she might come unglued, and Cole almost felt sorry for her. She probably thought he was here to blackmail her or pull some other devious stunt. She'd never believe he was here to protect her. And so far she hadn't let him near enough to tell her.

Frances Kincade put on a tiny frown. "Don't be difficult, Laurel. There's no time like the present."

"Mother." Laurel was smiling, but there was panic in her eyes. "I don't want to leave everybody hanging. This is supposed to be a family time."

The implication being that Cole, most assuredly not family, was unwelcome.

He gave her a measured look and buttoned his jacket. Fine. If she wanted him gone, he'd leave her to Hogan's mercies.

But Frances took his arm. "Nonsense. The more the merrier, I always say." She smiled up at Cole. "Come join us. I want you to meet my husband and my father, Judge Gillian. He was quite the political mover and shaker in his day."

Cole made up his mind. *In like Flynn.* Ignoring Laurel's muffled gasp, he grinned at the grande dame. "I'd be honored."

Frances Kincade might be the quintessential steel magnolia, Cole thought, but the blossom didn't fall far from the tree. To his amusement, Laurel marched into the café ahead of her mother and planted herself at the head of her family's table.

Head up, she gestured toward Cole. "Daddy, Fafa, Renata— this is Cole McGaughan. He's here from New York to cover the supreme court race."

Cole held a chair for Frances Kincade as she seated herself like the Queen of England, then shook hands with Laurel's father. Her grandfather sent a startled look from Cole to Laurel, who gave a tiny shake of her head. The old man frowned but took Cole's hand in a surprisingly strong grip. The young black woman who'd interceded for him in the rotunda gave him a blatant once-over, which he returned with a civil nod.

"Cole, this is Renata Castleberry, Laurel's campaign manager." Frances fluttered her fingers at her daughter. "Sit down, Laurel. You know how I hate it when you tower over everybody."

Laurel hesitated, then chose a seat next to her father, as far away from Cole as the rectangular table allowed. Cole took the only empty chair, across from Renata.

"How nice to see a young man with such exquisite manners," cooed Frances. "They don't teach that in New York. When I sang with the Met, we girls would have to fight to get a place at the table. And get a man to hold a chair? Glory, you might as well wish for the moon."

"Fraternity etiquette classes paid off, I guess," Cole said, ignoring the diva's narcissistic conversational ploy. Laurel hadn't acknowledged any previous acquaintance, apparently had never told her family about him or even showed his picture. Not one of them—with the exception of Judge Gillian—showed any sign of recognizing him. Despite the accident that had scarred his face, he didn't think he'd changed all that much. "Thanks for letting me barge in on a family gathering, Judge Kincade," he said evenly. "I would've been happy with an interview at a later date."

She looked away, expression guarded. "I'm afraid I don't have time for another interview. I have to get back to Mobile for court in the morning."

Clearly he was on sufferance here. "Then I'd better make the most of the time I have." He looked around the table and found every eye trained on him—an assortment of Kincade and Gillian eyes, all variations of Laurel in one way or another.

Frances, hyper and self-absorbed, was the least like her, though it was easy to see where Laurel's fine bone structure and dark eyes came from. Dodge had obviously bestowed the stillness, the common sense and humor lurking around the mouth. His thin hair was a faded auburn that must have been at one time the red-tinted dark brown of Laurel's thick mane.

The grandfather—Judge Gillian—was harder to peg. He was looking at Cole with a kink in his thick snowy brows. "That accent sounds like you might've been brought up somewhere in the South, boy. Where are your people from?"

Cole was certain the old man recognized more than his accent. "Good ear, sir. I'm from Mississippi. My father and his family still live in Tupelo, and my mother's in Hattiesburg."

"Divorce is such a blight on society." Frances sent her husband a flirtatious smile. "Dodge and I just celebrated our fortieth last month."

Laurel flushed. "Mother."

Frances blinked. "I didn't mean—"

"Never mind." Laurel sighed. "Mr. McGaughan, have you eaten? I'd be happy to treat you to lunch."

Mr. McGaughan. Nothing like starting over. But at least she was being polite. "I didn't come here for food." Her eyes widened, and he realized his adopted New York bluntness had been interpreted as a threat. "I mean, I'm not hungry." He and Hogan had grabbed a couple of breakfast burritos on the way to the courthouse this morning, and that would tide him over for a while.

Laurel was the only one of her family not eating—nervous over his presence, no doubt, but probably he shouldn't mention it. Food, the southern equivalent of love. "Thanks, though," he added belatedly, for the benefit of the Queen Mother.

Laurel stared at him for a moment. "All right." She ran her tongue across her lower lip. "Then what can I tell you that I didn't already cover in my speech?"

He flipped open his notebook and tried to ignore the fact that he was going to have to holler questions down the length of a six-foot table. "Let's start with this one. How is a thirty-two-year-old woman with less than two years of judicial experience qualified for the most important seat in the state's highest court?"

The espresso-colored eyes narrowed. "Hardball, huh?"

"Nothing like a good cliché to get the party started." He smiled, tapping his pen against the pad.

When Laurel hesitated, Renata butted in. "Judge Kincade has been preparing cases for trial since she got out of law school, many of which have gone before the state supreme court. She spent two years in the state attorney general's office, and the governor appointed her to her current judicial position in Mobile. Her experience has been concentrated and focused."

"Yeah." Cole waved a hand. "I got all that off the website. I want to know what's in your boss's heart and mind that's different from the other guys throwing a hat into the ring."

He met Laurel's eyes. He wanted to know what was in her heart and mind period. At the very beginning he'd lost a piece of the Laurel Kincade jigsaw puzzle and never found it.

Laurel laced her fingers together on top of the table. He noticed she had an antique cameo ring on the index finger of her right hand. No wedding band or engagement ring. "Well, for one thing, I've had a lot of experience dealing with the media. As you—" She stopped, continued smoothly, "I wrote for the *Daily Mississippian* while I was in law school, and I was media liaison for the attorney general. So when I say I'm tired of the mainstream press leading the judiciary around by the nose, I know what I'm talking about. It's time we started expecting judges to interpret the law and not rewrite it."

Cole scribbled, hiding a smile at her near blunder. "You don't think the media has a right to report what it sees? And comment on it?"

"Of course it does. But individual reporters shouldn't use their forum to scream when their personal beliefs differ from a judge's decision."

He looked at her hard, ignoring the fascinated gazes of her family and campaign manager. People at tables around them were listening as well. "Is your intent to reform the media, or the judiciary?"

She raised her brows. "Neither. My intent is to be the most competent and unbiased judge I can be."

Well, what had he expected her to say? He'd find out more about her from watching and listening than in an open confrontation in front of all these people. "Fair enough, Judge. Why don't you tell me a little bit about what you'll uniquely bring to the court as a woman? And don't give me that Dianne Feinstein look. People want to know how a young single lady deals with hardcore stuff like sex offenders, domestic violence, juvenile crime."

What he really wanted to know was how a woman who wouldn't undress in the light could listen to those cases without covering her eyes and ears. He found himself hungry to know her—where she'd been in the eight years they'd been apart, what she'd experienced, who she'd become friends with. It suddenly occurred to him that, despite the ringless hands, she probably at least had a boyfriend. A woman like her wouldn't have stayed single so long.

And he had no right to ask about it.

"Mr. McGaughan, as awful as those things are, I deal with them—as any judge would, male or female—with common sense and compassion and, in my case, a heavy reliance on my faith. Besides, I think I can safely say I'm not as sheltered as you seem to think. The voters would be amazed at the kind of people I've encountered."

The implication was that knowing *him* gave her insight into the worst of the worst. The gavel had come down. He wasn't going to get anything else out of her like this. No matter what she thought, he would never have stooped to blackmail, even in his BC—before Christ—days. And he sure wasn't about to do so now.

Still, if she imagined he would slink off like a whipped puppy, she *really* didn't know him.

"Judge Kincade, I think *I* can safely say you ain't seen nothin' yet."

Fafa accompanied Laurel to her car, parked in front of the old Scottish Rites Temple. A dirty-gray building, which had at different times housed both the state government's judicial branch and a brothel, it was one of the more interesting historical ironies forming the mythos of the state capital.

But right now she had her own historical irony to deal with. She braced herself for the inquisition.

"Are you going to explain what that fellow is doing down here?" Fafa opened the door of Laurel's red Maxima and fixed her with his trademark steely-eyed stare. He didn't mean it to be intimidating, but she always had to remind herself that she wasn't a felon facing his Yazoo County Circuit Court bench.

"Exactly what he said, Fafa. He's writing an article about the campaign." She glanced at her wristwatch. "Goodness, look at the time. I'd better hurry so I can beat the traffic—"

"Not so fast, young lady." Fafa didn't let go of the door. "I told you I'd respect your wishes about keeping that whole imbroglio quiet. But I'd assumed he'd stay away from you. Did you know he was coming?"

Trying to hold on to her breathing, Laurel looked at her hands. "No, sir. But it's not such a big deal. We've gone our separate ways, and he's just here on business. I can take care of myself. You don't have to worry." The words were meant to reassure herself as much as her grandfather.

Fafa didn't seem to be buying it. "Say the word, and I'll haul him into court for breach of contract."

"Fafa ..." Laurel smiled a little. "The last thing I need right now is the publicity of a court battle. Please. Let me handle it."

Fafa regarded her with focused concentration. After a moment he grunted. "You'll let me know if he gives you grief?"

She lifted her shoulders. "Cole's left me alone for eight years. He's not likely to stir up anything now." She hoped. Repressing a shiver, she kissed her grandfather's thin, papery cheek. "I've got to go. I'll call you when I get home."

He didn't let go of the door. "Have you called the campaign consultant I recommended? I can make the first meeting if you want me there. They're the best in DC, but it never hurts to have an experienced head in the game—somebody with your personal interests in mind."

Laurel stifled a sigh. No wonder Renata always teased her about her overprotective family. "I already met with them. They sent a guy down last week." She rested her arms on top of the car door. "Are you sure they're worth their fee? I'm asking people to give up hard-earned money to support me, and I want to make sure I spend it in the best possible—"

"You get what you pay for." Fafa patted her wrist. "Don't ever be ashamed of asking folks to put their money where their votes are going. You've got to be passionate about what you believe in, and you won't be in a position to make a difference if you don't get elected. Simple as that."

"You know I'm passionate, Fafa. But Renata's got me lined up next week to judge the Spam cook-off at the Peanut Festival in Dothan. Please tell me how that's related to serious politics."

Fafa chuckled. "Think of it as a cultural experience, honey. Maybe some of the places you're going are a bit off the beaten path, but you're in good hands with Derrick Edes's firm. Remember— you've got to get your name out there to win, so go eat lots of Spam and have fun." With a wave he headed for his Caddy, parked a few slots down the street.

During the two-and-a-half hour drive home, Laurel had plenty of time to envision all the reasons Cole McGaughan might have taken it into his head to leave New York to scope out an Alabama judicial campaign. Didn't he have enough to keep him busy without coming down here and stirring up all the feelings she'd so carefully stuffed into a box with her law school memorabilia?

Surely by now he had a string of girlfriends ready to be suckered in by that crooked smile, slightly bent nose, and diabolically twisted personality.

Stop, Laurel. You're over him.

Yeah? Then why, even after eight years, did it feel like a body slam to be in the same room with him? Robert Prescott, the former coworker she sometimes dated, never made her feel that way. Robert was organized, thorough, and loyal. Safe. Of course she'd never been intimate with him. He might take her arm or put his hand against her back as they walked into a building. And they pecked one another on the lips when they said goodnight. Like most men, he'd tried early in their relationship to see what he could get away with—then seemed relieved that she didn't want a permanent tie. They both enjoyed busy, career-saturated social lives with a dependable date when the situation required it.

The idea of Cole McGaughan putting up with such a platonic relationship for three years was laughable.

She parked in the driveway of her tiny midtown cottage, unlocked the front door, and punched the code to turn off the alarm. She loved this little brick house—loved its hardwood floors, its jewel-toned accents, and the handmade drapes in its tall arched windows. She loved the screened porch out back and the kitchen she'd just spent a good chunk of change remodeling.

Sometimes, though, not having a roommate got a little lonely. Growing up she'd been close to her sister Mary Layne, and her brother Michael, despite the fact that they'd each had their own rooms in the Castle, as Gilly liked to call it. Gilly, who'd come along late in their parents' life and reigned as princess du jour.

"Charles Wallace?" she called, shedding her heels inside the living room and carrying them into the kitchen. "Where are you, baby?"

A loud mew followed by the galumphing of paws on hardwood announced the presence of Laurel's only true soul mate. White Siamese with charcoal points and eyes the color of periwinkles—and the muscle tone of an Olympic discus thrower—Charles Wallace had adopted her six months ago at a local Humane Society event. She couldn't imagine life without him now.

"Hey, handsome!" She bent and scooped the cat up, letting him butt her hard under the chin. He didn't know his own strength and often woke her up at night jumping in the center of her chest looking for love. "Been a good boy today? Ready for your treat?"

His enthusiastic *mmrrow* had her laughing and hunting a bag of kitty treats under the buffet.

The phone rang. Jimmy Choos dangling in one hand and the heavy cat tucked under the other arm, she ran to answer it before the machine kicked in. "Hello?" She dropped into the antique telephone chair in the tiny foyer.

"Aunt Laurel, Parker's playing his bagpipe thing again, and I can't stand it. Can I come spend the night with you?"

"I don't know, Dane." Laurel was glad her ten-year-old nephew couldn't see her smile. Life for a firstborn was serious business. "It's a school night. What's your mom say about it?" She'd thought about taking in a movie with Renata, but she'd never been able to say no to Mary Layne's kids.

"She said if you weren't doing anything tonight, and if you'd bring me home on your way to court in the morning, she didn't care. Come on, Aunt Lolly, I found this really cool hammerhead shark on the PBS website I want to show you."

Sharks before bedtime. Lovely.

In the background she heard the screeching wail of Parker's chanter, the practice pipe he was learning to play in preparation for the adult bagpipe. It sounded exactly like Charles Wallace getting his tail stepped on.

"Okay," she sighed. "I'll come get you and we'll hit the Dew Drop for supper. Let me change clothes first, though."

"All *right*!"

Laurel hung up the phone and carried her shoes into the bedroom, where Charles Wallace had already taken over the center of the bed. Stretched out like Yul Brynner in *The King and I*, he gave her a come-hither look.

"Not now," she said, lining up the Jimmy Choos in the closet with the rest of what Mary Layne deemed an obscenely large shoe collection. "I have to go rescue a young knight in distress. You and I can snuggle after I eat hot dogs and gawk at marine life on the Internet."

The doorbell rang, and she paused in the act of yanking on a pair of Levi's. What now? She quickly found a long-sleeved pink T-shirt that only moderately clashed with her hair and went to the front door.

Her sixteen-year-old baby sister stood on the small front porch with her feet arranged in fifth position, two short red ponytails sprouting from the sides of her head. She had on baggy cargo shorts, an off-the-shoulder yellow cashmere sweater, and Doc Martens. The diamond chip piercing her small nose glittered in the late-afternoon sun.

"Hey!" Laurel stepped back to let Gilly in. "What are you doing here?"

"I got done with my class and decided to stop by to see if you were back from your thing."

"My thing." Laurel grinned. Gilly's interest in politics was right up there with moon rocks. "Yeah, I'm back. I was just heading out to pick up Dane. Want to join us for hotdogs and Monopoly?"

Gilly's pale green eyes lit. "Can we get milkshakes?"

If Laurel spent three hours a day at a ballet barre, probably she, too, could eat like the Auburn football team and still weigh a hundred and ten pounds. She shrugged. "Sure. Why not?"

Since his inversion, Cole didn't frequent bars anymore.

He always thought of Christ's coming into his life that way — a turning upside down, with everything he'd once considered important shaken down to the bottom like silt. Nothing but pure fresh air at the top.

But when Hogan insisted on meeting in the hotel lounge, Cole followed him in without protest. Meeting Laurel's family had more or less screwed his head on backwards. He could use a distraction.

They found a table looking out on the pool, and Hogan ordered a beer. Cole wondered what the waitress would do if he ordered a Sarsaparilla like some hick in a Disney western, but she didn't seem to be in the mood for a joke. She looked like she'd been on her feet for at least twelve hours.

He smiled at her. "Could I have a ginger ale?"

She raised her brows, but plopped a bowl of mixed nuts on the table. "Sure, honey," she answered and limped off.

Apparently too distracted to make his usual joke about Cole's alcoholic abstention, Hogan leaned forward, hands flat on the table. "So you got an interview with the judge's whole family, huh? Spill it, man. What'd you find out?"

"Well, it was like you thought." Cole leaned back in his chair, rubbing his neck. Tension had given him a nasty headache. "They're interested in helping her get all the free press she can get. So Judge Gillian—that's her maternal grandfather, the old gentleman with the cane—sent her mother back to the courthouse to find me. Apparently they didn't tell Judge Kincade they were going to do that. She was—" he hesitated—"surprised to see me."

The waitress came back with their drinks, and Hogan sent her off with a wad of bills on her tray. He slugged back some of his beer. "I haven't seen a woman with such a virtuous persona since Laura Bush." His lip curled. "Nobody's that perfect. Field thinks there's something in her past he can latch onto, something he can bring out in a negative ad."

Cole's headache took a field trip from the base of his skull to his temples. "I don't know, Hogan. I wasn't sure I could help you to begin with, and I'm even less certain now. Judge Kincade is ... well, she's got a pretty tight fortress around her, just within her family."

"Why do you think I brought you down here?" Hogan waved the bottle. "I couldn't get near them, but all you have to do is turn on the good ol' boy southern charm, and the Kincades invite you to lunch."

Cole pressed the cold ginger ale bottle against his forehead. It felt good. "It's not quite that simple. Judge Kincade is a very private woman, and she wouldn't tell me anything I couldn't easily get off her website."

Hogan's thick brows twitched together. "Are you hot for this lady? Because if you are, that's okay—I mean, she's a looker all right—but don't go feeling sorry for her and play dumb on me."

Cole almost wished there were something a little more potent in his bottle than fizzy syrup. Almost. "I'm not playing dumb, Hogan. I swear she didn't tell me anything useful. Here." He set down his drink, grabbed his portfolio off an extra chair, and tossed it onto the table. "Read my notes."

Hogan skimmed the notes, then frowned at Cole. "Right there with her parents, her grandfather, and her campaign manager, and you're telling me this is all you got? They didn't invite you to come down to Mobile for another interview? Follow her for a few campaign speeches or *anything*?"

"She shut me out like an elevator door." The words ground out of Cole. "There was no invitation for anything else."

Hogan seemed to realize he was getting the blunt truth. "Man, McGaughan. Talk about crash and burn." He shook his head. "When we ran around together in Memphis, you used to be the slickest piece of work I ever saw. What's happened to you?"

Words hovered on the end of Cole's tongue. *Inversion.* Hogan wouldn't understand, might even think of it as failure. "Being a political reporter is more than talking up beautiful women."

This whole idea of coming down South and looking up Laurel had been crazy. Hogan had called last week and asked him if he'd ever heard of Judge Laurel Kincade—knowing they'd both been at Ole Miss around the same time—and explained he was being paid to investigate her by her opponent, Mobile County District Attorney George Field.

After recovering from his initial jerk of surprise, Cole had responded with outward interest and inward dismay to Hogan's proposal that he help dig up dirt on the lovely Laurel. "There's all kinds of rumors circulating about Judge Kincade's love life," Hogan had declared. "Anybody that squeaky clean has got to be hiding something. If it's not a lover in the closet now, it's something in her past. I want to know what it is."

At the time it had seemed like a good idea to keep Hogan under his supervision to make sure the PI didn't bumble onto something Cole didn't want unwrapped. Now he saw with twenty-twenty hindsight that not only had he considerably increased that likelihood, he might have made a Faustian bargain.

It looked like the best way to protect both Laurel and himself was to leave before Hogan realized the true depth of his interest in her.

"Well, good luck, buddy." Cole jerked the notebook from Hogan's hands. "My vacation time's up, so I'm going back to New York." He pushed away his drink and stood. "I'm sorry I couldn't be any more help than this."

If one couldn't have a big-screen revival of *The Princess Bride*, the next best thing must be Monopoly with a ten-year-old shark enthusiast and a teenage ballerina.

Laurel rolled the dice and raised a fist. "Hah! The Aunt of Doom buys Park Place, Mr. Banker." She handed Dane a five-hundred-dollar bill.

He slid it into the bank, a distinct pout marring his mustard-stained mouth. "It's not fair — you get that whole side of the board. You'll load it up with hotels and bankrupt me and Gilly."

"Nah." Gilly blew an enormous pink bubble and sucked it back in with a bang. "She doesn't have enough cash left. You'll catch her with one of those railroads and she'll be mortgaging right and left."

Laurel threw her a mock frown. "I thought creative people were supposed to be bad with money."

"That's a myth. Myth! Oh, myth! May I have thome thugar?" Gilly cracked up. "Ha! I kill me!"

Dane made a face. "Gilly, you're so silly. You rhyme all the time."

Laurel smiled. Gilly had been saddled with their mother's maiden name, Gillian, but of course nobody called her that. Unless she was in trouble. She poked Dane. "Back to the subject. Park Place, shark boy."

"Oh, okay." Dane handed over the deed. "Your turn, Aunt Gill."

Gilly rolled double twos and landed on income tax. "Erg. So, Laurel, you're all official now, huh? You never said how the big announcement went today."

"I didn't stutter or anything, if that's what you mean. Plenty of press showed up."

Gilly looked up, coppery brows wrinkled. "You're not surprised, are you? You're big news. The judiciary's a controversial topic, especially when you've got a judge who comes out and says what she believes."

"Not exactly surprised." Laurel hesitated. Apparently sixteen-year-old Gilly paid more attention than she'd thought. "But I ran into an old acquaintance who's now a reporter. It was just kind of weird seeing him, that's all."

"*Him*? A guy? A hot guy?" Gilly's eyes sparkled like peridots. "I always miss the good stuff. Too bad about my class this afternoon or I'd have been there." Gilly's ballet classes were de rigueur. If she missed one she would lose her solo in *The Nutcracker* this season.

"We missed you," Laurel said, avoiding her sister's question.

Cole's looks had nothing to do with anything. It was his ability to fling disaster around like a rodeo bull that still twisted her stomach in a knot. That veiled threat he'd muttered—*you ain't seen nothin' yet*—might have been only an attempt to throw her off balance before he went back to New York and wrote a scathing article about southern-hick female judges. But what if he intended to get personal?

She caught Dane sliding his battleship off Boardwalk onto Go. "Hey, dude. Penalty for cheating is going to jail and losing two turns. Pay up."

Pay up—the story of her life. Oh yeah, it was time to toss money in that piper's hat, and she had a feeling the tune wasn't going to take her anywhere she wanted to go.

chapter 3

January

It had been snowing all day, and Cole pulled up the collar of his jacket against the miserable January cold as he flung himself onto a freezing wooden bench in Tribeca Park. People in Mississippi would laugh at the idea of calling this little triangle of grass a park, but it served his purposes. After a day in the office editing copy, he craved fresh air. Still ... it was good to get back to work. Christmas had been a disaster, and he was almost sorry he'd gone home.

He peeled the cellophane off a thick turkey on rye sandwich, which he'd bought at the Bread Tribeca under his apartment on Church Street. Sandwich for lunch, sandwich for supper. His mother would be appalled.

It occurred to him he hadn't talked to her since he'd gotten back from Tupelo. He finished his supper in a few hungry bites, tossed the wrapper at a nearby trash bin, and fished his phone out of his jacket pocket.

"Hey, Mom," he said when she answered. "What's up?"

"Cole! Where are you, honey?"

"Sitting in the park watching the world go by. Just finished work and supper, thought I'd check in with you before I go turn on the basketball game."

"This is Wednesday. I wish you'd join a church that has a choir. As much as you enjoy music—"

Cole laughed. "Mom, I don't have time. I just wanted to apologize for not making it down to Hattiesburg during the holidays. Tucker was home from school for the weekend, and I wanted to spend as much time with him as I could."

"It's okay. Your grandma and I went to see Aunt Colleen in the nursing home and started a quilt. Besides, I had to work a weekend shift or two at the hospital. We missed you, but we'll see you next trip."

"It may be a while, Mom. Plane fare's astronomical, and you know I don't take money from Dad." He let the silence hang.

His mother sighed. "How bad was it, baby?"

He watched a couple of pigeons scuffling over a paper sack and debated lying to her. It wasn't her fault the rest of the family constituted a southern gothic tragedy. "Well, let's see. Dad took me golfing and told me I swing like a hockey player. Teri shopped, as usual. She's compulsive." He let out an exasperated snort. "How many Nile green towels does one family need? And then there's Tucker ... "

His younger half-brother was drifting away like a piece of flotsam on a Mississippi River current, showing all the signs of washing up like Cole had. Why Dad made the kid major in business management defied explanation. Tucker was into music, always had been. He kept slipping off to jam in bars and juke joints, smoking pot and no telling what other illegal substances to gain some control over his life.

But Tucker wasn't his mother's responsibility, so he didn't go into detail.

"Oh, Cole, I'm sorry," said his mother. "You of all people should know that lost people act ... well, lost."

She should know it too. Cole's father — Davis McGaughan III, MD, premier plastic surgeon of Tupelo, Mississippi — had executed the ultimate cliché, leaving his wife in favor of his nurse, a young blonde with a curvy figure and no facial stress lines carved by hardheaded preteens. Cole was aware how hard his mother's life had been made by his father's selfishness.

And his own.

"Yes, ma'am," he said softly. "I'm not giving up on them. I've just got to regroup a little before I tackle another trip back to Dixie. Keep praying for me, okay?"

"You know I do. Every single day." His mother's voice brightened. "So what story are you working on now?"

"I'm following up on a story I wrote back in November about a conservative judge in Alabama. She's running for state supreme court chief justice."

He'd filled his mother in on the trip to Montgomery without many details. Laurel was part of the shipwrecked part of his life that he'd just as soon leave buried.

"That sounds interesting." They talked for a few more minutes, then she paused. "Listen, sweetie, I've got to let you go. Choir practice starts in thirty minutes and I still have to let the dog out and scrape the ice off the car. You wouldn't believe how cold it is down here."

"Okay, no problem. I'll call you this weekend." Closing the phone, Cole got up and strode, shivering, toward his building. The temperature had dropped several degrees while he sat outside. The apartment was going to be frigid. Maybe one day his thin blood would get used to this climate.

He walked in and pushed the thermostat up to around seventy-two, then wandered over to sprinkle a little food into his fish tank. A Red Fire Guppy swam with a Golden Veil Angelfish and a Betta named Bilbo, who was a finicky eater and twice had given him a scare by floating to the top. People said you couldn't keep Bettas with other fish, but he'd read up on it and found they'd play nice with everybody except their own kind. So far so good.

One day he was going to get a dog. The other day in the park he'd seen a blonde in a jogging suit being walked by a gorgeous golden retriever. What Cole wouldn't have given to have played Frisbee with that dog. The girl he'd barely noticed. For some reason, he still had an eye for red-headed southern Amazons.

He walked over to the corner where a punching bag hung from the ceiling and gave it a series of swift jabs before shucking out of his button-down shirt and khakis. Both his pairs of good pants were getting threadbare around the hem. Next paycheck he was going shopping.

Living in the city had turned out to be a lot more expensive than he'd expected when he arrived two years ago, but once he found this apartment above the restaurant, he'd been reluctant to give it up. In spite of the nasty weather, he liked the energy of the city. He liked access to Broadway and Times Square and people who read something besides hunting and fishing magazines.

Okay, so he was pretty fond of throwing a hook in the water himself, but he didn't have time for it anymore, so there was no point in wishing his life away.

He pulled on a pair of Old Navy cords and a formerly red Ole Miss sweatshirt that had been washed so many times it was now a splotchy pink, then sat down on the bed to change his socks. His eyes fell on the banjo case in the corner. His mother's mention of the choir had set up an odd, guilty itching at the back of his neck. A guy at church, apparently responsible for making sure new members got plugged in somewhere, had discovered Cole had a musical background and nearly gone into cardiac arrest. It hadn't been easy to convince him that Cole was just a hack bluegrass player from down South and wouldn't fit into the slick urban feel they were going for in their worship services.

If he got the thing out and practiced a little, he might not be such a hack. It had been a long time since he'd felt musical. Maybe since the Laurel Incident. *Could it be, Quad, old man, it's time to move on? Or move back to who you were before?*

Not in the spiritual sense. He wouldn't want to go back to who he'd been without the Lord. But in the last few years he'd certainly isolated himself from most of the things he used to love. His family. His music and art. His writing.

Which was a ridiculous thought. He spent eight to ten hours a day writing.

The itchy feeling somehow worse, he rose and picked up the banjo case. A thick coat of dust exploded in his face, making him sneeze as he took out the instrument. The strings lay limp against the pegboard. The last time he'd played, he'd loosened them before putting the banjo away, to keep the neck from bowing. Leaving the case in the bedroom, he wandered back into the living room and plopped down on the sofa with the banjo across his lap, bare feet on the brass seaman's trunk he used for a coffee table.

Plucking the strings as they slowly tightened into correct pitch, he laid his head back against the sofa. *Tune me, Lord. Seeing Laurel again set me all out of whack.*

Going down to Alabama had been an act of obedience — look how that had turned out. She'd all but shoved him on a plane and told him to get lost. She wasn't going to let him back in her life. Hadn't even given him a chance to apologize.

Lord knew he had a lot to make up for where she was concerned. But some people just weren't open to forgiveness.

His cell phone rang. Muttering, he carefully laid the banjo on the trunk and padded into the bedroom, where he found his phone still clipped to his belt loop. He looked at the ID. Caller unknown. "Hello?"

"Hello, is this Cole McGaughan from the *Daily Journal*?" It was a husky female voice he didn't recognize. Southern, maybe black.

"Who wants to know?" He'd learned caution the hard way.

The woman laughed. "You may not remember me, but this is Renata Castleberry from Mobile, Alabama. Laurel Kincade's campaign manager?"

The pretty lady with the braids and high-class suit. Relaxing, he sat down and found a notepad to doodle on. "Yes, ma'am. What can I do for you?"

"Boy, you can turn that stuff on, can't you?"

"What do you mean?"

"Never mind. I just wanted to thank you for the kind mention of the judge's campaign in your article last month."

Oh that. Yeah, that had been a real ad seller. A one-inch column right between a handbag sale and "Don't Let Allergies Stop You from Adopting a Pet."

"I assure you, it was no trouble at all."

"Well, Mr. McGaughan, since you expressed such an unprecedented amount of interest in Judge Kincade ..." She paused as if expecting him to acknowledge some kind of deep dark passion.

Get real, lady.

She cleared her throat. "Anyway, I've got a proposition for you. The Alabama judicial race looks like it's developing some interesting twists—especially in the primaries this spring. Definitions of marriage should come into play. Family values. Stuff that's of strong national interest right now." She paused for a breath. "In case you didn't pick up on it, Judge Kincade is a candidate who's solidly in the Christian camp. She doesn't hide the fact that her faith informs every decision she makes. Since you're a religion reporter, I thought you might be interested in doing an exclusive series on her campaign."

An exclusive series? Laurel's clean profile appeared on the notepad. He erased it.

When he didn't immediately answer, Renata rushed to clarify. "I mean, come down here and follow Laurel on the campaign trail, at least until the primary is over."

Cole stood there speechless for a moment, then realized his ear was hurting. He relaxed his grip on the phone. "That's an interesting proposal," he said mildly, though every instinct screamed *Run, Forrest, run!* He'd given Laurel an opportunity to listen, she'd shut the door in his face, and he'd fulfilled his obligation to the Holy Spirit's prompting. This woman had to be an emissary from the Dark Side.

"I think it's a *brilliant* proposal," she said cheerfully.

He had to smile at her effrontery. "The problem is, I already have my regular column, and what you're suggesting would require quite a bit of time away from the city."

"Wait, don't turn me down without at least hearing the whole idea. Laurel's—Judge Kincade's—conservative opponent is playing some dirtbag games with her reputation. The people of Alabama need to see her for the gifted, straight-up woman she is, and they won't get to do that if we don't somehow get a little corner of the media."

Cole sighed. "Ms. Castleberry, as much as I enjoyed talking to Judge Kincade, I don't skew my stories for anybody." What was he, crazy? He wasn't going back down to Alabama. Why was he even discussing this?

"For heaven's sake, we don't need you to skew anything. We just want you to report on the truth. That Laurel Kincade has got her stuff goin' *on* and deserves to go down in history as the first woman elected to the chief justice seat on that court."

Cole walked over to the one window in his apartment and looked out on the traffic going by on Church Street. The great wrought-iron clock of the Tribeca Grand Hotel, directly opposite, bonged eight o'clock as the doorman, nattily dressed in a black and red uniform, opened somebody's limousine door. Further down, bleary lights from Chinatown speckled a mosque and a couple of mainline denominational steeples.

"Okay, look." He imagined Renata Castleberry sitting on her front porch in southern Alabama with a glass of iced tea in hand. "I'm not giving you a yes or no right now. It's an intriguing idea, but I want to run it by my editor. If he gives me the green light, I'll call you."

He sensed her impatience. "Don't take too long. The primary is June fifth, so we'll start heating up the campaign by the first of April."

"Give me until the end of the month. I'll need to do some research." Call Matt Hogan, for one thing. Find out where he was in his investigation.

"Fine. You've got my number, Mr. — is it all right if I call you Cole?"

"Of course."

He couldn't help wondering if this was Laurel's idea. Maybe she'd had a change of heart. If not, she was going to go up in red-hot flames when she found out her manager had gone behind her back to bring Cole back to Alabama.

He picked up the banjo and began to pluck a rusty version of "Honey, Open That Door." A slow smile spread across his face.

The following week, Aaron Zorick scanned Cole's proposal, then gave him a classic beady-eyed-editor stare. "Why pick a judge in Alabama? We got plenty of crooked politicians right here in New York."

Cole resisted the urge to loosen the knot of his tie. "There's no evidence she's crooked. But she's running on a family values platform with a strong religious stand, and you never know what might turn up. Her opponents are going to do their best to bring her down. This is going to be one of the most interesting campaigns this year."

"Hmph." Zorick adjusted his glasses and leered at Laurel's photo, which Cole had scanned into the document. "She's a mighty good-looking lady."

"She is that." He couldn't slug his boss for looking at a beautiful woman's perfectly modest head shot. "The thing is, I've already met her—remember last fall when I took vacation days and went down there? Her campaign manager invited me to follow the campaign." He cleared his throat. "Also, the judge's mother took a liking to me."

Zorick leaned back in his chair, eyes twinkling. "I bet she did. You're a piece of work, McGaughan." He flipped the proposal onto the desk toward Cole. "All right, let's see what you can do with this. I'll send your regular assignments, and you can do them remote—just email them in."

"Okay, chief, but just to clarify—are you saying if this series goes well, you'll move me over to the political page?"

"It depends on the strength of the story." Zorick shrugged. "I'll put it this way: you make me look good, I'll make you look good. *Capisce?*"

"Yes, sir. Gotcha." Cole picked up his proposal and stared at Laurel's smile. Truth or consequences. Truth *and* consequences. He hoped he was doing the right thing.

chapter 4

Clutching his cocktail, Matt Hogan skirted the edges of the ballroom, looking for a way to get himself introduced to the judge's hangers-on. He'd never been comfortable in a milieu like this hootie-tootie Mardi Gras crowd. Unlike McGaughan, who'd grown up all but choked on a drawerful of silver spoons, Matt had been reared in rural Illinois, the son of a minister and a secretary. He'd gone to a public high school and worked his way through Northern Illinois University, then followed a girlfriend to Memphis. He'd hooked up with a private investigations agency there and stayed until his dad had a heart attack. Going back to the harsher winters of the Midwest hadn't been easy, but he'd managed to make it work.

Not that he ever stayed in Chicago more than a couple of weeks at a time. Just long enough to check his mailbox, say hello to his mom—who'd drive down for a meal if he let her know he was there—and hit some of his favorite clubs. This time, it looked like it might be months before he could go north again. The client, George Field, had plenty of dough and was determined to win the election.

You had to respect a guy like that. Matt couldn't imagine putting his own life under the microscope of public service. But to each his own.

Field was the one who'd gotten him the invitation to this ball. It had arrived in the PO box he'd rented for his short stay in Mobile—engraved on yellowish paper with those raggedy edges that meant it cost more than Matt's last meal. This was exactly the kind of shebang he would've sent McGaughan to, if the guy hadn't left him in the lurch and headed back to New York. Mc-Gaughan had grown up in an aristocratic southern family, and he'd know what to do with the bizarre foods on display at the buffet tables around the room upstairs.

Matt would have been happier with a hunk of rare steak and a baked potato. Eventually he was going to have to go up there and poke around until he found something edible. It was nine o'clock, and his stomach was howling for food.

His wardrobe was a problem too. The shoes he'd rented with his tails were a size too small, and the pants a tad too big, necessitating a hitch when he was sure nobody was looking. Oh well, he didn't look any different than any other man in the room. One monkey suit was about as goofy as the next.

Taking a position in front of the bandstand, he tipped the wine glass to his mouth but didn't swallow. He never drank when he was working—too much at stake. Every tidbit of information he heard was important, and he had to be able to remember it all.

Frankly, it had been a surprise to discover Judge Kincade planned to attend. Her reputation for strict moral rectitude was legendary. Evidently the opportunity to glad-hand in favor of her campaign had trumped virtue.

She stood a few yards away, the sparkling center of a circle of black tuxes. The four men around her—all lawyers, no doubt—

hung on her every word, watching her unconsciously graceful movements. Her beautiful dark red hair was dressed loosely on top of her head, confined with a simple jade clip that matched the color of her dress. Slender straps left her shoulders bare, the modest cut following her beautiful form and flaring slightly at her calves. As he watched, she threw her head back to laugh and lifted her hand to skim a strand of hair out of her eyes. The gesture was wholly feminine but somehow unstudied, and her companions were eating it up.

McGaughan could have been there in the inner circle, elbowing the others out of the way without even trying. But he'd decamped, the rat.

Well, Matt had been born with chutzpah—everybody said so—and he would eventually track down somebody willing to spill the beans on the judge.

Lifting his drink to his lips again, he scrutinized the women in the judge's vicinity. If he'd learned anything in six years of following cheating spouses, it was the power of jealousy. His gaze skimmed over a cluster of women, tipsy already, giggling together about their husbands' bosses. Moving further into the crowd, he passed two middle-aged couples in earnest conversation about a new health club going up at a midtown hospital.

Then two women—one black and one white, both attractive— caught his attention. Matt stopped. If he wasn't mistaken, the young black lady was the judge's campaign manager, Renata Castleberry.

But what hooked him was the way the other woman, a blonde with improbably generous assets and a dress cut low enough to advertise them, glanced at Judge Kincade from the corner of her eye. It was exactly the expression he'd been waiting for.

Score. Matt moved in.

"Judge Kincade, we're so happy you could join us tonight. The Krewe of Vulcan is proud to host the first event in the Convention Center since it reopened."

"I'm honored to have been invited," Laurel yelled over the band blasting "You Take My Breath Away" from the bandstand in the corner. She brushed her hair out of her eyes and smiled at Mayor Posey. Renata had promised she wouldn't have to indulge in any of the excesses associated with these functions. Put on a pretty dress, arrive on Robert's arm, say hello to as many people as possible, and call it a night.

She sneaked a glance at her watch. Nearly nine-fifteen. She had missed first-round auditions for the spring musical at the Popcorn Playhouse. Bummer. How was she going to help choose soloists if she hadn't heard them all?

Plus, her hair was driving her crazy. She'd gotten it cut that afternoon, and Tricia had thought it would be cool to leave a layered swag hanging over one eye like some TV soap opera queen. Poking at it untangled it from her eyelashes, but she probably looked like she had a twitch.

Or maybe the twitch resulted from the Medusa glare of Brandy Turner's hard blue eyes. The radio talk show host had a talent for showing up when Laurel was on public display and feeling insecure. So far Renata had fended her off, but Laurel was braced for attack.

"Laurel, would you like something to drink?" Robert gave her his avuncular smile.

If he weren't so pompous he would be cute.

"Just some club soda, please."

As he ducked away toward the bar, Brandy Turner moved in. "Laurel, I'm liking that dress, hon. It looks like a Vera Wang I saw on somebody on *ET* not too long ago." Brandy smiled, all but showing fangs. "Must be nice to be able to shop in the boutiques."

"It's a knock-off, but I like it." Laurel held her tongue with an effort. A notorious liberal, Brandy had more than once dripped poisonous barbs on air about Laurel's political affiliations.

"So, how's the push toward the Judicial Building coming along? Should be a shoo-in. You religious people are taking over Montgomery."

"We 'religious people' currently represent a majority of the state. That's how our electoral system works. The majority gets a voice." Laurel tipped her head. "At least, the last civics class I took said so."

"And the majority runs over the rights of folks with no power." Brandy wasn't even pretending civility now.

Laurel stared at her, nonplussed. "Do you really see me as a power broker?"

"Yes. And worse, you try to hide it. I don't think I've ever heard you come out and say what you believe about reproductive rights, for example."

"You know I can't speak on that kind of topic. It would compromise my impartiality in cases I might have to decide later." Laurel looked at the men around her. They all looked fascinated, but nobody offered to jump into the debate.

Brandy openly sneered. "Your partiality is already compromised. What you're worried about is the public's perception of you, and how they might vote if they knew what you really believe."

Laurel lifted her chin. Participating in a catfight wouldn't help anything. "What the public sees is exactly what it gets. I'm not hiding anything." She caught Renata's alarmed gaze across the room. "Excuse me, Brandy. If you want a debate on the air, call me sometime."

She headed toward Renata, who had been in conversation for several minutes with a sandy-haired young man in an ill-fitting tux. As Laurel approached, the guy—who possessed one of those

boy-next-door faces nobody in her right mind would trust—
suddenly pulled out his cell phone and slipped into the crowd.

How rude. "Who was that?" Laurel glanced at the exit where
the young man had disappeared.

Renata waved her hand. "Never mind him. What's Brandy
TWO got her panties in a twist about now?"

"TWO?"

"T. W. O. The Wicked One." Renata made a face. "One day a
house is gonna fall on her and relieve the world of an unnecessary
talk show."

Laurel covered a smile. "Renata. She's a very sad woman."

"If I had to lug that front load around day in and day out, I'd
stay in a bad mood too."

"Renata!"

"Okay, okay. I'm sorry. I'm not as virtuous and forgiving as
you."

"I'm not virtuous, I'm just ..." Laurel sighed and hooked an
arm through Renata's. "I just want to have fun tonight. Let's go
find Robert and see if we can teach him the electric slide."

Renata snorted. "That'll be the day."

"Sorry, Mr. Field, hold on a sec while I get out of the noise."
Matt hitched up his pants and tried not to shuffle in time to KC
and the Sunshine Band as he exited the ballroom. Left, right, left,
right. Four years of high school band had left an indelible mark.

When the client called directly, you'd better find a way to talk
to him, inconvenient or not. Matt headed for an unoccupied niche
near a window, where cell reception should be decent. The view
across Mobile Bay was staggering. Lights strung along the bridge
and suspended from the battleship *Alabama* floated in the mist
like—well, Matt was no poet, but they were pretty.

He turned his back to the window and focused on his caller. "Now. What can I do for you, sir?"

The sonorous voice, trained to carry across a courtroom, boomed in Matt's ear. "You can tell me what in Sam Hill's going on down there, young man. I'm not paying you to drink and carouse."

If he closed his eyes, Matt could envision the colored shirt, winter white suit, and eelskin boots the lawyer affected. The guy definitely had his quirks. "Sir, I might mention that you're paying me to follow this lady around, which is exactly what I'm doing." He took a breath. "Was doing. I had just connected with her campaign manager."

There was a short silence. "Oh. Young woman with more hair than brains. Hispanic-sounding name, but she's black?"

"Renata Castleberry. She seems pretty bright to me. And extremely loyal to Judge Kincade."

"That's the problem with these inbred old families. Extremely difficult to find a chink in the armor because they're related to every other person you meet."

"I'm not sure I follow—"

"Hogan, you're not from the South, you wouldn't understand. The Castleberry woman's relationship to the judge's family probably goes back several generations."

"But I think it has more to do with—"

"Never mind," Field said impatiently. "Give me the *Reader's Digest* version. How're you going to work her?"

Matt shifted and toed off one of his shoes. Relief. "I told her I represent some business interests looking at investing in the judge's campaign. Gave her my number and told her I want to meet with her sometime."

"Huh," Field grunted. "Have to say, that's not a bad idea. Interview her, then disappear."

"Right. And I made sure she knew not to say anything to the judge, in case it doesn't work out. Wouldn't want to get her hopes up."

"Boy, you're nearly devious enough to be a lawyer." Field chuckled.

"Too bad I'm not getting paid like one," Matt muttered. Ending the call, he crammed his foot into his shoe and limped back to the ball.

Maybe he could talk the busty blonde with a vendetta against the judge into another dance. Compensation came in a variety of forms.

chapter 5

Mother Superior's wimple took a drunken sideways slide as she crossed the Popcorn Playhouse stage warbling "Climb Every Mountain" in an unsteady teenage soprano. "'Til ... you ... find ... your ... dream!" The chunky young actress lifted her arm and pointed to the ceiling. Hiking her black habit to expose a pair of enormous purple Crocs, she vaulted into the wings.

Laurel, front row center in the newly remodeled theater, had been sitting on her hands through the entire excruciating length of the song. Opening night was eight weeks away, but the kids had a long way to go. As the community youth theater's main vocal coach, she was responsible for all the soloists as well as the big choral numbers. Musicals like *The Sound of Music* were their bread and butter.

"Jamika, that was ... well, we need another rehearsal or two." Laurel went to the foot of the stage and laid her notes on the floor. "Come here and let's chat."

The wimple peeked around the backdrop, beneath it two dark brown eyes sparkling in a mocha-colored face. "I been practicing with my CD, Miss Laurel. Grandmama says I should go on *American Idol*."

"Let's conquer the Gulf Coast before we take on Hollywood, honey." Laurel smiled to take the sting from her words.

Jamika's big white grin appeared as she clumped over and plopped down cross-legged in front of Laurel, the habit hitched above her knees. "Did you ever have to wear one of these skanky outfits when you was a kid? I bet you got to play Maria."

"Actually, in college I was Mother Superior myself." Laurel straightened the cockeyed headpiece. "My sister was chosen for Maria. It hurt my feelings until I realized I had one of the best solos in the whole musical."

Jamika thought about that, head to one side. "How come you decided to be a judge, instead of a famous singer?"

"I couldn't handle the pressure," Laurel said with a straight face.

"You think I could be a judge?"

"I think you can be anything you want to be."

"Huh." Jamika sat up. "Reckon I could."

"Laurel?" called a husky voice from the back of the theater. "Is that you?"

Laurel turned. "Renata! I thought you had a real estate meeting tonight."

"I did." Renata swayed down the aisle, sandals slapping against her heels. "It's over. I wanted to catch you before you went home. Want to grab a bite to eat?"

Laurel looked at her watch. Jamika's grandmother would be here to pick her up any minute. "Haven't eaten since breakfast. That would be great."

Twenty minutes later they were in O'Charley's with salads.

"You know you're going to have to cut out some of these extracurriculars when the campaign heats up in a week or two." Renata, always a bulldog, pointed her fork at Laurel. "You won't have time for singing and dancing and playing with the munchkins."

"The extracurriculars are what make me different from the other guy." Laurel speared a cucumber and a section of red onion. Her breath would stink, but Charles Wallace the Tuna-Breath wasn't likely to care. "Anyway, I'm committed through the end of the season. That's May fourth."

Renata frowned. "What makes you different is the fact that you're brilliant, your judicial experience is stellar, and you're female. Not the fact that 'no' isn't in that gigantic vocabulary of yours."

Laurel shrugged. She didn't feel so brilliant. In fact, she hadn't slept last night for thinking about a teenage boy whose case had come before her bench yesterday afternoon. Weighing her responsibility to the public against sending a kid to prison for the first time required the wisdom of Solomon.

Renata's dark eyes narrowed. "You do it on purpose, don't you? Keep yourself all tied in knots so you won't have time to think."

Laurel sipped her sweet tea, avoiding Renata's gaze. "I don't know what you mean." No amount of busyness would keep that kid's pale freckled face out of her dreams.

Renata sighed. "Okay, fine. The land of denial is a beautiful place, Judge Laurel."

Nobody was more aware of her deficiencies than Laurel herself. "Did you have something about the campaign you wanted to discuss?"

"As a matter of fact I did." Renata picked up her BlackBerry and poked at it with the stylus. "I've arranged for some really good publicity. Our top gun consultant approved it—so you don't get a veto."

Renata looked so smug that Laurel put down her tea glass. "Renata, what have you done?"

"My job." Renata sat back, folding her arms. "Why? What's the matter?"

"You know I like you to run things by me before you commit my sched—"

"I haven't committed your schedule to anything. He'll be completely at your disposal." Renata tapped the table with half-inch white nails. "Just hear me out. First of all, he promised to keep your private life off the record, unless you give him permission to print it."

"Him? Him who?" Alarm had heat rushing from Laurel's chest to her eyebrows. "Print what?"

"Okay, baby, breathe. It's gonna be all right. Remember that good-looking reporter from Tupelo-via-New York who ate lunch with us back in November?"

"Cole McGaughan." Laurel could hardly get the name past her numb lips.

"I didn't think you'd forget a pair of shoulders like that." Renata grinned. "Well, I called him up and offered him a shot at following your campaign. He gave me a tentative yes the first of February, and just confirmed this morning. He's doing a full series for the *Daily Journal* on Christian politics in the South."

"You—you called *him*?" Laurel shut her eyes. "What possessed you to do that?"

"Common sense. The guy was obviously hot on you, and I thought, what the heck—let's just see what he says if I invite him back for a little southern hospitality. The *Journal*'s fairly even-handed in their reporting, right? Besides, even bad press is better than no press." Renata cleared her throat. "Laurel? Are you okay?"

Laurel opened her eyes. "He said he's coming?"

"I *told* you—What's the matter with you, girl? Didn't you hear me? He'll be here in two weeks."

"Do you happen to know of a Baptist convent?"

Cole stayed at his desk over his lunch hour, turning down an invitation to go for drinks and pizza. He had about a million details to take care of before he could leave the city. Sublet his apartment, find a home for the fish, wrap up the articles he was working on for upcoming issues.

Call Hogan.

Leaning back in his chair, he propped his feet on the desk and reached into a drawer for a pack of Nabs. Peanut butter and cheese crackers. Yeehaw. He was looking forward to getting back to the South and hooking up with some sweet potato casserole, pot roast and gravy, maybe some banana pudding. His stomach gave a mighty rumble, and he shoved two whole crackers into his mouth. Sometimes his imagination was a curse.

When the Nabs were a sad, distant memory, he decided there was no point putting it off any longer and flipped open his cell phone. Hogan's number appeared in the display and rang once before his friend picked up.

"McGaughan, what's up? Thought you'd taken an assignment in Zanzibar or something."

"Zanzibar is no longer a country."

"How do you *know* these things?" Hogan demanded. "Don't you get tired of correcting people?"

Cole shrugged. "Not really. Are you busy?"

"I'm sitting outside the courthouse where Laurel Kincade is presiding over some juvenile misdemeanor hearing." A cracking yawn came across the phone. "I'd rather watch paint dry."

"Why don't you just tell your boss the lady's a dead bore and leave her alone?"

"Because he's paying me good money to *not* leave her alone. Besides, there's something funny about the way she avoids certain questions."

Cole stopped squeaking his desk chair. "What questions?"

"I don't know. Questions about her young adulthood. Maybe college days. There's a gap of information there. Something happened, I'm just not sure what. Or when, exactly."

"Well, maybe I can come down and give you a hand after all. Our lady judge's campaign manager called me a couple of weeks ago and offered to trade a series of insider interviews in exchange for a little free publicity for Her Honor."

Hogan let out a string of excited profanity. "That's great! When are you coming?"

"I should be able to wrap things up here and get a flight out in a couple of weeks. You want to meet me once I get there?"

"Sure, man. Listen, I'm glad you're coming. This place is a psych ward. Hardly anybody speaks regular English." He muttered another curse. "Look, I've got to go. I see the judge's retinue. Call me when you get to town, okay?"

"All right." Cole closed the phone and rooted around in the drawer for a bag of stale Doritos. As he munched, he thought about Hogan's comments. Up to now he hadn't been seriously worried about the PI discovering anything damaging. Laurel's grandpa was too good a lawyer. But if Hogan somehow managed to turn over enough rocks, Laurel could be in a lot of trouble.

It was a good thing Cole was headed down there to keep an eye on her, whether she liked it or not.

Licking his fingers, he gathered the last few crumbs in the Doritos bag. First thing he was going to do when he got to Alabama was find a good catfish restaurant. A man had to have his priorities straight.

chapter 6

"Mom thinks I should be home helping her polish silver," Gilly said as Laurel opened the Nissan's small trunk. The two of them began to unload Ziploc bags full of brownies they'd baked the night before into a cardboard box.

Every other Saturday the sisters helped with PBJ—Peanut Butter and Jesus—Day. At six o'clock that morning, Laurel had picked up Gilly and driven downtown, where they were to meet sixty other church members for the project sponsored by their church choir.

"Mom should be down here helping *us*." Lugging the boxful of brownies, Laurel led the way toward the Water Street Mission, housed in an old warehouse near the State Docks. "It's not like she couldn't run one of those home tours in her sleep."

"I know. But she told me to remind you the caterer would be at the Castle at nine, and you're in charge of keeping an eye on them."

The sisters exchanged an eye-roll. If anybody understood Laurel's impatience with their mother's obsession, Gilly did.

While growing up in Mobile, a city rich with historical heritage, all the Kincade progeny had been steeped in Indian, French,

Spanish, and antebellum lore. As high school seniors, the older two girls had been chosen as Azalea Trail Maids—aka Girls in Big Poufy Dresses—the city's PR ambassadors. The Mobile Historical Preservation Society, their mother's hobbyhorse, had been an important family outlet—including fundraisers like the home tour at the end of March and participation in Civil War reenactments at nearby Forts Morgan and Henry.

Laurel still appreciated the impact of the past on the present. But in the last few months she'd been looking at lots of things differently.

Specifically since Cole had burst back onto the stage of her life.

The night Renata told her he was coming back, she'd gone home and gotten on her knees beside her bed. When that didn't seem to adequately express her confusion and desperation, she'd flattened herself facedown on the rug. With Charles Wallace perched in the center of her back, she'd cried a little and asked God what he was doing. And asked for new eyes.

And to her complete surprise, he had done just that. As if someone had installed a high-def camera lens inside her head, capable of capturing minutiae she'd never noticed before.

Laurel glanced at her younger sister, skipping beside her with two shopping bags full of brownies. Gilly's nose-stud was an example. Six months ago when she'd first seen that delicate little diamond chip—paid for with Gilly's birthday money—Laurel had been horrified. "No pun intended, but why do you want to deface yourself that way?" she'd demanded. "Are you trying to grab attention? How come Mom let you get away with that, when she'd have grounded me or Mary Layne for life?"

Gilly had just smiled. "I like it. It's me. Doesn't hurt anything, so get over it."

For a while Laurel had watched in anxiety, praying her sister wouldn't start doing drugs like Michael, or sleeping around like many of the kids she saw in court every day. That hadn't happened. To the contrary, Gilly loved Jesus passionately and often set an example of servanthood for her older sisters. The PBJ idea was her brainchild.

New vision. Which meant that some aspects of launching a political campaign presented difficulties. Laurel had never had any trouble making friends—she'd inherited enough of her mother's social acumen to place her in the ranks of "Most Likely to Succeed" in *Who's Who*. But flattery was not her style. And a recent study of the first few chapters of Daniel cemented her determination to set herself apart from the obsequious brownnosers of the political world.

In the most ladylike Christian way, of course.

"Hope Marjean managed to get plenty of bread." She held open the Mission's front door for Gilly. "She and Dewey were in charge of sandwiches this time."

"I'm sure they did. You worry too much, Lolly." Gilly stopped and took a deep breath. "Pew. Stinks in here." She cheerfully headed for the kitchen, where the rest of the group had begun to gather. "Hey, why didn't you bring Hot Reporter Guy along with you? He could've done a story on your charitable contributions to the community."

Laurel grimaced. "That is exactly what I'm *not* going to do. Make a big deal out of stuff like this for political mileage. I'm picking him up at eight-thirty, and he's coming to the home tour."

Gilly looked over her shoulder, eyebrows raised. "Does Renata know?"

"She knows about the tour." Laurel had wrestled with this very issue in her quiet time with God this morning. Renata had agreed that her private life could stay private. What Laurel did with her church was just that. Private. And if Cole McGaughan knew about it, he'd write about it.

She'd found this out doing a Google search on him some time ago—a compulsively nosy dig into what he'd been up to for the last eight years. He'd been in Memphis for four years, writing for the *Commercial Appeal*. Then he'd suddenly moved to New York, where he'd been absorbed into the messy, massive soup of national news. Gradually his name had begun to surface more often until he was winning awards, gaining the respect of his peers.

Successful journalist. Who would've expected him to dig himself out of the hole he'd plowed into?

Two things she was sure of: She didn't trust him. And he wasn't going to take her under again.

Cole stood in front of the hotel waiting for Laurel. He hadn't been sure how to dress for a historic home tour—and southerners could be funny about sartorial etiquette—so going for safety, he'd strait-jacketed himself into a blue button-down and a tie. Expelling a breath of irritation, he loosened the knot at his throat. No sense asphyxiating himself before lunch.

He bounced a little on his toes. *Nerves, man.* Who would've thought he'd be this rattled by the thought of seeing Laurel again? She'd been avoiding him for the most part, letting her manager pick him up at the airport and maintain all ensuing contacts. Either Laurel was extremely busy—which was likely—or she was just a bit freaked over his presence—also likely.

Not that he didn't like Renata, who was bright, outgoing, and as organized as a team of NASA engineers. But he'd been on edge ever since the Chief had green-lighted the series. The night before he left he'd even taken "the box" down from the closet shelf and opened it up for the first time in years. Then put it right back. Some things he still couldn't deal with, even though he'd come a long way on his spiritual journey.

A car horn honked. He started and looked up. He'd been staring at the Colonel Reb on his tie like an idiot savant.

Framed by the open car window, Laurel wasn't pretty in the traditional way. But the angular chin, deep widow's peak, and dark eyebrows marked a face that was strong and sexy and confident. He'd never been able to capture it properly with words or paint.

To cover his elation he frowned at her. "It's not like you to be late."

"I know. Traffic on Airport ... " She gave him an apologetic smile. "I told Renata we should let you meet us there."

Belatedly he realized her campaign manager was peering at him over the tiny backseat, eyebrows elevated. "'It's not like you?' Have you two been spending time together without telling me?"

"We've spoken on the phone a few times," said Laurel, punching the unlock button. "Hop in—unless you want me to get out and open the door for you."

He fell into a rabbit hole of memory—of standing on the front steps of the Sigma Alpha Epsilon house one night in May of 1998. The last stop on Laurel's designated-driver Good Samaritan route (he assumed she'd been delivering in order of sobriety), he'd been able to stand without swaying. Much. With a veneer of insolence and a good deal of buried shame, he'd eyed his erstwhile transportation, which she'd left parked on the street.

"Who drives a minivan to law school?" He leaned back against the apartment door for support.

Laurel twirled her keys. "A person with a lot of friends."

"I have plenty of friends," he said, ignoring the lurch of his stomach. Maybe he wasn't so steady after all.

"Yeah, and they're all passed out back at the Warehouse."

"So—so were yours."

She sighed. "Not all of them. Just the ones I needed to watch out for tonight."

He eyed her with a perception that seemed to come from some spotlight inside his brain. A Laurel spotlight he hadn't been aware of until that moment. "Who watches out for you?"

"Not drunk frat boys, that's for sure." She took his keys out of his hand and unlocked his door. "Go to bed, junior."

"How old do you thing—think I am?" he stammered, looking down at her. A tall girl, willowy as a sugar cane reed, the top of her head still only reached his chin.

She'd squinted up at him. "Twelve?"

Shaking off the past, Cole stepped off the curb and opened the car door. Though the spotlight hadn't gone away, he was no longer slave to his emotions. It had been a long dark battle to overpower them, but he knew now where his strength lay. *Help me, Lord.* "Thanks for picking me up." He got into the front seat and felt the air conditioner blast him in the face. He glanced at Laurel in surprise as he put on his seat belt. He remembered her being extremely cold-natured. "Thanks for the air. It must be mid-eighties today."

"No problem." She shrugged. "I figured you might be in shirt and tie."

"I wasn't sure what to wear." He slid a glance at her full turquoise skirt and fitted cotton sweater. "What exactly are we doing today?"

"I'm hostessing my parents' open house for the home tour. Mom's rabid for historical preservation." She checked traffic and moved onto Airport Boulevard. "I'll shake hands and give out my materials to everyone who goes through the tour." She glanced at Cole's tie. "You look fine. Just don't go shouting 'Hotty Toddy' in public, okay?"

"Think the Alabama fans might not appreciate it?"

"We'd find you painted crimson and tied to a flagpole," Renata said with a laugh. "How's your room?"

"A hotel's a hotel." The *Journal* was paying for it, and Cole could stand anything for three months. He turned sideways so he could talk to both women at once. "How's the campaign going? What do your polls say?"

"Laurel and Field are running neck-and-neck so far," said Renata. "We have a pollster at the University of South Alabama who's really good. The numbers are telling us we need to focus more on the business community. Play to Laurel's strengths."

Laurel's strengths? "I wouldn't have thought they would lie in business. How do you propose to do that?"

Renata leaned forward. "We're using her dad's contacts to line up speaking engagements with chapters of the Business Council all over the state."

"Isn't Field going for the same vote?" Cole loved the interplay of politics. If he didn't have so much fun writing about it, he'd consider running for office himself. Maybe in Mississippi first, then on a national level.

"Of course. Field's no dummy. But some of his actions as DA over the last few years have put him in conflict with several major players, at least in this county. He's going to have a hard time winning them over." Renata grimaced. "We hope."

"The guy seems like a qualified candidate," Cole offered.

Laurel took the bait. "Oh, he's qualified, all right. Qualified to take some trumped-up charges and indict the most straight-up governor we've ever had." She scowled. "It was a vicious personal vendetta."

"I came across Thorndyke's indictment in my research. You were a partner in the law firm he founded, right? How'd you avoid being implicated yourself?"

"Believe me, I was investigated. There was nothing to find." Laurel took her eyes off the road long enough to shoot a glance at

Cole. "Which is why the charges didn't stick to Governor Thorndyke either."

"Personal vendettas and oily governors." Cole hooked an arm across the back of the seat. "I'm interested in hearing your take on the whole thing."

Those strong brows pulled together, and Cole couldn't tell if Laurel was resentful of his skepticism or simply irritated by his presence. Without answering, she stopped the car at a traffic signal where the road ended at a major thoroughfare. To his right was a triangular median with a Civil War–era cannon monument; past it stretched a small city park, green with spring. Across the wide boulevard in front of them, which was lined with huge, gnarled ancient oak trees dripping with Spanish moss, a white-pillared mansion housed a fine restaurant. Fan-leaf palms and azaleas choked the fenced yards to the left.

After the concrete and pavement of New York, it was nice. "Where are we?" he asked. Laurel was going to ignore any question she found uncomfortable.

Renata jumped into the silence. "Laurel grew up in the Oakleigh district. Her parents still live in the house, mausoleum that it is."

"Hey, you're talking about my family home!"

"Oh, like you haven't complained about the prehistoric plumbing and skimpy insulation and miniature closets since I've known you." Renata leaned forward to talk to Cole as Laurel turned left onto the broad tree-lined boulevard. "The Kincades bought the old Elmore mansion with Miss Frances's trust fund when Laurel was a baby. Mr. Dodge is in the construction business, so they've been gradually restoring it. It's a real showplace now. You'll see."

In less than ten minutes they turned into an established neighborhood full of clapboard, brick, and Spanish plaster mansions.

Cruising down quiet shady streets, Cole took note of yards guarded by oaks and azalea bushes nearly as tall as the second-floor balconies crowding every corner. Green in every possible shade of the palette, with flowers blooming everywhere—pink and red camellias, magnolias, daffodils, and others he couldn't put a name to. He immediately wanted to paint.

Halfway down a narrow street cobbled by tree roots, Laurel turned left again.

Cole caught a glimpse of the street sign and did a double take. "Church Street!"

Laurel braked. "What?"

"I live on Church Street."

"You live in the Holiday Inn."

He smiled. "No, I mean in New York. My apartment's above a bread store on Church Street, in Manhattan."

"No kidding!" Renata laughed. "How weird is that?"

Downright spooky in Cole's opinion, but just then Laurel pulled into a driveway that led to the back of a gray-green antebellum monstrosity in the center of the block. It featured a deep porch, gingerbread trim, a gazillion dormer windows, and a weathervane perched on its high-peaked central roof.

She parked in front of a restored carriage house that already housed a Lexus sedan and a Ford SUV. "Here we are. The tours start at ten, so we'll have to hurry. Mama wants me to talk to the caterer."

"Why do you have to talk to the—"

Laurel was already out of the car, and Cole had to jog to catch her before she skipped through the back door without him. He found himself in a big, sunny kitchen with heart-of-pine floors and white-painted cabinets. Gleaming stainless steel fixtures made it modern enough to be functional and old-fashioned enough to avoid the look of anachronism.

Renata came in behind him, shaking her head. "Always on a tear, that girl."

He frowned as Laurel ducked into a serving anteroom between the kitchen and what looked like a breakfast nook. "I thought you said she was okay with me coming down here to follow her campaign."

"She'll be fine. You just leave the judge to me."

"She'll *be* fine?"

Renata edged toward the anteroom. "Don't pay her any attention if she seems a little hostile right at first. She's working through some issues that got nothing to do with you. I think."

Cole gave Renata a long look and stalked after Laurel. He was beginning to sympathize with Woodward and Bernstein.

"And the chiffonier here in the foyer was brought from Paris by the Lamar family in 1860, just before the late unpleasantness with our northern cousins." Laurel cast a droll look at the crowd of tourists, who tittered.

"That's the woman who's running for supreme court," someone said as if Laurel were one of the stone statues in the garden. "Isn't she beautiful?" A camera went off and Laurel blinked against the flash of light. Was that Renata waving at her from the back of the crowd?

"All right, folks, that's it for the ground floor." She laid a hand on the chiffonnier's gleaming surface. "If you'll move up the staircase to your left—the mahogany banister of which, I assure you, my posterior polished to a blinding shine when I was young—you'll be met by one of our city's lovely Azalea Trail Maids. She'll take you through the bedrooms on the second floor as well as the upper gallery." She smiled at a teenage boy with ear buds sprouting from his head. "Y'all have a good day—and

Alabama residents, don't forget to come out and vote on June three."

Renata shouldered past the last grandma in line for the stairs and leaned in to murmur in Laurel's ear. "Are you done here? We need to talk."

"I think this is the last group before lunch. What's the matter?"

"Come here." Renata pulled Laurel into the study off the front parlor, a room her mother had decorated in the Louis XIV style. It was exquisite, but its main charm was a door that closed without squeaking. Renata shoved Laurel onto a fragile-looking silk ottoman that had survived two civil wars and the great Chicago fire. "Okay, I have to know what's going on in your brain before I explode from curiosity." Renata propped both hands on her hips.

"I have no idea what you're talking about." Puzzled, Laurel folded her hands. Renata should have been the one on the stage.

"I went to a lot of trouble to talk that man into coming all the way from New York. He's been following you around like a lost puppy, waiting to get a private word with you, and you literally *run* every time he gets within hollering distance. How's he supposed to interview you if you won't stand still long enough?" The toes of Renata's pointed, bejeweled sandals tapped with impatience.

Laurel shrugged. "If he's so interested in an interview, where is he now?" She'd been aware of Cole shadowing her all morning, and she'd walked around with her stomach in a fizz of half-thrill, half-terror. Funny how you could pray and release fear, then snatch it back like a best friend.

He'd signed the contract, she reminded herself, and the past was the past. Besides, she was a different person than that innocent, scared girl who'd gotten mixed up with him so long ago. She could be a grown-up and talk to him about her campaign.

Her fear was that he'd want to talk about more than the campaign.

Still, when he'd wandered off after the first tour group left ...

"I don't know where he went." Renata lifted her hands. "Maybe he decided your mother would be an easier target." She sat down on the fainting couch across from Laurel. "Baby, I tried to be patient. I didn't push you for information when you got all weird about Cole coming down here in the first place. I thought, okay, she doesn't like to be forward with a good-looking guy—got the perfect lady stuff going on, whatever. But this is too strange, even for you."

Laurel studied her fingernails. Her behavior had to look strange. It *felt* strange, like walking underwater, movements sluggish, vision distorted.

"I know if you had some kind of background with this man you'd have already told me."

Laurel glanced up from under her lashes. Renata's ruby-colored mouth was turned down. Her best friend knew almost everything about her. But this was not the time and place for true confessions. On the other hand, Laurel wasn't going to lie. "There's something about him that gives me the heebie-jeebies, Renata. I'll talk to him with you or somebody else around, but I don't want to be alone with him. Okay?"

Renata rubbed her forehead. "I don't get it. He seems like a perfectly nice man. Your mama thinks he's a doll. He's been talking cars with your dad."

"I can't explain it." Laurel clamped her lips together. "And I can't change my feelings. Just please—Renata, if you love me, don't leave me alone with him."

Renata sighed. "You are one weird white chick. But okay."

Cole drained his fifth cup of strawberry punch and looked around for a place to set it—besides the top of some priceless antique. For the past hour or so, he'd been skulking amidst a crowd of tourists in the green salon in an effort to keep up with Laurel, who had been moving smoothly from group to group. Shaking hands and introducing herself, she would stay a few minutes to talk, then move on. Keeping an eye on his elusive quarry, he edged past a couple of middle-aged matrons with large handbags and large plastic fingernails.

He saw a tray on the buffet between the scarlet-and-gold brocade-draped floor-to-ceiling windows and headed for it. Ditching the tiny crystal cup, he followed as Laurel approached a group of seniors conversing in front of the fireplace.

"Are you folks enjoying the tour?" Her smile was warm, not a bit forced, as if she had all day to talk about AARP and the best buffet discounts in town.

"Lovely old place, my dear," said a silver-haired lady in white stretch pants and a floral top. "I've lived in the area all my life but never got a chance to come downtown this time of year. Do you still live here?"

"No, ma'am, but my parents do. They taught me to love Mobile history."

"Bet you did the Azalea Trail Maid gig, didn't you?" Cole kept his expression bland, but couldn't resist tweaking Laurel a bit. "Was your dress peach, strawberry, or orange?"

Stiffening, she looked over the head of the silver-haired lady and met his gaze. As he'd intended, she was remembering flavors, not colors, and a certain ice cream party on the back patio of the SAE house. He could see flares of alarm going off in her eyes.

After a frozen moment she let out a breath. "With this hair? Pistachio."

He could visualize her in one of those gong-sized hats and a ruffled dress that would take up half a room. He could also see that the old ladies in the group were eating out of her hand.

"In any case," she continued, unperturbed, "as I said, I've always loved history and politics, which is one reason I'm running for a place on the supreme court. I want to make a difference in my home state."

She was a genius, and she just might win this thing.

His phone vibrated on his hip, and he moved away to answer it. "McGaughan."

"Hey, it's Hogan. Where are you?"

"The judge's old family home." Conversation droned in the background. Plugging his other ear with a finger, Cole moved toward the French window. "I hate to tell you this, but there's nothing to report on the lady. She's a born politician, and her family is one of those rare intact units. Even if there were any skeletons in the closet—which I doubt—they wouldn't break ranks for a stranger." He opened the window and stepped outside, squinting against the sun. It was a bright spring day, and the garden was full of lush plants and blooming annuals. He took a deep, appreciative sniff. Nice. His mother would like this place.

"Well, you're just going to have to figure out a way to weasel information out of them. You be the guy who's *not* a stranger." Hogan's voice grew more animated. "Listen, I just left the courthouse in Biloxi. There's a smokin' hot little blonde clerk I've been having coffee with all week, and she finally let me have a look at the computer. I told you I'd found a gap in the judge's records. Well, it's not accidental. McGaughan, her records were erased."

Mouth dry, Cole turned to look at Laurel, standing just inside the window, laughing at something her father had said. She had no idea Matt Hogan was on her trail like a bloodhound. Ironically, it was Cole she was avoiding.

"That's a pretty wild assumption. You might be getting all excited over something as simple as a bunch of unpaid parking tickets."

"Parking tickets?" Hogan made a rude noise. "Why would she go to that much trouble?"

"You don't know this woman. Her reputation is everything to her."

"Maybe so. But she has no right to defraud the public of information it needs to make an informed decision regarding the judicial race." Hogan's tone sharpened. "Don't you agree?"

"Of course I do. Who's the reporter in this conversation?" Cole walked toward the house, relieved when the connection fractured. "Hey, I need to go. The party's breaking up in there, and I have to make sure I don't get stranded here without a ride."

"Okay. Have to admit you're in a useful spot. Just keep your eyes and ears open." Hogan paused, letting anxious silence hum across the line. "McGaughan, you wouldn't screw me over, would you?"

"Why would you ask me something like that?" Cole opened the French window, letting the noise of the crowd serve as drone accompaniment to his words. "I'll let you know if somebody in Judge Kincade's family tells me what you want to know."

Which would happen when the moon turned to green cheese.

chapter 7

"Laurel, I don't understand why you're doing this to yourself."
The Reverend Wade Theissen surveyed the salad bar with a jaundiced eye, then went straight for the pork chops and mashed potatoes. "I wouldn't get out of the electric chair just before they threw the switch to run for public office."

By dint of long practice Laurel refrained from riposting to her brother-in-law's barb. She needed to concentrate on the speech she would shortly give for Mobile's Christian Legal Society, which immediately followed the buffet lunch. She selected a veggie-stuffed bell pepper and bent down to whisper in Mary Layne's ear. "Does he think he's being funny?"

"I'm sorry," Mary Layne muttered, perpetually guilty. "I got a babysitter and told him where I was going, and he invited himself along."

Laurel shrugged. "It's okay. It's just that he never approves of anything I do."

"That's because you intimidate him." A crease appeared between Mary Layne's straight dark Kincade eyebrows. "Which seems to be a chronic problem between you and most men. I'm beginning to think Mom's right—"

"Stop. Just stop right there." Laurel widened her eyes in mock alarm. "Do not channel Mom, or I'll let you and Wade spring for your own rubber chicken lunch. I refuse to take responsibility for the general lack of testosterone in the single male population of Mobile County." She glanced at Wade, now working his way through an array of lemon meringue pie, bread pudding, and chocolate-chip brownies. He was starting to get a nice little paunch above his brown leather belt. "Or the married ones, for that matter."

Mary Layne giggled. "When I tell you what I found out at the doctor this morning, you'll have to change your mind, about Wade at least."

Laurel stared at her strawberry-blonde younger sister, nearly a head shorter and soft from already having borne four children. "Are you telling me—"

"Yup. Bun number five is officially in the oven. Due in December." Mary Layne's brown eyes had a sleepy, pleased droop. "The kids are all thrilled."

Laurel had reservations about that. Dane, for one, regularly complained about the overcrowded Theissen household. But Mary Layne, the quintessential earth mother, ran a graphic arts business so she could take care of her husband and homeschool her children without working outside her home. If she wanted to run herself crazy changing diapers one more go-round, who was Laurel to knock the butterfly off its flower?

"That's wonderful, sweetie." Laurel leaned down to kiss her sister's cheek. "I'm happy for you."

"Mom thinks we should exercise some restraint." Mary Layne's smile wobbled, and Laurel feared she might have to mop up an emotional outburst. But her sister visibly recovered her sunny temper when a dark-haired giant carrying a computer backpack entered the room. "Speaking of testosterone"—Mary Layne cut a glance at Laurel—"when are you going to bring your hunky reporter home for the rest of us to meet? Mom says he's charming."

"He's not *mine*, and he's *not* coming home with me. There are some things that should stay—Mary Layne! Where are you going?"

Her languid little sister was hustling across the room, where she proceeded to flash her dimples at Cole McGaughan and introduce herself with wholly unnecessary animation.

Later Laurel found herself seated across from Cole at a round banquet table—close enough to have to endure the heat of his silvery eyes, but too far away to control the conversation. Having successfully avoided close contact with him for a week, she chafed at this enforced proximity, especially when her brother-in-law discovered fresh religious meat. The last thing Cole McGaughan would be interested in talking about would be church.

On the other hand, maybe it would serve him right to squirm. She sipped her tea and let it happen.

Wade pushed back his happy plate and leaned his elbows on the table. "My wife tells me you're a New Yorker, Mr. McGaughan. What do you think about the South?"

Cole smiled. "Since I'm told 'Hotty Toddy' doesn't play well on this side of the state line, I guess I'll just let my accent speak for itself." He glanced at Laurel. One eyelid flickered. "Please, though, call me Cole."

Laurel felt her cheeks heat. He'd better not start in on the Push-Up flavors again.

"I grew up in Mississippi, but this is my first visit to Mobile," Cole continued smoothly. "Beautiful city."

"You just missed azalea season," said Mary Layne. "But still, there's a lot to see this time of year."

Wade patted her hand. "If you're going to be with us any length of time, Cole, I hope you'll join us at our church. I'm the pastor of a new congregation on the west side of town. Lots of young people like us, and the worship style's cutting edge."

To Laurel's astonishment, Cole looked interested. "Maybe. I visited the big church on the interstate near my hotel last Sunday. I liked it a lot."

"What in creation possessed you to go to church?" she blurted. Mary Layne and Wade both frowned, while Cole's eyes lit with amusement. "I mean—I'm sorry I didn't think to invite you to my church. I attend one of the oldest Baptist churches in Mobile—it's in the Spring Hill area—and we have a lovely service."

For a moment she and Cole stared at one another. Years rolled back to the first time she'd seen him—amplifiers blaring rock 'n' roll across a jewel-green quad, multicolored flags snapping in a spring breeze, a sizzle of attraction arcing in response to the swaggering confidence of the born athlete.

No. No, no. No matter what had happened eight years ago, they were now essentially strangers. She didn't want to start over with him, but she'd just extended an olive branch. He could take it, he could throw it away, he could even hit her with it. She clenched her fingers in her lap underneath the table.

Those magnesium eyes softened, his mouth curled a little, and he looked so unlike himself that she blinked. His smile grew until he was grinning broadly. "Why, Judge Kincade," he drawled, "did you just invite me to come to church with you tomorrow?"

Caught, she shook her head. "I just said you might enjoy our services if you like traditional music and the great hymns of the faith. We have a Gottfried pipe organ built in Erie, Pennsylvania, in 1929. It was rebuilt about five years ago by the Dobson company, and our organist is a professor at the seminary in New Orleans.

She drives over every Wednesday and Sunday." *And I'm babbling, Lord help me.*

Someone tapped her on the shoulder. "Laurel? Are you ready for your speech?"

Laurel looked up to find Robert Prescott hovering over her. He was the president of the Christian Legal Society chapter. She pushed her chair back. "Yes, I'm ready."

She was more than ready to get out from under the amused gray gaze across the table. She prayed she could get through this speech without forgetting that her ultimate goal had everything to do with moving to Montgomery and nothing to do with impressing an irrepressible reporter.

Cole exited the Spring Hill Baptist Church balcony during the final prayer and vaulted down the wooden stairs as fast as he could without sounding like a herd of stampeding buffalo. In the foyer he passed a five-foot septuagenarian with blue hair and the most immaculate white skin he'd seen outside of a mortuary. He screeched to a halt. "Excuse me, ma'am, can you tell me where the choir goes when they exit the loft?"

The elderly lady leaned on her cane and gave him a quizzical look. "Wire goats in your neck fell off? Young man, have you been drinking?"

Cole blinked, but when the woman surreptitiously tweaked a hearing device in her ear, he grinned. "Never mind." He dodged for the interior of the building, going on instinct. The choir would have to doff their robes and music folders somewhere in that vicinity.

Nope, drinking wasn't his problem at the moment, just one elusive southern belle. He'd called Laurel last night, hoping to wrangle an invitation to sit with her in church this morning, but he'd gotten her voice mail, and she hadn't returned his call. So he came by himself, arriving early in hopes of catching her. He hadn't counted on this being such a massive congregation and church plant. There must have been a thousand souls just in the service he'd attended, and there had been two others — one before and one after. The parking lot was full, and though he'd asked the red-vested parking volunteers if they knew Laurel, nobody had been able to tell him exactly where she could be found.

So he'd accepted a worship bulletin, wandered up into the balcony, and sat by himself, surrounded by strangers.

Laurel's church was as different as night and day from his small, intimate fellowship of believers in Manhattan. His church rented space in a theater and leaned toward ultra-modern music, high-tech production, and a rather loose, unorthodox structure. Christians in New York tended to stick out like rocks in pea soup. Not so here in the jewel of the Bible belt buckle. Cole felt like he'd been swallowed whole. Maybe he'd get used to it.

Maybe not.

One thing for sure — watching Laurel and listening to her sing with that massive, robed choir under a stained-glass rose window had been a revelation. He'd felt the serenity of the Holy Spirit enter through the music, wash him, subdue him for the first time since he'd left New York. Connecting Laurel with that spiritual gift did something soft to his insides. He wasn't entirely sure he liked it or trusted it.

But he trusted the Giver of the gift. *Help me, Lord, to reach her — if you want me to. Make Laurel listen to me.*

He found a hallway that seemed to lead along the outside wall of the sanctuary, toward the choir loft. Passing through a nursery wing brightly painted with murals of biblical scenes, he smiled at the shrieks of children overlaying the piped-in strains of the final hymn from the end of the service. Eventually he found himself in another small entryway facing a door marked "Choir Room."

Bingo.

The choir room door suddenly opened, and people flooded out on a noisy tide of conversation. Cole stood like a rock in a creek bed and let them flow past—people dressed in snazzy spring suits, all smiling and discussing lunch. No tall, red-haired judges.

He was just about to give up and head for the Piccadilly by himself when he saw her. She came out detached from the rest of the crowd, head down as if she were checking a button on her dress—a red trench coat affair with a wide belt that cinched her small waist and drew attention to her curvy shape and long legs.

She looked up and saw him. She stopped, Bible held against her stomach. "Cole! What are you doing here?"

Hurt blindsided him. Ever since he'd arrived a week ago he'd been nothing but kind and considerate, following at a distance, respecting her desire for privacy. Couldn't a man come to church without being treated like a stalker?

"You invited me, remember?"

"I know, but you never said you were coming and—"

He turned on his heel and headed for the exit to his right.

"Cole! Wait, Cole—come back!"

He paused with a hand on the door, shoulders tense. He didn't want to fight on the Lord's day. He didn't want to fight with Laurel at all. Pushing open the door, he walked out into a bright spring noontime sun.

Halfway to the parking lot she caught him. Her hand on his upper arm went through him like a two-hundred-volt charge, stopping him in his tracks. The last time she'd touched him ...

He jerked out from under her hand, wheeled. "What, Laurel? I'm leaving you alone. I'm booking a flight back to New York as soon as I can get back to the hotel and boot up my computer."

"You don't have to—Cole, I'm sorry, you just caught me off guard. I told you, I wasn't expecting to see you." Laurel's milky skin was even paler than usual, and she was chewing on her lower lip. She had a bit of lipstick on her teeth.

"If you'd answered your phone last night you'd have known I was coming. But it's too much trouble to return a phone call from me—isn't it? In your estimation, I'm the off-the-charts bad boy who doesn't deserve the time of day, much less the grace of God's family." Over the top, maybe, but resentment had built up until he could no more have put a lid on it than he could have turned the sky purple. He was peripherally aware of a young couple with toddlers in tow, glancing at him and Laurel as they got into their SUV a few spaces away. *Enjoy the show, folks.*

Laurel opened her mouth, but no words came out. She finally put a hand over her lips. Her eyes swam with tears.

Cole wasn't in a mood to feel sorry for her. "If you could've stood still long enough for a meaningful conversation, there are some things I'd like to have told you. Like the fact that I committed my life to Christ three years ago and I've never looked back, never been the same. I'd have told you I came down here—twice—to tell you how sorry I am for everything that happened between us eight years ago. But I wanted to tell you to your face, not leave it on some answering machine."

"Cole." Laurel dropped her hand to clasp her Bible in both hands, shieldlike. He waited, but she just shook her head.

"For a woman who's so good at verbal communication, you're mighty inarticulate, Judge Kincade. You might want to work on that." Hurt nearly stopped his lungs. He made himself exhale. "Anyway, I just wanted to say I forgive you for what you made me do. I'm moving on, lady." Backing up a step, he turned and headed for the parking lot. He didn't look back.

He'd said all that to Laurel, expecting to feel lighter for having unloaded it. All he felt was sad.

Laurel sat in the Bonefish Grill parking lot with the sun roof open, letting the April sunshine bake the top of her head. The rest of the family had already gone inside. She couldn't join them until she'd dealt with that awful confrontation with Cole.

She looked at her hands on the steering wheel. They trembled.

What on earth had made him speak to her that way? Forgive *her*? For crying out loud, what did he think she'd done to him? A miraculous conversion? How could she have known? He'd never said a word about it in a week of following her around.

True, she hadn't given him much chance to talk about anything personal, but the message on her answering machine could have warned her he was coming to church this morning. Appearing like a paparazzi outside the choir room door ... Dressed up in neat black slacks, a crisp pink oxford shirt, and a charcoal-and-pink patterned tie that, so far from looking feminine, only served to exaggerate the shadow of incipient beard and the strength of the hands stuffed in his pockets. Like he wanted to grab hold of her and—and—

And that was the root of her conflict. Attraction going both ways. Attraction that had nearly snapped her in half once upon a time.

At least ... at least he was gone for good now. She'd finally been so rude to him that he was bound to be on a plane back to the Big Apple in the morning.

Gone. Which should make her feel relief. Happiness. Delirium even.

Instead—guilt.

She put her head in her hands. "Oh, God, what's wrong with me?" she whispered. "I'd moved on. I hadn't even thought about him in years. Well, not much."

Cole's dark face played in her brain, an angry film noir. Yes, angry, but he was hurt too.

She could understand it to a degree. For a long time she'd resented the fact that Cole had always had everything he wanted. Money. Education. Good looks and perfect physique — he even went to college on a wrestling scholarship. He'd apparently arrived at a job with one of the most prestigious newspapers in the country. But confusing the issue was his claim of regeneration. He wanted her forgiveness.

No, that wasn't what he'd said. He expected to forgive *her*.

"God, I've got to have help," she said aloud, looking up through the sunroof, where a fleecy bank of clouds drifted overhead. "I can't figure this out by myself."

Cole had been sitting in Starbucks all afternoon, mainlining espressos until he was just about as high speed as the café's free Internet service.

The more he thought about Laurel Kincade and her hypocrisy, the madder he got. If only the rest of the world knew what he knew about her.

Worse still, due to thunderstorms in Atlanta, he couldn't get a flight out of Mobile tonight. So he was supposed to just sit here in this poky little southern city with its lazy, drawling, flower-scented religiosity and let that woman pretend to be Miss High-on-a-Pedestal Snow White. Let her travel all over Alabama kissing babies and glad-handing bumpkins who were looking for leaders with "family values." Let her use that beautiful innocent face, that God-given intellect, to make them believe she deserved to judge them.

No. Not gonna happen. Not while he was on the field.

He unzipped his backpack and took out his computer. After booting it up he stared at the blinking cursor on a blank Word document. He thought best through his fingers on a keyboard.

It's me, Lord. What do you want me to do? I thought you sent me down here, but I've been beating my head against a wall. I'm tired. This is stupid, if you'll excuse my frustration. The woman is impossible.

He stopped with his fingers on the keys, closed his eyes, and sighed. Phrases from the music at church sifted through his mind. *From everyone who has been given much, much will be demanded. Forgive and you will be forgiven.*

Forgive, yes, but he didn't have to let Laurel off the hook. He didn't have to let her con the good people of Alabama, who thought they were getting something they weren't. That wouldn't be right or ethical.

A twinge of conscience was interrupted by a young woman pushing a baby in a stroller, who gave Cole a curious glance as she cruised to the counter. He blinked—realizing he must look like a catatonic drunk. Downing the cold dregs of his fourth double espresso, he closed the prayer document without saving it and opened a fresh one.

He'd come down here to write an article, and by golly, he was going to write one that would turn this Alabama judicial race upside down. The dateline and his name went at the top of the page, then he stared at the cursor for a moment. Taking a deep breath, he plunged in.

MOBILE—Judge Laurel Kincade, appointed last summer by Governor Nels Thorndyke as a district juvenile court judge in Mobile County, is seeking election in the June primary as Alabama's first female supreme court chief justice. In January, surrounded by family and supporters in the rotunda of the Judicial Building in Montgomery, Kincade announced her decision to run for the seat vacated by retiring Judge Clyde Barron.

Though initially a long shot for the post, Kincade, 32, has steadily gained popularity in local and statewide polls. As the daughter of longtime Mobile residents Dodge and Frances Kincade, owners of Kincade Construction, and granddaughter of Yazoo County, Mississippi, Circuit Court judge Pete Gillian, Kincade has a wealth of financial and political backing at her disposal. Governor Thorndyke, as well as several conservative state senators and high-profile Alabama church leaders have endorsed the judge's candidacy.

Unfortunately, it turns out that Alabama's sweetheart "Christian family values" judge has been hiding quite a healthy skeleton in her closet.

Somebody was pounding on the hotel room door. Cole rolled over and cocked a bleary eye at the clock. Six a.m. Good grief. He'd been up half the night perfecting the article. And then a bunch of teenagers on spring break had decided to host a party at the pool right outside his balcony door. He'd finally had to call management to make them give it up and go to bed.

The banging on the door kept up until he flung back the sheet in disgust. After yanking on a pair of jeans he'd dropped on the floor last night, he opened the door yawning.

Laurel stood in the hall with her hands loosely clasped in that beauty pageant way of hers. At the sight of his bare chest, her eyes went wide. She immediately slammed them shut. "I woke you up." Her voice was husky, embarrassed.

Have mercy. "I told you I'm leaving town, Laurel. What else do you want me to say?" He rubbed his bristly jaw. Lord, he probably looked like an escaped convict.

Laurel, on the other hand, was her usual perfectly groomed self. She had on one of those flowing ankle-length skirts she favored, this one in earthy brown tones, with a silky, clingy beige top that made him want to touch. He clutched the doorframe instead.

She gingerly opened her eyes. "I was afraid you'd already be on the way to the airport."

"Yeah, well, I couldn't get a flight. So. Lucky you." He squinted at her. "What are you doing here this time of day? God doesn't even get up this early."

"Yes, he does." She licked her lips. "I know because I've been talking to him for quite some time. And he says I need to talk to you."

"Huh?"

"Cole, would you just put your shirt on, and come somewhere with me so we can ... " She looked around. "I shouldn't be here at your hotel."

"Now's a fine time to think of that."

A tide of red washed up from the V-neck of her top, all the way to her widow's peak.

"Oh, okay," he sighed, backing up and scratching his chest absently. "Wait right there."

He shut the door in her face, an action that gave him a certain satisfaction, then fished under the bedspread for his shoes. As he sat down to put them on, he glanced at his computer. The article was finished, but he wanted to read through it one more time before emailing it to his editor this morning.

Wonder what Laurel would say when she discovered he was about to throw a rock right through the window of her career ...

Laurel stood on first one foot and then the other, wishing she'd elected to wear flats instead of these silly two-inch heels.

And why had she bothered to paint her toenails? Cole wasn't going to look at her feet.

But it had somehow seemed important to look put-together this morning when bearding the lion in his den. The lion who ate Christians for lunch.

No, wait, Cole had become a Christian himself. Or so he said. Talking to him on a spiritual level was going to be so odd, like discovering an extraterrestrial visitor had learned English overnight.

She leaned against the wall, staring at the 223 on Cole's door as she lined up her arguments—excuses, really—in her head. *You took me off guard. I was afraid you'd tell my little sister what kind of trouble I got into, and I didn't want to be a bad example. I didn't trust you because you hurt me—*

She winced. That was the one she couldn't, wouldn't, articulate out loud.

The door opened, and Cole came out stuffing a set of car keys into the back pocket of his jeans. He still looked stubbly around the jaw, but he'd combed his hair and smelled like toothpaste. And he'd pulled on a mint-green polo. She'd seen him without a shirt before, so she shouldn't have been so shocked.

She sneaked another glance at him.

He didn't smile. "Can we go to Waffle House or something? Seeing as I've had about three hours of sleep, I need coffee."

"I'm sorry to have gotten you up so early. Like I said—"

"I know, Laurel, it's okay." Cole pressed a thumb and forefinger against his eyelids. "I'm—" He sighed. "Can we just please go to Waffle House?"

A smile broke through as she led the way toward the elevator. "You still have a penchant for fried eggs and biscuits and limp bacon?"

"Guess so. Remember the time after Elise's bowling party?"

"You bowled a three hundred."

Cole grinned down at her as he punched the elevator button. "Your best score was a hundred and fifty. Not bad for a girl."

Something inside Laurel's stomach zipped upward as if she were already on the elevator and it had taken off without her. After all that had happened between them, how could they stand here and tease one another like this?

Her expression must have reflected her confusion; Cole's grin faded. In silence they rode the elevator down to the lobby, then walked side-by-side out to the parking lot.

"Let's take my truck," he said, pulling the keys out of his pocket. "I rented one big enough for my long legs."

"All right." Laurel followed him to an enormous gray Ford and waited for him to open the door for her. He took her elbow and gave her a little boost up onto the high seat, his palm warm and rough on her bare skin. She peeked at him. "Thanks."

In the driver's seat beside her, he started the ignition, and country bluegrass blared from the CD player. He turned it down, glancing at her. "Sorry. I still like it loud."

"I'm surprised you have any hearing left."

"What?"

"I said—" She caught the white glint of his grin and stopped. She fell for that one every time. "You used to like the White Stripes."

"I grew up, Laurel." There was reproach and regret and maybe a lot of other stuff she couldn't identify mixed in his tone.

She didn't look at him again until they got to the little diner and sat down across from each other in a booth. Then she had to face him.

But he zeroed in on the menu and gave the waitress his charming, crooked smile. "Hey, how are you? I need three fried eggs over light, grits, toast, and bacon—can you make sure it's not overcooked? Oh, and give me an IV of coffee. It's been a long night."

The hard-faced waitress smiled and picked up the menus. "Sure, hon. Next time don't wait so long before you come see us." She turned reluctantly to Laurel. "For you, ma'am?"

"Just a small orange juice, please." At the woman's disdainful look, Laurel blurted, "And waffles with sausage." What was wrong with her? She never ate fried meat. And processed starches for breakfast? She was going to gain five pounds before noon.

Cole had that little glint in his eyes that told her he'd somehow read her mind.

She stared him down. *Get this over with, Laurel.* "I wanted to apologize for freaking out on you yesterday at church. I was just—surprised to see you."

"We had to come all the way to Waffle House for that?" Cole looked up when the waitress set a mug in front of him. "Thanks." He picked up the coffee and sipped it black, then looked at Laurel across the top of the mug. "I told you I'm not gonna worry about it. I'd thought since we were old friends I might be able to write a top-notch series about your campaign and help you out in the bargain. But you've obviously got some issues with me. If my being here makes you that uncomfortable, I'm going back to New York. Simple." He smiled a little. "And I told you I've moved on."

"But you didn't mean it."

"I promise you, Laurel—"

Laurel held up a hand. "I'm not blind. I can see the way you're looking at me. And you're right, I haven't gotten over my bitterness either. Here's the thing, Cole. You promised to stay away from me, and when you suddenly violated that promise, I felt threatened. I didn't know anything about you had changed." She frowned. "I *still* don't know it for sure, no matter what you say."

Cole nodded reluctantly. "Words are cheap, I guess."

"Yes. But I will give you this. In spite of the loud music and fried eggs, what I've seen of you so far is light-years away from the spoiled frat boy I used to know."

"I don't know how you could tell," Cole muttered. "You make me feel like Pepé Le Pew." He put on an exaggerated French accent. "'You are my peanut. I am your brittle.'"

Laurel had to laugh. "If it's any consolation, you don't stink."

"I'd say he smells pretty darn good, if you ask me." The waitress plunked down their plates. She ripped off the ticket and laid it on the table, then flounced off to the other end of the diner.

Laurel pursed her lips. "I think you've made a conquest." Another in a long line, which was at least half the problem here. She surveyed her meal and found to her surprise that her appetite had returned with a vengeance. Maybe reconciliation was good for the constitution. She picked up the syrup pitcher. "So why don't you start by telling me more about how you came to know the Lord? I'm curious."

Cole had already dug into his own meal, mixing eggs and grits and bacon into a primordial soup that would have been completely disgusting if Laurel hadn't been distracted by that pale scar on his face, pulling slightly as he chewed.

"I should have told you first thing, I know." He caught her looking at his cheek and grimaced. "After you left Oxford, there was a ... an incident, involving a case of beer, my Beamer, and William Faulkner's gravestone. Messed up my face pretty bad. This is sort of part of the journey back, though." His lips curved as he traced the scar with a finger. "Some of us are pretty hardheaded."

"I'm not perfect either, Cole."

"That's true." His eyes twinkled. "*Mon petit* buttercup. Okay, okay, I'll leave you alone. So you want to know what it took to turn the reprobate wild-man wrestler, Quad McGaughan, into the mild-mannered reporter you see before you today."

"Yes."

He pushed away his empty plate. She'd barely made a dent in her waffles. "Hey, sweetheart, could I have a refill?" he called, holding up his coffee mug. The waitress nearly hurt herself running back to fill it again. Cole winked at Laurel. "A man needs his strength for telling tales."

Laurel steeled herself. This was how it had happened the first time. Teasing, intimate looks, inside jokes, leashed masculinity. "Don't tell me any tales, Cole. Tell me the truth."

He sobered. "You know what the Bible says about the truth. But you pay a price for freedom." He looked at her from beneath heavy black lashes. "Think you're ready for it?"

He was enjoying her undivided attention, the rat. Still, she nodded. "I'm not going anywhere. I don't have to be in court until this afternoon."

"Won't take that long. Pretty straightforward story. About three years ago, I was writing for the *Commercial Appeal* in Memphis. Prison Fellowship has an operation in the Tennessee penal system, and I was assigned to research it when some of the bigwigs came to town for a summer crusade. Having been—" he cleared his throat and looked at the ceiling for a moment—"intimately acquainted with a jail cell myself, I found the interviews particularly challenging. Didn't take me long to realize I couldn't shake or rattle these guys, no matter what kind of questions I asked. They knew what they were talking about regarding prisoner rehabilitation—and not only that, they genuinely cared about the men and women they were preaching to and teaching in those Bible studies."

"I've done some jail ministry myself." Laurel sipped her juice. "In college. And lately, before I started getting busy with the campaign."

"Huh." Cole blinked. "Well, it was a revelation to me. I couldn't help being impressed by the results I saw, and one time I actually got to meet Mr. Colson." He shook his head. "I've never seen such a changed life. And I thought, if a brilliant guy like that believes, then maybe I should check it out for myself—you know, what the Bible claims about Jesus."

"Cole, surely that's not the first time you heard the gospel." She didn't know a lot about his family, but she thought there were at least a couple of Christians in his pedigree.

"Of course not. My mom and my uncle Zane had been trying to talk to me about it since I was a little kid, but there were too many other influences drowning them out. I wouldn't listen. But that year in Memphis, I had been through so much stuff that I was broken down to a place where I could hear what God was trying to say to me. I saw where I was headed and decided I didn't have anything to lose by asking the Lord to forgive me and rescue me." Cole smiled, a luminous smile that made Laurel blink tears away. "And he did."

"Oh, Cole. I'm so glad."

"Yeah. It was pretty cool." Cole leaned forward, his expression eager. "I wrote that article, and it was good enough that a couple of wire services picked it up. The *Journal* ran it and wound up offering me a job for their religion beat. I think I'm up for a promotion." He looked at her expectantly, as if waiting for her to jump up and cheer.

Laurel still found herself unable to instantly cast aside eight years of distrust. "That's wonderful."

"But ..." Cole sat back, lips flattening. "You think I don't deserve any of the good things that have happened to me."

"I didn't say that!" Laurel picked up her napkin and twisted it. "The apostle Paul got a second chance. Jonah did. Like you said, even Charles Colson did." She closed her eyes. "We all do."

"Then why can't you forgive me, Laurel? Why can't we start over and be friends?"

An image played across the backs of Laurel's eyelids—Cole advancing toward her from across a New Orleans bar, the expression in his eyes sending terror burning up the alcohol in her stomach like a residue of fuel in an empty gas tank. If she'd tried to explain it, no one would have understood why she should be afraid of Cole McGaughan. That night she'd been mourning Michael all over again. Vulnerable. And somehow he'd known and taken advantage.

Forgive? Start over?

For heaven's sake—*friends*?

The idea made her stomach churn.

Yesterday she'd sung the words, "Forgive as I have forgiven you." Had she meant them, or had that just been a platitude, a sop for Sunday morning choir?

Somewhere she'd read that her own strength was insufficient for such requirements—but Jesus had a big, deep well, full of living water. *Lord, please fill me up. I'm empty. I can't do this.*

She opened her eyes and looked at Cole, who regarded her with caution rapidly melting into disappointment. "Okay," she said before she could change her mind. "My feelings aren't there yet, but my brain says yes."

Cole's lips parted. "Yes, what?"

"Yes, I'm going to forgive you. Although, I'll be honest—you'll still have to earn my trust. I want you to—" She swallowed, had to force herself to continue. "You can stick around and write this series of articles. That is, if you still want to. I promise I won't shut you out anymore."

Cole's astonishment was palpable. He grinned, eyes crinkling. "Really?"

"Really. But Cole—writing about anything that happened between us in the past is strictly off-limits. Off the record, if you will. Is that clear?"

He saluted. "Yes, ma'am, Miss Scarlett."

Cole regretted writing that article about Laurel, even if every word of it was true. Skewed toward vengeance, it was unworthy of any journalist with professional ethics.

Thank the Lord he hadn't sent it. And he wasn't going to—not when she had apologized so sincerely and all but given him carte blanche into her campaign.

She was still wired pretty tight, but that was Laurel. He actually liked the challenge of making her crack a smile. One day he'd get a laugh out of her and the world would shift on its axis.

He was about to call for a celebratory third cup of coffee when his cell phone blared at his hip. Since Laurel was tucking into her waffles and sausage with gusto, he checked the ID. Hogan. He shouldn't answer it, but the guy would keep calling until Cole picked up.

He caught Laurel's gaze. "I'm sorry, I need to take this call. Will you excuse me for a minute?"

She shrugged. "Sure."

Cole walked outside and flipped open the phone as he sat down on a bench beside the door. "What's up, Hogan?"

"I'm back in Mobile. Just checking in." Hogan sounded like a sailor on board after a three-day leave. "Where are you?"

"Having breakfast with Judge Laurel."

"Well, it's about time."

"Get your mind out of the sewer, boy. We're at Waffle House, and everybody slept in their own beds."

Hogan sighed. "Wish I had."

"What do you mean?"

"I've been out on surveillance all night."

"Surveillance? Surveilling who?"

"Your lady's best buddy. She's quite the get-around girl."

"Renata? That doesn't sound like her."

Hogan gave a sour laugh. "I'm here to tell you, what people put on the surface is never what's going on underneath. That's why we've gotta keep digging on the judge. Sooner or later we'll hit pay dirt."

Cole didn't want to hear it. "So where'd you track down Renata?"

"Little rhythm and blues club on Dauphin Street. And you'll never guess who she was hanging out with."

The back of Cole's neck tightened. "I'm sure you're gonna tell me."

"The judge's campaign consultant has contracted out to a local guy for some marketing stuff. Up-and-coming young guy named Derrick Edes. Little Renata's got a hot boyfriend."

Cole relaxed. "So? They're socializing to make plans for the judge's campaign. People mix business and pleasure all the time."

Hogan chuckled. "Don't I know it. But you get people socializing, and information eventually starts to flow. Especially when alcohol's involved. You might want to try a champagne dinner with the lovely judge instead of a pancake breakfast, homeboy."

"Look," Cole interrupted, trying to figure out how to say what he needed to say without sounding pious. He wanted to bring Matt along with him spiritually, but there were things holding his friend back, things only the Holy Spirit could free him from. "Just remember that an alcohol-induced flow of information is a two-way street. And before you know it, you're out of control and facing a head-on collision."

He had to hold the phone away from his ear to soften Hogan's spew of sewer language. "McGaughan, it's way too early in the morning to get preached at."

"Yeah, and my grandma always said cussing is a mark of a weak vocabulary."

"Tell your grandma I don't give a flying flip about my vocabulary." But Hogan chuckled. "All right, Cornbread, help me out here. Field is threatening to fire me if I don't find something on this lady soon."

Cole shut the phone, returned it to the clip on his belt, and went back inside the restaurant.

Laurel was absently spinning her orange juice glass against the table. She looked up. "Everything okay?"

"Yeah, that was a friend who's in Mobile on business." He sat down again and snitched a piece of sausage off Laurel's plate.

She smiled and pushed her leftovers to his side of the table. "You should bring him by the house sometime. I want to hear more about what you've been doing in the last few years."

Cole shrugged. "Maybe."

The rat's nest of ethical issues involved in this situation made his head threaten to explode. He had no intention of telling Laurel he'd originally come down here to help her opponent investigate her for a tell-all story, not when they were just getting back on cordial footing. If he warned her about Hogan, Cole would be tarred with the same brush. The best he could do was commit himself to his job and write the best story possible about a female judge's political campaign.

And if the judge just happened to be a beautiful lady he was falling in love with for the second time ... Well, God help him.

c h a p t e r 8

Cole woke up early Wednesday morning intending to write up what he'd learned about the Alabama judicial campaign so far. Turned out he had a good deal of information on Laurel Kincade and very little on her opponent.

He stared at his notes. Time to rectify that situation.

He got dressed and headed for the truck, which he'd left in the rear parking lot of the hotel. Just about to get in, he heard an odd noise coming from the Dumpster at the corner of the building. If the hotel had rats, they were Rodents Of Unusual Size. He hoped he wasn't going to have to wrestle one of them for the princess's hand like the hero of *The Princess Bride*. Laurel used to love that movie, had it memorized back to front, and he'd often teased her by quoting obscure lines.

His smile faded when the ROUS suddenly yelped—with a tone remarkably like a dog.

What the heck? A dog in the Dumpster?

He shut the door of the truck and cautiously approached the garbage receptacle. The smell was overpowering, and the noise was getting louder. Maybe he should call animal control. Taking a breath and holding it, he peered over the open metal door.

A pair of distressed brown eyes in a long, sad canine face peered back at him. The rest of the dog's body was buried in a pile of shredded trash bags and unmentionable refuse. It released a long, miserable full-throated howl.

Cole released his breath in surprise. "Well, hey, buddy. What's a nice ROUS like you doing in a place like this?"

Laurel knew everybody in her courtroom well, except the defendant.

Marjean Brock, who was in the choir at church, considered herself the Christopher Columbus of the Internet and would stay up all hours of the night surfing eBay. Which explained why she was currently yawning over her steno machine at nearly five in the afternoon.

Then there was Deputy DA Adair Fanshaw, slouched behind a table stroking his long, scanty sideburns with thin fingers. Just a year out of law school, Adair needed to make his mark quickly or he'd find himself pinned in position, doomed to years of saying "yes, Your Honor" to a female judge.

Laurel frowned at the top of Adair's head, a trick she knew would drive him crazy. He brushed at the thinning brown locks tied at the back of his neck with a red rubber band.

Meanwhile the boy's court-appointed defense lawyer, Douglas "Doogie" Sherill, listed all the reasons Laurel ought to dismiss the charges. Too young for a record. Only a third offense. Mr. Goldsmith was overreacting to a childish prank. Yada, yada.

She'd heard it all before.

She was interested in the kid himself. He reminded her of a half-grown puppy braced for the next boot aimed his way. Small and hungry-looking for his age—her notes said he was fourteen. He'd been engrossed in the circling of his thumbs, but suddenly he looked up and met her gaze. Narrow blue eyes in a winter-white face, with a wide mouth clamped in defiance or fear, or maybe a combination of the two.

There had to be a better way to help this kid. Nothing anybody had tried so far had worked. She broke eye contact with young Marty Welch and removed the pewter-framed reading glasses perched on the end of her nose.

"Mr. Sherill, I'd like some time to review my notes and speak to Mr. Goldsmith again before I rule on the charges."

Doogie blinked. Judge Kincade never interrupted. "Yes, Your Honor." Yanking on his tie, he glanced at Adair.

Adair shrugged and tried not to look irritated.

Laurel folded her glasses and slid them into their metal case. "We'll convene again in the morning. Make sure Marty has everything he needs for the night, will you, Mr. Sherill?"

The boy exhibited a remarkable lack of gratitude for her concern, but Doogie nodded and touched his shoulder. Marty flinched.

Sighing, Laurel pushed back her squeaky but comfortable chair, stacked her notes, and watched her party disintegrate.

Was she ready for the bigger responsibility of the supreme court? Administrative duties, the teamwork with eight other judges, writing opinions that would decide cases. She thought so, but sometimes fear took her unaware.

She stepped down off the platform behind the bench and was about to head for her office when she realized Marjean was standing in the courtroom door, an expression of deep concern marring her pudding-soft features. Her steno machine in its case waited at her feet. "Judge Kincade, may I ask you something?"

Laurel paused, a hand on the door. "Of course. What's the matter?"

"Who's going to care about these kids when you get elected to the big court and move up to Montgomery? They'll put some hard-nosed twerp in here who'll send 'em all to juvie and won't take time to figure out how to rescue them."

"A hard-nosed twerp may be just what this place needs." Laurel smiled, pulling her hair off her neck with her hand. The robe got hot and itchy after a long day. "I'm not the only good judge in this state."

"You're one of the best I've seen, and I've been around since the ark landed on Ararat." Marjean hoisted the steno machine and blew a trail of gray-streaked hair out of her eyes. "Well, better get home to the mister before he starts rooting through the freezer for frozen pizza. Take it easy, Judge, you're looking a tad washed-out these days. Toodles."

Shaking her head, Laurel slipped out of her robe and draped it over the hanger on the back of the door. Was it any wonder she looked washed-out? She'd stayed up late last night practicing the commercial she was scheduled to record tonight. That would probably go late too. Recording engineers all seemed to be part vampire.

Grabbing her purse, she went out the side door into the hallway. She smiled at Paul Nunnely, the burly African American security guard posted at the exit.

"Have a good evening, Judge Kincade," he intoned with a little salute.

"Thanks. You too, Paul."

"I told your gentleman friend he could wait by your car."

She halted in her tracks. "My *what*?"

"Big dark-haired guy." Paul's mustache pulled down. "Showed me a press ID and *said* he was a friend. Here, I'll walk you out there. I won't let him bother you—"

"Is his name Cole McGaughan?"

"That's it. So you do know him?"

Laurel sighed. "I know him. You don't have to come with me. I'll be fine."

"You sure? I got nothing else to do right now."

Laurel smiled up into Paul's heavy dark face. He never failed to offer her a caramel as she walked through the security check-point every morning. She'd bought christening gifts for his two new grandbabies last year. He was a good man, and she was going to miss him as well as Marjean when she moved to Montgomery. "Mr. McGaughan is a reporter who's been doing a series of stories on my campaign. But if it'll make you feel better, you can watch me walk to the parking lot."

"You got it." Paul smiled and waved her off.

Laurel clutched her handbag under her arm and headed for her car.

The evening was a bit cool for early April, with a fresh breeze drawing the scent of spirea and viburnum from the hedges around the parking lot. No reason to get all hot and bothered.

Especially not the sight of Cole leaning against the hood of her car, long legs stretched out and crossed casually at the ankles. He sat relaxed with his hands in the pockets of his khakis, the sleeves of a pale blue button-down rolled to the middle of his fore-arms. He was whistling.

She got closer, and the tune drifted at the edges of her recog-nition. She frowned, trying to recall what it was.

Cole pushed away from the car. "Sorry, I should have called, but you were in court and your secretary said I'd better wait for you out here if I wanted to catch you."

"No, it's okay." She stopped a couple of yards away. "I was just trying to figure out what you're whistling. It sounds familiar for some reason."

He stared at her. "It's 'I Only Want to Be with You.' It was in my tape deck all the way down to—"

"I remember now." She hardly knew where to look. Just when she got back onto a normal footing with Cole, he lobbed something else at her. Now it was Hootie and the Blowfish. "I don't mean to be rude, Cole, but I have to go home and get ready for the radio spot we're recording tonight. Did you need something?"

"Yeah, as a matter of fact I do." He ran a hand around the back of his neck, rumpling his already rumpled hair. "I was wondering what your thoughts are on bloodhounds."

Matt Hogan was kicked back with a beer at a table outside a little pizza joint called the Mellow Mushroom when Wallace Field's ID popped up in the display screen of his cell phone.

He decided to let it ring this time. He'd set up a little opposition research with Renata Castleberry, who was due to show up any minute, and he didn't want to have to explain anything. Field was driving him crazy, calling twice a day wanting to know how the Kincade case was progressing.

Like a snail on BZDs.

The problem was McGaughan. Matt couldn't figure the guy out. One day he was promising to help with the case, eager to load up enough ammo against the lady judge to strip her naked—figuratively speaking, of course—and hand this judicial race over to the guy who deserved it. Well, as much as any ambulance-chasing attorney deserved anything good in this life.

Then, before you could say "Boo Radley," McGaughan was all but sitting in Laurel Kincade's lacy pocket, eating bonbons and drinking tea with the Mobile high society elite.

Matt took a slug from the sweating, icy brown bottle on the table and morosely scanned the parking lot again. Women. Always late. The University of South Alabama main campus was just across the boulevard. He could make better use of his time by checking out the library archives. You never knew what you could dig up from old lady librarians showing off their research skills.

Plus, he could have scoped out the hot coeds, who'd apparently left everything but their underwear at the beach during spring break. No explaining the exhibitionistic tendency of girls these days, but it sure was entertaining.

Fifteen minutes later, a white soft-top sedan pulled up with a screech of brakes, and Renata Castleberry flung herself out of the driver's seat. She slammed the door on her purse, uttered a rude word, and extricated herself before she saw Matt.

"Sorry I'm late," she said, huffing. "I was showing a house over in west Mobile, and the lady wouldn't turn me loose. I kept telling her I had another appointment, but—"

"Never mind." Matt smiled his forgiveness. "I'm just enjoying the breeze and my beer. You want to go inside?"

"No way, I've been stuck in this car all day. I'm glad to sit out here. I'm hungry, though. Let me go order a drink and a pizza, and I'll be right back." Renata disappeared for a few minutes and came back with a glass of iced tea. She plopped into the patio chair under the shade of the plastic mushroom-shaped umbrella and sucked down half the contents of her glass. "Umm. That's good. I was parched."

"The real estate business keeping you busy, huh?"

"Yeah, baby. Towards the end of the school year the market picks up with people ready to think about moving." She shrugged, her dark-brown shoulders smooth and toned in a sleeveless pale green top.

She was a pretty lady. Matt would have tried for a little action, but she was a bit standoffish, in spite of her vibrant way of moving and talking. Besides, she seemed to be fairly taken with the bald black guy, Edes.

"Thanks for taking time to meet with me," he said. "The group of businessmen I represent are keen on finding out about Judge Kincade's campaign platform."

"Well, you know, that's my job. Laurel doesn't like to deal with the money." Renata grinned. "And I do."

"So how do you have time to work with the judge's campaign?" He offered her a slice of cheese bread he'd ordered to tide him over.

"I *make* time for Laurel. I don't trust her affairs to anybody else."

"Affairs?" He sat up. "What kind of affairs?"

Renata laughed. "Not *that* kind of affairs. We're talking Laurel, here. I can't even remember the last time she had a date that wasn't associated with some kind of business function."

"Who does she go out with when she does those business things?"

Renata made a face. "Different men. Usually it's Robert Prescott. She used to work with him in the AG's office, and he's now an attorney for the Army Corps of Engineers. But they're extremely platonic. I personally think she's holding out for something better."

"Don't blame her for being picky. Woman like her could get anyone she wanted." Matt steepled his fingers under his chin. It was time to go fishing. "I was over in Jackson, Mississippi, at a conference last week and ran into a lady who says she knew the judge in law school days. What was her name?" He pretended to think. "Teresa? Diane? Man, I'm drawing a blank now."

Renata's snapping dark-brown eyes lit. "Could it have been Monica? She lives in Biloxi. I met her one time when I went up to Ole Miss for a football game."

"I don't know. She might even have been her roommate, now that I think about it."

"I doubt that." Renata shook her head. "Right after Elise grad-uated, she married a dentist named Brent Vanderbecken, and they live right here in Mobile."

"Huh." Matt scratched his head. "Must've been Monica."

Elise Vanderbecken. The interview list was growing by the second.

Judging by the look on Laurel's face, Cole could have used a little of his famous slick-willy charm right about then. Where was the rewind button when you needed it?

"My thoughts on bloodhounds," she repeated. "You mean, as in dogs — like the one on the *Beverly Hillbillies*?"

"Yeah," he said, relieved that she understood. "Only this one's name is Rebel. Which should tell you why I couldn't leave him in the Dumpster."

"In the — the *Dumpster*?" Laurel put her hand to her head, nearly coldcocking herself with that forty-five-pound handbag. She dropped her arm, frowning. "What were you doing in a Dumpster?"

Her expression was really making him uneasy. "It's a long story, and I'll be happy to explain, but why don't you come meet Reb first, then let me buy you supper, and we'll figure out what to do." He smiled at her, as honest as he knew how. No more putting one over to gain an advantage, no more lying to get his own way.

"Where is it?"

"In my truck." Cole jerked a thumb over his shoulder. He hoped Rebel had quit slobbering on the windows. He wasn't sure he'd be able to see through the windshield as it was.

Laurel stood on tiptoes. Her eyes widened. "Gadzooks. Is that a *tongue* hanging out of its mouth?"

"Well, of course it's a —" Cole turned around to look and winced. "He seems to like the way the glass feels on his — Never mind. Come on, you've got to pet him." Desperate, he took Laurel's arm and towed her toward the truck. Rebel started barking, going crazy with joy. Already he'd adopted Cole as liberator and idol.

Laurel balked. "Cole! Wait a minute." She dug in her heels and jerked her arm out of his hand. "If you found him in a Dumpster, how do you know he doesn't have rabies or mange or—or scurvy or something?"

"That's one reason I needed to talk to you. I hoped you'd recommend a good vet. So I could get him checked out. But he seems perfectly healthy. He's already been neutered. And he had on a collar with his name engraved on it, so somebody was taking care of him at some point in the distant past. He's just all skinny and lonesome and his tag is missing." Cole unlocked the truck, the window of which he'd left cracked to let fresh air get to the dog. "Hey, Reb, old buddy, how ya doing?" He opened the door and dodged a tongue to the cheek and chin. "Chill, dude, a little decorum when you meet a lady."

"He looks hungry." Laurel stood several feet away, but her eyes were alight with amusement.

Cole took that as a good sign. "I fed him half a bag of dry dog food and most of my hamburger from lunch. He's just really"—he wiped his face—"affectionate."

Laurel's laughter erupted, the full-bodied belly laugh he'd been waiting to hear. Warmed to the core, he joined in, tussling with Rebel to hide his pleasure.

"He looks like he's not much more than a puppy. Reminds me of one of my nephews." Laurel leaned around the door of the truck and cautiously put out a manicured hand to scratch behind the dog's long, floppy ears. "Aren't you the handsome boy?"

"And here I was thinking I needed a haircut." Cole gave Laurel a grin, moving aside to let Rebel press his bony head against her immaculate charcoal suit jacket.

"Guess I'm headed to the cleaners in the morning." She stroked the thick sorrel-colored fur above his collar. "You do realize you can't hide a dog this big in a hotel room. He probably howls."

Rebel stared up at her adoringly, smiling mouth open, tongue hanging halfway to the ground. He seemed utterly unaware that his fate hung in the balance.

Cole leaned on the open truck door. "I know," he said with a sigh. "The guy at the hotel desk said if I couldn't find a place for him by tonight I should take him to the humane society." He ducked his head and looked at her through his lashes. "Is your yard fenced?"

"No! And Charles Wallace would come unglued at the very suggestion."

"Oh." He scratched his nose. "Didn't know you already had a dog."

"Cat." Her frown dared him to comment. "And he doesn't like to share, so don't even think about it." But she looked down at Rebel, who gazed up at her with saggy, baggy soulful brown eyes. Her expression softened. "Okay, I'm thinking. Maybe I have a temporary solution."

"Really? Hot dog."

Rebel closed his eyes in ecstasy and pressed his long snout into Laurel's stomach.

"Maybe," she repeated firmly, "but Mary Layne's going to kill me."

"Wow, Rebel's gonna love this place." Cole looked around in satisfaction as he pulled the truck up in the Theissens' circle drive.

Laurel wrinkled her nose. "Yeah, if we can get him past my sister."

Cole wasn't worried, now that he'd gotten this far. He and Laurel were even on coconspiratorial terms. He'd followed her to her house and sat outside while she changed clothes, thanking God his gut had told him she'd have compassion on this tall, skinny, most likely wormy canine. No, probably the Holy Spirit had prompted him.

The more he learned about the Christian life, the more he understood God's deep desire to will the best for him. And the more he listened. God was good, and for whatever reason, seeking out Laurel was something he'd been commanded to do. For his good and hers.

He had to keep reminding himself of that.

He looked over his shoulder at the dog, sprawled across the backseat of the truck. "It'll be okay, old man. Just act natural." Rebel whined, and Cole reached back to ruffle his ears. "Well, maybe not *too* natural."

Cole got out of the truck, grabbing Rebel's collar to keep him from running off, and surveyed the sparkle of water beyond the house — a sprawling split-level farmhouse with a freestanding garage and a couple of outbuildings. The Theissens owned a ten-acre hunk of land on Bayou Sara just north of the Mobile city limits, far enough out to be charmingly rural but close enough to enjoy the city's amenities. Cole would've given his right arm for his fishing pole.

He turned to look across the back of the truck when he heard the sound of children's shrieks and running feet coming from the direction of the woods.

"Aunt Lolly! Whose dog is that?"

"We didn't know you were coming!"

"Aunt Lolly, hug me first!"

"Did you know we was getting a new baby?"

Four of them, best Cole could tell, ranging in size from gangly preadolescent male — wearing what looked like a skunk on his head — to miniature princess in a fairy costume, barely able to remain upright in a pair of adult-sized stiletto heels. The younger three gathered around Laurel in a group hug, while the older boy, who was probably around ten years old, sidled toward Cole. He stared open-mouthed at Rebel.

Cole tried not to return the favor. That skunk hat was something else.

"This your dog?" The boy extended his knuckles for Rebel to sniff. Rebel obligingly gave them a lavish slurp.

"Kind of." Cole glanced at Laurel, who was still occupied with the three munchkins. "We're, uh, trying to find a home for him."

The boy's brown eyes, which showed a strong family resemblance to Laurel's, widened. "No way!"

"Way." Cole cast caution to the wind. If Laurel didn't have this in mind bringing him and the dog out here, she should have. "Would you like to adopt him?"

"Would I?" The boy's eyes glistened. "Oh, man." He fell to his knees and flung his arms around Rebel's skinny neck. "This is better than a shark!"

chapter 9

Cole sat under a canvas awning on the Theissens' boat dock watching the sun set with a hook in the water, a root beer next to his hip, and Madison, the fairy princess, in his lap. Her red-gold curls were tickling his chin and the stilettos kept banging into his kneecaps, but he couldn't find much to complain about.

He looked over his shoulder at Laurel, sitting in a lawn chair sipping a diet soda. She had on the skunk hat, which her nephew Dane had abandoned when Rebel showed signs of eating its head off.

"So is somebody going to explain what's the deal with the unique chapeau?" he asked, amused all over again at Laurel's unselfconscious flair for entertaining the children. She had been periodically squeezing the black-and-white tail dangling over her shoulder, to make it perform a sort of snuffling grunt, which never failed to make Madison giggle.

"It's part of Dane's curriculum vitae."

"Okay, my high school Latin's pretty fuzzy. Translation, please?"

"Basically a homeschool résumé. Mary Layne makes Dane volunteer at the library, only he didn't want to wear one of the librarian's 'cheesy old stupid girl hats.' So Mary Layne let him pick one out at the toy store." She squeezed the tail. The skunk grunted, and Madison's laughter sent her heels into Cole's knees again.

He winced. "As long as he doesn't have an authentic smell, we're cool." Cole peered over the child's head at his watch. "What time is your session tonight?"

"Nine. No rush. The studio's downtown, so we can zip down the Pritchard connector and get there in about ten minutes."

"Okay." From the direction of the woods he heard a boyish cowboy whoop, followed by a cacophony of barking and the shrieks of the two middle children. "You think your sister and brother-in-law are mad at us for dumping the dog on them?"

"Mary Layne owes me a favor or two," Laurel replied, dodging the question. "You never did tell me what you were doing hunting through the Dumpster."

"I was headed out to do some research on your opponent. My truck was parked in the back parking lot. Must've been a divine appointment." The three children raced by, followed by the long-legged puppy. "I'm sure Rebel thinks so. Come to think of it, I never did catch up with Mr. Field. I'll have to call him tomorrow."

"I know my phone number." The strawberry-haired elf in his lap looked up at him and reeled off the number.

Cole gently pinched her nose. "Good job. I'll give you a call sometime." The pole jerked in his hand. "Hey, sissy, I think we've got a bite. Let's pull 'er in."

"Ew! I don't like fish." She scrambled out of his lap and trotted off toward the house, gauzy skirts trailing and heels wobbling. "Mommy! That man's got a fish!"

Chuckling, Cole pulled in a miniscule crappie, which he threw back. He turned to look up at Laurel. "I like your family. Reverend Wade's a little stuffy, but he seems like a good guy."

Laurel smiled. "I like them too. Wait 'til you meet Gilly. She's a hoot."

"Is that right?" He laughed, the sight of dignified Judge Laurel in a skunk hat too much for his composure.

She wrinkled her nose. "Oh, shut up."

"Did I say anything?" He looked at her, smiling. "I'm discovering that I really didn't know you at all."

She propped her chin on her fist. "I tried to tell you that."

"So when do I get to interview you?"

"Good grief, Cole, you've been following me around for almost two weeks—"

"*Oui, ma petit chou*, your Pepé 'as given ze grand chase—"

Laurel hid a smile. "I'm not going anywhere at the moment. How about now?"

"I don't have my notebook and pen." He considered her for a moment. "I'll drive you to the studio tonight, and we'll get a cup of coffee afterward. Okay?"

Caution flared in the soft brown eyes. He regretted it, but realistically couldn't blame her. He hadn't done much to earn her trust so far.

She sighed. "We'll see. Hey, looks like you've got another minnow on your line. At this rate we'll be here until midnight trying to get enough to make a decent meal."

He gave her a measured look, then lifted the pole. Sometimes it was better to cut bait.

The recording studio was in an industrial section of town that Laurel didn't frequent unless she had the car windows rolled up tightly and the doors locked—and that was in the daytime. If Cole hadn't been with her tonight, she might have bailed.

The muscular shoulder above hers made her feel safe as they walked together from the small, dark parking lot behind the old brick building. The front door was unmarked because, in the proprietor's words, "Why advertise all this high-dollar equipment anybody could walk in here and steal?" Only a coat of lurid orange paint and the black stick-on numbers 742 distinguished it from the sidewalk.

Cole held the door for Laurel, peering up a set of narrow dark stairs at the naked bulb dangling from the frayed ceiling. He sniffed. "Mildew. You sure this is the right place?"

"After Katrina, everything in Mobile smells like mildew." She tried to keep her voice light as she started up the creaky wooden stairs. Maybe high-heeled sandals hadn't been the best choice of footwear for tonight's venture. She glanced over her shoulder. "Renata's meeting us here. Derrick Edes, the guy from the publicity firm, made arrangements for the recording. He said this is a reputable company."

"I'm sure it'll be fine." Cole stuck close, and she let him.

At the top of the stairs a locked glass door discreetly advertised "Port City Productions." Laurel pushed a buzzer and waited. Through the door she saw an empty carpeted hallway. In fact, there was carpet everywhere — ceiling, walls, floor. Soundproofing, she supposed.

After a moment a slight young man with thick, wavy black hair and a disarming smattering of freckles unlocked the door. "Hey, y'all. I'm Noah, the engineer. Come on in." He shook hands with Laurel as she stepped into the hallway. "You must be our famous candidate. Welcome, Judge Kincade."

"Thanks, Noah." Laurel glanced over her shoulder. "This is Cole McGaughan. He's a reporter doing a series of stories on my campaign. Do you mind if he sits in?"

Noah looked up at Cole, who towered over him by half a foot. "No problem as long as you keep quiet when I tell you to."

"You're the boss," Cole rumbled, somehow managing to efface his large person as they followed Noah into a small conference room, where Renata and Derrick were already poring over notes at one end of a table.

Derrick, a handsome black man with a shaved head and al-mond-shaped eyes marked by slashing black brows, was dressed in a pumpkin-colored collarless shirt with a black sport coat. A discreet gold ring pierced one ear, a sophisticated look that drew the eye. Renata had been interested in him since the consulting firm had hired him in January.

He rose and shook hands with Laurel. "Judge Kincade, good to see you again." An open smile creased his lean face. "Sorry about this thing getting started so late. Thanks for working with my whacked-out schedule." He offered a hand to Cole as well. "You must be McGaughan. Glad you could make it."

"Me too."

Cole held a chair for Laurel, then seated himself next to her. He really did have lovely manners. For a New Yorker.

Okay, she was daily revising her opinion of him. Minute by minute in fact. She kept picturing him digging that eighty-pound bloodhound puppy out of a Dumpster, feeding and bathing it—he had yet to explain how he'd managed that feat—and hauling it around in his truck all day just so he could find it a good home. And then there was that little time-out at Mary Layne's house with the children. Madison had glommed on to Cole as if he were her favorite uncle, and she was notoriously choosy about whom she bestowed her favors upon. Even eight-year-old Cheri had shyly hugged him and asked him to come back again.

Laurel waited for Renata to settle some issue with Derrick, very much aware of Cole's quiet presence. What was she going to do about him? There was a spark of ... something in his eyes when she caught him watching her. Something that reminded her of the way he'd looked at her eight years ago. Piqued interest, maybe. She was afraid to call it attraction. Whatever it was, it created a chaos of emotion she'd learned to dispense with long ago.

Noah the engineer poked his shaggy head through the doorway. "Hey, you guys about ready? I've got the mikes and headsets hooked up."

Renata looked up. "Laurel, have you been practicing? We've got plenty of studio time, so we can do as many cuts as you need to."

"I'm ready." She made herself let out her breath. No reason to be nervous. She spoke in front of hundreds of people every week. This was just a canned statement.

She put her hand over her fluttering stomach.

Cole touched her shoulder as he got to his feet. "You want to practice on me one time?"

"Sure, that's a good idea." Accepting his proffered hand, she rose, smiling at Noah. "Which way is the studio?"

"Come on, I'll show you."

Momentarily Laurel and Cole, along with Derrick and Renata, stood in the hallway outside the door of a small, carpeted soundproof booth. Laurel glanced at Renata. "Can I practice with Cole before I go in?"

"Yeah, no problem. Derrick and I will be in the control booth. There's a window so we'll be able to see and hear each other. Cole, you just come on down there after you and Laurel get done, okay?"

"Okay." His gaze remained on Laurel as the others left. "Are you all right?"

"I'm fine." She had to be fine. But what if she sounded like one of the Lollipop Kids from *The Wizard of Oz*?

"You wowed everybody that day at the Judicial Building."

"Did I?" She blinked at the compliment.

"You know you did. You saw my article." He smiled, magnesium eyes soft, then gestured into the empty sound booth. "This should be a piece of cake. No audience."

She laughed. "I keep picturing the thousands of people who'll hear it on the radio."

"Okay then. Start by explaining to me—in just a couple of sentences—why you want this job."

"I—" She stared up into his eyes, caught by her own reflection in their dark silver, black-shot irises. For a moment she couldn't have said what her name was. She moistened her lips. "I want to make a difference. I want to bring the integrity and family strength and education and experience I've been blessed with, to serve the people of Alabama. To make sure justice is served for all its citizens. Fairly. Consistently. Applying the law without rewriting it or legislating from the bench."

Cole briefly touched her shoulder with an almost affectionate playfulness. "See? That's what you do. Tell them that." He smiled at her and backed toward the control room next door to the sound booth. "Go get 'em, princess."

After the taping session—which proceeded in three takes with a smoothness Laurel had not anticipated—Noah invited her into the control room to listen back to the recording. By this time the college student was on a comfortable, first-name basis with his clients. Derrick had made a Starbucks run, and the whole crew was loaded up on caffeine, silly and in no mood to go home and go to bed.

"I'm very impressed, Ms. Judge Lady," Derrick teased, handing Laurel a caramel macchiato. "You should've gone for a job in broadcasting."

"I don't think so." Yawning, she sank onto a saggy velour couch. "I couldn't take the hours."

"She'd be wasted behind a microphone." Renata's look was as full of pride as any stage mama. "You should see this lady sort out a bunch of strutting lawyers with their own agendas to push. She can cut 'em down to size by just staring down her nose through those little half glasses."

"That's not what I—"

Renata waved a hand. "No, but it's not a talent to be sneezed at." She grinned at Cole. "Apparently you saw that right off. Great couple of articles you've written so far. The one last weekend was right on the money."

"Thanks." Cole looked uncomfortable. "I just write the truth. Laurel, I've been meaning to ask you something."

She jumped. Was he going to interview her right here in front of everybody? "Sure. What is it?"

"Your opponent. You never say a word about the guy. What do you know about him?"

"Wallace Field? He's the Mobile County DA."

Cole made a face. "I know that. I mean his background. Where did he practice law before he took over the DA's office?"

"He's a lawyer from Citronelle. Practiced privately there for several years, then became assistant DA here in Mobile before he was elected as the top gun."

"What kind of guy is he?"

Laurel shrugged. "Nice enough. I don't run into him a whole lot socially."

"Give me a break." Renata folded her arms. "Field is the ultimate power broker. Puts on his own show and runs over anybody who doesn't give him top billing."

"You just described most American politicians." Cole grinned. "Nothing new under the sun."

Renata scowled. "Well, he's been running some underhanded little scams to get where he is, and there's proof out there—if Laurel would just let us advertise it."

Cole raised his brows. "That true, Laurel?"

Ignoring him, she stared Renata down. "I'm not going there. If I can't get elected because of my qualifications, then I don't want the job."

Derrick kicked back in his chair and propped his feet on a battered coffee table. "Sounds real sweet, Judge, but you know Field is gonna drag you around by the hair if he gets half a chance. You better be ready to play hardball yourself."

"I conduct my trials with professionalism, and I abide by the canon of judicial ethics. Regarding my reputation, there is absolutely nothing for Mr. Field to grab onto." Laurel found herself locking gazes with Cole. The smile in his eyes was shadowed, but not with the mockery she might have expected. Instead there was sadness, maybe regret.

God, please don't let him tell.

The Mobile Bay bridge was afire with lights as Cole turned the truck out of the studio's parking lot and headed toward Laurel's house. The skyline in the rearview mirror was a fairytale display blurred by fog and intermittently colored by downtown neon signs staggered like a first grader's drawing. He felt the intimacy of being alone with Laurel in the dark vehicle and was almost surprised she'd allowed it.

As he cruised through a blinking yellow light on Government Street, he glanced at the clock on the dash. Nearly eleven. "What time do you have to be in court tomorrow?"

Laurel sighed and laid her head against the back of the seat. "I'll have lawyers and clerks and psychologists and police swarming my office at eight." She rolled her head to look at him. "Why?"

"You said you'd let me do the interview tonight. But you look tired."

She yawned behind her hand, then laughed. "Guess I am. Even my court reporter's been telling me I look like a hag lately."

"Hardly that." His glance skimmed her strong, angular profile. Certainly her hair was messier than he'd ever seen it; a long hank had fallen out of its clip and was now tucked behind her left ear, tangled in the jade and silver beads of her earring. "But I won't keep you up if you need to get to bed. We can do it another time."

She was silent so long that Cole wondered if he'd offended her. He turned onto her street, dodging the gnarled roots of an oak tree that interrupted the pavement, and parked in front of her house. He found Laurel studying him, eyes half-closed.

He frowned. "What?"

"I'm thinking it's real after all."

"What do you mean?"

"The newness. The ... differentness. I can't get used to this unselfish streak, Cole."

He gripped the steering wheel. Purplish light from a streetlamp washed across his knuckles, making his hands look huge and ham-fisted. "Man, I must've been a first-class jerk."

"You just wanted what you wanted and did what you needed to do in order to get it. I never did figure out why you wanted me."

"Come on, Laurel, you know why I wanted you."

She grimaced. "You could've had any girl you wanted back then. And I'm guessing you probably did. I was not the kind of material that would have made you look twice."

"Laurel—"

"I'm being perfectly sincere. Realistic. I was tall and skinny and bosomless, with all this red hair ... " She pushed the fallen swathe behind her ear again, smiling at him with a sleepy, vulnerable shadow in her eyes, lips pursed a bit.

He suddenly, insanely, wanted to lean over and take her mouth with his and make her remember why he had wanted her.

Yeah, that would help the situation. "I was probably short on redheads in the little black book. I don't know. Doesn't matter, because for all practical purposes, that guy is dead. I really need you to get that, Laurel—understand that I'm treating you differently because I *am* different." He lifted his hands. "I knew this was going to be hard, but I didn't realize ..." He let out a frustrated breath. He'd just have to keep showing her. "Never mind. Good night. I'll meet you at Renata's for the drive up to Enterprise on Saturday."

"But—what about the interview?"

"You're going to bed," he said gruffly.

"No, I want to get it over with. I mean—" He could see her blushing even in the darkness of the cab. "I mean, this is a good time. I'm not that tired."

He just looked at her for a moment. In spite of her political background and experience, she'd faced little real opposition. Naturally she was a bit naive. But as Cole knew all too well, Hogan was out to get her. A real professional would insist on a public place in daylight hours.

On the other hand, selfish or not, he wanted more than anything to be with her. He was honored and pleased that she wanted his company. And nobody had to know he'd been here tonight. "Okay then," he said. "Let's do it."

He followed her up the sidewalk to her front door and waited while she fumbled with the lock and ran to turn off the alarm. Good thing she took safety seriously. He hated to think about her living in this old neighborhood all alone with nobody to watch out for her but the big Siamese cat twining around her ankles.

"This is Charles Wallace"—Laurel bent to pick up the cat before she turned on a lamp—"who thinks he's master of the universe. Don't tell him any different."

"Wouldn't dream of busting his kitty bubble." Cole looked around. Aside from white cat hair everywhere, it was a nice place.

Laurel seemed to be into antiques, which didn't surprise him. Fit the style of the old house.

"You want to sit down while I make coffee?" Laurel had backed into the dining room doorway, hugging the cat close.

The defensive pose tugged Cole's heart. "No, I'll come watch."

"Okay." She swallowed, then turned and led the way into the kitchen, a warm, honey-toned room with a red-curtained bank of windows on one side and gleaming appliances.

He leaned against a counter and watched her sort out coffee-making supplies, her movements awkward enough that he cleared his throat. "Laurel, you don't have to do this just for me."

Red climbed her white throat. "I drink herbal tea most of the time, but I'm not opposed to coffee on occasion." She smiled. "Just don't crucify me if it's not Starbucks perfect."

He picked up the cat, who had been rather violently butting his head against his shins. "Hey, dude. You not getting the adulation you deserve?" Charles Wallace purred like a lawn mower and Cole laughed.

Laurel pushed the button to turn on the coffeemaker, smiling at the cat, who blinked up at Cole in utter adoration. "You're not allergic, are you?"

"No. I've been around animals all my life." He scratched the cat under his white chin. "I used to escape to my uncle Zane's farm during the summers when I was a kid."

"Escape?"

He sighed. "You haven't met my family."

"No ..." She turned, opening the freezer to store the coffee. Face hidden and voice muffled, she said slowly, "I never had the chance."

"You'd like my mother. She lives in Hattiesburg. And Uncle Zane's a pretty cool guy. But when my parents split, for reasons unknown, the judge awarded primary custody to my dad." He traced the charcoal edges of the cat's ears, watching them twitch. "Probably because he had the most money."

"That's a cynical thing to say." Laurel came out from behind the freezer door. "A judge takes everything into consideration—"

"Yeah, like who's gonna pay for the prep school education, right?" Cole stared at Laurel. "And build your stock portfolio, send you to college, and put you up for the family fraternity so you can pickle your brain in beer before you turn twenty. And buy your first and second and third car after you wreck them all, and bail you out of jail, and scrub your DUI records so nobody ever finds out."

He clamped his teeth together against the bile spewing out onto the last person who needed to hear it.

Laurel's mouth opened and shut a couple of times. "How old were you when they divorced?"

"Nine." He looked down. "But I'm not blaming my dad for everything I did wrong. I made my own choices."

"I know, but—" Laurel took a step closer. "Look, Cole."

He did. The aroma of hazelnut coffee filled the room, and he knew he'd forevermore associate it with her and this moment. Her eyes were soft and almost tender. His heart cracked. Of all the mistakes he'd made in his life, throwing away Laurel Kincade's regard had been the most colossal. Something quickened in him, a longing to repair the damage he'd done.

Careful, though. He mustn't make assumptions. He waited, let her choose her words.

"Don't you think your dad did all those things because he loved you?"

"He did those things because he couldn't stand the thought of one of his possessions—that would be me—taken out from under his control. If I looked successful, he looked successful. Then when I landed in trouble, that reflected on him too." How could he explain his messed-up, dysfunctional family to a woman who had been raised by Dodge and Frances Kincade? "Now he's doing it again to my little brother, and there's nothing I can do about it."

"You have a little brother?" Laurel had moved to lean against the counter next to him. Her presence was warm and comforting. She smelled nice too, kind of like light sandalwood.

Cole nodded. "Tucker was born when I was eleven, so I guess he's ..." He squinted, thinking. "Nineteen. He's a freshman at Ole Miss this year."

"You never told me that."

"There were a lot of subjects that never came up."

"What *did* we talk about?"

"Books. When I found out you'd read the entire Lord of the Rings trilogy, plus *The Hobbit*—"

"And finding somebody who understood the structure of *The Princess Bride* was incredible. I could hardly believe it when somebody told me you were a journalism major. You were such a—a frat boy jock." They stared at one another. A smile curved Laurel's mouth. "So tell me about this dysfunctional family of yours. Your dad's a plastic surgeon, right?"

"I'm supposed to be interviewing you." Cole rubbed a hand along his bristly jaw. "How'd you know that?"

"The first time you ... " She looked away, face rosy. "Once you said your father would have people lining up to copy my cheekbones."

He studied her. "That's right." He reached out and traced the pad of his thumb across her cheek, then brushed the trembling corner of her lips. His mouth suddenly went dry. This had been a very bad idea to come inside so late at night. They were both tired, and defenses were down. He watched her eyelashes flutter, heavy and unintentionally seductive.

She'd never understood her own sensuality. But he did.

He withdrew his hand and reached for the coffee carafe. The timer was beeping loudly. "I think we're coming in for a landing here. Got a mug handy?"

Laurel blinked and jerked upright. "Of course. Why don't you get the milk out of the fridge, and I'll scrounge us up some cookies. Might as well do this right."

chapter 10

She had to get him out of here. If she hadn't insisted he stay and then plugged in that doggone coffeemaker, he'd already be back at his hotel. What had she been thinking?

Well, she'd been thinking she was over him. She'd been thinking after he dropped out of her life eight years ago that she'd never find herself attracted again. But here he sat on her living room sofa, vital and good-looking and, yes, *different*.

Cole-not-Cole. Cole as he was meant to be. A thread or two of silver above his ears, attractive little crinkles at the corners of his eyes, and a shadow of regret underlying the joy in his expression. Maturity. Maybe that was it. In the days when she'd first met him, if she'd been able to telescope to a view of this moment—things might have been very different.

As it was, she'd learned not to trust her feelings. Fafa always said if anything seemed too good to be true, it probably was.

Heart-scarred by Cole, she'd never been quite satisfied with later romantic relationships. Before Robert, there'd been a guy at her church in Atlanta, a divorcee with middle-school-aged kids. Ultimately, she didn't love him enough to get comfortable with ex-wife and child custody issues. Besides, every time he kissed her, she remembered being one flesh with Cole. Finally she realized it wasn't fair to tie herself to any man as long as old sensations dogged her with images inked in her mind like tattoos.

She blinked as Cole set down his coffee mug—a souvenir from Pike Place Market in Seattle—and reached for his notebook and pen. He also pulled a small recorder out of his pocket. "Mind if I record this?"

Laurel's stomach lurched. "I guess not."

His eyes narrowed, quizzical and humorous. "You've been interviewed before."

"Not by you."

"Last January in Montgomery—"

"Oh, yeah. I'm sorry I was so ... " She looked for Charles Wallace and found him batting at the tassels on Cole's loafers. "Do you want some more coffee?"

"Thanks, I've had enough." He turned on the recorder and laid it on the sofa. "Let's start with your experience. I know you graduated from Ole Miss law school and clerked for the Eleventh Circuit Court of Appeals. How did that prepare you for serving on the bench?"

Matt sat in his car outside the judge's house with a box of Krispy Kreme doughnuts and a jumbo coffee. It was nearly midnight, and he'd been watching through the window as she entertained McGaughan—him on the sofa, her in a wing chair across the room, like a couple of senior citizens in the retirement home. What the Sam Hill was McGaughan thinking, not to take advantage of the situation?

He'd seen the guy operate. Back in Memphis they used to cruise the clubs on Beale Street, and McGaughan was good at picking up women. Almost as good as Matt—not that he would brag or any-thing. Back propped against the door, he took a slug of his coffee. It was sad, really, that McGaughan had lost his edge. Just went to show what happened when you let religion strangle the life out of you—and there was no doubt McGaughan had gotten religion lately. Where was the fun in sitting next to a hot tamale like Laurel Kincade without at least *trying* to shuck her out of her clothes?

Or maybe McGaughan had a strategy going. Maybe the recent go-to-church thing was part of it. The judge seemed to be one of those wound-tight women who might require a little finesse to undress. He smiled at his mental rhyme. *Finesse to undress. Yes. You, Matt Hogan, are the best.*

And he, unlike McGaughan, was enjoying his life.

He squirmed to find a more comfortable position in the seat, banged his funny bone on the steering wheel, and sloshed coffee on the camera in his lap. Swearing, he checked to make sure the lens cap was on.

Spying on people and taking sleazy pictures. What a great way to make a living.

By the time Laurel had recounted for Cole what she'd done with her life during the eight years since they'd been together at Ole Miss, she lost some of her jitters. She even managed to relax enough to laugh at his questions regarding her three years with Thorndyke, Hope, and Diemert. "I was the youngest partner in history there."

Cole stopped scribbling and stared. "No way."

"Maybe something to do with being in the right place at the right time." Laurel shrugged. "Anyway, I spent the next two years in the attorney general's office. When I wanted to come home to Mobile, the governor appointed me to my current post."

"Forgive my pointing out the obvious, but you've come to your position in a relatively short amount of time, and via a rather truncated process. Your opponent says you may not be up to the weight of the higher court. How do you counter that?"

"I've had plenty of experience handling matters of the judiciary, and I'm uniquely gifted in administration." Laurel folded her hands on top of her knees. "This has been demonstrated from my earliest days in college and law school." She smiled, turning it inward. "Some people have even called me a control freak."

Cole abruptly stopped the recorder. "You think that's a good thing, Laurel?"

Suddenly her energy seeped out as if a bathtub plug had been pulled. She sighed and looked away. "I'm beginning to think not. Are we almost done? I'm really tired."

"One more question." He turned the recorder back on. "You're not married, Judge Kincade, and there's been no mention of anybody special in your life—besides your family, that is. Our readers will want to know if you'll be leaving anybody behind if you're elected and move to Montgomery."

He held his pen in one big fist, the little rectangular notebook in the other, and regarded her with what she could only call polite disinterest. But for some reason the question left her airless, broadsided. "You mean like a—like a boyfriend?"

"Or a girlfriend." When she gasped, he grinned. "Kidding. Seriously, though, you're a family-values candidate, and people are going to be curious."

"That really isn't anybody's business."

"When you declared your candidacy for public office, you made your entire life everybody's business." He said it matter-of-factly, without any heat.

There was a moment's silence as their gazes held. Laurel clenched and unclenched her fingers. He was right, but she didn't have to like having him poke into her love life. Or lack thereof.

"I'm not dating anyone seriously at the moment."

Something flickered in his gray eyes as he looked down at his notes. "Okay. Noted. The judge is available."

"I'm not—" She stopped when the flicker turned into a twinkle. "Argh. Cole McGaughan, what am I going to do with you?"

"How about putting a dozen of those cookies in a bag to go?"

Thursday morning Cole was researching George Field's résumé in the downtown library's special collections division when his phone vibrated against his hip. In spite of the late night with Laurel, which he didn't mind, he'd gotten up early to go to the gym, then decided to get some work done while Laurel was in court. Mumbling under his breath, he placed the microfiche he'd been viewing on hold with one of the librarians and went outside to return the call.

He plopped down on the damp concrete steps. It had rained before daybreak, and puddles stood on the uneven sidewalk. There was still a smell of rain in the air. "Hogan, you have a talent for interrupting when I'm in the middle of something."

"First of all," Hogan said in an aggrieved tone, "this is a telephone. *Phone* meaning audio. I cannot see you. Second, old buddy, old pal, you owe me an update every now and then, so I won't have to wonder what's going on."

Stalling, Cole watched a couple of cars whiz past on Government Street. Finally he picked out an answer. "I recorded an interview with Judge Kincade last night."

"Well, it's about time. You learn anything interesting?"

"I think it's interesting that she isn't dating anybody special at the moment."

There was an incredulous silence. "Now there's a piece of headline news. So what are you planning to do about it?"

"Do about it? What do you mean?"

"McGaughan, I cannot believe I'm having to suggest that you move in on empty turf. The woman is all but advertising. *Vacancy. All applicants welcome.*"

Cole pictured Laurel's vulnerable expression as she'd let him out the front door last night. He hadn't touched her. But he'd wanted to. "I'm thinking about it."

"That's it? You're thinking about it?"

Cole shrugged. "Yeah. Hogan, you're just going to have to let me handle this my own way."

"All right." Hogan's reluctance was obvious. "But I've got one more major bone to pick with you."

"Yeah?"

"Yeah. I want to know why you didn't tell me Laurel Kincade's law school roommate is right here in Mobile. By this time you should have already interviewed every local person of interest in the judge's background. I'd say a law school roommate would be of extreme interest."

Caught flat-footed, Cole ran a hand around the back of his neck. It hadn't even occurred to him that Elise Bell might be living in Mobile. She'd been a shallow, air-headed piece of fluff—a nonentity compared to Laurel, and he'd paid little attention to her back then. And in the detritus of his own life after college, he couldn't have cared less what happened to her.

Selfish, maybe, but there it was.

Besides, he'd become way more interested in getting to know Laurel again than letting Matt Hogan have at her. Playing both sides of the fence was getting tricky.

He said a quick prayer for guidance. "Matt, honestly the subject of law school hasn't come up yet, beyond general questions about educational background. But if you want me to interview the Bell woman, I will."

"Bell? Renata said her name is Vanderbecken."

Cole froze. What had he just done? "Bell was her maiden name. You said so, right?"

"If it is, it's the first time I've heard it. Renata said she married a dentist named Brent Vanderbecken. I'm sure she never mentioned a maiden—" Hogan's tone sharpened. "McGaughan, you're lying to me. You already knew about this roommate, didn't you?"

"I knew about her, but I didn't think it was a big deal. I didn't know she was living in Mobile."

Cole could hear Hogan seething on the other end of the line. "For some reason you're protecting the judge. You know what I think? I think you're screwing up the best career shot you're ever gonna get because of a redhead with a great pair of legs and—"

"Hogan, shut up." In the old days Cole would have said something a lot stronger than that. Agitated, he got up and paced down to the street corner. "Look, if you're so interested in Judge Kincade's law school career, I'll find the Vanderbecken lady and talk to her. Married to a dentist? Please. She's probably a soccer mom who doesn't even run in the same circles as the judge anymore."

Hogan remained silent for so long that Cole wondered if he'd lost the connection. Finally, however, the PI let out a breath. "Okay, McGaughan, find out what you can from her, since you're the one with the open entrée. I'm still tracking down the court records or I'd do it myself." He paused again. "Dude, I'm worried about you."

Cole forced a chuckle. "It's probably the humidity. My brain's mildewing. Hey, I'm going to church Sunday. You want to come?"

"Are you kidding? That's my only day to sleep in."

Well, it had been worth a shot. "All right, but call if you change your mind. I'll let you know what I find out from the roommate."

"Sure, man. Take it easy."

Cole returned the phone to the clip on his belt and mounted the steps to the library. The past was getting all balled up with the present, and pretty soon it was going to be impossible to unsnarl. When a guy like Matt Hogan started psychoanalyzing you, it was time to get help.

"So the farmers switched their cash crop from cotton to peanuts—now a multimillion-dollar industry in Alabama—which would never have happened without the scourge of the boll weevil." With a grand gesture, the retired gentleman conducting the tour of Enterprise's Depot Museum invited his captive audience to gaze in wonder at the glass-encased Lady of the Boll Weevil statue. The statue gazed in dismay at the amputated arms and huge metal bug lying ignominiously at her feet.

Cole bent down to whisper in Laurel's ear. "Is it any wonder the rest of the world thinks we don't wear shoes down here?" Along with Renata, Derrick Edes, and Laurel's sister Gilly, they were winding up a tour of the city in conjunction with one of Laurel's campaign functions. "Not only do they have *one* of these creepy things, they've got a replica out in the town square."

"Stop." Laurel put a finger to her lips. "I have to give a speech in about five minutes and you're gonna make me laugh. Besides"—head canted to one side, she surveyed the armless statue—"I think she's got a certain melancholy beauty."

Cole snorted. "Yeah, if you can ignore her fetish for a seventeen-pound beetle squatting on a UFO."

Laurel's smothered laugh collected an annoyed look from their tour guide as the group shuffled out into the warm spring sunshine. Cole had no objection to spending a lazy Saturday morning exploring the curiosities of Coffee County. The square had a café where the Rotary Club would treat them to lunch, and he'd discovered a bluegrass festival going on nearby. Maybe he could talk Laurel into sliding over there with him after her speech.

"What are you two snickering about?" demanded Gilly as they passed the boll weevil monument replica rising from the center of her iron fence and fountain. "I want in on the joke."

Cole grinned down at the willowy young teenager, the top of whose head barely reached his armpit. Gilly and Laurel were about as different as it was possible for two sisters to be and still be biologically related. The family resemblance was there in the swoop of the eyebrows and the extravagant bow of the upper lip. But Gilly's blue nylon basketball shorts, sleeveless white lace top, and brick-colored camisole made a fashion statement that would never have occurred to her older sister. The flaming shag-cut hair was tied back with a Barbie-pink bandanna, and she skipped along in a pair of camouflage-print sneakers.

"We were just discussing the family resemblance between Our Lady of the Boll Weevil and that green Statue of Liberty chick," Cole said in an undertone. "I think somebody should get slammed for plagiarism."

Gilly wrinkled her nose. "Can artwork be plagiarized?"

"Come to think of it, I don't know if I'd call that art." Cole pretended to flinch when she socked him in the arm. "Laurel, your sister's hitting me."

Laurel, who had walked ahead to talk to Derrick, cast an amused look over her shoulder. "He's too old for you, Gill."

"Not hitting *on* me," said Cole. "I meant taking punches." He winked at Gilly.

She stuck out her tongue, green eyes sparkling.

What a great kid she was. With a weekend off from school and ballet responsibilities, she'd chosen to tag along with her older sister. The more Cole got acquainted with the members of Laurel's family, the more he liked them. No wonder she'd been so horrified eight years ago to wake up and realize—

He stopped that train of thought dead in its tracks. No going back.

Onward and upward.

He could have predicted that his cell phone would vibrate right in the middle of Laurel's speech after lunch. He was going to kill Hogan. But when he saw the caller ID, he excused himself to Renata, the only one of their party who noticed his departure, and went out onto the sidewalk outside the café.

His neck muscles had already tightened. His stepmother never called unless she was fighting with his father and needed a referee. Cole had learned not to intervene, though Teri had it in her head that Cole was her ally in some sort of invisible war.

He answered just before it went to voice mail. "Hey, Teri, I'm kind of busy right now, unless this is an emergency." He'd learned, in fact, to be psychologically ruthless.

"I'm sorry, but it *is* an emergency." The tears in her voice were nothing unusual. She was generally in a state of perpetual PMS. "Davis—your dad, I mean—said you're down in Alabama again—and I know you're working, but it's Tucker."

"What's the matter?"

"I've been calling his room number and his cell all week, and he won't return my calls."

Cole walked toward the boll weevil monument in the center of the square. "What do you want me to do? He probably just forgot to charge the battery. Or maybe just didn't want to bother answering. You know how he is."

"No, I—I called the RA in the dorm. He went down to look in Tucker's room, and his roommate says he hasn't been in since *last* Friday. That's over a week! As far as anybody knows, he hasn't been to class either." Teri burst into sobs.

Frowning, Cole sat down on a bench along the sidewalk. He had to admit that didn't sound good. "I don't mean to scare you, but did you call the hospitals? Did you call the police to see if they'd maybe found his car?"

"I called the hospitals, but for obvious reasons, your father didn't want to involve the police."

Of course his father wouldn't call the police, even if his son had been reported missing. Davis McGaughan guarded his reputation like the Hope Diamond.

Cole reined his anger in. No use blasting Teri. "I understand why you're concerned, but I'm at least eight hours away from Oxford. I think you'd better call the police, no matter what Dad says."

"I will, but you're close to Tucker. He loves you, I mean. Would you at least try tracking him down by phone first? Maybe he'll return your call."

Cole rose, wishing he'd never answered his phone. No, if something had really happened to his brother, he should try to help. Frankly, he could understand why the kid might want to run away. He sure felt like doing it himself on a number of occasions while growing up.

"All right. Sit tight for an hour or so, Teri. If I can't get hold of him by then, you'll have to call the police, okay?"

"Okay." Her drawling husky voice wobbled like a child's. "Thank you, Cole."

He sighed. She'd broken up his parents' marriage, but he was beginning to see that she needed his compassion. If he could just locate where he'd put it.

Laurel was talking to the mayor of Enterprise when Cole came back into the room. His relaxed, teasing expression had disappeared. The thick brows were lowered, and concern bracketed his mouth. He folded his arms and leaned a shoulder against the wall. His eyes told her he needed to talk to her.

Distracted, she answered at random the mayor's questions about the progress of her campaign before excusing herself and going to Cole. "What's the matter?" She laid a hand on his forearm.

He didn't seem to notice. "My stepmother called. My younger brother's disappeared. He was in class at Ole Miss last Friday, but nobody's seen him all week."

"Oh, no. What are you all going to do?"

He cracked his knuckles, the most agitated gesture she'd seen in him since their truce nearly a week ago. "I called his roommate. He likes to hang out with musicians in all kinds of dives—and you can imagine what some of those people are like—but to this point he's been conscientious about going to class. I'm afraid something's happened to—hang on." He snatched the vibrating phone off its clip and glanced at the ID before flipping it open. "Tucker! Where are you?"

Laurel ignored the babble of voices in the crowded room, concentrating on Cole's strained face. From the corner of her eye she saw Gilly entertaining a farming couple with tales of performing as Scout in *To Kill a Mockingbird*, while Renata and Derrick passed out "Kincade—Justice for Alabama" bumper stickers.

Cole slumped against a table, relief written in every line of his big body. "What in the *heck* are you thinking—taking off like this in the middle of the semester? Spring break was two weeks ago." He listened for a moment, scowling. "I know Teri's a worrywart, but you can't just punt school whenever you feel like it. How're you going to make up the work?" Another pause. "I get what you're saying, but this isn't the best—Tucker, wait—"

"What's the matter?" Laurel asked.

Cole glared at the phone. "I've got to get back to Mobile."

Laurel raised her brows. "Well, sure, we're wrapping things up here—"

"No, I mean right now." He stuffed the phone into his pants pocket. "Laurel, please. I need to get there before he decides to take off to somewhere else."

She shook her head. "What's he doing in Mobile?"

"Apparently playing a gig with the Black Bottom Boys."

Her brow wrinkled. "Who're they?"

"Some band he's hooked up with that needed a guitarist."

She saw that he was perfectly serious. "Cole, what do you think you're going to do? Pack him up and haul him back to school yourself? He's nineteen years old. That's a grown-up."

He sighed. "Nineteen is not a grown-up. Nineteen is a train wreck looking for a place to happen."

Clearly he was remembering his own trip through the pits. Sympathy welled in Laurel. "All right, then we'll go. Let me collect everybody else. Meet me at the car, okay?"

Gratitude swam in his eyes for a moment before he looked down. "Thanks, Laurel," he muttered.

She beckoned Gilly and made her way toward Renata and Derrick. "Hey, guys," she called, "something's come up and we need to get back to Mobile a little early. Let's pack it in."

Lord, she prayed, *help me give Cole wise counsel. Help him do what's best for Tucker.*

chapter 11

If he hadn't been so aggravated with his little brother, Cole would have enjoyed the company of the two beautiful Kincade sisters — Laurel, tall and elegant in jeans and a rust-colored beaded top, and Gilly a pint-sized firecracker in white drawstring pants and a red T-shirt.

At least Zuzu's Fish Shed on the Mobile Bay causeway seemed to be a local family restaurant rather than one of the dives Tucker sometimes played. Built up on pilings with a covered deck extending out onto the bayou, it was constructed of rough-hewn boards that looked like the first strong wind might shove the whole pile into the bay. Cole suspected it had withstood a hurricane or two, and would probably last far into the century.

The three of them followed a young waitress dressed in shorts and "Shed Head" T-shirt out to the deck, where the bandstand was set up in the far corner. The setting sun smeared popsicle-colored light across the bay, and a fresh breeze chased away heat and mosquitoes. Seagulls, laughing like children, played in the water, dive-bombing for fish and detritus floating away from shore.

"Y'all want to sit next to the water?" the waitress yelled over the music blaring from three-foot speakers in every corner.

"How about over by the band?" Cole jerked a thumb over his shoulder.

The waitress shrugged as if he were taking his hearing into his own hands and led the way toward an unoccupied rough-hewn table.

The four-man band was playing a funky country-rock instrumental, but Cole's full attention was on his brother, seated on a stool with his lean body crouched over an acoustic guitar, shoulder-length dark hair a curtain over his face. The kid was so into the music he didn't even seem to notice when he was left to play an extended ad lib solo. The music pulsed from Tucker's fingers, from his entire body, piercing Cole with golden, aching sound. He seated Laurel and Gilly at the empty table, then sank into a third chair. When had his brother turned into this freaking genius?

When the drums, bass, and keyboard cranked back up, Cole looked at Laurel. Her lips were parted, eyes wide. She felt it too. Gilly had her hand over her mouth.

Oh, man. His dad was going to have a cow.

Laurel saw it coming the second Tucker McGaughan pushed his hair back from his face with one hand and bestowed a mischievous second grader's smile on Gilly. He set the guitar in a stand and slid off the stage with the unstudied cool that some men are born with and others sell their souls trying to attain.

"Hey ..." He grabbed his brother in an unembarrassed bear hug. "Didn't know you were coming."

If the smile hadn't already done it, the drawl and a pair of translucent blue-gray eyes would have sealed Gilly's fate. To give her credit, she maintained ladylike composure, waiting to be introduced.

Cole stepped back. "You should have known, doofus. Is your set done?"

"Yeah. Twenty-minute break. Hold on, I need something to drink." Tucker hailed the waitress. "Hey, Bethany, I need a bottle of water, and bring these folks whatever they want, okay?" He slouched in a chair, casting a curious glance at Gilly and Laurel.

Cole made an awkward gesture. "Tuck, this is Judge Kincade and her sister, Gilly."

Tucker looked confused for a moment. Then he focused on Laurel. "Wait—*you're* the judge?" The grin appeared. "Whoa. You can put me in handcuffs anytime you want to."

Cole scowled. "Have a little respect, Squirt."

"Just call me Laurel." Laurel felt a smile tugging at her mouth. "Anyway, I don't do handcuffs. That's the police." She looked for signs of drugs in the boy's nearly colorless eyes. The pupils were tight, the expression bright and focused. He didn't seem to be high.

Tucker looked up and smiled at the waitress as she served their drinks. "Thanks, Bethie. Okay, so, Laurel, what'd you think about the music?"

"I see why you'd rather do this than sit in a business law class," Laurel said slowly. Cole had explained the situation between Tucker and their father on the way back from Enterprise.

"Wrong answer." Cole set his soda glass down hard. "You've got to finish school before you take off on the road."

The bright look faded from Tucker's olive-skinned face. "Says who?"

Laurel could all but hear the underlying message: You're not the boss of me.

Cole gave Laurel a pleading look.

"Did you write that last piece?" Gilly picked up a spoon and fished the lemon slice out of her tea. "I liked the way you put the theme from *Firebird Suite* in the countermelody of the bridge." She sprinkled salt on the lemon and began to suck on it.

Tucker watched in apparent fascination. "I don't know anything about a *Firebird*—ugh, how can you stand that?" His lips puckered. "I heard that tune in a Disney movie when I was little."

Gilly took the lemon out of her mouth. "I dance to classical music all the time. That was not Walt Disney. It was Igor Stravinsky."

Tucker's brows lowered a notch. "I'm pretty sure it was *Fantasia*."

Gilly laughed. "Oh, well, then. I forgot about *Fantasia 2000*. *Firebird Suite*'s the finale."

"Sheesh, what a know-it-all," Tucker muttered, but he winked at Laurel.

"Unfortunately, that sort of runs in my family." Laurel glanced at Cole, who had been listening to the musical tennis match with his mouth open. "And we're all pretty partial to education too," she added for his benefit. "Gilly's headed for Spring Hill College, where I went."

"No, I'm not."

Laurel's head snapped around. Her little sister was tossing the lemon rind across the rail into the reeds, where a couple of seagulls went to war over it. "What do you mean? Have you decided to go somewhere else?"

"I'm not going to college at all." Gilly sipped her tea. Her cheeks were pink, but there was not a grain of indecision in her face or body. "At least not for a while."

"But—"

"Lolly, you haven't been paying attention. I'm a dancer. Next month I'm auditioning for the School of American Ballet, and if I make it and finish there, I'll be a ballerina for the New York Ballet. Or on Broadway. Wherever God opens a door."

"I knew I liked this chick." Tucker grinned at Gilly in wholesale admiration.

"When did you decide this?" Laurel felt as if somebody had turned her brain wrong-side-out.

"I've known it since I was about six years old." Gilly's eyes were serene as green glass but held an odd sort of ancient compassion. "You don't just wake up one day and decide to be a ballerina. It's what I was created to do, just like you're created to be wise and help people straighten out their lives."

"But … I assume you've discussed this with Mom and Dad. You'd have to live in New York. Isn't that where the School of American Ballet is? How on earth—"

"They're going to help me figure it out—if I get into the school, that is."

Awkward silence fell, filled by conversation from surrounding tables, the water lapping against the pilings under the deck, and the cry of the gulls.

Finally Tucker let out a breath. "Well, I hate to bust up this jammin' party, guys, but my break's about up. Coleman, you mind if I come crash with you tonight? I slept in Spiro's van last night, and it wasn't any too comfy."

Laurel could tell Cole wanted to straighten his brother out right now, but the wisdom of waiting until they were in private won. "Sure, man," he said mildly. "Call me when you're done, and I'll come back to get you."

"Can we stay a while?" Gilly pleaded. "I'm hungry."

Laurel feared it wasn't the crab claws her sister was interested in.

But Cole had already grabbed a stack of paper menus from the metal bucket in the middle of the table. "Dinner's on me," he said. "What's good?"

"'Night, Cole, 'night, Lolly—see you in church in the morning!" Gilly hopped out of the truck, blew a kiss, and skipped up the driveway. Slipping through the wrought-iron gate, she disappeared into the Castle's backyard with a last wave.

Cole backed the truck into Church Street and headed toward Laurel's house. He glanced over and found her staring out the side window. "Your sister is one fine young lady."

"Yes, she is." Laurel's voice was pensive. "And I hate to see her falling for a rock star."

Cole snorted. "Tucker's hardly what you'd call a rock star."

"To Gilly he is. And I'm not sure there's not potential for it anyway." She looked at him. "He's awfully good, Cole."

Cole hunched his shoulders. "You think so?"

"You know he is. Once I heard Dave Matthews live. There was that same electric shiver in the air."

"That's very poetic." Cole smiled. "I know what you mean. It's just hard to think of my little brother in those terms. When I left for college, he was only in the second grade. I used to call him the Toothless Wonder. Granted, he was already plunking around on this banjo Uncle Zane bought me as a consolation prize when my parents split up. But who knew it would get to be an obsession?"

Laurel gave a startled laugh. "You play the banjo?"

"Well, I play *at* it. Not like Tucker. He can play anything with strings. Dad finally caved in and bought him a guitar for his tenth birthday, so we'd jam some when I came home for holidays."

Laurel was silent as he drove a couple of blocks, crossing Government Street and turning onto her street.

Finally he glanced at her. "What's the matter?"

"I was just thinking. That must've been around the time you and I ..." She sighed. "When are we going to talk about that, Cole?"

"I don't know. I thought we already did." He stopped the car in front of her house. "It's a pretty high-voltage subject, and I ... I don't feel like ruining the evening."

She sucked in a breath. "We're not having an 'evening,' Cole. We just went to hear your brother's band play."

"I know." But hearing her say so left this miserable wad of loneliness stuck under his ribcage. "I mean, you're right. I should let you go in and get to bed. You have to get up and do the choir thing in the morning, after all." She was the busiest person he'd run across in a long time. Maybe she filled up every waking minute with activities because she was lonely too.

She reached for the door handle. "Are you coming to church tomorrow?" Her voice was soft.

"Maybe. If this redheaded lady in a choir robe doesn't throw me out." He grinned at her and grabbed the hand she threw up in mock outrage. "You and your sister. Violent women. Violent, I tell you." He tugged her toward him, noting the ambivalence in her eyes. He was making progress.

Progress toward what? What exactly did he want from her?

Emotions crashed through him along with physical sensation. It had been a long time since he'd let himself linger near a woman he was attracted to without some kind of buffer. He knew himself, knew his weaknesses. He couldn't be sure, even though he was a new man in Christ, that those weaknesses were truly gone.

Apparently they weren't, completely, because just the feel of Laurel's smooth fingers cupped in his hand made his mouth go dry.

Then she laced her fingers into his. For once she didn't back away. "Not tonight, Cole, but we are going to have to talk about that time a little more. We left scars on each other, and—and some of mine were so well-hidden I didn't know they were there until you came back."

He turned her hand over, uncurling the fingers, and brought it to his mouth. "I want it to be better." He kissed her palm, felt her tremble.

She slowly withdrew her hand. "I'll be praying for you and Tucker. Good-night, Cole." She opened the door and slipped out into the night.

He watched her walk up the sidewalk, enjoying the gentle sway of her hips and the way she bunched her hair at the back of her neck, then let it go. After she'd gone inside and turned off the porch light, he put the truck in gear and headed back toward the causeway. In the old days he would have needed a stiff drink. Now he needed ...

Now he needed what was always at hand. The Comforter, the Counselor, his best friend.

God, I'm falling here. It's almost worse than the first time, because now I understand the consequences. This time we're both gun-shy, and I don't know if we'll ever get past what happened before. Please shut my feelings down if this is not your will. I can't take another crash and burn.

Please ...

Laurel scooped up Charles Wallace and curled on the living room sofa in the dark. The cat snuggled under her chin, purring loudly.

"Yeah," said Laurel. "I need a hug too. I thought he was going to ... " *Kiss me on the mouth.*

He would have too, if she hadn't acted like a sixth grader on a first date. Why had she pulled away? Self-defense, probably.

She turned her hand over and examined the palm, half expecting glow-in-the-dark marks to appear. Phosphorescent, like those stamps she and Mary Layne would get at the fair when they were kids. Nothing showed up, but her skin felt his presence anyway. Cole managed to mark his territory, no matter what.

She could almost smell him, masculine and heady.

Wrong. Don't concentrate on the physical, Laurel. You promised to pray.

She closed her hand over Cole's imprint.

Oh, God, here we are. Give me clear eyes to see the truth. Please don't let me be fooled. Please protect me and Gilly. Protect Cole and Tucker, and may your will be done in our lives.

She pressed her face into Charles Wallace's soft fur.

And one more thing. About the election. May your will be done in that too.

"You're sure the little red-haired chick will be here?" Tucker twitched at the rolled-up cuffs of a yellow-striped button-down shirt. It looked like he'd slept in it.

Cole jostled his brother's shoulder as they crunched up the gravel drive toward Mary Layne and Wade's house. "Laurel said the whole gang's coming." Laurel's mother had invited him and Tucker to the Kincades' after-church lunch. "Church girl made an impression, huh?"

"Church girl? You think she's serious about that stuff?"

"Dead serious."

Tucker visibly swallowed. "Well ... we can't all be perfect." He brightened as a tall, gangly puppy came running from the direction of the pond. "Hello, is that a dog or an anorexic calf?"

"Tucker, meet Rebel the Wonderdog." Cole stopped and braced himself for the onslaught. "Hey, old man—how's life on the farm?

Down! Behave yourself." He pushed the dog's paws off his stomach and bent to scratch him behind the ears.

"Holy flapping ears, Batman, it *is* a dog"—Tucker crouched and instantly found himself thrust onto his rear—"who doesn't know his own strength." Laughing, he shoved Rebel away and rolled to his feet.

"Mr. Cole, come push me!" Madison, violently pumping the swing on the gym set beside the house, kicked up a cloud of sand and dust with her little bare feet.

"Not now, Maddie." Cheri stood on the front porch, still in her Sunday dress. "Mama said to let our guest-es come in for something to drink first." She backed against the door and smiled shyly at Cole and Tucker. "I made the sun tea. And I picked some mint from my herb garden. Do you want some?"

"Sounds good, please, ma'am." Cole paused. "Tucker, the elf on the swing is Madison, and this one's Cheri. Martha Stewart Junior."

"I could iron your shirt for you." Cheri looked up at Tucker with large, serious brown eyes. "I just learned how."

Tucker smiled. "Thanks, I kinda like the wrinkled look. But I'll take a glass of tea if you can spare one."

Cheri's eyes sparkled. "I'll be right back."

Summarily abandoned in the foyer by their small hostess, Cole and Tucker looked at one another.

Fortunately Laurel wandered in from a doorway to the left, dabbing at the front of her lacy white blouse with a damp washcloth. "Confrontation with Rebel," she explained, smiling a welcome. "Come on into the kitchen. Everybody's in there hammering Wade on the virtue of short sermons."

Cole followed her through a huge great room, notable for its indistinct decor unless you counted the musical instruments. An antique upright piano took up half of one wall, a guitar leaned in a corner, and a couple of miniature violin cases lay open on the sofa. A drum set flanked an old red recliner on the other side of the coffee table.

When Tucker's wistful gaze landed on the guitar, Cole grabbed his brother's elbow. "Later. Let's go be sociable."

The sea of humanity in the kitchen seemed to overwhelm Cole's introverted younger brother. His ability to put himself on public display on stage had never transferred to social situations. Tucker allowed himself to be introduced to Mary Layne and Wade—he'd already met grandparents Dodge and Frances at church—then tried to blend into the wallpaper by backing into a corner.

Gilly was having none of that. She lit up when she saw Tucker, pushing him into a chair at one end of the kitchen table. She stood with a hand on his shoulder as if he were a prize student. "Mom! Do you know he writes actual music? And he's got a cult following on MySpace? And a single from his CD's getting some radio playtime?"

Frances, standing at a counter making roses out of radishes, looked intrigued. "I did not know that. Not that I know exactly what a MySpace cult following is, but I assume that's a good thing. What music school are you studying with, Tucker? Who's your vocal coach?"

Tucker pushed his hair out of his eyes. "Well, ma'am, I don't exactly have a vocal coach." He glanced at Cole. "And I'm not exactly in school right now."

"We're working on that," Cole said, folding his arms. He'd found a seat on a stool at the breakfast bar, next to Laurel. "He's going back tomorrow."

Tucker's brows pulled together. "No point in that," he muttered. "I sold my books a couple of weeks ago."

"You sold your books?" Cole shook his head. He'd done some crazy things in his time, but some of his younger brother's stunts were just plain weird. "Why would you do that?"

"I had a chance to get front-row tickets to a Rascal Flatts concert." Tucker looked up at Gilly. "Wouldn't you have done the same thing?"

"She most certainly would not!" gasped Frances Kincade.

Gilly pursed her lips. "I think I'd better not answer that question in mixed company—parents and regular people, I mean." She patted Tucker's shoulder and sat down beside him. "Plead the Fifth, right, Laurel?"

Laurel cleared her throat. "Here's a suggestion. Take the money you get from this weekend's gig and buy your books back. You've only missed a week of class."

Tucker sat silent for a moment, probably out of respect. Finally he shrugged. "I'll think about it."

Cole touched Laurel's knee in gratitude. If that suggestion had come from him, his brother would have thrown it back in his face. "Look, man, there's a lot to be said for growing up before you jump in the deep end of the entertainment pool. No question you've got the talent, but there's some sharks out there who'll eat you alive."

A sly grin tugged at Tucker's mouth. "Sharks in the pool? Dude, don't be writing lyrics anytime soon. Talk about mixed metaphors."

"Daddy used to be a pool shark." Gilly nudged her father's elbow. "Didn't you, Pop?"

"Now wait a minute—" Dodge's naturally high color deepened to beet-red as laughter filled the small kitchen. "Just because I won a tournament or two when I was in the service—"

"Which branch were you in, sir?" Cole asked, letting the conversation flow away from his younger brother. Continued counseling for Tucker would be better accomplished in private anyway. Preferably with Laurel present. He'd be an idiot not to take advantage of her knack for connecting with kids, which had been honed by years of experience in the courtroom.

And despite all the evidence to the contrary, Cole was not an idiot.

"Can you make a cup and saucer, Aunt Laurel?"

"Let me see. Maybe I can remember." Laurel took the circular length of blue yarn from Cheri, who was snuggled under her arm in the squishy upholstered armchair, and began to twist it around her fingers.

After a gargantuan meal of pot roast and mashed potatoes, everyone had taken a bowl of Mary Layne's killer banana pudding to the family room. Now Madison lay asleep on the sofa with her head in her grandmother's lap, Mary Layne was knitting in a corner, and Wade had disappeared behind the newspaper. Grandpa Dodge had taken on Gilly, Parker, and Dane in a cutthroat game of Parcheesi at the schoolroom table near the window.

"Whose guitar is that?" Tucker, who'd appointed himself busboy, stood in the kitchen doorway eyeing the instrument in the corner.

Wade peered out from behind the newspaper. "Mine. I jink around on it some—used to be a youth pastor, and playing guitar is required—but I basically know just enough to be dangerous. I hear you're quite the virtuoso. Want to try it out?"

Laurel smiled as the boy's face lit. This soporific Sunday afternoon atmosphere had to be death for a restless youngster like Tucker. In fact, even Cole had already decamped, taking the family four-wheeler to run Rebel through the woods.

Tucker took the guitar out of its case and sat down cross-legged on the rug in front of the empty fireplace. He played a soft experimental chord, then began to tune. "Won't it wake up Little Bit over there?" He nodded at Madison, curled like a kitten next to Frances.

"Hardly." Mary Layne adjusted her needles with a smile. "She's been known to fall asleep in a New York subway. Let 'er rip."

Laurel soon let the yarn fall into her lap unnoticed as the spell of the music wrapped her like gold threads of a fairy tale. Tucker played haunting, minor-keyed old songs that Frances and Dodge knew, as well as silly children's songs that had Cheri, Parker, and Dane singing along. Then he entertained them all with a fresh-sounding ballad with romantic, I-miss-you lyrics.

"I like that," Gilly said, chin on fist. "I've never heard it before."

"You wouldn't have. It's mine." Tucker looked down as his fingers rippled a scale.

"You mean *you* wrote it?" Laurel stared at him in amazement. "Words and all?"

"Sure." The translucent eyes were matter-of-fact. "Something hurts me, I write about it." A little grin curled his mouth. "While I was still in high school my girlfriend went off to State, and after a while I didn't hear from her. So finally I called and found out she'd had, like, three other boyfriends since school started."

Gilly winced. "Ouch."

Tucker laughed. "Yeah, well, I got music out of it, so everything's cool."

"Play it again," Gilly demanded.

Laurel listened to the wry, oddly mature lyrics, thinking there must be a lot of assumptions she made on a daily basis that, colored by her own experience, fell short of real understanding. She threaded the yarn through her fingers, enjoying its slightly scratchy texture. When her hands were connected by a loose web of blue, she stared at the pattern. What good thing was God up to in her life?

Music from pain. The idea was suddenly profound.

She stuck her thumbs in the net of yarn, slipped her middle fingers free, and a cup and saucer appeared. Order from chaos. Her pastor had talked about the concept that morning in his sermon.

"Ooh, pretty." Cheri poked a stubby finger into the middle of the cup. "Teach me."

Laurel hugged her niece. "Okay. Then I want to go make sure Rebel hasn't dragged Mr. Cole into the pond."

Maybe she'd let fear entangle her long enough.

chapter 12

She found Cole parking the four-wheeled ATV in Wade's shop. Rebel's reddish coat dripped brown water onto the grass as he lapped thirstily from a stainless steel bowl just outside the garage-style door. By dint of some fancy footwork, Laurel managed to avoid contact with his muddy snout as she entered the stuffy, wood-scented building.

"Did you and Rebel get your fleas worked out, as my Grandma Kincade used to say?"

Cole looked up from checking the vehicle's brake. "Don't know about the dog, but I feel better for a little fresh air." His amused gaze traveled down her burgundy pantsuit to her black leather pumps. "Want to go a round with me?"

"Rain check." She brushed a hand over the dusty surface of the table saw as she walked by. "Next time I'll bring my jeans and take you up on it. I like the woods, but Dane's kind of a wild driver."

"I bet." Cole stood up, the ATV forming a barrier that Laurel could only be grateful for. He walked around it. "This whole crew is something else. I wish I'd known where you came from, Laurel. I thought you were a spoiled, old-money Mobile girl."

"That's mostly true." She picked up an unfinished wooden top Wade and the boys had been working on and gave him a crooked smile. "Is that why you went after me? For my money?"

"I told you why I went after you." Cole perched on a stool beside the saw, hands clasped loosely between his knees. Mud was spattered all up and down the legs of his black slacks and covered his leather shoes. "There were just some things about you that didn't quite jive, you know what I mean? Smart enough to get into a competitive law program. Always dressed to the nines. But that minivan you drove ..." He shook his head, smiling.

Laurel laughed. "The DD-mobile. They called me Doodah."

"The designated driver."

"Or, as the case may be, the dead duck."

The gray eyes went taut. "What do you mean by that?"

"Nothing." She looked away, appalled that her feelings had come blurting out. Somehow it always went back to the night she'd received Michael's letter. To that point she'd been telling herself Cole was too immature—a heartthrob frat boy with the attention span of a butterfly, a waste of perfectly good oxygen. He always flirted, because he flirted with anything in a bra, and she would give him her trademark look of patronizing amusement which sent most men running, tails between their legs.

But not Cole McGaughan—Q the guys called him, short for Quad because he was the fourth installment of Coleman Davis McGaughan. No, Cole would not run. Drunk as he was, he'd seen past her pain and recognized that she was pulled to him like steel filings to a magnet.

She never accompanied her friends to the Warehouse, a local club where students went for loud music—which she hated—drinks—she was a teetotaler—and dancing—Gilly was the ballerina of the family and Laurel had two left feet. But she'd just found out Michael's death wasn't any accident, and she couldn't stand reality anymore, so she walked freely into the smoke- and alcohol-infested dive, accepted the drink Elise handed her; one sip, two, then down it went until she fell into sweet oblivion.

Except oblivion brought a collision with Cole, who did not run. She'd had to literally wrench him out of her life, make it impossible for him to return.

Yet somehow he'd defied the impossible, ignoring her wishes.

His expression gentled. "What is it about me that sends you into such a tailspin, Laurel? I promise I'm not waiting to trick you into some indiscretion." He humorously began to unbutton his cuffs. "Look, nothing up my sleeves." Opening his hands, he held her eyes.

"I need a date," she said before she could change her mind.

"You need a—" His mouth opened and closed. "What?"

"I know you think I'm crazy, but there's this reception I have to go to next weekend, and I don't have a date yet. It's by invitation only, and I wondered if you'd like to go."

"Well, sure, I—"

"But it's a formal event, so you'll need a tux. Is that a problem?"

Cole got up off the stool and took one step. Only a few inches separated them now. His smile was soft, almost tender. "I'll wear tights and a red cape if you want me to."

Laurel swallowed, looking up into his eyes, drowning in ocean-gray depths. She was going to regret this, she was sure.

But she was going to enjoy it first.

After leaving the Theissens', Cole took Tucker back to Ole Miss. In typical McGaughan fashion, the six-hour drive to Oxford was accomplished in laid-back camaraderie, with the MP3 player blaring favorites in every genre. By the time Cole dropped his brother off at the dorm, Tucker seemed reconciled to going back to class and finishing out the semester in his current major.

By the light of a streetlamp in the dark parking lot, Cole studied his little brother's tired, washed-out face. It was nearly midnight, and the kid needed to get to bed. He also needed a lecture. "Man, you're going to have to talk to Dad about letting you switch to music. You can't expect the old man to keep footing the bill while you goof off like this."

"Why not? You did." Tucker dodged the playful fist Cole swung at his shoulder. "Seriously. It's easier to just go with the flow. Besides, I'm not sure I could cut a real music program. I never did read worth a flip."

"Yeah, but what if you want to compose for, say, movies or TV or something? You need to understand theory and instrumentation and stuff."

"I don't know." Tucker shrugged. "That's not important to me right now. I just want to play my guitar. Sing a little."

Cole clenched the keys in his hand. At one time he'd been this short-sighted and dumb. And he'd nearly killed himself too. "Did I ever tell you how much I regret all that goofing off I did? How much pot are you smoking?"

"Not enough to hurt anything." Tucker folded his arms, a gesture both defensive and divisive. "Don't tell me you never piped a little weed."

"Actually, I did—and like I said, I regret it. But alcohol was my ball and chain. God gave us inhibitions for a reason, Tuck. To protect us. I don't want to see you get in the same jam I wound up in. Jail is not fun."

Tucker slung his hair out of his eyes. "You need a box of soap for that speech?"

Cole sighed and gripped his brother's tense shoulder. "Did it sound like that? I'm sorry. You know I love you, man." To his chagrin, his voice cracked. He cleared his throat and stuck his hands in his pockets.

Silence fell, the humid night dark and quiet except for distant voices and laughter from an open window in the dorm. A couple of cars drove past. One honked.

Finally Tucker sniffed and wiped a hand under his nose, softly cursing. "I can't believe you made me *cry*. Get your butt out of here before I call security." He flung his arms around Cole, hard and brief, then snatched his guitar out of the truck. "G'night, Clark Kent. Good luck with the judge lady."

Cole squelched the urge to follow his brother into the dorm and make sure he studied for his economics test. He'd done every-thing he could for Tucker—except pray for him. That he could continue to do. And he had a long, lonely ride back to Mobile to accomplish it. Laurel had offered to come with him, but she was scheduled to preside in court in the morning. She was undoubt-edly in her bed fast asleep by now.

As he drove, sweet images played across his mind. Laurel jok-ing around with her dad during lunch, quoting parts of an Abbott and Costello routine word-for-word. Singing along with Tucker in a rather wispy soprano as she braided cornrows into Madison's hair. Changing her mind about the four-wheeler ride and hanging onto Cole's waist for dear life as they bumped over muddy country roads for a solid hour.

He could still feel the imprint of her arms around him.

He didn't know when exactly it had happened, but he had fall-en in love with Laurel all over again. Keeping Hogan's intentions from her was an impossible assignment. If he was going to win her back, he was going to have to cut himself loose from Hogan.

The sooner the better.

Matt Hogan shaved with one eye on the mirror and the other on McGaughan, sprawled in the only comfortable chair in his hotel room. He knew a man on a mission when he saw one. He also recognized a man in love.

Not that he'd ever been there himself. Commitment was a country he hoped never to visit—at least not until his hair started turning loose and he'd passed Candy Land on the board game of life.

He rinsed the razor and stuck it back in his shaving kit, a beat-up leather bag his mom had given him for high school graduation. Surreptitiously he tugged the lock of hair that fell from a rather spectacular cowlick across his left eyebrow—just to make sure it was thick as ever. He did this every day since he'd read in *GQ* that the hair gene passed through maternal lines. His mother's dad had been bald as a billiard ball by the age of forty.

Reassured that his follicles remained intact, he grabbed a hand towel to wipe his face. McGaughan waited impatiently, tapping his fingers together, tapping his feet, all but squirming in the chair. Well, tough. Wake a guy up from a dead sleep before seven a.m. and you deserved to twiddle your thumbs awhile.

"Come on, Hogan, I've got deadlines to meet." McGaughan picked up a pile of papers Matt had left on the table and flipped through them. "Comb your curly locks later."

Matt dropped the towel on the bathroom floor and sauntered to the desk to unplug his cell phone charger. "Maybe you don't mind looking like a *Survivor* reject, but some of us have a little pride in our appearance." He turned on the computer and gathered his keys and change.

McGaughan looked up from perusing one of the documents. "Huh? Oh." He rubbed his knuckles across his unshaven jaw. "I told you, I drove all night to get back here. Haven't had time to go back to the room and shower yet. I wanted to get this behind me."

"Get what behind you?" Matt didn't like the way McGaughan's eyes were moving. Shifty. Definitely shifty. "What's the matter with you?" He yanked open the curtain, letting a flood of early-morning sunshine awaken dust mites in the air and reveal the chaos of the desk, table, bed, and dresser.

McGaughan blinked against the sudden light, his expression … weird. Eager and happy, if one could apply such sappy emotions to one of the most hardboiled reporters in New York. Well, he *had* been, at one time. Lately McGaughan was—

Weird just about covered it.

"I'm okay," McGaughan said. "In fact, everything's clear for the first time." He replaced the papers on the table and lurched to his feet. "Matt, I need to talk to you about something important."

"Oh, really?" Matt looked at the door. When a guy went postal, you'd better know where the exits were. "You've already talked to the judge's old roommate?"

"Haven't had time. I've been busy." McGaughan paced over to the dresser, picked up a *Playboy* magazine, and turned it over. He stared at it for a moment, then closed his eyes. With a grimace, he slid it under a T-shirt Matt had left there last night. "No, it's this thing with Laurel. Judge Kincade."

Taking a chance, Matt sat in the chair McGaughan had vacated. The guy looked restless but not exactly dangerous. "Laurel." Matt grinned. "Sounds like you took my advice and scored."

McGaughan scowled. "It's not like you're thinking. But we have become … friends. I've spent a lot of time with her, and I brought you the interview recording so you could hear for yourself." He pulled a cassette out of his pocket and laid it on the dresser. "She's as principled and upright as any politician I've ever met."

Matt snorted. "That's not saying much."

"You know what I mean. There's a line I'm not crossing over on this one, Matt."

"I knew it. You're falling for her." Matt sat up, staring hard at McGaughan. "Don't you care about the glitch in her background? What are you gonna do when somebody else—and I hope it's me—pulls down the curtain and exposes the truth?"

"The truth is nothing to be afraid of." But McGaughan glanced at his watch. "Look, I've got a column due by noon. I've got to go. Let's just leave it at this—Don't expect any more information out of me. I'm writing what I see and hear, and that's it. Read my articles if you want to know anything else about Laurel Kincade."

"Hey, whose idea was this in the first place?" Matt protested, but McGaughan slipped out the door with a final wave.

Steamed, Matt grabbed the T-shirt off the dresser and tossed it over his shoulder. He flipped over the magazine and glared at the sultry beauty on the cover. Fantasy was a whole lot more fun than reality. Too bad it didn't pay the credit card bills.

Wednesday afternoon Cole sat in his room staring at his computer screen. He had a nasty suspicion that he had to confirm. He flipped open his phone and speed-dialed Hogan.

Hogan picked up immediately. "Hey, McGaughan, I thought you were pretending I didn't exist. Where've you been?"

"Following up phone calls to a couple of Anglican bishops. They're spearheading relief projects after that tornado in Oklahoma last weekend. Gotta write a couple of other related articles later this week. Listen, I have a question for you. What do you know about Derrick Edes?"

There was a moment's pause. "You're expecting information out of me when you won't return the favor?"

"Come on, Hogan, this is important."

"Oh, all right. But all I know is what I've told you. Edes seems to know his stuff and he's tight with Renata Castleberry."

"Have you seen him in contact with Field?"

Hogan made a disparaging noise. "Why would she hire a consultant with ties to her opponent?"

"She wouldn't knowingly. It's just that I saw Edes's name on some papers on your desk the other day. Looked like a report on Laurel's personal finances."

At the time, he hadn't thought much about it. After all, Hogan would be interested in everybody connected with Laurel's campaign. Besides, he'd been snowed under with extra assignments since Monday.

But this afternoon he'd finally had a chance to google-search the slick publicity manager. So far all he'd found was a brief reference to Edes's employment several years ago by the firm who handled the publicity for Field's race for the DA's office. Campaign management was a notoriously fickle profession, and there could be nothing to this ticklish feeling at the back of Cole's neck.

"Why were you rifling through my stuff, anyway? *I'm* the investigator." Hogan laughed. "Edes is her consultant, McGaughan. Of course his name's going to pop up here and there."

The ticklish feeling mutated to raised hackles. Hogan had not answered the first question at all. And he'd deflected the second accusation. If Cole challenged him, he'd lie. Simple as that.

"Okay, if you say so." Cole bookmarked the site he'd been searching and logged off the Internet. "I've got to finish this article and see about getting hold of a tux for a ... thing I have to do this weekend." Hogan didn't need to know he was escorting Laurel to the reception. He ended the call and sat there absently spinning the phone on the desktop.

If Edes had been feeding information about Laurel's finances to Matt, who then sent it on to her opponent, he was an unmitigated snake. Matt could be excused, since he was doing what he'd been hired to do and made no pretense of friendship with Laurel or her campaign. But for Edes to play both sides of the fence in a political race was despicable.

Cole picked up the phone and dialed Laurel's cell number. When her voice mail picked up, he hung up without leaving a message. She'd been tied up all week with a full docket, trying to get her caseload cleared before the hottest season of the campaign descended. He'd see her on Friday anyway. Better to tell her what he suspected in person.

She had to be warned.

Laurel had to keep looking up at Cole to make sure she hadn't stepped into some Ozland where up was down, inside was out, and the sky was really black velvet pinned with diamonds. The historic Saenger Theatre glittered with jewelry and beaded gowns and reeked of flower arrangements and expensive perfumes that would normally have given her a headache; awareness of her tall, dark escort eclipsed all other sensation as if he were a particularly luminous moon.

Or perhaps he was the solar center and she the pale satellite. The social situations in which she and Cole had been together to this point had been either campaign-oriented or pure fun. Dressed in a tux for this elegant, formal occasion—a reception sponsored by the Mobile Arts Council in honor of a world-renowned cellist who would perform in concert tomorrow evening—Cole emitted a subtle, almost sensual power.

Earlier when he'd picked her up in a brand-new silver sedan, he'd smiled at her confusion. "Tired of that gas-guzzling truck," he'd explained, but she knew somehow that he'd traded in his vehicle with her in mind.

"You look ..." She'd swallowed and looked away, unable to express how the fit of expensive broadcloth across those powerful shoulders affected her. "I'm glad you decided to forego the red cape."

His laugh had rumbled as he'd clasped her hand lightly to help her into the car. "Figured the tights might cause a scene. You look pretty amazing yourself." His eyes warmed her, skimming her shoulders and face. He reluctantly released her hand. "Guess we'd better get going."

Now his touch lingered protectively on the small of her back as they stood talking to her mother and the president of the council, Louise Bartikowski, wife of a prominent local doctor.

"How is the campaign coming along, dear?" Mrs. Bartikowski, who had connections all over the county, laid a friendly be-ringed hand on Laurel's wrist for a second. "Jerry was just asking about you the other day. He said he'd be happy to help in any way."

Laurel smiled. "Thanks, it's going well."

Frances interrupted. "I have to confess I have three most brilliant daughters. Besides Laurel, there's Mary Layne winning graphic arts awards, and Gilly off to audition for the ASB." Preening, Laurel's mother adjusted the crystal beads at her neckline. "We're all going to miss Laurel when she moves to the capital."

"And I don't know how those children at the Popcorn Playhouse will get along without you either." Mrs. Bartikowski, used to ignoring Laurel's mother's self-absorption, smiled kindly. "Have you thought about who'll take your place?"

Laurel had indeed lost a bit of sleep over that very question. She'd mentioned the idea to Gilly—

"What's a Popcorn Playhouse?" Cole reached into his pocket as if he might take out a notebook and start taking notes.

"It's the community's youth theater." Mrs. Bartikowski, who had contributed thousands of dollars to the program, lit up at the opportunity to endorse her pet project. "They do musicals mostly, since that's what sells tickets. Laurel performed there herself as a child and went on to win a few starring roles until she went away to law school. She's been coaching soloists and the chorus since she moved back to Mobile two years ago."

Cole moved to look down into Laurel's face, his expression quizzical. He seemed almost offended. "You didn't tell me about that."

"I'm uncomfortable with putting my charities into public custody."

Frances sighed. "I keep telling her it's good publicity, and she needs to let people know." She turned to Cole. "Maybe you could talk some sense into her."

"Maybe I can." Leaning down, he murmured, "I need to talk to you about something else anyway, Laurel."

"What is it?"

"Not here. Is there someplace more private?"

She forced her eyelids up to meet his gaze. Her stomach quaked. The gravity of his expression made her forget the crowd in the room, the soaring ceiling with its glittering chandelier, the grand marble staircases spiraling up to the balcony. "Mom, Mrs. B, will you excuse us?" She tucked her hand in the crook of Cole's arm and led him toward a shadowed nook behind one of the stairwells. "Tell me."

He smiled a little. "Nobody's dying. Relax."

"Sorry." She hastily released his arm and clutched her tiny beaded bag with both hands. "You're scaring me."

He lifted a hand as if to brush her face, then stuck it in his pants pocket. "I don't mean to. It has to do with your campaign, and I was going to wait and tell you about it later, when I took you home. But I ..." He looked away. "Laurel, your mother's right. Somebody needs to talk straight to you."

"About what? My campaign's going fine, and I've got a first-class consultant handling the details." She took a breath. "Cole, as much as I appreciate your interest, you of all people should know that some aspects of my private life have to stay that way. Private."

He eyed her for a moment, lips pinched together. "What if I know something you don't?"

"It depends." She gestured with the little gold bag. "Quit being so mysterious and just spit it out. I'm a grown-up now, remember?"

He smiled, grimly. "Yeah, I guess you are. I'm sorry to bring it up here, but we've both been busy this week, and this is something that shouldn't wait. I believe Derrick Edes has been doing opposition research on you. He's a mole for George Field's campaign."

chapter 13

Cole watched the color drain out of Laurel's face, leaving the beauty mark under her left eye to stand out in bold relief.

"What? How do you know that?" The shock in her voice went straight through him.

"Let's just say I followed up on a lead."

A little of Laurel's color came back. "You have to tell me how you know. Otherwise, it's just hearsay."

He rolled his eyes. "Might have known you'd think like a lawyer."

"I *am* a lawyer." If she'd been any stiffer he could use her for a doorstop. "Renata vouches for Derrick, and I've known her for a very long time." *Longer than I've known you*, being the implication.

"Yeah, and Renata herself is hanging out in some places you'd probably be surprised to find out about."

"I don't listen to gossip." Laurel leaned against the wall behind her, less than a step away from him, but he felt the leap backward in their relationship.

Her loyalty to her friend was a beautiful thing, but he wanted to punch the wall in frustration. Without breaking Matt's confidence, how was he going to convince Laurel to watch out for herself? One thing a reporter didn't do was reveal the source of his information without permission. And Hogan wasn't somebody Cole chose to either confide in or cross at present.

He gripped one fist inside the other. "Okay, you're right. I shouldn't have said anything if I couldn't prove it to you. Just ... Laurel, will you be careful and keep your eyes open to what's going on around you? No matter how brilliant you may be in the court-room, you've always been a little naive about your friendships."

He saw that he'd hit a nerve. Her eyes widened just a bit, be-fore the extravagant dark lashes swept down to cover a vulnerable expression he was all too familiar with.

"Unfortunately," she said huskily, "that's true. Warning taken."

He almost let her slip away. But if he was going to chide Laurel for an excess of trust, he'd better be honest enough to admit the opposite fault in himself. Time to repent. Past time.

"I didn't mean me, Laurel. Wait, not me." He slipped an arm around her where the shimmering green gown clung to her nar-row waist, catching her against his side as if they were stopped in a tango. She turned her face away. "Look at me. Please."

There was a full minute of background noise — laughter and conversation and a harpist playing from a far corner — counterpoint to their silence, before she raised her eyes. Mute, she stared at him. He could see her mouth tremble at the corners. "I don't know what you want from me," she whispered.

"I want to start over," he said. "I want to learn who you were and who you've grown to be. I think I might ... I think I ..." He couldn't say what he felt, because it was too huge, and the timing was too soon. But he saw that she understood.

He also saw that it scared her to death. She shook her head, jerkily, biting her lip as she often did when she was upset. But she didn't walk out of his arms.

"I won't hurt you again, Laurel," he said as steadily as he could, considering his breath was backed up in his throat, and his chest felt like it might explode. "I'm asking you to give me another chance."

Her eyes dampened, and he had no idea what that meant until she said, "Okay. I'll try." Then she smiled a little. "But we have to get out of this dark corner before my mother starts sending out bridal shower invitations. I don't think you're quite ready for that."

He smiled. "Don't sell me short."

To ease the silence between herself and Cole on the way home, Laurel turned on the radio. Hoping for classical music, she got Brandy Turner instead.

"Friends and neighbors, get ready for the onslaught of the right-wingers into your living rooms, your mailboxes, and the airwaves." The brash, slightly nasal voice bled sarcasm. "The primaries are upon us in only six weeks."

"This chick is a real piece of work." Cole turned up the volume before Laurel could snap the button off. "Have you ever listened to her?"

"Only when I'm in the mood for indigestion," Laurel muttered. "How can people take her seriously?"

As if Brandy had heard her and sought to prove her point, the tirade continued. "If you're smart, folks, you'll safeguard your minds against the elitism bound to surface from the conservative camp. Tonight we'll be talking about the judicial race for a couple of seats on the Alabama Supreme Court, including that of chief justice. Let's just hope the good guys win. Give me a call if you'd like to vent." Brandy rattled off the station's toll-free number.

Cole snorted. "She's just trying to stir up controversy. That's what talk show hosts do."

Laurel stared at him, indignant. "I've met this woman, Cole, and she hates my guts. You should hear some of the things she's said about me. Said *to* me."

Cole's expression was skeptical. "Come on, Laurel, I doubt if it's personal."

"Oh really? Well, listen to this." Laurel dug out her cell phone and dialed the number for the radio station. After several rings, she got through and was put on hold.

As she waited, Brandy took a call from a woman who responded to the talk show host's greeting with the honeyed tones of Old South Old Money. Probably one of Laurel's mother's contemporaries. "Yes, I'd just like to say I've had—" the woman cleared her throat, as if to make sure she wasn't misunderstood—"personal dealings with Judge Kincade. At least, a friend of mine has. Back when she was just a lawyer up in Montgomery, Laurel Kincade represented my friend's ex in a custody suit. The presiding judge walks in and says, 'Oh, hi Laurel, how's your grandpa doing?' and proceeds with business as usual." The woman's cultured voice paused for dramatic effect. "Now I ask you—was that fair?"

While Brandy responded in gleeful outrage, Laurel waved her free hand at Cole, phone pressed to her ear. "See what I mean?"

"Okay, she's a little intense." He parked the car in front of Laurel's house and killed the ignition but left the radio on.

Just then the call screener spoke to Laurel. Within moments she was patched through to Brandy. She took a deep breath for calm. "Hi, Brandy. This is Laurel Kincade. I'd like to respond to your previous caller."

"Judge Kincade." Brandy drew out the name as if she could hardly believe her good fortune. "Long time no see. What's it been? A couple of months?"

Not long enough, Laurel thought. "About that," she said evenly. "It seems you're a little misinformed."

Brandy laughed. "And you're a little sensitive. If you're serious about running with the big dogs, honey, you're gonna have to get a tougher hide." The radio squealed. "And turn your radio off— you're interfering with the broadcast."

Eyes alight, Cole snapped off the radio and leaned closer to Laurel.

She pushed the speakerphone button so he could hear the conversation. But when he didn't move away, she was grateful. "Is that better?"

"Much. So you take exception to being called on your little nepotism problem?"

"If I walked out of every courtroom where my grandfather is known, I'd have to move to California." Laurel kept her voice calm.

"So you admit it."

"I admit that my job as a custody lawyer in Montgomery was to make sure the unhappy little kids who came through my office wound up in the best possible situation. I had a remarkable amount of success, but I happen to believe that building strong and healthy families is the only way to prevent the sort of misery and loss I saw every day. If I'm chosen to apply the laws that are already on our books to protect Alabama families, I'll be honored."

"Folks, isn't that the sweetest and most patriotic thing you've ever heard?" Brandy's voice took on a coat of saccharin. "I might just break out in 'Sweet Home Alabama.' While I'm wiping my eyes, let's take a short commercial break."

Laurel heard the phone click. Her audience with Brandy TWO was over. She closed the phone and palmed it.

She didn't realize her head was bowed until Cole lifted her chin with one gentle knuckle. "Hey, you did good," he said. "I'm proud of you."

"I guess it was a waste of time." She released a breath. "Her audience doesn't like me anyway."

"I dunno. You converted me."

Her eyes flashed to his, and she found him smiling. Something latent in his gaze set her skin to tingling. She dropped the phone in her lap and clenched her hand—the hand he'd kissed less than a week ago. Her palm burned as if his mouth still touched it. "I've got to go, Cole."

"I know." But he took a tress of her hair that the stylist had left dangling against her shoulder—most of it had fallen out of its knot by now—and twisted it around his finger. His hand wound up close to her ear and trailed down her jaw. "I think we're having an evening."

"Wha—What?" Her breath had stopped somewhere high in her chest.

"Last Saturday you said we weren't 'having an evening,' we were just listening to Tucker's band." He paused and studied her lips. "This is different."

"I think you're right." She closed her eyes, unable to bear the soft way he looked at her. If she kept looking, she'd have to think about the ramifications of letting Cole kiss her. Inviting him. Because that was what she was doing. Part of her brain said, *If you don't want this to happen, get out of this vehicle right now, sister, while the getting's good.*

And she'd been right here once before, though under quite different circumstances.

He must have been thinking about the same thing. Just before his mouth closed on hers, he breathed, "I told you I won't hurt you again, Laurel."

Yes, and this time she was quite sober. She was a mature woman who had not kissed a man properly in, oh, too many years to count. This one knew what he was doing, and she was being turned inside out with the diamond-spangled black velvet sky under her feet like a magic carpet. He was still the man she loved, even after all he'd done to wrench her life apart at the seams. Oh, no, it didn't hurt.

When he stopped and laid his forehead against hers, she took his rough jaw between her hands to pull him back, but he resisted. "Wait, sweetheart. I need to ... Okay, look, you're the most beautiful thing I've ever seen, but you're killin' me." His voice was slightly slurred, and she could feel his lips smiling against her fingers. "You know what I mean?"

Her eyes opened. "Oh!"

"Yeah. So ..." He quickly kissed the side of her mouth and pulled away, groaning. "I told you I'm a new man." He rubbed the heels of his hands against his eyes. "I can't believe I'm saying this—but go inside, Laurel. And I'm going back to the hotel to take a cold—Never mind. Just call me tomorrow morning, okay? Right when you get up. I want to hear your voice."

She really wanted to kiss him again, but he was right. Staying any longer would be dangerous.

Besides, there was always tomorrow.

Laurel called as Cole was pounding up the stairs after an hour-long workout in the hotel fitness center. It wasn't a full-fledged gym but contained enough weights and cardio machines to keep him in decent shape until he could get home to his Y membership.

He stopped in his tracks in the stairwell, letting the echo of his steps bounce off the metal stairs. Or maybe that was his heart chugging like a printing machine at press time. "Hey ..." He sat down right where he was. "You decided to sleep in."

"No, I decided I needed some time in the Word before I called. I've been up since six or so."

He couldn't tell from her voice—breathless? thoughtful?— what she was thinking. What the heck did he know, except that he was glad she'd called. "Yeah, I was just about to do the same thing. I went and pumped some iron first, ran a few miles to get me going." He paused, wiping his face with the towel around his neck. "Are you okay?"

This time he could hear a smile. "I'm good. Very, very good. I just wanted to, you know, check in with the Holy Spirit about ... everything."

"Everything. You mean me?" He knew how *he* felt about it. God had rocked his world through a beautiful woman. And not just any beautiful woman. Laurel. He knew her well enough to know she wouldn't give her kisses lightly. She had as good as told him she was serious about him. Could a man ask for a greater gift outside of soul salvation?

"Yes, of course, about you." Her voice was soft with that husky undertone that slid under his skin and made him want to go run another mile or two. "But there's so much else going on in my life ..." She sighed. "It only complicates it all. For one thing, how are you going to write objective articles about me if we—"

"Let me worry about that." Cole stood up and continued the climb up the stairs. He might have known Laurel would overanalyze the situation, thinking herself into a snarl of doubt. "You concentrate on being your smart, gorgeous self and winning the election." He opened the door to his floor and headed for his room. "Have you thought any more about what I told you last night? About Derrick Edes?"

She hesitated. "I've thought about it. I just don't know how to approach Renata yet."

"You've got to confront Edes. If you don't, you could get yourself into trouble. The guy's got access to all your personal records."

"Cole, I promise you I'll be careful. I'll deal with it."

"I guess that's a start." He'd have to double up on watching her back. Masking his frustration, he forced an upbeat tone. "Now what are you up to today?"

"Playhouse rehearsal at ten. You want to come watch?"

"I have a couple of pieces I need to write. When I get done I'll give you a call."

"Okay. Cole, I need to go wash my hair."

"Brother, the classic brush-off—no pun intended." He laughed with her. "No problem, I'll talk to you later."

Silence hung, neither of them willing to say goodbye, neither ready for words of commitment.

Finally Laurel cleared her throat. "Okay then. See you." The line went dead.

Smiling, he stuck his keycard in the lock, went into the room, and turned on the shower. He'd told Laurel he was headed for Bible study, and he would do that before he sat down to write, but first he needed a serious talk with the Father.

A year or so ago he'd read a Christian actor's testimony of figuratively ripping out his heart and daily standing with his arms lifted, blood running down. Offering up the most vital organ to God, like some native in a ritual spiritual exchange. The graphic image fired Cole's imagination and resolve when milder admonishments would have blown right past his strong will. Particularly on days like today when he sensed his life in crisis.

He stood under a needlelike spray of hot water, feeling it pound his head and sluice down his body as he prayed.

Transplant my heart, God. Take my will, replace it with yours.

Give me Laurel was what he heard in answer.

His mouth opened, he took a breath and choked on shower spray. Coughing, he swiped water off his face with both hands.

"You don't mean that," he said aloud. He never argued with God. But generally what God said to him was written down in the Bible, and there was no arguing with it anyway.

The feeling of private battle persisted. He wanted Laurel—he admitted it—on a fleshly level, as well as on an emotional and spiritual level. How could he even consider giving her up on the day after she'd begun to soften toward him? But he sensed God wanted—no, demanded—his willingness to do so.

I'm bleeding, Lord. Would you really do this?

There was nothing tame about the God he now served. Maybe he still got dressed up in a tuxedo occasionally and drove a nice car, maybe he earned his living banging out sentences on a computer keyboard. But God was the heart hunter and demanded it all.

Cole knew this.

He flattened his hands against the shower stall, bowed his head under the water, let it wash him. "Okay," he said. "I'm ready. Whatever you want." He didn't know what the decision meant, but he knew he was different. Every day he went a little deeper, found a little more richness.

When he'd dried off and dressed, he piled up on the bed to scan his email. He read a forwarded funny from his mom, a brief note from Tucker, and a notice reminding him to pay his rent back in New York. The last one was from Aaron Zorick.

McGaughan,

The work's been good so far, but I think you can dig a little deeper. You're soft-pedaling this gal. Find some kind of flaw or nobody's going to believe you're a serious journalist.

And that was it.

Muttering under his breath, Cole hit "reply."

Mr. Zorick,

This world has a big problem with cynicism. I hope you'll let me write the truth as I see it and not force me to invent scandal where there is none. If you want a tabloid-style exposé, you should recruit another reporter.

Sincerely and respectfully,
Cole McGaughan

He sat back and reread his words. He'd written his gut reaction but knew better than to hit "send" without some serious thought. Instead, he opened a blank Word document and journaled what had just happened between him and the Lord.

As he finished, someone banged on the door. "Just a sec!" he hollered. Boy, the maids were getting aggressive these days. Opening the door he found not the five-foot-nothing Hispanic woman who'd been making his bed for the last three weeks, but a six-foot, knobby-kneed PI dressed in a pink Hawaiian shirt, canvas shorts, and rope sandals.

Hogan flashed a peace sign. "Aloha, dude."

"The pineapple field's that-a-way." Cole hiked a thumb over his shoulder.

"Come on, man, it's Saturday. Let's go play golf or something. Maybe hang out at the beach and watch the babes—I mean the waves." Hogan executed a passable hula move.

Cole pinched the bridge of his nose. Hogan could be a lot of fun, but how could Cole explain his complete disinterest in ogling half-naked women who were not Laurel? Okay, he repented of that thought too. He didn't have the right to think of Laurel unclothed to any degree until they were married. And she was a long way from thinking of *him* as husband material.

Hogan's smile faded. "You feeling all right?"

"I'm feeling fine, but I'm working." Cole gestured toward his laptop, still open on the unmade bed.

"Okay. Whatever." Hogan dropped his hands. "Working. You just seemed, you know, a little tense the other day, and I thought you might want to take a break."

Cole would have taken the cue, wished Hogan all happiness in his babe-hunting, and shut the door, except for one thing. There was the slightest hint of loneliness—with a soupçon of curiosity—coloring the guy's expression.

Cole remembered feeling lost and curious about religious people himself. There was no way his conscience would let him shut the door on a chance to make a difference in his friend's life.

He stepped back and widened the opening in the doorway. "Come on in, Hogan, while I shut down the computer and find my shoes."

chapter 14

Matt walked in with every intention of making himself at home. He'd been thinking about the situation with McGaughan off and on since Monday. There was no reason a guy with all that potential should throw away his career for some black-robed, pucker-mouthed legal eagle, no matter how hot she might be. It was the signal duty of Matthew Christopher Hogan to toss a rope to the drowning man.

All he had to do was remind McGaughan of all the fun he was missing. He'd come prepared for guerilla warfare. Step one: doubt.

He pulled a cassette tape out of his pocket and rattled it. "Hey, one of the reasons I came over was to play this thing for you. I think you'll find it interesting."

McGaughan was sitting on the bed putting on his sneakers. He glanced up and frowned. "Is that the tape I gave you of my interview with Laurel?"

"Nope. You were right—that was a total bust. But this . . . this little baby's got some juice."

"What do you mean?" McGaughan reached for the cassette.

Matt chuckled and backed away. "Not so fast. This is valuable property. Where's your cassette player?"

"Over there." McGaughan gestured toward the desk.

"Oh, right." Matt plugged the tape into the deck, checked to make sure it was cued, and punched the "play" button.

Looking confused, McGaughan sat there, one shoe off and one on. Matt let him alone. After all, this was for the guy's own good.

A soft, drawling female voice began to speak. Matt had hidden the microphone, so the sound quality was a bit muffled, but the words were clear enough. "Yes, I knew Laurel back then," the woman said in a sweet potato casserole soprano. "We were roommates in law school. If you're asking about that last year, I'd say she *was* a little strange at times."

As his own voice came through on the tape — "What do you mean, strange?" — Matt glanced at McGaughan.

There was little expression on the hard face, but the tips of his ears were pink. "Stop it. Stop the tape." McGaughan dropped the shoe in his hand and braced his hands on his knees. "Was that Elise Bell?"

"Vanderbecken. Remember? She got married."

"Whatever. When did you talk to her?"

"Monday, after you told me you weren't going to do it."

"I never said—"

"You made it clear you didn't want to hear anything negative about your girl. So I did it for you."

McGaughan passed his tongue across his lower lip. "Sooner or later Laurel's going to find out Field has a hound dog on her tail. She could have you locked up for harassment."

Matt laughed. "I haven't bothered her one bit. I'm just talking to some nice southern folks who happen to know her."

McGaughan stared at him for a moment. "Okay, so the roommate thinks she was a little strange. Whoopee-doo."

"Listen to the rest of it." Matt pushed the "play" button again.

"I mean," continued Elise Vanderbecken, "Laurel was the most dependable, conscientious person I ever met in my life. She studied, she went to class, she went to church, and not much else. She had some wild friends who hung out at this dive called the Warehouse, but as far as I knew, she never went herself." The honeyed voice paused. "Then one weekend she went with them down to New Orleans for Mardi Gras. It was February, and cold as a frog's heinie in Oxford. I almost wished I could go with them, but my sister was getting married and I had to go home. I still don't know why Laurel went—it wasn't like her. I think something must've happened, because she was crying when she left."

There was a pause while the young matron apparently rescued one of her progeny from the distress of a cartoon program that ended too soon. Matt hit fast-forward, and the tape continued.

"Sorry about that." Elise sounded flustered. "Anyway, I got back from the wedding expecting Laurel to be waiting on me in the room, holed up in her bed with a book, just like usual. But she stayed gone for another three days. Finally she dragged in looking all pale and tired. She never told me one word about where she'd been or what happened down in New Orleans. I asked other people who went, and they just said she'd disappeared. The second day she was gone, Laurel called Tiff Carter to say she was fine and not to worry. That they should all go back to school without her and she'd be back in a day or two." Elise heaved a loud sigh. "Don't you think that's a little bit odd?"

Matt stopped the tape. He could tell McGaughan had heard enough. He looked sick.

"That *does* sound a little bit odd, if you ask me." Matt folded his arms and propped a hip on the desk. "What do you think, McGaughan?"

McGaughan visibly pulled himself together. "I think you don't have enough to keep you busy, if that's the only dirt you've collected on the woman."

Matt laughed. "Come on, McGaughan, you know something happened while she was in New Orleans that week. All I have to do is talk to the right people and find out what it was. She's toast."

"What do you think she did, commit a murder and hide the body?" McGaughan managed to look amused.

"I don't know, but if you're smart, you'll think twice about putting all your career eggs in that particular basket. In fact, if you're *really* smart, you'll change your mind and help me smoke her out."

McGaughan bent to stuff his foot into the other sneaker. "It's not gonna happen, Matt. We'll play golf today, but Laurel means a lot to me, and if you have any respect for me, you'll find another job and leave her alone."

"Dream on—" A sudden pounding on the door halted Matt in the process of removing the cassette from the tape deck. "What the heck?"

"Must be the housekeeper." McGaughan yanked open the door. "See, I told—"

A small dark woman in a maid's uniform burst into vociferous Spanish, wringing her hands.

McGaughan glanced at Matt, who shrugged. "*No hablo español*," McGaughan stammered.

Then the woman began to cry. And mew. "*El gato*," she blubbered.

"That means 'cat,'" said Matt, fascinated. "One of the few words I know. There's this great little cantina in Houston—"

"Cat?" echoed McGaughan. He *mewed* back at the maid.

Matt nearly wet himself laughing, especially when the woman stopped crying, grabbed McGaughan by the arm, and tried to drag him out into the hall. "*Sí, sí,* cat." She launched into another string of Spanish words.

"I think she wants to show you something," Matt managed after he'd caught his breath. "You might want to take your pistol, though. Man-eating kittens, you know."

McGaughan scowled at him as he gave the woman an awkward pat on her plump shoulder. "Hey, she's obviously upset about something, so I'd better go down to the desk with her and see if I can help. At least get somebody to translate." He grabbed a keycard off the dresser and stuck it in his pocket. "Don't go anywhere, I'll be right back."

Matt snickered. "Trust me, I'm dying to know what's going on, and why she picked *you* to dump on."

After McGaughan and the Mexican crazy-woman had disappeared behind the closed door, Matt cast himself into the armchair to wait. He linked his hands over his stomach, propped his feet on the bed, and circled his thumbs. He'd have to admit, even when McGaughan got religious, he wasn't boring. One thing after another, from leggy redheaded judges to bloodhounds in a Dumpster.

So what was it about this turn to God? What made a smart guy like McGaughan suddenly go all woo-woo and give up some of the most fun stuff in the universe, like laying back Jack Daniels and chalking up women?

He spent a whole minute puzzling over the question, came to no reasonable conclusion, and quickly got bored. So if, for the moment, he wasn't going to be whacking two-inch balls into a four-inch cup from four hundred yards, and there weren't any magazines with pretty pictures to look at—nothing but a copy of *Newsweek* and yesterday's *Daily Journal* lay on the table—then Matt really ought to be working. McGaughan's computer sat open on the bed, right where he'd left it. Maybe there were some notes about the lady judge he'd neglected to share.

The issue of invasion of privacy flitted across Matt's brain and, as usual, drifted away like barroom smoke. How else were you supposed to do your job if you didn't snoop when you had the chance?

Without a second thought, he picked up the laptop, sat back down in the chair with it, and moved the mouse to wake up the monitor. Bingo. Several documents sat on the desktop.

First he read what looked like a blog entry. It was full of religious imagery and made very little sense. Offering up your bloody heart? What in Sam Hill was that all about? But there was one line that did catch his attention.

"I want to make a difference in Matt's life. I want him to know you like I do."

Holy cow. He suddenly felt like a stag caught in the sights of some hunter's gun. And he'd put himself squarely in the middle of the target.

Matthew, baby, you're the bull's-eye.

Oddly, he didn't feel angry. He felt sort of flattered. Lately McGaughan had been calling him "Matt" more often than "Hogan" — like a brother rather than a friend. He knew McGaughan wasn't weird or gay or anything; it was just some subtle change in their friendship. Intimacy of any sort made Matt uncomfortable. But since McGaughan didn't make a big deal out of it, he'd let it slide, pretended not to notice.

This, though ... this reference to him personally in a prayer to God, made him feel loved in a way that wasn't like anything he'd known since he left home. Since the last time his mother had hugged him.

When his eyes started to water, he muttered a curse, sent the blog document down to the dock, and fished around on the desktop some more. To his delight, the email program came up without a password, and he found a couple of items addressed to

McGaughan's editor at the *Journal*. Apparently Zorick thought McGaughan was sloughing off his opportunity too. No surprise there. And it looked like McGaughan was getting ready to commit the ultimate stupidity of quitting a perfectly respectable job with one of the best papers in the country.

Matt looked at his watch. McGaughan had been gone for ten minutes. No telling when he'd come back. But this was too interesting. No way was he going to sit here playing solitaire with this goldmine right in front of him. Within a folder titled "Articles," he found a subfolder labeled "Laurel Kincade." He opened it and found a series of documents that had already gone into print in the *Journal*. He recognized all the titles — except for one entitled "Alabama Family Values Candidate Hides Disreputable Past." He let out a whistle of surprise.

The first two paragraphs told him what Laurel Kincade was running for and a bit about her background — nothing, of course, that he didn't already know. But the third paragraph widened his eyes.

Unfortunately, it turns out that Alabama's sweetheart "Christian family values" judge has been hiding quite a healthy skeleton in her closet. According to a firsthand source who wishes to remain anonymous, eight years ago Laurel Kincade participated in a drunken elopement after a Mardi Gras celebration in New Orleans. Ms. Kincade and her lover took advantage of a loophole in the Louisiana marriage license laws, whereby the required blood test and seventy-two-hour waiting period may be waived for out-of-state tourists. They were married by a well-known French Quarter minister who advertises his services on the Internet. Two days later, apparently sober enough to be humiliated by her lapse in judgment, Ms. Kincade appealed to her grandfather, Mississippi Judge Gillian, who personally annulled the marriage. Judge Gillian subsequently pulled strings to cover up both the marriage and the annulment.

"Holy cow," Matt said aloud.

McGaughan had known this all along. The article was dated April 6, two weeks ago. Which begged the question—*Why?* Why hold onto information this explosive?

Matt pulled his earlobe. McGaughan had feelings for this lady and had changed his mind about letting anything damage her reputation.

He skimmed the rest of the article, which was a bit editorial in nature. Statistics on candidates claiming tenure to the family values platform. Voting records of several prominent representatives already in office. Enumeration of judicial decisions in Alabama during the past five years, related to religious and moral issues. Blah blah blah.

Upshot: buyer beware.

Society's moral climate being what it was, Matt supposed, Laurel Kincade's behavior wasn't any worse than any other college student who had gotten loaded and run off to get married. At least she'd *gotten* married. The damning thing about it was the cover-up.

Everybody loved to shoot a hypocrite. Everybody, it appeared, but McGaughan. He was going to let this woman get away scot-free with her butter-wouldn't-melt-in-your-mouth, holier-than-thou attitude, when she'd been just as much a hellion as the next coed. The difference being, she had the money and connections to bury the evidence.

Almost.

Matt had it right here in his hands—not only the stuff George Field had been paying him for six months to find, but also what, for all he knew, could be a Pulitzer-worthy article. If he were really McGaughan's friend he'd send this puppy off to New York and let the feathers fly.

McGaughan's editor would have to check the sources, verify the facts, but the article held the ring of absolute truth. His gut told him so.

Quickly, before he could think twice—and before McGaughan could come back in and catch him—he typed up an email to Aaron Zorick. He attached McGaughan's article to it and hit "send."

He replaced the computer on the bed exactly as he'd found it and brushed off his hands. Job well done.

"McGaughan," he muttered, "you don't know it, but I've just done you the biggest favor of your career. You can thank me later."

He plopped himself down in the chair, propped his feet on the bed, and began to circle his thumbs again.

When Cole had offered his heart up to God in the shower that morning, he had pictured himself accomplishing something along the lines of wrestling tigers in the wilds of Africa.

He had not imagined fishing headfirst in the Dumpster again, trying to coax a feral mama cat into giving up her kittens. The high-pitched remonstrance—encouragement—cursing, for all he knew—of Lucia Ochoa, who stood at the Dumpster's opening, narrating his efforts in Venezuelan-inflected Spanish, didn't make the situation any easier.

"Come here, you reeking, flea-bitten scrap of dog food," he coaxed, softening his voice despite an overwhelming urge to puke on the odor surrounding him. "I'm trying to rescue your babies before the lot of you get carted off to the landfill."

The mama cat, a calico with smears of something indescribable matting her coat, hissed at him with singular lack of gratitude.

"Look, I know you're scared, but this is the way it's going down. Either you come out like a lady, or I come in and get you. And if I have to mess up these leather shoes, one of us is going to the vet for an operation. Which is probably going to happen anyway, huh?"

Lucia politely tapped him on the butt, which was undoubtedly all of him she could reach. She said something in Spanish.

Cole twisted his head. "What?"

She said it again. Big help, since his Spanish vocabulary included *taco, amigo,* and *tequila.*

After she'd appeared sobbing at the door of his room, he'd let her tow him down the elevator to the front desk, where a bilingual clerk explained what had her so upset. When he'd assured her, through the young clerk, that he indeed had a soft spot for dogs, but pretty much considered cats to be target practice, she had burst into fresh wails of distress.

Of course he'd immediately felt like a heel. Now here he was, literally waist-deep in garbage.

Shrugging, he reached for the cat. And got a five-inch claw mark from his wrist to his third knuckle. "Yow! You wretched feline demon, don't you know Superman when he stares you in the face?"

He shoved himself backward out of the garbage bin to examine his bleeding hand. He was probably going to get lockjaw.

Lucia tapped him on the arm. "*Señor.*" She showed him a thick towel and repeated whatever she'd been saying for the last five minutes. When he looked blank, she rolled her eyes and wrapped the towel around her hand. She grabbed his arm with her towel-wrapped hand and tugged. "*Sí?*"

The light came on and Cole took the towel. "Why didn't you suggest that before?" Taking a deep breath, he plunged into the bin again. Hanging there, eyeball-to-eyeball with a cat suffering from postpartum depression, five bald newborn kittens, and a ton of human detritus, a sudden intuition came to him.

This is what you did for me, God. Plopped right down into my garbage when I didn't really want you, and offered to save me.

He would have wept, except it would have used up the remaining available oxygen. So he hitched himself as close to the cat as he could get without falling in completely and wrapped the towel around his scratched hand. "Need a little help here, Lord," he muttered and cautiously reached for Mrs. Calico. "Here, kitty, kitty."

To his astonishment, she let him stroke her head with the towel. Wait, was that a purr? Holy smoke, she was *licking* the nubby nap of the towel. In less than a minute he had all six cats out of the Dumpster, nesting on the towel in a box, with Lucia crooning over the nursing kittens like a black-and-white-uniformed Madonna.

Cole stood over them, arms folded, feeling pretty darn satisfied with himself. "God, please don't let Hogan find out what I just did," he muttered.

chapter 15

The theater was buzzing with mamas and costumes, kids and props. "Cockroaches," set-changers dressed in black, ran around raising and lowering backdrops, shoving set pieces around. Sound and lighting techs adjusted levels, periodically precipitating earsplitting squeals through the amplifiers.

Surrounded by all the elements of a musical production she loved, Laurel couldn't stop thinking about a big, dark-haired writer who made her feel like spinning in circles on top of a mountain, arms flung wide, singing "The hills are alive ..."

Crazy. She smiled, and a couple of little girls skipping down the aisle past her grinned back.

Jamika stopped and struck her trademark hands-on-hips pose. "Miss Laurel, you look like you been smokin' something. You better go get you some air."

Laurel laughed. "Honey, I don't need to smoke anything to feel like this." She put an arm around the child, and they headed for the backstage door. "Are you ready to put on the show in a couple of weeks?"

"Yes, ma'am. Grandmama bought out the whole first two rows for our family." Jamika tugged one of her beaded braids. "I almost told her not to, 'cause I'm a little scared."

Laurel pulled her into a hug. "That's normal. Once you get onstage you'll be fine. That's what happens to me when I'm in court sometimes. I'm scared until I start talking. As long as I'm prepared, the Lord takes over and helps me."

"Yeah, that's what Grandmama says all the time. 'What time I am *afraid*, I will trust in *thee*.'"

Jamika's declamatory flair made Laurel smile. "She's exactly right. That's one of my favorite verses."

The girl sniffed. "If you got half as many favorite verses as my grandmama, we gonna be here all day. I gotta go find my wimple. See ya, Miss Laurel!" Jamika scooted off into the costume room, leaving Laurel to answer her cell phone.

Hoping it was Cole, she looked at the ID display. Renata. "Hey, girl," she said, looking in vain for a quiet corner. "What's up?"

"Did you see the article in the paper this morning?"

Laurel sat down on a speaker case behind a curtain. "What article? I skipped the paper and went for a walk."

"I hate to tell you this, but somebody's been scuttling through your private records and spilled a bunch of stuff to the *Register* about your finances."

Laurel swallowed. "So? I don't have anything to hide."

"New paintings in your office and the trip to Brazil last year?"

"The paintings were gifts of the artist, who is a lifelong personal friend, and I went to Brazil on a mission trip!"

"I'm just saying, whoever dug this stuff up is trying to make you look bad. Like a spoiled rich girl, freeloading off the county's money."

"Who wrote the article?"

"The political guy at the *Register*. Want me to track him down?"

"You can meet with him if you want to. But it's really not a problem, Renata. You know me. I keep meticulous records, and I've got receipts for the Brazil trip." Hopefully her supporters would pay no attention to such tripe.

Renata sounded dubious. "Derrick thinks you should write a counter to the article, submit it for the editorial section."

"I suppose I could." The mention of the publicity guru reminded her of another issue. "Renata, how much time have you been spending with Derrick?"

"Some." Renata sounded coy. "I have to say, the man's got charisma. And potentially, I could go long-term with this thing."

Laurel's stomach got queasy. "*You* could. But what about him?"

"Oh, Laurel, you'd be a lot happier if you just relaxed a little."

If one more person told her to relax, she was going to scream. Still, she wasn't going to repeat hearsay evidence. Not until she'd proved it with her own eyes. "I'm not saying you shouldn't date the guy and have fun. I just think before you get serious, you ought to do a little research. Find out if he's married, whatever. Business is one thing, but—"

"Laurel." Annoyance colored Renata's voice. "Just because you're an anal-retentive worrywart doesn't mean the rest of the world operates that way. Look, I gotta go. Derrick's coming to pick me up in a few minutes, and I need to fix my face. I'll let you know what I find out from the reporter. Bye now."

Renata was gone before Laurel could either apologize or explain. "Ouch," she muttered. *Anal retentive? Worrywart?* She looked at the phone hopefully. Maybe Cole would call and cheer her up.

Rather like Alexander, hero of the story his grandchildren liked so much, Aaron Zorick was having a terrible, horrible, no good, very bad day. After he'd suffered through a cold shower due to the fact that some idiot had jinked with the plumbing in his building, his wife had decided she was in the mood for cheese toast for breakfast. If there was any substance that smelled worse than rubberized processed cheese spread on charred Wonder Bread, Aaron had yet to inhale it. The lining of his nose still stung, six hours later.

As if that weren't enough, the subway had been clogged with a hundred or so Hoboken seventh graders on a field trip to the Central Park Zoo. Aaron heard words that would have made P Diddy-Diddy Bang-Bang, or whatever he was calling himself these days, blanch snow white. And then a veritable parade of reporters had come through his office, whining about how hard it was to get good news. Nobody wanted to talk to the press anymore, yada yada, on and on. Aaron wanted to gather the whole crew, crack their heads together, and yell *What would freaking Lois Lane do, you bunch of crybabies?*

So when his email alert chimed Saturday afternoon, he growled and turned up the volume on the TV set in the corner, where a *Seinfeld* marathon had been soothing his nerves. Who needed more bad news in a day that had gone so far south it was falling off the edge of the map? On second thought, that would put him in the same class with the tribe of the world-class slackers he had to ride herd on. He stubbed out his cigarette, moused the icon, and braced himself for more hassle.

After skimming the headline of the article attached to Mc-Gaughan's email — "Alabama Family Values Candidate Hides Disreputable Past" — he nearly stuffed it in a holding file. After all, he'd just run the last piece McGaughan sent — and the only reason the *Journal* was footing the bill for the guy's extended tour through Dixie was because Aaron was a pushover. A soft, marsh-mallow-on-a-stick pushover.

Then he changed his mind and opened the article. Though McGaughan's work on the Alabama series hardly warranted a Pulitzer nomination, it was competent. Maybe he'd managed after all to open up his lady judge and produce some real news. Aaron put on his glasses and started to read. Then, halfway through, he sat up and hit the print button.

Once he had the hard copy in his blunt, arthritic fingers, he laid it on the desk and pored over it, mesmerized. Not only was it a piece of solid, tight writing, but it also had the ring of absolute truth. Aaron blindly reached for his cigarette and stuck it in his mouth unlit. *Scoop*, his brain screamed. The Sunday morning political page was laid out and ready for print, but a story this big could bump something else. A flush of victory surged from the soles of his feet to the top of his head where the hair disappeared into freckled skin.

The *Times* was going to eat his journalistic dust. His day had suddenly turned very, very good.

Cole was putting through on the second green when he remembered he was supposed to call Laurel back.

Fine enamored swain you are, he told himself, making an excuse to Hogan and sliding off to mend fences. He had a lot to learn about maintaining a serious relationship. If that was where this one was going.

"Hey, lady," he said when she answered on the first ring. "What are you doing?"

She whispered, "Having a powwow with the kids before we send them home for the day. I meant to turn my phone off—sorry, I can't talk right now."

"That's okay," he said. "I won't keep you, I just wanted you to know I probably won't be coming by tonight. A friend of mine showed up, and I think I ought to spend a little time with him."

"Okay, don't worry about it—I'll see you at church in the morning." She paused. "Bye, Cole."

She was gone before he could tell her how much he regretted not seeing her, how he'd been thinking about her all day, how he'd been praying for her.

Maybe, though, it was good he didn't have to tell her what God had said to him in the shower. Maybe he should keep that to himself until he figured out what it meant.

Sunday morning when Laurel walked into the choir room for preservice warm-up, she had the feeling of being in one of those Marx Brothers movies where the eyeballs in picture frames followed a character everywhere he went. People were talking, looking at her surreptitiously, and avoiding her glance. She looked down to see if her slip was showing, then remembered she was wearing pants. As she climbed to the third row of the soprano section, she checked her neckline and found to her relief that all buttons were buttoned and all lace tucked in.

Relieved, she sat in her usual spot beside Marjean Brock. "Hi, Marjean. How was the antique show yesterday?"

Marjean, who had been reading a printout of what looked like an Internet news article, looked distracted. She removed her big black-framed Canasta glasses and let them drop onto their chain. "Had a ball. I found out that ugly brooch my great-aunt Ludell gave me for my wedding is worth six hundred dollars." Giving Laurel a concerned look, she rattled the paper in her hand. "So what do you think about this article?"

"I don't know. What's it about?"

Marjean gave a theatrical gasp, putting a hand to her pouter-pigeon bosom. "You haven't seen it? I've been subscribing to RSS feeds on your campaign since the first of the year. This one showed up this morning, and—oh, Laurel, it's not good."

Laurel tried to get a glimpse of the paper in Marjean's lap, but it was upside down. Odd that something as minor as her campaign finances would be national news. "Oh, that. Renata told me about it yesterday. What's the big deal?"

Marjean blinked. "Well, I suppose you could look at it that way. I mean, you got it annulled and everything ..."

"Annulled?" A twinge of misgiving settled in Laurel's stomach. "Aren't you talking about the article about my trip to Brazil?"

Marjean shook her gray head. "This one's by Cole McGaughan. He claims you had a drunken elopement to New Orleans and covered it up with an—"

"Let me see that!"

With a reproving look the choir director rapped his baton against the music stand.

Marjean whispered out of the side of her mouth, "Okay, but you have to promise not to scream." She handed over the paper as if it might blow up in her hand. "Don't say I didn't warn you."

The pianist burst into the introduction of the morning's anthem and the director motioned for the choir to stand. Laurel rose with her eyes on the paper. When she saw the headline followed by Cole's byline, however, her knees buckled. Her fanny hit the chair hard. Violet waves buzzed across her vision.

Kincade women do not faint, she told herself. *We wobble, but we don't fall down.*

Oh, God, she prayed, some part of her wishing she *could* black out. *Help me not throw up.* People were staring, and Marjean was fanning so vigorously with her choir folder that Laurel's hair whipped against her cheeks.

"I told you it was bad," Marjean hissed over the music, which swelled in a great tide of choral praise. "I'm so sorry, Laurel."

"I've—I've got to go to the bathroom," Laurel mumbled, lurching to her feet. She stumbled over people to reach the stairs down out of the choir room risers. In the hallway, all was eerie silence. She slid down, back against the wall, until she was sitting on the floor with the paper pressed flat to her knees. Her hands shook so that she could hardly hold onto it.

Cole. Oh, Cole, how could you do this to me? He'd gotten under her skin, made her fall in love with him for the second time, and hung her out to dry like a wet bathing suit.

Anonymous source. Of course he wouldn't name himself. Now that he was building a reputation as a Christian journalist, he wouldn't want to be implicated with a wild party girl like Laurel Kincade.

Asinine. Just ridiculous. In today's liberal world, who was going to care that some young law school student had gotten a quickie New Orleans wedding? Especially when that person had clearly become a responsible, mature adult. But the grinding point of this article was the hypocrisy angle. She had covered up what she'd done, pretended like it never happened, hoped nobody would ever find out. Presumed to pass judgment on the rest of the world.

The rules were for everybody but Laurel. Consequences? Walk a straight enough line and you avoid most of them. The trouble was, like the Bible said, your sins would find you out. Usually in the most inconvenient and public place imaginable.

Pharisee.

Alone in the hallway, just her and God, she held the crumpled paper against her face. Whenever Daddy used to lecture her and Mary Layne and Michael about some childish antic, he would call it a "come to Jesus meeting." Now she knew why.

"Lord, this isn't fair," she whispered. "I'm so embarrassed. I trusted him again. Against my better judgment, I trusted him."

She smoothed the paper against her knees again and made herself read it. *Skeleton in my closet? Lapse in judgment?* Cole himself constituted her biggest skeleton to date. And he had chosen to betray her by yanking her past out in the open, putting her most private emotions on public display.

Tears backed up behind her eyelids. *Don't cry. Don't even. Not here, where everyone will see.*

Throat aching, she held onto the wall and got to her feet like an old woman. She swayed for a moment, took a deep breath, and headed for the parking lot. She had to get out of here before her mother and Gilly caught her and made a scene. She had to get herself together first.

Oh Lord, help.

Cole paced the hotel lobby cracking his knuckles. Rage, blacker than the Tallahatchie River at flood stage, nearly stopped his breathing. At every turn he made himself draw in air because it was the only way to keep himself from hitting a wall with his fist.

He'd started calling Hogan's room at six, the second he'd laid eyes on that wretched article. Front page of this morning's political section—exactly where he'd always dreamed of seeing his byline. But not at the expense of everything important to him.

Laurel. He was going to have to see Laurel and try to explain.

But first he was going to kill Hogan. As soon as he found him.

When he couldn't get Hogan to answer the phone, Cole had gone down to his room to bang on the door. No answer, so either Hogan was hiding under the bed, or he'd made a run for the border.

And Cole was too agitated, too angry, too worried about Laurel, to sit in church. So he'd asked at the desk to make sure Hogan hadn't checked out, then spent an hour pacing the lobby and calling Hogan's cell phone every ten minutes. Sooner or later he was going to answer, and when he did—

Lucia Ochoa came by, headed for the elevator with a cartload of clean folded towels and bottles of water. She smiled at him and said something he now recognized as "kittens" in Spanish.

He gave her a distracted wave. The problem was he'd sabotaged himself—leaving an amoral private investigator alone in his room with the computer on. He didn't even have to call Aaron Zorick and ask how it had happened. There was no other explanation.

"*¡Disculpe, Senor!*" Lucia had abandoned her cart and stood in front of him, attempting to thrust a Post-It note into his hand.

"Hi, Lucia. Something wrong?" Cole accepted the note as Lucia rattled off something in Spanish. "I'm sorry, I don't—" Holy cow, this was from Hogan, saying he'd be waiting in the hotel's business center. "Thanks, Lucia. *Gracias.* I've got to take care of something important. I'll see you." He gripped the maid's shoulder and charged toward the stairs.

He found Hogan sitting at a computer, dressed in a sport coat and slacks with a tie that looked like a Crayola storm. Hogan wheeled around when the door opened and beamed a welcoming smile. "McGaughan, what took you so long?"

"I've been looking for you all morning. Why are you not answering your phone?"

Hogan slapped at his pocket. "Must've left it in my room. I didn't want to wake you up, so when I saw your little Mexican jumping bean out in the hall, I told her to give you a note."

"She did. What are you doing in here all dressed up?"

"Thought I might go to church with you this morning. I'm working in here because lightning hit my computer last night."

Hogan paused, eyebrows raised, expectant. "The story's all over the wires." He frowned. "Sit down, McGaughan. You're looking a little green."

"This is the color of unqualified rage." Cole cracked his knuckles again. "Do you know you have just destroyed any chance I ever had of winning back my wife?"

Hogan blinked. "I didn't know you had a wife. What does she have to do with—" Comprehension visibly and volubly dawned as surprise colored Hogan's language blue. "You wrote that article about yourself? You and the judge were *married*?"

"What do you think?" Cole gave one of the other desk chairs a violent spin. "What possessed you to break into my computer—my private email—and send that piece to my editor? Are you insane?"

Hogan shut his mouth and shrugged. "I thought I was doing you a favor. You left the room, open invitation. When I saw it, I thought, cool—here's what I've been looking for. The public needed to know, McGaughan. Field is pretty happy, by the way."

"I would guess he is." Cole flung himself into the empty chair and plowed his hands through his hair.

"Wow, you and the judge." Hogan shook his head. "Who woulda thought? She doesn't seem like your type at all. I thought you were just, you know, jackin' around."

"Maybe I was, way back then. Before I really knew her. Before I came to know Jesus." Cole looked up. "Matt, you may not understand this, but you've got to believe me when I say I'm not the same guy you knew in Memphis." He spread his hands. "I'm not the same guy who screwed around with Laurel Kincade's feelings and hauled her off drunk to a French Quarter preacher eight years ago. I'm not even the same person who wrote that article."

Hogan reached for the knot of his tie. He looked away. "Come on, McGaughan."

"I mean it. I've been a Christian wuss around you, so this is partly my fault. You see the things I *don't* do anymore, and you vaguely know it's because I'm religious, but I never sat down and explained *why* I go to church on Sundays." Cole sighed. "I wrote that article in a fit of hurt and disappointment over the fact that Laurel didn't want to be around me. Yeah, maybe I had in mind taking her down a peg or two, proving she's no better than anybody else. Let's face it, Christians act like jerks sometimes." He thumped his chest. "Exhibit A. Classic jerk. But because Christ is inside me, and I'd prayed about it, he intervened before I sent that thing off to New York. Laurel came to see me and apologized. We decided to give one another a fighting chance to prove we'd grown up."

"But you kept it," Hogan said, looking bewildered. "It was still in your computer."

"I put it aside and forgot about it." Cole smiled, the irony and frustration of the situation almost humorous. "I feel like one of the guys that got to the edge of the Promised Land and had to go back to wander around in the desert until their midlife crisis was over."

"Huh?"

"Never mind." Cole stood up, anger spent. Being mad at Hogan was like whipping a puppy who'd chewed up your underwear. He didn't get it. "I've got to go find Laurel and see if there's anything I can do to repair the damage. Just don't do me any more favors, okay, Hogan?"

chapter 16

Laurel's emotions ranged all over the map as she drove through Municipal Park. As she'd left the church the sound of the choir singing that big, bombastic opening anthem had stung her heart. She hadn't felt much like praising God, and she certainly hadn't felt like enduring her mother's histrionics. Given the way gossip infested some of the women's Bible study classes, Mom would almost certainly have seen the article.

So Laurel got in the car and drove all over Spring Hill for nearly two hours. No, she didn't want her family right now. She wanted her best friend.

Renata lived in an old established neighborhood near Shaw High School in a low-slung brick ranch with thick, well-tended grass, flowers around the mailbox, and a brand-new roof. The cool, soothing peace of arching oaks and magnolias and lacy dogwoods hardly penetrated the miasma of disappointment and embarrassment that threatened to drown Laurel. So far she'd managed to push away the anger boiling beneath the surface.

Keep a lid on it, Laurel, she told herself. *You've survived bad things before. Perspective, right?*

She pulled up behind Renata's green Saturn and got out of the car, relieved not to see Derrick's black Cherokee in the driveway. She took a breath and punched the doorbell.

"Hey, girl!" Renata, clad in white shorts and a neat persimmon-colored blouse, pulled her inside. "What you doing out this way?"

Laurel breathed deeply of the dark odors of fried vegetables and pork emanating from the kitchen. "Are you finished with lunch?" Renata's church services often went late into the afternoon.

"Yes, but I've got leftovers if you're hungry." Renata led the way into the breakfast nook off the kitchen. White eyelet curtains in the bay window let in buckets of afternoon sunshine, which poured across the oval maple table. "Sit down and I'll fix you a glass of tea. You in the mood for lemon?"

"I'm in the mood for the strongest thing you've got," Laurel said with a weak laugh. "How about arsenic?"

Renata crossed her arms. "That's not funny. What's wrong with you?"

Laurel knotted her hands in her lap. "You haven't seen the Internet news, have you?"

"I've been in church all morning. Why?"

Laurel looked away. "I've been driving around since right after Sunday school. I need to talk to you."

Giving Laurel a sharp look, Renata brought over the two glasses filled with strong sweet tea and fragrant slices of lemon. She sat down at the table. "Here. Tell Aun*tee* what the matter is, and we'll fix it."

Laurel took her tea glass in both hands, slowly rotating it back and forth. Finally she looked into dark eyes soft with compassion and not a little curiosity. "I don't think you're going to be able to fix this one, Renata. I have to share something with you. And you have to promise you won't tell anybody unless I give you permission."

Renata's eyes narrowed. "I don't think that would be wise."

Laurel tensed. "I need counsel, but I need you to be on my side." She pushed her chair back.

"Okay, wait." Renata grabbed Laurel's hand. "Hold on, baby. You know I'm on your side."

"You promise?"

"Laurel, I've always kept your confidence. Now what is it?"

Laurel looked away, let several seconds tick past. She swallowed. "Okay, here's the truth. Cole McGaughan was my husband."

Renata's mouth fell open. "He was your—Huh?"

"Nobody knows this but my Fafa. He had to take care of the annulment."

"Annulment?" Renata jumped out of her chair. "Are you out of your *mind*? You got married and unmarried without telling me?"

"It was while I was in law school. It was a mistake."

Renata's eyes bugged out. "I feel like somebody just shoved me off a cliff." She sat down abruptly. "I think you'd better start at the beginning. Why are you just now telling me this?"

"Because I never thought I'd see him again after we split up. He promised he wouldn't—Can you imagine how *I* felt, seeing him that day in the courthouse last fall? Without any warning? And then you call him up and invite him back down here, after I'd managed to get rid of him!" Laurel put her fist to her mouth.

"I didn't know! How was I supposed to know, when you didn't tell me? I *thought* there was something fishy about the way you were avoiding him, and the way he looked at you, like—like—"

Laurel couldn't stand it. "How was he looking at me?"

"Like a gladiator looks at a lion in the arena. At first. But the last couple of weeks, he's been all moony-eyed, and I thought we'd made a real convert." Renata laid her beautiful dark hands flat on the table. "Laurel, what have you done?"

"It's not what *I've* done that's the problem." Laurel opened her purse and took out Cole's article. "Read this."

Renata took the article, emitting little squeaks of dismay as she read, until she reached the bottom of the paper. She tossed it onto the table as if it were on fire. "Oh my gosh! That scurvy rat! He didn't even name himself as your lover—he wrote it like he's some detached reporter just barfing up news."

Laurel nodded miserably.

"You'll have to sue him."

"I can't sue him. It's all true."

"Okay, well—well, we'll just do what we were going to do with the other article. You write a dignified response, explain why you did what you did, how you've grown up and changed—"

"I don't want to answer questions that haven't been asked."

"Laurel—"

"My reasons for that trip to New Orleans are nobody's business."

"Why'd you come over here then, if you're not going to listen to anything I have to say?" Hurt filled Renata's brown eyes.

"I just wanted some unbiased sympathy." Laurel blinked against tears of her own. "I knew my life would be a public exhibit when I decided to run for this office. But I wasn't expecting it to be so hard to keep my past private. I wanted to do something extravagant, something only the Lord could do through me. Believe me, I know my faults. But I thought his power would be enough—that he'd smooth the way for me if I committed every part of the race to him." She spread her hands. "It hasn't turned out that way at all, and I don't understand it."

"Huh." Renata tapped her long nails against the table. "I want to know where it's written in the Bible that the devil lays down his pitchfork and sings hallelujah when God's children announce they're up for serving Jesus."

"I don't—what do you mean?"

"Look, white girl, you know I love you, but you've had a mighty easy ride on this planet up to now, if you don't mind me pointing it out. What makes you entitled to a free pass from Go to Board-walk without hitting a luxury tax once in a while?"

If Renata had physically slapped her, Laurel couldn't have been more shocked. She sat there with her mouth open, unable to speak.

"All I'm saying," Renata sighed, "is don't be shocked when the world persecutes you and hates you for his name's sake. It's in the Book. Go read it."

No argument occurred to Laurel at the moment, debate team president that she was, so she simply nodded and stood up. "I'm going home. Thanks for listening, Renata."

"You're welcome," Renata said cordially. "Come any time. You want to take some of these rutabagas with you?"

"No, thank you." Laurel hated rutabagas almost as much as she hated public embarrassment.

Renata walked her to the door. "Look, I understand your emotions getting all shanked by this jerk." She shook Cole's article. "But this isn't just paintings and a trip to Brazil. You don't leave something like this out there without telling your side of it. Not smart. We've got to deal with the press, do some damage control here."

"I know." Laurel rubbed her eyes. "I understand. I've just got to get myself together first."

"Sure." Renata reached for Laurel and pulled her into a warm hug. "You love me?"

"I love you," Laurel said, numb to the lips. "I don't like you very much right now, but I love you."

Renata laughed and let her go. "Call me when you figure out what you want to do."

"I will." Laurel slipped out the door.

"Laurel, come on, I know you're in there." Standing on Laurel's doorstep with a bunch of flowers clutched in one hand, Cole punched the doorbell for the third time. If communicating with her had been difficult before — when all he'd done was seduce her, marry her, then let her go in the space of three days — getting an audience with the queen of lifelong grudges appeared to be out of the question.

He stepped back into the yard and looked up at the dormer window above his head. The curtain twitched open, then dropped shut. Oh, yeah, she was there all right. And refusing to acknowledge the blockhead banging the door down. He felt like Charlie Brown wooing his little red-haired girl.

Okay, so he'd have to concede she had a good reason to be angry with him.

He'd tried calling, but the phone stayed busy all Sunday afternoon. Finally he'd concluded the phone was off the hook, and he could hardly blame her. She probably had local reporters harassing the daylights out of her. Maybe he could take the stinger out of the bite if he went to the press again himself, this time with a fair and balanced — and up-to-date — version of the story, including his own part in Laurel's fall from grace.

Maybe he should pray about that before he did it.

The immediate issue was getting her to talk to *him*. Not as a reporter, but as her ... well, what was he? Doubtful if she'd consider him a friend. Ex-husband? He winced. Ex-lover? Even worse.

Lord, what should I do?

He sat down on the step, with the flowers across his knees. He'd carefully picked them out with the florist's help — gladiola, pink roses and purple hyacinth, bluebells and gilly flowers, and of course, forget-me-nots. He had a feeling if she would just talk to him, let off some steam, maybe he could get her to listen long enough to understand how much he regretted what had happened. That this time it wasn't his fault.

Unfortunately, he was helpless to get through to her. If she didn't want to listen, he couldn't make her. Besides, some barely awakened wisdom told him he didn't want a woman who wouldn't listen. Maybe last time she'd relented and come to him with an apology, but he couldn't live this way long-term, never knowing what would send her incommunicado.

Was he being unfair? Did she have a case for throwing him out for good this time? After all, if he'd never written the article to begin with, Hogan wouldn't have had anything to send to Mr. Zorick at the *Journal*.

All he knew was, his brain hurt and his heart hurt. He sensed a battle going on, of which he was only a part. There was an enemy who wanted division between him and Laurel, an enemy who'd do anything to keep a godly, Bible-believing woman out of that judicial seat. Who would also be thrilled if Cole gave up and quit praying.

So he just wouldn't.

There had to be some way to repair the damage done to Laurel's campaign. To bring something glorifying to God out of this whole situation. Even if Laurel decided she couldn't love him.

So, Lord, what do you want me to do? I don't think it's your will for lies to win the day. I know I can't control whether or not Laurel believes me and forgives me, but if you'll walk me through this, I can act with integrity and courage. Just show me. I'm listening.

Feeling marginally encouraged, he heaved himself to his feet and laid the flowers on the step. "See ya, Laurel. I'll be back."

Deep in the polar icecaps of his mind, where dwelt the frozen, outcast ghost of conscience, Matt Hogan's dreams conjured a certain chilling whisper. He tossed and turned and beat his pillow as the whisper grew. Finally, as he settled in for breakfast and popped open the Monday morning newspaper, it became a whining nag that penetrated the inhabited reaches of the Siberia of his soul. By the time he read three articles indicating Laurel Kincade's downhill slide in the polls, Matt was experiencing a full-blown howl right in his ear.

How was a man supposed to enjoy bagels and eggs with that racket going on in his head?

He flung down the paper and hit George Field's speed-dial number. What he needed was somebody telling him how brilliant he was.

"Hogan!" There was a definite chortle in Field's voice. "I was just about to call and congratulate you on a job well done."

Smiling, Matt pushed back his plate. "So you're pleased?"

"It's a good start," Field allowed. "I'd be happier if this had come out closer to the primary. She's still got six weeks to recover."

"Wha—?"

"People can be surprisingly forgiving. It depends on how she handles it. Bill Clinton wiggled out of some deep doo-doo in his time, and remember what happened when news of W's DUI hit. If she flat-out denies it, and it can't be proved with photos or hard evidence—or if she comes clean and apologizes—we could be right back where we started."

Matt snapped his plastic fork in two. McGaughan, of course, could prove the allegations in the article. After all, he had been the party of the first part. And if McGaughan refused to back up the story, Matt could always do a little more digging and come up with photos and hard evidence of his own. He could always make a trip to New Orleans and find the preacher who had tied the knot.

Something, though ... something kept his mouth shut. For the moment. Maybe it was the uncomfortable shouting match going on in his head.

With friends like you, Hogan, who needs enemies?

Shut up—I've got to take care of Number One.

Oh, really? And what happens when Number One gets in trouble? Who are you going to call if you've alienated every buddy you ever had?

I did it for McGaughan's own good!

He sure didn't look very happy about it yesterday. In fact, he looked like he wanted to beat the snot out of you.

"Geez, Field, you might show a little appreciation. I'm working my tail off down here in this godforsaken swamp. The least you could do is send me a check."

Field chuckled. "If Laurel Kincade drops out of the race, there's a ten-thousand-dollar bonus waiting for you. Now go follow up on this story and see if you can get some photographs to go with it."

With the phone safely out of reach in his pocket, Matt picked up the newspaper and stared at the file photo of Laurel Kincade's campaign announcement. Suddenly he wondered how she felt about this whole thing. All he knew of her was what he'd observed from a distance and what he'd learned from research. Old articles, interviews with friends and family. He'd never talked to her personally.

No doubt about it, she was a good-looking chicka. That was the first thing a man noticed about her. Smart too—you'd have to be, to advance to that kind of position at the age of thirty-two. But what would possess a bright bombshell like that to do something so utterly stupid? Not the part about running off with McGaughan. Alcohol, as he knew only too well, could take a person's inhibitions down to zero and precipitate any number of catastrophic situations. The cover-up was what interested him.

Why hide a ho-hum, everyday occurrence like marrying the wrong person?

Now curiosity was clamoring along in a duet with his conscience, and there was no living with himself. Matt disposed of the newspaper along with his breakfast trash and headed for his car. The only way to satisfy curiosity was to ask questions.

Laurel was beginning to think that staying home and refusing to answer the phone yesterday had been a serious mistake.

Well, one more mistake in a series that began with saying hello to Cole McGaughan when she was a third-year law student.

As she tended to the business of running her court on Monday, she tried to pretend that everything was normal when nothing was normal. First thing this morning, she'd tried to diffuse the situation by calling a staff meeting. Her two assistants, her clerk of court, and a couple of interns entered her office bearing expressions varying from avid curiosity to sympathetic respect.

"I know you all saw the article in the paper this morning." The *Register* had picked up Cole's story, which had been on the wires—and variations of it had been in papers all over the state. "I will eventually respond in print, but the heart of the story is true. I was briefly married, it was annulled, and my behavior has been completely circumspect ever since. As is obvious to anyone who knows me. I have nothing else to say. Is that clear?"

The assistants looked at one another and elbowed the interns.

"Perfectly, Judge Kincade," said the clerk.

"Good. Please send in the lawyers from the first case." Laurel waved her hand, and the five of them drifted away like a puff of smoke.

Only it hadn't been quite as smooth as she'd hoped. First her mother caught her in between cases. "How dare that man betray our confidence?" Frances dissolved into noisy tears. "He seemed like such a nice young man from a good southern family. And so attractive! And those shoulders!"

Laurel couldn't help but notice that the content of the article didn't seem to faze her mother one bit. Maybe she hadn't actually read it. "Mom, I'm afraid I'm pretty busy here. Can I call you back tonight?"

"Oh, certainly. Never mind how embarrassing this is for the family, and not a word of explanation from you. Laurel, how could you?"

"I'm sorry, Mom. You don't know how sorry. I'll call you later."

Then her grandfather jumped on the bandwagon. "I knew he was out for trouble when he showed up back in November. Why didn't you tell me he was threatening you, Laurel? I'd have gotten rid of him somehow. Bought him off or something."

"Fafa, he didn't want money. His family's loaded anyway." She couldn't explain how Cole had tricked her with personal charm twice in one lifetime. It was too humiliating.

"We'll sue him for breach of contract. We can't let him get away with destroying your reputation like this."

"My reputation can handle it." She hoped. "Besides, can you imagine the media circus if I took him on in a lawsuit?" She shuddered. "It's bad enough as it is. The phone's been ringing off the hook, Brandy Turner's on the warpath, and the attorneys are giving me either pitying or sneering looks, depending on how much they like me. But—" she took a deep breath and released it—"I can handle it. In a day or two, somebody else will brew a tempest in a teapot, and my little scandal will blow over."

"I hope you're right." Fafa sounded doubtful. "And I hope it happens before your poll numbers slide beyond redemption."

Laurel hoped so too.

She got through three hearings before lunch, sent her crew off to scavenge the downtown eateries, and shut her office door. A pile of briefs, files, and computer printouts on her desk waited for her attention, but she needed a moment of peace before tackling them. Tossing her robe across the back of a chair, she lay down on the sofa with a cushion under her head and her knees across the end. Her eyes closed.

She hadn't slept much last night. She'd kept thinking about the flowers she'd found on the front step when she opened the door to take a bill out to the mailbox. A miscellany of color and size and texture, wrapped in pastel cellophane and gauze, the luscious scent of them had begged her to pick them up and sniff.

Cole had apparently left them when she wouldn't open the door to him. She considered throwing them in the street so somebody would run over them, but she took pity on the flowers and carried them into the house. Picturing Cole in the yard, tall and forlorn, she sat down on the sofa to look at the multicolored bouquet. The only other time he'd given her flowers was in New Orleans, the night before they got married. He'd bought a bouquet from a street vendor—pure blood-red roses, a violent declaration of passion that she'd been too distraught to comprehend.

These were different. The note said so. Standing in the kitchen, she'd fingered the card, tied with a pink satin ribbon to the long stems of the gladiola. *"Each one means something. Please call me."* She didn't think she'd ever seen his handwriting before— large, spiky print, perfectly legible.

What was she supposed to do with them? Stick them in a vase and moon over them? As if. She wound up laying them in a leftover Wal-Mart bag and bringing them with her to work. Maybe she'd take the flowers to the nursing home, so somebody could get some enjoyment out of them.

She was almost asleep when her intercom buzzed. "Judge Kincade?"

Her eyes flew open. That sounded like Marjean. What was she still doing here? She got up and hit the speaker button. "Yes?"

"There's a gentleman here to see you. I told him you were on your lunch break, but he insists."

"Who is it?" If it was Cole—

"He says his name is Matthew Hogan."

The name meant nothing to Laurel. "He's not a reporter, is he?"

There was a brief silence, then Marjean cleared her throat. "He's a private investigator. He says he's the one who sent the article to the *New York Daily Journal.*"

Laurel sat down abruptly. "Send him in."

chapter 17

The young man who walked into her chambers was nearly six feet tall and carried himself with a pirate swagger. However, his face was put together in such a pleasantly nondescript way that Laurel probably would have walked right past him without a second glance.

Matthew Hogan offered his hand. "Judge Kincade, thanks for seeing me."

"Have we met before, Mr. Hogan?" As she shook his hand, Laurel studied him. His sandy hair, cut in one of those messy, stick-out-in-odd-places styles, fell over one hazel eye from a deep cowlick. He had on khakis and a plain blue oxford shirt.

"Call me Matt." Deep dimples grooved his cheeks in a grin that erased all blandness. "If I look familiar, it's because I've been following you around since November."

"Oh, really?" Laurel gestured to one of the chairs in front of her desk. "Maybe you ought to sit down and explain why I shouldn't have the bailiff come in and arrest you."

"McGaughan said you might say that." He took casual possession of the chair, crossing an ankle over the opposite knee. "Won't wash, judge. I have a private investigator's license. I'm just doing my job."

"I suppose I don't have to ask who hired you." Laurel picked up her favorite gel pen and prepared to take notes on a legal pad. She wished she had a recorder.

"I can't divulge who my client is, but it wasn't McGaughan, if that's what you mean." Hogan's foot began to jiggle.

Was he nervous or just hyper? Laurel suspected the guy's client—whoever he was—wouldn't be happy to see him in her office.

Which only served to further pique her curiosity. "Mr. Hogan, I have no earthly idea what to think. Why don't you tell me why you're here?"

He grabbed hold of his ankle, stopping its jiggling. A photograph on her credenza of Gilly posed in her tutu seemed to fascinate him. "The only reason I'm here," he muttered, "is because the voice won't shut up."

The *voice*? "Mr. Hogan, do you mind if I call in the court reporter to make a few notes?"

A flush washed up the tanned column of his throat. "I knew you'd think I'm a nutcase. You'll have to take my word for it, this whole thing's completely out of character. But if I don't tell you McGaughan had nothing to do with that article in the *Journal*, I'll be wigged out anyway. I sent it." His square jaw jutted. "So go ahead. Sue me."

Laurel stared at him, trying to read the cool hazel eyes. "It's very kind of you to take the blame—I assume you're a friend of Cole's—but I'm afraid *that* won't wash. The only person who knew that story was Cole, my grandfather, and me. It had to come from Cole."

"Well, of course he wrote it. Lord knows I can't put a sentence together and make 'See Spot run.' But the story was just sitting in his computer, not hurting anybody. I'm the one who attached it to an email and sent it to his editor at the *Journal*."

"How on earth would you send it without his knowledge?"

Hogan's face all but went up in flames. "He went down to rescue a litter of kittens, and while he was out of the room, I ... sort of poked through his computer files." The foot started to jiggle again, madly. "I know it sounds bad, but that's how you find information—you take advantage when people aren't looking. McGaughan knew I was investigating you, so he should've turned off the computer before he left, right?"

Laurel frowned. "I'm going to pretend I didn't hear that. Your ethics, Mr. Hogan, are abysmal." She rubbed her forehead, where a solid ache was building behind her eyes. What was she going to do with this confessed sneak-thief who was trying to get his friend out of a jam? "I—appreciate your candor." The words came out as if prized by a crowbar, but she said them.

Hogan looked alarmed. "Hey, that's not good enough. McGaughan's beyond mad at me—I've never seen him like this. And I have to say I don't exactly blame him. Judge Kincade, he's the best friend I ever had. I might not've sent the article if I'd known he was your—the husband in the story."

Laurel tipped her head. "What difference would that make to you?"

"You'd have to know McGaughan. Well, I guess you *do* know him—" He uttered a raw word and laughed sheepishly. "Man, what a strange situation. I keep forgetting ... Anyway, trust me, you're the *only* chick the guy ever committed to, even for three days. He was a real player back in the day."

"Am I supposed to be impressed?"

"No, no! I just meant—" Hogan swore again. "You should have seen him when he realized I'd sent that article without him knowing about it. I know seriously upset when I see it, and the only reason he should be upset would be because of hurting you. A byline like that is gold for his career."

Laurel frowned. There was no reason to believe this guy. She didn't know him from Adam. "I'm sure it is."

"So you're gonna let McGaughan off the hook?"

"I told you I'd think about it." She gave him her narrow-eyed, judge-on-the-bench look. "I wonder if there's anything else you're not telling me."

Hogan's brows rose. "I like the way you think. If I tell you who else is messing with you, will it convince you McGaughan's on your side?"

She wasn't conceding so easily. Cole had destroyed her reputation. "Who is it?"

"Look, I'm not giving up my boss. But I don't mind ratting on somebody else who's making money on both sides of the table." He leaned forward. "You might want to keep an eye on your girlfriend Renata."

Horror snaked through Laurel. "Renata would never betray me."

"I'm not saying she would. But she's in bed with somebody who'd serve you up on a platter in a New York minute."

Laurel swallowed. "Can you prove this? How do I know you're telling the truth?"

"Feed the guy false information. Watch what he does with it. If it shows up in certain places you'll know exactly where it came from."

She stared at him. "You're a devious man, Mr. Hogan."

Hogan sighed. "It's my job, judge. Not always pleasant, but it's the only way to help McGaughan. Now—" he set both feet on the floor and stared her in the eye—"if you find out I've told you the truth on this, you can believe what I said about McGaughan too."

"I suppose," she said slowly.

Hogan nodded. "All right then. I got stuff to do, so I'm jettin'." Giving her that dimpled smile, he shook hands and sauntered from the room.

Laurel stared after him, nonplussed. What an odd man. And what a perfectly weird conversation.

She'd put off the visit to the Castle long enough. It wasn't going to be pretty, but her parents deserved an explanation.

So Laurel drove around back and went in through the kitchen, calling, "Hey, Mom? Dad, where are you?"

Hearing a halloo from the family room, she dropped her purse on the breakfast table and marched through the dining room. She found her parents watching the evening news, her mother with a cross-stitch project in her lap and her father flat on his back on the sofa, feet propped on its arm. They both sat up straight as she entered the room.

"Laurel! Honey, how are you?" Mom yanked off her reading glasses and laid them with the cross-stitch on the lamp table. She got up and launched herself at Laurel, who allowed herself to be hugged and crooned over for several minutes before disentangling herself.

Dad waited on the couch, hands awkwardly dangling between his knees. He looked as if he'd like to hug her too. When she dropped down beside him, he sat back with an arm around her and let her drop her head onto his shoulder. "Hard day, baby?" he murmured into the top of her head.

She wanted to cry all over again. "You just don't know."

Mom stood in front of the TV, hands on hips. "Well, we might have known, if you'd had the sense to tell us about this monstrous situation eight years ago. What possessed you, Laurel Josephine

Kincade, to hide something like this from the whole family? And, by the way, is it true?"

Laurel rubbed her eyes. "Yes, Mom, it's true. I didn't tell you because you and Dad were still dealing with—with Michael. I couldn't add to it. So I got Fafa to take care of it."

Her mother stared at her while her father silently squeezed her shoulder. "But ... it's just so unlike you! The whole thing. I just don't know what to say."

Laurel thought about telling her the obvious solution was not to say anything. Since that wasn't likely to happen, she made herself sit up and clasp her hands on her knees. "Where's Gilly?"

"In her room, studying for a test." Mom shook her head. "Which is where she's going to stay. You're not involving the baby in this."

"Laurel's right, Frances," Dad said, patting Laurel's back. "Gilly needs to be able to defend her sister if she's questioned."

"No." Laurel gave her father a sharp look. "Nobody has to defend me outside the family. But Gil does have a right to know the truth."

Dad's heavy steel-gray brows lowered, but he reluctantly nodded. "Whatever you want, babe." He looked at Mom. "Go get Gilly, honey."

Her mother rarely questioned her father's judgment. Lips tight, she left the room. Laurel could hear her calling up the stairs for Gilly.

Within a few moments Gilly bolted into the room ahead of her mother. "Lolly!" She flung herself onto her knees and grabbed Laurel's hands. "Oh my gosh, what's going on? I can't believe you did something as romantic as eloping. Who was the guy? And what happened to him? How come you never told us about him?"

Laurel would have given her soul not to have this conversation. The disappointment and distress in her parents' faces reminded her why she'd kept it from them all these years. She licked her lips. "It wasn't romantic, Gilly. Getting married on a drunken binge was very stupid, which is why I had Fafa annul it immediately." She took a deep breath. "The guy was ... it was Cole McGaughan."

Gilly let out a little shriek. "You were married to *Cole*? No *way!*"

If there'd been a hole in the carpet, Laurel would have crawled into it. "Yes." She looked at her mother, who stood in the doorway, a hand over her mouth. "I'm afraid so."

"So he wrote that article out of revenge?" Dad's voice was grim. "He'll be sorry he messed with my daughter."

"But I like Cole!" wailed Gilly.

Laurel gripped her father's knee. "Daddy, I told you, I don't want this to escalate. It's important that you let me deal with Cole in my own way."

"But—" He scowled. "I don't understand this at all, Laurel. He seemed like a nice enough guy. And he seemed to admire you, the few times I've been around him. Why would he do something like this?"

Laurel closed her eyes, pain and anger slamming her all over again. "He must have been terribly hurt when I severed our relationship without seeing him again. And I've been in the legal profession long enough to know that people do outrageous things when they're hurt. I can't justify his behavior or mine. The whole thing's just ..." Her throat clenched for the millionth time that day. She looked into her little sister's wide, innocent eyes. "Gilly, learn from my mistakes, okay? You find a guy like Daddy from the start, and don't give your heart to a man who doesn't know the Lord."

"But I like Cole," Gilly whispered again. Her eyes filled with tears. "I think there's some explanation. Some reason he—"

"Like I said, there's no excuse for it." Laurel gripped her sister's hands. "I'm so sorry I lied to you all." She looked at her mother and then her father. "I'd go back and change it if I could, but I can't. So I'm counting on you all to pray for me until we weather this. In the meantime, I'm begging you not to interfere. All right?"

Her father looked as if he'd argue, but after a moment he gave a jerky nod. "Whatever you want, Laurel. You're an adult now."

"I hope you know," Laurel's mother said, chin up, "I won't let anyone speak badly of you."

Laurel found a sad smile. "Mom, you can't control public opinion. But I love you for backing me up." She bent to kiss Gilly's cheek. "It'll be all right. Eventually."

"She actually let you into her office?" Cole stared incredulously at Hogan. He had avoided the guy for two days as he tried to overcome his rage and disgust. By Wednesday he was willing to discuss this balled-up situation over lunch at El Chico.

"I think she was as curious about me as I was about her." Hogan chomped on a *queso*-covered tortilla chip. "You know, we're going to have to start patronizing the Golden Arches if Field doesn't reimburse me for some of my expenses pretty soon."

Cole raised a brow. He figured Hogan deserved to suffer a little. "So what did she say? When you told her you sent the article, I mean?"

Hogan looked away. "I don't think she believed me. She's pretty PO'd at you, brother."

"Learn from this. Women do not like to be lied to. They do not like to find out there's another woman on the side. They do not like to be used for cheap entertainment."

"You mean ... they're good for something else?" Hogan grinned when Cole scowled. "Relax. I take your message loud and clear. Not that I ever plan to fall for just one. Man, there's too many pretty flowers in the garden of life to pick just one. I prefer to walk around and ... smell them all."

"Now there's a nice sentiment." Cole snorted. "I'll tell you what's wrong with it. By the time you realize there's one rare bloom you want and everything else looks like weeds, your smeller is all jaded and you wish you'd focused your energy on being the kind of gardener who could take care of that particular flower, and—" He crammed a chip into his mouth. Hogan was looking at him like he'd lit up a hash pipe and started chanting "Desiderata."

"There are definite drawbacks to friendship with a writer." Hogan shook his head. "Anyway, as far as the lady judge is concerned, your shish is kebabed for now. I advise you to enjoy the professional kudos from your boss and move on."

Aaron Zorick had called that very morning, informing Cole he'd been moved to the political beat as of today. Victory had a taste remarkably similar to ashes. He said through his teeth, "I didn't want a promotion at the expense of Laurel's career."

Hogan looked uncomfortable. "Doesn't necessarily have to be. Depends how she handles it. Like Field said himself, she could come clean, admit everything, and have plenty of time to recover before the primary."

"You talked about this with Field? When?"

"The same morning the article hit locally. He wasn't quite as pumped as I thought he'd be."

"That's because he's a slick politician. He knows this campaign can turn on a dime. And you can bet he's got a few other tricks up his sleeve. Matt, you better get out from under this guy's thumb before he nails you to the wall too."

"Not until he pays me." Hogan sat back as the waitress refilled their drinks and brought their entrees. "The guy's loaded with cash, and he needs me. I don't care who wins. As far as I'm concerned, all politicians are sleazebags to one degree or another."

"Laurel's not."

Hogan snorted as he dipped a flauta into a bowl of salsa. "Like I said, watch how she handles the truth. Clay feet in Gucci sandals, man. Just watch."

"Get out of my way, lady, we were here first!" Renata, all of five-foot-five, stared down at the diminutive soccer mom trying to plant a "Field for Chief Justice" campaign sign in a fire ant mound along the interstate between Prichard and Chickasaw.

Laurel, watching through the open window of Renata's Saturn, covered her eyes with her hand. "Renata, come on. We'll move down the road a little way."

Renata's lips pressed together. "This spot's visible from every direction. We move down, your sign'll be hidden by the exit ramp."

The other lady suddenly shrieked. "Ow! They're in my sandals!"

"Serves you right." Glowering, Renata refused to back up. But Laurel noticed she'd planted her feet carefully on either side of the ant mound the other woman's feet had found.

Swatting at her ankles, the soccer mom grabbed her sign and scuttled to her SUV, parked behind the Saturn. The SUV bumped onto the interstate and took off, pouring black diesel smoke into the bright Saturday morning air.

Triumphant, Renata shoved Laurel's sign into the soft center of the mound, hammered it in with a couple of solid whacks, and hurried back to the driver's seat. "We've almost covered this side of the interstate," she said, putting the car in gear. "We're close to Mary Layne's house. You want to go by and say hello?"

"Sure, why not." Laurel hadn't seen much of her family this week. She'd been desperately keeping herself busy.

"Girl, I'm getting so excited. We launch the direct mail campaign on Monday, and that'll put us in the five-week countdown."

"I guess I'm ready." Laurel hesitated. "I wish the thing about me and ... you know ... would blow over. The local press has been beating my door down for interviews."

"I told you you should've responded." Renata sent her a jaundiced look as she took the Saraland exit. "You missed your chance to come clean and admit a youthful indiscretion. The polls indicate loss of confidence in your judgment."

Laurel stared at a church steeple as they passed. "It's just not something I can talk about openly. I wish Alabama judges were appointed and not elected ..."

"Well, they're not, so you deal. The public's got to perceive you as a person of absolute character and integrity."

"I *am* that person, and I would have been perceived that way—I *was*, until Cole McGaughan decided to sling mud at me."

"He says he didn't do it, right? What about that guy, Hogan, who came to see you?"

"I'm supposed to believe some shady Inspector Gadget who admitted he's been watching me through the windows for four months?" Laurel shook her head. "Cole's going to have to get a better advocate than that, if he wants to convince me he's straight up."

"Well, you know, other than that one article—which, I admit, was a pretty big punch in the gut—he's written some very fair copy on you. He's been just as hard on Field—"

"He's trying to get back in my good graces because it's to his advantage somehow. That's how he is, Renata. I'm telling you, I've known him for a long time, and people don't change overnight."

"Okay, you're gonna have to help me out here, because there's something that still doesn't make sense to me. If you distrust the guy so much, what made you fall for him in the first place?"

Laurel sighed as a vivid mental slideshow blinked through her mind. "We had mutual friends, so I knew him at a distance for a couple of years. You know that good-looking bad boy who shows up in every crowd—the one with enough intelligence and humor to be charming? That's Cole." She pressed her lips together. "I wouldn't let myself think about him for a long time. But even though I knew he didn't have a spiritual bone in his body, I got sort of fascinated in spite of myself. He's a smooth talker. And he has a way of looking at you that makes you feel like you're the only woman on the planet. And he writes poetry and draws funny pictures ..." Laurel stopped on a gasp. She was about to burst into tears. "But he's a self-absorbed jerk," she said threadily. "Let's don't forget that. When I woke up on my honeymoon morning, there was a call on his cell phone from a girlfriend back in Oxford. While I was in the bathroom, puking my guts out from a hangover the size of Tokyo, he was calling her back."

"Oh." Renata bit her lip. "I can see where that'd make you a teeny bit ill."

"Rather. So don't lecture me on forbearance, okay? I've spent about all I can afford on one man."

"*T*his is Laurel Kincade. I'm sorry I can't take your call right now. Please leave your name and number after the beep, and I'll get back to you as soon as I can.*"

Yeah, sure she would. Just like she'd answered the five other messages Cole had left this week. He was getting the big polar freeze, and this time it wasn't going to end.

He yanked the earphones out of his ears and tossed them onto the car seat.

Love is patient, always hopes, always perseveres, he reminded himself. *Love never fails.*

There must be some question about the quality of his love, because his was about to fail. How could he keep on when she wouldn't let him near her? *Give me Laurel*, God said. Sometimes the Almighty had a way of forcing his hand.

He pulled the car into the Mobile courthouse parking lot and pulled up the Bible program on his PDA. 1 Corinthians 13. Here was the rest of it.

"Love is patient, love is kind. It does not envy, it does not boast, it is not proud. It does not dishonor others, it is not self-seeking, it is not easily angered, it keeps no record of wrongs. Love does not delight in evil but rejoices with the truth. It always protects, always trusts, always hopes, always perseveres." Then you got to the *love never fails* part.

He put the stylus away and laid his head back against the seat, letting the air conditioner blast him in the face. How was he going to protect Laurel from this distance? And should he, really? Was he striving toward a relationship where God had closed the door?

Something didn't feel right about that assumption. Particularly in light of the admonition to persevere.

Breathing another prayer for guidance, he turned off the ignition and checked to make sure he had his notepad and pen. He liked the PDA for keeping track of his schedule—and the electronic Bible was handy—but for interview situations he still preferred good old paper and ink.

He had Hogan to thank for the heads-up on this Tuesday afternoon press conference. While working with Matt earlier, he'd learned things about George Field that would curl most people's hair—if they were aware of it. The guy was a self-promoting megalomaniac. Even if Laurel never spoke to him again, Cole had a responsibility to make sure the public was fully informed about her opponent.

Mobile County Government Plaza was a ten-story granite-steel-and-glass complex that sprawled over two city blocks on Government Street downtown. Cole crossed the walking mall and entered the soaring atrium-style foyer. Administrative offices were on one side, the security line for the elevator up to the courts on the other. He saw a few television cameras already set up near the far side of the atrium, with print reporters hanging out in conversation and the TV people doing mike checks. He headed over to join them. He was early, but within a few minutes the spacious lobby was crowded with reporters, gophers, and cameras.

Almost everybody was local, of course, with a few journalists from Montgomery, Andalusia, and Selma sprinkled in. A couple of guys had driven all the way from Birmingham—Cole surmised Field had scheduled the press conference for the early afternoon to give the TV stations time to get the piece on the air. As far as he could tell, he was the only out-of-state correspondent.

Reminded him a bit of Laurel's coming-out party back in November. He smiled, remembering the expression on her face when she'd recognized him. The phrase "shoot to kill" came to mind.

His ruminations came to an abrupt end when the doors to the administrative offices burst open, and a cadre of county officials in power suits and ties strode through flashing cameras. Cole recognized George Field, in the center, from news clips. Fifty-eight years old with electric blue eyes and thick gray hair, Field had a gorilla-like build with long arms, short legs, and barrel chest. He might as well have had "Napoleon Complex" stamped on his craggy forehead.

Field wasted no time explaining the purpose of the meeting, announcing the indictment of former Speaker of the Alabama House of Representatives Krenshaw Grogan, on thirty-six counts of graft and fraud. Grogan would be charged and held on $500,000 bond.

As the crowd muttered its collective shock, Cole took notes. He was much more interested in Field's demeanor than the case itself. There was a flame of pride, almost glee, in the back of the man's sharp blue eyes. Every bit of attention in the huge room was focused on his dramatic announcement, and the cameras were rolling—Wyatt Earp, Batman, and Sonny Crockett all wrapped up in one bad lawman.

"In conclusion, our office would like to emphasize that we've never tolerated graft in Alabama. It's been the signature crusade of our administration to end the practice for good." Field rocked back on his heels. "Ladies and gentlemen, I'll be happy to take questions."

There were of course several questions about Mr. Grogan's future, as well as his interactions with other parties in Alabama government. What channels the Speaker had used to funnel money through, how it had managed to find its way into his pockets, and exactly what measures would be taken to ensure that all guilty parties were apprehended and appropriately punished.

Cole scribbled Field's answers, deeply appreciating the irony of this man presuming to prosecute corruption. During a split-second lull in questions, Cole stuck his hand in the air.

Field acknowledged him immediately.

Not for the first time, Cole gave thanks for his unusual height. "Cole McGaughan of the *New York Daily Journal*, sir. I'd like to ask a couple of questions regarding your bid for the supreme court, if you don't mind a slight detour in topic."

Field's eyes widened, then narrowed as he recognized the author of the "Kincade article." "Of course, Mr. McGaughan. I'm happy to touch on any topic my constituents feel relevant."

"Thank you, sir." Cole flipped to a clean page in his notebook. "Your ratings in the polls have taken a dramatic upward turn in the last week, while those of your opponent have tumbled. To what do you attribute this?"

Field looked down for a moment. Hiding a smile?

When he addressed Cole, his demeanor was appropriately grave—and modest. "Well, with all due respect for my lovely opponent, it was a given that voters would eventually focus on my experience and ability to get things done." With the attention of a journalist from a national paper—as well as all the state media—focused on him, Field gestured grandly. "As this indictment today illustrates."

"You may be right, sir. On the other hand, I'm interested in rumors that you hired a private detective to investigate Judge Kincade's finances and background. I'd like your comments on the subject." Silence sucked all the air out of the room. Field's mouth opened and closed a couple of times. Cole could hear the soft click and whir of camera lenses, the scratch of stylus and pen.

"Well—I have no idea where you heard something like that, but there's absolutely no truth to it. Of course I deplore such political maneuverings. I have the highest respect for Judge Kincade's reputation, and I was terribly disappointed to hear of that embarrassing hoopla last week. In fact, I believe you're the one who wrote it, aren't you? Maybe Judge Kincade's former husband could answer your questions."

Cole figured he'd rarely seen a more masterful job of deflecting an attack. He nodded. Two could play the game. "Since that's a protected source, I'll give you one more instead. I'd like to know if you authorized the push polling which has lately negatively affected public perception of Judge Kincade."

All but apoplectic, Field waved his hands. "No! No, of course there's nothing to that rumor either. I'd never authorize—Rumor! Just a rumor. Now if you'll excuse me, the conference is over. Thank you for your attention, ladies and gentlemen." He turned on his heel and disappeared through the doors to the administrative wing, his flunkeys on his heels like Flying Monkeys following the Wicked Witch of the West.

Cole tucked his notebook and pen away, smiling a little. The questions had been asked.

Everywhere she went, he was there, like the cloud of dust that followed Charlie Brown's buddy Pig-Pen. And this despite her plea to Renata to keep her schedule full so she wouldn't have to sit home and face the blinking red eye of the answering machine. In typical Cole fashion, he had wormed his way into the good graces of everybody she knew.

Well, except for her immediate family. He hadn't yet breached that fortress.

When she spoke on rehabilitating juvenile offenders at the Mobile Exchange Club meeting on Wednesday, he wangled an invitation through Mrs. Bartikowski, charter member of the Cole McGaughan Fan Club. Even when she drove all the way to Demopolis on Thursday to address the Associated Builders and Contractors, he showed up just a few minutes late, hauling Matt Hogan along with a camera. The ABC guys were thrilled to have a member of the press give them coverage, so what could she say other than, "Hi, guys—there's a seat on the front row"?

So far she had managed to avoid one-on-one interviews, but it was getting harder and harder to ignore his patient good humor. Everything he had written about her had been fair, balanced, and no-spin. Including that elopement article—which the rest of the press wasn't going to let her forget.

Even his hard questions seemed to be for her benefit. They kept her from settling in and getting careless. He wanted to know if she'd heard the latest poll results indicating her faltering ratings—she had, and it worried her, though she responded with composure. He asked if she'd had professional help completing the questionnaires submitted by various voter coalitions—she had not; it hadn't occurred to her to do so. He inquired if her presence at a Baldwin County Save-a-Life banquet indicated her personal conviction about the abortion issue—she replied that people were free to read her actions any way they chose.

On the last Friday in April, on her way to an appearance at the Alabama Chicken and Egg Festival, she called Renata. "You've got to do something about him."

"Who?"

"You know who. He's conned you into giving him my schedule."

"The schedule is on your website, Laurel. Remember, we want the press to show up—it's free publicity."

"Renata—"

"Anyway, did you consider the fact that if people see you together, the talk about you is more likely to die down?"

"And did *you* consider the fact that seeing him everywhere I go makes my brain freeze? How can I concentrate on what I'm supposed to say with him lurking in the crowd like Paul Bunyan?"

"Paul Bunyan?"

"The giant with the big blue ox—"

"I know who Paul Bunyan is," Renata said with some irritation. "I just don't know what a mythical lumberjack has to do with a mild-mannered reporter from New York. Tupelo. Wherever." She sighed. "Look, I think he's already headed up that way, but I'll try to head him off the next few places you go. Problem is, it's a free country, and he's a member of the press. We can't exactly ban him from your public appearances. Or most of the private ones, for that matter."

Laurel bit her lip. She might as well accept the fact that she had an unwanted shadow. "You're right. I'm sorry for complaining, just ignore me. I'll handle it."

"What does that mean?" Renata sounded suspicious.

"It means I'll be good. I know when I'm beat. Metaphorically speaking."

"You sound stressed. I should have come with you."

"I told you, I'm fine. Talk to you later, Renata."

She closed the phone. So Cole was coming to Moulton. At least she was forewarned, and thus forearmed. Time enough to get prayed up.

～℃～

On his way out of Mobile on Friday, Cole passed the Sara-land exit. He decided to take his life in his hands and swing by to shake hands with Rebel. If you couldn't have your girl, at least you could have man's best friend, right? Assuming Laurel's sister didn't spray him full of buckshot.

It was a close call. He got out of the car and heard the littlest widget shouting, "Mommy, it's that man again!"

He looked around and couldn't find the widget herself. Then he saw two little bare feet hanging down from the bottom limb of a magnolia tree near the house.

"What man, honey?" he heard from the vicinity of the open garage.

"The one that brung us Rebel."

"Brought, not brung." Mary Layne appeared in the garage opening. Seeing Cole, she scowled. "What are you doing here?"

"Checking on my dog."

"He's fine. The boys took him down to the pond to chase a tennis ball tied up in a sock." Mary Layne's Laurel-like brown eyes softened. "Dane checked a book out of the library and learned how to build a doghouse. You should see it."

"Oh." So Rebel was all moved in, a permanent fixture. There went the idea of taking him back to New York when this episode was over. *Right, like that dog would make it in the concrete jungle.*

Mary Layne's expression and body language let Cole know there was a war going on in her brain. Clearly she remembered she was fraternizing with The Enemy. But she was also a pastor's wife. "I'm very ticked off at what you did to my sister," she said, hands on hips, "but I've been married long enough to know there are always two sides to a story. Would you like to come in and have a glass of tea or something?"

"I'm on my way out of town, so I can't stay long. But yeah, I'd like to tell somebody my version of what happened. Laurel sure isn't listening."

"If you heard the baloney she has to listen to all day every day, you'd be cynical too." Mary Layne waved him into the garage. "Come on in."

A few minutes later the two of them sat on the back porch with glasses of iced tea, watching the two boys and the dog play near the pond. Inside the house, ragged piano scales staggered through the open windows. Cheri was practicing, her lack of skill equaled only by her determination to get it right.

Mary Layne propped her tea glass on her round tummy and raised her reddish eyebrows.

Cole began to sweat, but resisted the urge to confess every misstep of the past ten years. "I wrote the article, but I didn't send it."

"Oh, really. Then how—"

"I have this 'friend' who thought he was doing me a favor by snooping in my computer files. Suffice it to say, he wanted Laurel to look bad, so he made sure she did."

"I find that singularly difficult to believe. If you were one of my children, I'd put you on TV restriction for a year."

Cole rubbed a hand across his mouth. He could hardly blame her. "I love your sister. I would like to marry her. Again."

Her eyes narrowed. "She told me you were the one. I just can't believe it took her all this time to come clean."

"See, that's what I don't understand. You two are obviously close. Why wouldn't she tell you something like that?"

"I'm not sure. I'm just as flabbergasted about this as anybody." She looked Cole up and down until he blushed. "So it's true? You two—you know—?"

He lifted his shoulders. "Afraid so."

Mary Layne shook her head. "I can't wrap my head around my perfect big sister and some wild frat-boy hauling off to New Orleans—much less getting married and unmarried and then hiding it all these years. How many years?"

"Eight." Cole watched some kind of realization kick in behind her eyes. He set down his glass. "You know why she did it, don't you?"

She hesitated. "Maybe. Maybe not. But if she doesn't want to share it, I'm not blabbing. There's been enough of that going on lately." She frowned. "The question is, what are you going to do about it?"

"I brought her flowers and tried to explain. There's not much else I can do—unless somebody runs interference for me."

Mary Layne gave him a thoughtful look. "Wade and I can pray."

"I'll take it," he said promptly. "In the meantime, if Laurel comes around and wants to talk about me—or *to* me, for that matter—will you let me know?"

"It depends. My loyalty is to my sister."

"Blood being thicker than water, huh?" He picked up his empty tea glass and stood. "Well, thanks for giving me half an ear at least. Better than nothing."

"You're welcome." She gave Cole a sympathetic smile. "We're taking good care of the dog, you know."

Cole tried to return the smile. He supposed that was one consolation.

Laurel spent the night at a hotel in Decatur, hub of the Alabama chicken farming industry. Unpacking her suitcase, she hoped she'd brought along the proper attire. A campaigning dignitary should look professional, but this was a family festival at a fairgrounds. She called Renata again.

"Tell me again why I'm doing this? What do I know about chicken and egg production? What in the world am I going to talk to them about?"

"What you say doesn't matter as much as the fact that they see your face and recognize your name on the ballot. Maybe you should let them ask questions. See what *they* want to know."

That sounded to Laurel perilously like a free-for-all. "I think I'll do a little research." She opened her laptop, jumped on the Internet, and squelched her childhood bird phobia long enough to research the production of chickens and eggs. Two hours later she was starving and still couldn't have answered the famous question about which came first.

And really couldn't have cared less. Boy, was she ever going to knock it out of the park in the morning. *Not.*

In this budget hotel, room service wasn't an option, so she grabbed the novel she'd been trying to read for six months and hooked her purse over her arm. Then nearly had a heart attack when she came face to face with Cole in the elevator.

"Oh!" She stood there so long, the door started to shut.

He quickly stuck his hand out to make the door bounce back open. "Laurel! Hey."

"Hi. Sorry, I have to ..." She stood there looking at him. He leaned against the back wall, dressed in jeans and a pink polo which was not in any shape, form, or fashion, feminine. A shadow of dark beard scraped his jawline, and he looked glad to see her.

She looked away.

The door tried to close again. He reached out for the "open" button. "Come on, where are you going?"

"To get something to eat," she mumbled.

"Me too. I'll take you."

Every instinct screamed for her to bolt. "I was just going somewhere for a salad."

"I can make that happen. Everybody's got salads." His gaze dropped to the book in her hand. "Unless you want to be alone."

She didn't want to be alone, but she was scared of being alone with *him*. A quandary Marilyn vos Savant couldn't have figured out. "No, I ... Okay."

Maybe she hadn't prayed hard enough this morning. Or maybe she hadn't been specific enough. Or maybe God had just had enough of her whining about Cole following her around. *Get it out in the open. Tell him to leave you alone and be done with it.*

She got into the elevator, every molecule of her body aware of Cole. His height. His bent nose, the way he cupped his hands against the elevator rail. She thought of the way he'd held her face when he kissed her.

Grow up, sister. He was just doing his job as a reporter, following the subject of a political race that interested him. Cole liked to kiss. He kissed lots of women. No way a guy like him had remained celibate for eight years. Her physical longing for him, and conversely, her shame, was exacerbated by the knowledge that he was an extraordinary lover.

After what happened between her and Cole eight years ago, she'd gone through major spiritual angst over the issue of her own purity. Was it worth holding onto at her age? Didn't she deserve to be loved? On more than one occasion she'd almost yielded ground, thinking to maneuver a man who hovered on the edge of commitment.

But a film of spiritual protection—instilled not just by the prohibitions and promises in God's Word, but by a loving earthly father's assurance that she was worthy of a man's full commitment unto death—kept her resolve firm.

Oh, yes, resolved, but no less vulnerable to emotional damage. She stood stiff as a maypole in the center of the elevator, which seemed to be running on chicken manure and not electricity.

Cole cleared his throat. "I went by to see Rebel this morning on my way out of town. He said to tell you 'Arf.'"

"You were at my sister's house?" If that wasn't just dandy. Now he was invading her family.

He rubbed the back of his neck. "She wasn't thrilled to see me at first, but she broke out the iced tea and we had a conversation. Nice girl."

"Yes, she is." The conversation stalled. When was this elevator going to reach the ground? "Rebel seems to like it there."

"Yep. I thought I might take him back to New York with me, but he'll be happier with your nephews. He's already got a dog-house and everything."

She didn't want to feel sorry for Cole, who couldn't have the dog.

The elevator mercifully opened. Laurel dug in her purse for her keys. "Want to take my car?"

"If you don't mind, let's take mine. Headroom, you know." He grinned a little.

Oh yeah. The Nissan nearly decapitated him. "That's fine."

They managed a whole meal at Wendy's without mentioning anything controversial or personal. They talked about Field's indictment of Krenshaw Grogan, Cole told her about the kittens Lucia Ochoa had sent to live with her family, and Laurel listened to his outline for the next article he planned to submit.

She had almost relaxed when he asked her how she felt about some conservative Christians treating her like a folk hero.

She sucked diet soda down the wrong way and started coughing. "Like a what?"

"You okay?" Cole handed her a napkin. "I see it all over the Internet. People are forwarding emails asking for prayer for you because you're being persecuted."

"You've got to be kidding."

He shrugged. "It's like you're the home team girl, and some outsider yanked your drawers down."

"As the outsider who did the yanking, maybe you could explain why my poll ratings are still so low."

"I wondered when we were going to get to that." Cole's ears reddened. "People don't know what to think, because you haven't come out and told them what to think. Nothing's worse than being wishy-washy or uncommunicative."

"Well, thank you very much, but there are some things I didn't choose to communicate to every Tom, Dick, and Harry on the street." Laurel kept her voice low, but gripped the edges of the table and leaned in. "When the choice was taken out of my hands, it upset me. Very much!"

"I can understand that. I've tried every way I know how to apologize. What did you do with the flowers—kick them into the street?" Cole's eyes burned.

"I'm not that childish. I took them to the nursing home."

"That sounds like you."

Laurel wasn't sure he meant it as a compliment. "They were beautiful, and I didn't want them to go to waste—"

"Oh right. Let's not get emotional. The only time that happens, bad stuff goes on. Like falling in love and getting married."

"I got married because I was drunk!"

"And why did you get drunk?"

"Because I'd just found out my brother killed himself!"

Cole stared at her, his face gone white. His mouth opened, then closed. "Your brother—"

"My brother, Michael." Tears slipped out in spite of her best efforts to contain them. "On New Year's Eve he'd flipped his car on Kalioka Road and died on the way to the hospital. They called it an accident. That was bad enough, but six weeks later, Elise, my roommate, gave me a handful of unopened mail she'd mislaid.

There was a letter from my brother, telling me he wanted to kill himself. He was hooked on crystal meth, depressed and ashamed, and just wanted out of life." Her breath began to hitch. Cole stared at her, but she kept on, dogged. It was an unutterable relief to spill her feelings about that awful day. "Six weeks too late to do anything about it. I didn't know how to tell my parents or even if I should. I loved Michael so much, and I'd been praying for God to get his attention. For this to happen—well, I was so angry at God, I thought why should I even try pleasing him anymore? What good does it do? My family didn't *deserve* to deal with any more tragedy." Her voice wobbled. "I'd been getting ready to go home, while you guys—all my other friends—were headed to New Orleans for Mardi Gras. Somebody asked me one more time if I wanted to come along, and I kind of wigged out and said okay."

"Laurel—"

"You wanted to know, and here it is." Crying, nose running, she looked at Cole, absorbing his genuine distress. "If you choose to print it I won't stop you, but you've got to know my family has kept this quiet for eight years and our good name is important to my parents and grandparents."

"I keep telling you I won't hurt you on purpose, Laurel." He reached for her hands, which she snatched away.

"Yeah, well, forgive me if I don't believe that anymore. I'm tired of getting my knees cut out from under me." She looked away from the compassion in his eyes. A couple of women at a nearby table were surreptitiously watching her. She lowered her voice. "Take me back to the hotel, okay? I have to get ready for tomorrow."

"So you're not giving me any more chances?"

"Cole, do you really *want* another chance? We're so messed up, there's no hope of salvaging this thing. I don't trust you, and you'd be crazy to waste your time on anybody as gun-shy as me." She closed her eyes, mopping her face with the napkin. "Please."

"Okay, Laurel." He sighed. "Come on."

They drove back to the hotel, walked side-by-side through the lobby, and rode the elevator to Laurel's floor without speaking. Laurel sniffled quietly into tissue after tissue.

Cole touched her arm as she got off. "I'm sorry I upset you, but I'm glad to finally know all the truth."

"It wasn't my secret. My parents . . ."

"I won't tell anybody."

He said something else as the elevator closed. It might have been "I love you," but she was crying too hard to know for sure.

chapter 19

Cole bumped the back of his head against the elevator wall as it crept toward the third floor. *Idiot.* Thump. *Idiot.* Thump. *Idiot.*

Why couldn't he ever think of the right words when he was with Laurel? Give him a computer or a piece of paper and pencil and he was flaming Victor Hugo. But face to face? He'd waited over a week for a chance to talk to her, and when he got it—what had he done? Made her cry.

He felt a little like weeping himself. Now he knew for sure why she'd eloped with him, not that he'd ever thought it had anything to do with his intelligence and character. At least he'd assumed it had something to do with personal charisma, maybe his sense of humor. Laurel herself had told him he was a good kisser.

But no, the simple truth was she'd been a twentysomething daddy's girl blind with grief and some obscure form of survivor's guilt. So blind she'd turned to the first presentable male to pour a couple of Hurricanes down her at Pat O'Brien's and offer a comforting shoulder.

Not that he'd had any intention of moving past the stage of rumpled sheets in a cheap hotel. His intentions, however, rammed full-tilt into the reality. Even with her considerable brainpower overcome by alcohol, there were some things Laurel wouldn't do without a ring on her finger and her name on a license.

And Cole had found himself so consumed by lust and selfishness—not to mention copious quantities of rum and fruit juice—that he'd figured it would all work out in the end. As had most things in his life to that point. His parents had divorced and seemed to recover just fine—which just went to show the true extent of his self-absorption.

He should have known. If he'd learned anything growing up in the shadow of Yoknapatawpha County, it was that there were wars and rumors of wars; there were facts conveyed by reliable witnesses; and then there was evidence you saw with your own eyes. And at the end of it all you might not see the truth until you woke up stone cold sober in a New Orleans hotel with a long-legged, angry redhead in your bed and a paper cigar band on your finger.

He walked into the room, passed up his computer, and yanked a pad of drawing paper out of his backpack. No more blogging his emotions into the computer. He flung himself into the chair and turned on the light. He sketched a cartoon likeness of himself, befuddled, looking up. "What, God, what?" he printed in the speech balloon.

Give me Laurel.

I can't give you what I don't have.

Laurel stood on an open-air platform just inside the entrance to the Lions Club Fairgrounds in Moulton, shouting an invocation over a cacophony of squawks, cackles, and crows coming from the pens behind her. She prayed with confidence, sincerity, and brevity. Presumably God wasn't offended by the smell of manure.

She'd arrived at the fairgrounds bright and early, dressed in tailored blue jeans, red denim jacket, and lacy white undershirt, to be met by the county extension coordinator for the Alabama co-op. After leading her to the platform where a crowd had gathered for the opening ceremonies, he introduced her and left her alone. The coordinator seemed to have little idea what she was doing there, and despite last night's research, she still wasn't sure she could have enlightened him.

Just as she said "Amen," the county agent came running up to give her a handheld microphone. Taking a breath for composure—why was she nervous all of a sudden?—she smiled. And jumped when the microphone squealed.

"You're too close to the speaker, ma'am," called out a man in the crowd. "Back that tractor up a little."

Laurel laughed and stepped back. "Is that better? Thanks for letting me come talk to you a little this morning. I've lived in Alabama all my life, and this is the first time I've been to the festival. I'm looking forward to tasting all the chicken treats before I leave. Until last night I didn't know the difference between a pullet and a cockerel, but I've enjoyed boning up on my chicken feed." She grinned. "And my chicken jokes. I hear you're having a contest."

"Why don't you tell us a lawyer joke, Judge Kincade?" suggested someone in the back. The voice sounded a lot like Cole McGaughan.

Squinting against the sun, she searched the crowd. Sure enough, a dark, rumpled head toward the rear towered over everyone else.

"Okay," she said promptly. "What's the difference between an attorney and God?"

"I don't know—what?" called the man who'd told her to back up the tractor.

"God doesn't think he's an attorney."

There was a collective groan from the crowd, but people were elbowing one another and grinning.

She smiled. "I have to tell y'all that as far as I'm concerned, the only good chicken's a dead one. When I was a little girl, my grandma Kincade, who lives over in Cullman, had a yard full of chickens, and I swear they chased me from the car into the house every time I came to visit. So I'm going to keep a safe distance from the live ones, and go for the ones cooked crispy on a stick, okay?"

Her audience laughed again, apparently unoffended to discover her deathly fear of their source of livelihood.

Relaxed now, Laurel briefly outlined what she hoped to accomplish on the supreme court. Halfway into the speech she realized, Cole or no Cole, she was having a good time. She wasn't going to let him ruin her life, and she certainly wasn't going to let him take over her campaign. Let him tell the world whatever he wanted to. There was a certain amount of freedom in not having anything to hide.

She kept her remarks short and to the point, relying heavily on the self-deprecating humor she'd learned from her father's parents. She was no stand-up comedian, but she could tell a good yarn. By the time she got to the end of her allotted time, her audience had doubled in size. A couple of TV cameras, local stations on-site to film the Little Chick Beauty Pageant, had sidled into the crowd.

"Do you have any questions?" She started to hand the mike off to the extension agent, who had appeared from somewhere like the Wizard of Oz. Surely these people had better things to do than discuss judicial politics on a beautiful spring Saturday with food and games and music all around.

"Wait, Judge—yes, I've got a question."

Laurel clutched the mike in surprise, looking for the source of the question. A female reporter stood at the edge of the crowd, PDA and stylus ready. "Okay," Laurel said. "Fire away."

"I read the article about you and the guy you ran off with in college." Curiosity was folded into every line of the woman's face. "What happened to him?"

Why hadn't she stepped off the platform when she had a chance? Things had been going so well. Laurel shrugged. "Nothing dramatic. We went our separate ways, and he went on with his life."

"Why did you decide to hide the fact that you'd been married until now?"

Laurel hesitated. "The legal definition of annulment is 'rendering a marriage void, as if it never existed.' So technically—" She stopped when a murmur of disapproval rumbled through the crowd facing her. She took a sharp breath. "Technically I wasn't married, but yes, I hid the annulment from my friends and family. For a long time. There were extenuating circumstances, you'll have to take my word for it. I'm not terribly proud of my behavior that week. It was reckless and dangerous to my health and safety. I'd counsel young people not to follow that example, but to listen to words of wisdom learned from hard experience. Alcohol on top of any emotional upheaval can result in lifelong negative consequences." She swallowed. "Consequences that reach beyond your personal sphere and damage every relationship you have."

The reporter stared at Laurel, then bent her head to scribble on the PDA pad.

Laurel let a short silence hang before she brought the microphone to her mouth again. "Thank you all for your kind attention. I hope you'll go to the polls and vote in a few weeks. I'd be honored to be elected your next supreme court chief justice."

"Wait, Judge Kincade, just one more question."

Laurel froze.

Cole had moved to the center of the crowd. He stood out like an oak tree in a stand of sugar maples. "This goes to motive," he said pleasantly, as if he were a lawyer with a witness on the stand. "I'd like to know if you loved the guy you married."

She literally forgot to breathe for several seconds as she stared at him. "I was beginning to," she whispered into the microphone. "But people sometimes let you down."

Matt sat on Elise Bell Vanderbecken's living room sofa, holding a ten-thousand-dollar photograph in his hand.

He worked hard; nobody could say he was a slacker. He endured endless nights of mind-numbing boredom and weeks of bad food and months of disrespect, just to make a decent living. Once a month or so, he would call his parents and remind them that at least he wasn't selling drugs, and hey, Magnum PI used to make a living doing exactly the same thing. Mom would sniffle and ask when he was coming home, and Dad would ask him if he still had his Bible.

Matt always lied and said yes. No sense offending anybody.

But a ten-thousand-dollar bonus was nothing to sneeze at. The old man would be proud.

At least, he should be. Pastoring his little church in northern Illinois, it probably took Ben Hogan six months to make that much money.

"So this is her brother Michael, huh?" He looked at Elise, who was jostling a whining infant against her shoulder. He hoped to goodness she didn't decide to whip open her blouse and start nursing it.

"Yes. I didn't get the connection until the article about her runaway marriage hit the paper. Then I realized I'd given her a letter from Michael the same week as that Mardi Gras trip. From what Laurel told me, Michael was sort of a troublemaker, and he was killed in a car wreck on New Year's. She'd been taking his death fairly well, so there had to have been something in that letter that made Laurel go off the deep end." She paused and wrinkled her freckled nose. "Are you *sure* this background check is necessary for the supreme court? This is really personal stuff."

Matt nodded gravely. "Yes, ma'am, I need all the facts I can get regarding Ms. Kincade's past history. If there's anything that would keep her from serving on the state court, we need to know it now."

"I understand." Elise nodded. "I grew up here in Mobile, but I didn't know the Kincades that well, except for Laurel. I apologized for losing the letter and asked if there was anything I could do to help, but she didn't want to talk about it. She's such a private person." Elise shook her head, jouncing the fussy baby. "You'd think somebody like that wouldn't want the exposure of running for public office. *I* sure didn't." She smiled with a certain amount of self-satisfaction. "I'm very happy being the queen of my own home. Nobody runs *my* life for me. Oh dear! There's Lily waking up from her nap. Sorry, I'll have to go. You can take the picture, as long as you get it back to me."

Matt found himself all but shoved out the door. He didn't care. He had the picture.

"Remember, though, this is a confidential investigation," he told Elise just before she shut the door on him. "Judge Kincade shouldn't know I came to talk to you."

Tuesday afternoon Cole parked at the end of a cul-de-sac in a west Mobile subdivision and walked up to a white Creole-style cottage with a For Sale sign in the yard. Renata had called that morning asking him to meet her in one of the empty homes she was showing. Curious, he'd agreed. Maybe he could probe into the question of whether she was feeding information—inadvertently or not—to Field's campaign.

Renata opened the front door before he could ring the bell and hauled him inside. "Hurry up. If Laurel accidentally drove by—"

"She's on her way back from Talladega." He yawned. "I just got back myself. That's a long drive to make in one morning."

"She's liable to call me any minute, though, and I wanted to talk to you first. Find out how things went on the northern tour, and see what you thought about ... well, how things are going." Renata led the way into the family room. There was no furniture, so she sat on the hearth, tugging her skirt down over her legs.

Cole simply stretched out on the floor. "Man, I'm beat."

Renata looked at him with little sympathy. "Think how Laurel feels. She's got to stay focused and bright for four more weeks. Good thing she handles stress well."

"Speaking of how things are going ..."

"What? I don't like the way you said that."

Cole rolled his head. "Oh, she handled things fine. But there were definitely some stressors."

"Like what?"

"Like the rooster that got loose and chased her into the Nerf ball pit."

"You've got to be kidding!"

"I fished her out, while some little kid took his prize Bantam back to the judging pens." Cole snorted. "And then there was the old man in the bad toupee who tried to take her home with him after church Sunday morning. Laurel was kinder to him than I was."

Renata put her head in her hands. "I keep telling her she's got to keep a little distance."

Cole grinned. "Okay, it really wasn't that big a deal. But she definitely has every intention of staying away from *me*." His smile faded. "Why is it everybody but Laurel can see how much I love her?"

"I had this sort of insight this morning," Renata said quietly. She looked down at him. "Sometimes it's harder for people who've been in control of their lives to let go. You find out there's one thing—one very important thing—out of your control, and it scares you. Really bad, you know?" She shrugged. "For sure, Laurel's afraid of her feelings for you. Maybe deep down she knows how much you love her, and that scares her too."

Cole felt his throat tighten. "I don't want to control her. I've tried to tell her that, but it never comes out right. I just want to help her and be her partner and love her." He sighed. "God's even as much as told me not to expect anything in return. Just stand my ground, do my job, and let *him* be the Man. Do you know how hard that is? He wired me to go after what I want, and now he tells me to back off."

Renata pressed her full lips together. "Brother, I suggest you do what the Man says to do. I wouldn't be messin' around with those instructions."

"How about you?" Cole sat up. Even a month ago he would have deflected such an intimate conversation with a joke. But it was time to call a spade a spade. "I believe you sincerely care about Laurel. Do you realize you're jeopardizing her career by allowing Derrick Edes to stay on her campaign?"

Her expression tightened. "What do you know about Derrick?"

"The question is what do *you* know? You're the one in his pocket."

"Not anymore. I shut that down last week after I talked to the reporter who wrote about Laurel's financial doings."

"What do you mean?"

"I wanted to make sure they got the straight about where her paintings came from, and who paid for her trip to Brazil. Of course the guy wouldn't tell me who gave him the false info, but while I was there he got a call. It sounded a whole lot like my *ex*-boyfriend." Renata brushed her hands together in exaggerated fashion.

Cole smiled. "Did you confront him?"

"Do I look like a woman who'd ignore a rattlesnake in the grass? Of course I confronted him. And of course he told me I was imagining things. I think that's what you call an impasse." Renata snorted. "But if he thinks he's getting any more goods off me, he can think again."

"I wish you'd convince Laurel."

"She'll come around once I can produce some hard proof." Renata shrugged. "I know we got this high-powered, high-dollar consultant pulling strings from DC, but so far I'm not too impressed. Hiring a guy like Derrick ..." She made a face. "You and I can do a better job. You said you had some ideas for getting her campaign back on track."

Cole shook off his lethargy and discouragement. "What we have to do is help her reverse public opinion. When people aren't paying attention to the issues, or don't care about them, the likeability factor's critical. And Laurel can do this. I've been out there with her and saw it firsthand. She had a bunch of farmers who couldn't care less about state judicial issues eating out of her hand."

Renata grinned. "In spite of being chased by Foghorn Leghorn?"

"Maybe *because* of it." Cole nodded. "People identify with a candidate who has compassion and humor and common sense. Laurel's got all that in spades. They don't care so much how smart you are, despite what a lot of national media would lead you to believe."

"Laurel's no dummy," Renata pointed out.

"You're right." Cole rubbed his eyes. "Somebody just needs to help her show off the parts of her character that are harder to put in a résumé."

"You know how to do that?"

"Yeah, but don't tell her it was my idea or we're dead in the water."

Renata, eyes twinkling, crossed her heart. "You're the boss."

Laurel picked up her mother after a Junior Miss coordinators' meeting Tuesday night. Mom tossed her satchel in the backseat, then got in the front, talking before the door shut.

"How was your trip, sweetie? You won't believe what Miss Kansas's talent is. She wants to twirl Samoan fire knives, which is completely against the fire code. So the committee deputized me to call her mother and talk her into regular double batons or something a little less—pyrotechnical. You were a Junior Miss fifteen years ago, and you've got such a way of talking sense into people, I wondered if you might …"

"You have got to be kidding." Laurel glanced at her mother. "I just got back from a six-hour drive after wrestling chickens and learning to speak NASCAR."

Mom batted her eyes hopefully. "It's so sweet of you to pick me up. Your dad dropped me off on his way to the country club, but his tennis game went long, and I didn't have the heart to make him leave in the middle of a set."

"No problem, Mom." Laurel sighed. "I wanted to talk to you anyway."

"Really?" Mom sounded pleased. "Lately none of us have managed to get much information out of you except what's in the newspapers. I swear Cole McGaughan knows more about you than I do."

Laurel flinched. "Mom—"

"Oh, you know what I mean. You're so busy running that campaign, talking to the press, chatting up voters … It's like your family hardly exists anymore."

"Mother, you sat in on that conference with the campaign consultant, way back in January. He warned us it would be a strain on our relationship, and that you and the others would have to be patient with me." Her mother had a knack for raising guilt like an allergic rash. "But since you mentioned Cole, I think I should warn you that I finally told him about Michael."

Mom gasped. "Laurel, that's *private*, and he's a reporter!"

"I know he is, but honestly I don't believe he'll write about that. If he does—" she shrugged—"we'll deal with it like we should have eight years ago. Goodness knows we're not the first family to have drugs and suicide in our history."

"Laurel!"

"Come on, Mom." Laurel pulled into her parents' driveway and put the car in park. "Let's be honest. This smiling facade of I'm-okay-you're-okay may look pretty on the outside, but it's cooked up some poison—in my life at least. Telling Cole was a way of lancing the boil. I think you and Daddy should consider doing the same. We all need a dose of the truth."

Laurel looked at her mother, who sat hunched in the passenger seat, picking at the fringe on her scarf. She looked very fragile. Laurel was about to relent and apologize when Mom angled her chin in that diva way of hers.

"If I promise to drag your daddy to the counselor, will you give Miss Kansas's mother a call?"

Field didn't want to meet in his office, so Matt said fine; they'd rendezvous in the park like a couple of thugs from an Oliver Stone movie.

"What's the secret password?" he whispered, and Field hung up on him. Matt didn't care. He was a bit perturbed with the guy by now. The last time he'd paid him with cash in a plain envelope—not entirely unexpected. What *was* unexpected was the amount: exactly one-third of what Matt had agreed to.

"I pay in full when the job's done," Field had said when Matt called to complain. "And don't forget—there's the bonus when she throws in the towel. I want this race all to myself."

Personally, Matt thought that attitude reeked of unsportsmanlike behavior.

He pulled into a parking space in the lot between Riverside Park and Water Street, next to the Convention Center. On a midweek afternoon the park was practically deserted; a couple of college-age lovebirds leaned on the waterside rail throwing popcorn to the seagulls, and a middle-school truant whizzed by on a skateboard. Matt sat down on a bench, looked at the photo in his pocket, and tried to remember that he loved his job.

Well, okay, he liked it. It wasn't too bad. Maybe he could stand it for another couple of years.

He was about to get up and ask the lovebirds if he could share the popcorn—he'd forgotten to eat lunch—when Field appeared, hurrying from the direction of Government Street, where his office was located in the courthouse plaza.

"Hogan, what's this all about?" Field cast himself onto the bench and yanked a protein bar out of his suit jacket.

Matt's salivary glands went into overdrive. "It's about a little thing called a contract."

"We didn't sign a contract." Field scowled as he bit into the energy bar. "This is all off the books, and you know it."

"I'm not talking about paper and ink. I'm talking about where two gentlemen shake hands on their word." Matt watched Field chew. "I don't know how you guys do it down here in Dixie, but in Illinois, when one of those gentlemen fulfills his part of the agreement, the other one pays what he owes."

Field avoided Matt's eyes. "Hogan, you're smart enough to know I don't carry that kind of cash with me. And it's not floating around where I can get hold of it at will, for that matter. I've got

PACs to pacify, the Secretary of State's office sniffing my funds disbursement trail, the press watching every move I make. You know what it's like. You'll have to be patient."

"While I'm being patient," Matt sneered, "how'm I supposed to pay my bills?"

Field bridled. "I assume a highly respected investigative agency like yours can get enough credit to subsidize expenses during the operation of a case."

Matt stared at him. "You assume."

"I assume," Field repeated. He got to his feet, cramming the rest of the protein bar into his mouth and talking around it. "Did you have anything productive to bring to my attention this afternoon, or did you get me out here to waste my time with a bunch of useless whining?"

Matt hesitated. He could give Field the photo, let him run with it, and most likely knock Laurel Kincade completely out of the race. But what if Field continued to stiff him?

The real question was did Matt really want to work for this insufferable jerk one moment longer?

The answer made him settle back onto the bench and cross his feet at the ankles. "I'm working on something," he said. "I'll let you know when it pans out."

"You do that." Field let the paper-and-foil wrapper drop on the ground. "I've got confidence in you, Hogan, you can handle this." He swung off toward the park exit.

Matt picked up the wrapper and tossed it in a trash bin on his way to the car. He had just discovered something important: he did not like this particular job at all.

Laurel was knee-deep in junior prima donnas when a team from Channel 4 News showed up backstage. She looked up in astonishment to find a camera zooming in as she pinned ribbons on "Brigitta's" bonnet.

Fashioning a bow under the little girl's chin, Laurel sent her off with a teasing pinch of her cheek. "Break a leg, Rosy."

The cameraman switched off the recorder and lazily waited for the reporter to approach Laurel.

"Hi, I'm Chelsea Stamper, Channel 4." The tall blonde beauty stuck out a hand and beamed at Laurel. "Wasn't she just the cutest thing?"

"Yes ... I'm sorry—" Laurel cast a distracted glance at the excited young actors standing on chairs and making guided missiles out of their props. "Did I know you were coming?"

Chelsea Stamper laughed. "Probably not. Your campaign manager called yesterday and said you'd be here getting ready for opening night. I thought it would be fun to catch you in a spontaneous moment with the kids. My manager and I have discussed covering the Playhouse for months, and this seemed like a great time to give the arts a little exposure."

Renata.

She hadn't told Renata she'd been rethinking her stand against publicizing her charities—after all, the exposure could bring in donations. Still, Renata could have at least warned Laurel to take her hair down from its ponytail.

Laurel smiled. "That's very kind of you. You're welcome to film the kids—"

"Oh, we will, but if you don't mind, I'd like to interview you as well." Chelsea blinked big blue eyes and wiggled a finger at her cameraman. "Come on, Wes, she says it's okay."

"It's okay," Laurel said, "but you're going to have to let me organize the children first. Give me half a minute." This was not in her plan. Boy, was it ever not. But *some* people thought she was wired a little too tight, and it was time to prove she could be flexible. She began to sing. "Doe, a deer, a female deer ..."

Within thirty seconds, all twenty children were singing along with Laurel, even the little blonde diva playing Maria. Trained to listen and respond to their teacher's voice, they clustered around her and began to sit cross-legged on the floor as she touched them one by one on the shoulder. By the end of the song, all were still and quiet, index fingers over their lips.

"Thank you so much," Laurel told the children with a smile. "I need you to listen while this nice lady asks me a few questions about your performance tonight. If you pay attention, she may want you to sing again." Laurel met Chelsea's delighted blue eyes and received a nod in response. "Perfect. Now what can we tell you about our program?"

Chelsea moved in with her microphone, and the camera followed. "Thanks so much, Judge Kincade. Before we talk about the program, though, you're in the middle of an exciting judicial campaign, and yet you're spending valuable time with these kids."

"Yes, I'm running for chief justice of the Alabama Supreme Court. The conservative primary is coming up in just three and a half weeks."

"That is so interesting!" Chelsea gushed. "You'd be the very first woman to serve in that capacity, right?"

"That's correct. There have been women on the court, but none have served as chief justice."

"What on earth makes you want to take on a job like that? Aren't you satisfied in your current post on the Mobile County Juvenile Court?"

Laurel looked down at the circle of upturned young faces. The children listened, full of pride that "Miss Laurel" was on TV. Her eyes stung. "I'm very happy in my job here in Mobile. My family is close, and I know my staff and I know I do a great deal of good in the juvenile court. It'll be hard to leave these boys and girls. But I try to teach them to stretch their wings and be eagles when they get a chance. What kind of example would I be if I stayed home like a big chicken?" Catching Jamika's dancing eyes, she flapped her elbows and let out a squawk. All the children burst into gales of laughter as they copied her. It had become a private joke since she'd gotten back from Moulton and described the rooster chase.

The reporter clearly didn't get it, but she played along, laughing. "Makes sense to me. So how long have you been working with the kids here at Popcorn Playhouse?"

"Since I was about this one's age." She tweaked one of Rosy's curls. "I graduated from the program and stayed involved, except for a few years when I was away at law school."

"That's amazing. Are there openings for people in the community who'd like to donate time or resources to the program?"

"Sure. They can call this number." Laurel recited the play-house phone number.

"Thanks, Judge Kincade. I bet everybody in town will want to call the box office and see the show." Chelsea reeled off the dates of the performances. "Now, could we have one more song?"

"Of course. How about 'Edelweiss,' boys and girls?"

When the song was over, Chelsea signaled the camera to shut down. She smiled at Laurel. "That's one of the best interviews I've ever done. It'll be on the ten o'clock news tonight."

"Wow. Cool." Laurel looked down at the children, hands on hips. "You hear that, kiddos? You're stars!"

A cheer went up.

The publicity would be great for the playhouse.

When she got home, Laurel climbed in bed with a cup of chamomile tea and turned on the late edition of the news. Charles Wallace hopped into her lap as the coverage of the play came on. "Look, CW. We're on TV."

Unimpressed, Charles Wallace pranced over to bat at a pillow tassel. Laurel rescued it as Chelsea interviewed a succession of parents who'd been loitering in the lobby before the performance.

"My granddaughter Jamika—" the elderly woman leaned into the microphone—"she was the Mother Superior, the one with the big solo. She just loves Judge Laurel. You couldn't ask for a sweeter, more patient lady. Gives up every Saturday and lots of evenings to work with these children. Makes 'em mind too. Respect themselves and each other. The fellow that started this program—he's a good guy too, but it wouldn't have its heart and soul without the judge and a few other adults who give their time and talent to help kids like my Jamika."

Laurel clicked off the television and sighed. "Well, Charles Wallace, I guess that's the price you pay, running for public office. I was hoping they'd focus more on the kids instead of me." The cat tried to wiggle his way into her embrace. She absently petted him, then turned off the light and flopped onto the pillow. "I guess Renata will be happy."

"When I said I'd help, I didn't know we were gonna be slinging peanut butter and jelly in a soup kitchen at the crack of dawn." Hogan crammed a sandwich into a paper sack and handed it to Cole, who added a bag of potato chips and a brownie.

Cole grinned at his friend's dismay. They'd been downtown since 6:30 a.m., packing lunches for the Water Street Mission. He fished a bottle of water out of the cooler at his feet and passed it to Hogan. "You wanted to see what she does on Saturday mornings," he said. "Can you picture your boy Field coming down here to do this, unless there was a TV crew around to film it? I don't think so."

"You think anybody would mind if I ate one of these?" Hogan, eyed the sandwich in his hand. "I never got around to eating dinner last night."

"Go ahead." Hogan's restless, tense expression worried Cole. He'd seen guys get that look and wind up wrecking their lives. "What's the matter?"

"Nothing's the matter." Hogan sounded almost sullen, most unlike his usual sunny temperament. He unwrapped the sandwich and put half of it in his mouth. Around it he said, "It's just that I never knew anybody that actually did stuff like this. Except maybe my parents."

"Really?" Cole didn't think he'd ever heard Hogan mention his family. "Where do they live?"

"Illinois. My old man's a preacher."

"No way."

"Yeah." Hogan chewed. "Behold me, the classic prodigal PK. The old man used to make me do stuff like this when I was growing up."

Cole silently packed a lunch sack. This put a whole new spin on the guy's lifestyle. Or maybe not. "I would never have been able to tell you had a religious upbringing. What happened?"

"Got off to college, drifted along with friends having a good time." Hogan shrugged. "Going to church was always this dull thing, at least the way my dad preached. When I was a little kid, he was enthusiastic but not too good at it. Then the enthusiasm turned into discouragement. The church never grew, and we were always dirt poor. Dad didn't know how to do anything else." He gave Cole a rueful look. "I told myself I wasn't going to end up like that. But look at me. PBJ and potato chips taste pretty doggone good right now."

Cole was about to answer when a slight commotion stirred at the doorway to the kitchen.

Amanda Downs, a reporter Cole had recently met from the *Mobile Register*, stuck her head in. "Hey, Cole, somebody said Judge Kincade was in here. Have you seen her?"

"She and her little sister went to Sam's for more chips. They'll be right—Oh, here she is." Cole beckoned Laurel, who had entered the back door carrying a box of potato chips. "Hey, Judge Kincade, your public has found you."

"Judge Kincade!" Amanda lit up. "Would you mind if I ask you a few questions?"

Gilly gave her sister a push from behind. "Go on, Lolly, we've got to get these things on the table."

Amanda rushed over to take Laurel's box and help her unpack it. "I'd appreciate it so much. I'm Amanda Downs, from the religion page. My editor liked what you said on the news last night about the playhouse, and she said if I could get you to talk about what your church does at the mission here, I could have a front-page byline."

Laurel glanced at Cole. "Did you tell them I'd be here?"

"Nope." But he'd give Renata kudos for a smart move.

Laurel looked at the reporter and shrugged. "It was my sister Gilly's idea. You should probably talk to her."

Cole wanted to shake her. Or kiss her.

"Oh, I will," said Amanda, pulling a notepad out of her purse. "I'm going to talk to the pastor and several of the other folks. But you've traveled all over the state, and you're in touch with other city officials all the time. I'm interested in your take on the homeless problem in Mobile."

While Laurel talked to the young reporter, Gilly moved in to help Cole and Matt finish up the lunch sacks. Matt remained uncharacteristically quiet, seeming to enjoy the banter and camaraderie of the team.

Gilly wedged herself between the two of them and looked up at Cole. "Are you going to tell me what's going on between you and Laurel? Because if you don't, I'm going to tickle you until you scream for mercy."

Cole shrugged. "What did Laurel tell you?"

"That you hurt one another a long time ago." She pressed the back of her hand to her forehead dramatically. "You're a lowlife scumbag, and I'm supposed to stay away from you and people like you." She shook her head and crammed a sandwich into a sack. "I'm sorry, but I don't go for the melodrama. There's got to be an explanation."

Cole's heart lightened. Somebody might actually believe his side of the story. "There is. Hogan, do you want to confess?"

Hogan started, a blush flagging his cheeks. "Do I have to?"

Cole wished he had a camera to capture Hogan's expression. The brave, mostly dead, Pirate Westley, stretched out on Prince

Humperdinck's Machine in the Pit of Despair couldn't have looked any more tortured.

"We are men of action," Cole said. "Lies do not become us."

"Oh, all right." Hogan took the sack Gilly handed him and placed it in the box. "I was the one who emailed that article to the *Journal*. It's my fault your sister hates his guts."

"I knew it." Gilly beamed at Cole. "When are you going to tell Laurel?"

Hogan shuffled his feet. "I already told her, and she doesn't believe me."

Gilly's smile faded. "Well, if that isn't just like Laurel. She's got to have proof for everything. One time Mom's little Yorkie carried one of her favorite sweaters out into the yard, and she blamed me for months."

"This is a little more serious than a sweater," Cole said, "but I appreciate the vote of confidence. Do you have any suggestions?"

Gilly grimaced. "I'm afraid you're just going to have to wait it out. Or somehow prove you're telling the truth. I'm so sorry, Cole." She reached out and hugged Cole around the waist.

He returned her hug, feeling remarkably comforted. "You're a good kid, you know that?"

"Of course I know it." Smiling, Gilly flirted her lashes at Hogan. "So, Matt, what do you do for a living, and do you also have a hot younger brother?"

Hogan's eyes widened. "Sorry, no, all I have is a bunch of sisters who used to make my life miserable. I'm a ..." He swallowed. "A private investigator."

Gilly blinked, pulling away from Cole. "How 'bout that. What are you investigating?"

Hogan glanced at Cole and sighed. "Up until about ten minutes ago, I was investigating your sister." His mouth tightened. "Now I'm—now I'm not."

Cole suppressed a whoop of victory.

Gilly's gamine face split into a big grin. "Cool!" She held up a palm. "High five, Matthew!"

Looking sheepish, Hogan slapped the girl's palm. "I hope I don't regret this."

"I knew I was going to regret this," Renata muttered Sunday afternoon, slapping the phone into its cradle.

Laurel, feet propped on the ottoman in front of Renata's living room rocker, looked up from the computer in her lap. She'd been reading comments on her campaign blog. Apparently Field had managed to spread a rumor that Laurel was overcompensated for several speaking engagements during the last few years, violating Canon 6A of the Judicial Code of Ethics. All she could do was write to people and deny it. "What do you regret?"

"Breaking up with Derrick."

"Whoa." Laurel involuntarily shut the lid of the computer. "When did this happen?"

"Last week." Renata got up to straighten a poster hanging askew over the sofa. "Don't get me wrong—I'm not sorry I sent the turkey back to the barnyard. But I wish it hadn't happened in the middle of your campaign."

"Well, you know I wasn't excited about you dating him."

Renata looked over her shoulder. "Laurel, I gotta tell you something. I didn't want to admit I might have made a mistake about him until your big goof-up came out. Then I did some checking and found out he's not what he seemed. You were right—he was just playing me. I was so flattered to have this good-looking, successful single guy pursuing me ... I let him lead me off into places I never should've gone."

"Renata ... everybody makes mistakes. Some of us more co-lossal than others. That's what forgiveness is for." Laurel looked away. "Did I ever apologize for keeping my annulment from you for so long?"

Renata shrugged. "Well, it's not like the whole world has to know your business. But when God teaches you something, you should probably share it with the people who love you." A glimmer of a smile appeared. "He's been taking me to the woodshed lately, how about you?"

"The Lord disciplines those he loves." Laurel shook her head. "He sure loves me a lot." She hesitated. "Do you think your relationship with Derrick—or lack of it—is going to affect the work he does for us?"

"I hope it means you're going to fire him."

Laurel frowned. "I'm sorry he disappointed you, but he's been doing a good job—"

"Yeah, for Field."

"According to Cole. But you know I don't believe anything *he*—"

"Laurel, I've got reason to believe Derrick's the one feeding lies to the *Register* about you."

" 'Reason to believe'? You can prove it?"

"Not yet. But until I do"—Renata paced across the room, twitched the curtain, and wheeled to face Laurel—"will you promise me you'll be really careful around him?"

"I'm going to be careful around everybody, Renata." Laurel opened the computer. "Count on it."

Matt had a bag full of tricks. Literally.

In his suitcase was a collection of microrecording equipment that would make the CIA proud. Most of it he had put together himself, a mixture of cast-offs from guys getting out of the business and stuff he had acquired at private investigator confabs. So he walked into a Baldwin County seafood restaurant on a rainy Friday afternoon looking like a seventh grade history teacher but wired like a Russian satellite.

"You're not here to dun me for more money, are you?" Field tucked his PDA in the pocket of his navy suit jacket lying across an empty chair. He already had a glass of tea at his elbow. "Where've you been?"

"I decided if I'm going to get paid, I'd better help you win." Matt yanked out a chair and dropped into it. He didn't apologize for keeping the DA waiting. The guy deserved all the inconvenience Matt could dish out. "I've been here, there, and yonder. Mostly following your lady around, trying to find out what makes her tick."

"Well, that's a hard one." Field snorted. "According to the press, she's into teaching kids to sing and feeding street bums. Putting criminals away and keeping them locked up doesn't seem to cross her radar screen."

Matt frowned. "Seems to me that's the job of the DA's office and the police. Why do you want to switch jobs?"

"Because nowadays the real power behind law enforcement is the judiciary. And with power comes privilege, my fine young gumshoe. There are a lot of folks with money willing to support the ones with power." Field caught a waitress's eye. "We're ready to order, hon."

When the waitress had gone, Matt pursued the previous topic. "So if you can't beat 'em, join 'em, huh?" This guy was dangerous.

Field shrugged. "I'm sick of this bleeding-heart family values junk. You get a woman like Laurel Kincade in charge of the court and she's gonna be all about homeschooling rights and protecting the environment at the expense of business, and letting preachers dictate to the rest of us."

"I've been doing my best to catch her inconsistencies."

"You may not be able to do that. Frankly, Kincade's a straight shooter. That's why nailing her for covering up that little law school indiscretion was a home run. If we could dig up something else like that ..." Field paused, eyebrows raised.

"Like you said—with Judge Kincade, what you see is what you get."

"Which would be a self-righteous, moralistic ..." Field proceeded to call Laurel Kincade a series of uncomplimentary names which Matt hoped she never had to hear. Winding down, the DA smiled sourly. "I feel better now. I'll be glad when this primary's past us. Then I can concentrate on beating the pants off the liberals." He emptied a couple of packets of sugar into his tea. "I'd figured the lady would be an easy mark, being so young and inexperienced—thought at the first show of fangs she'd turn tail and run. I'll have to give her credit for guts."

In Matt's opinion Laurel had more than that. She had integrity, a commodity he'd discovered to be as rare as snowmen in Florida. "So if we can't get her on moral issues, I'm assuming you have other plans."

"Who says we can't get her on moral issues?" Field chuckled. "Follow her when she's with her campaign manager, take pictures, and we'll see what we can do with Photoshop. Two single women spending that much time together ..."

Matt swallowed a sudden urge to punch the guy's dirty lights out. He couldn't make himself agree, so he pretended to take notes. "How's the push polling going?" Push polling was a way of manipulating voter opinion by asking questions loaded with negative information about an opposing candidate.

"Not as successful as I'd hoped. The real polls are showing her numbers improving every day. We're trying Internet rumors. Hard to trace the root of that stuff, and she's too naive to turn the trick."

Matt looked up. "What do you mean?"

"She has yet to spring a negative ad against me." Field shook his head. "'Course there's not much she can pull out there." He grinned. "I'm a pretty standup guy myself."

"Yeah, you're a real prince," Hogan said without a trace of sarcasm. "Hope the good guys win."

"Look, Hogan, I *am* a good guy, but I'm in this thing to win. I've got eyes and ears in places you can't go."

Matt leaned in and lowered his voice. "What are you talking about? *Wire taps?*"

Field just smiled. "Let's just say Laurel Kincade's private life is a little more interesting than you'd think. Your reporter buddy apparently fell for her in a big way, but she's not returning his calls. I want you to follow up on that, see if you can figure out what's going on."

For a split second, Matt saw himself and Field as in a still-frame photo. The image made him cringe. He'd been working for a criminal, and now he could prove it.

Make it right, Matt. For once in your life, do the right thing.

He gave Field a lazy smile. "Ah, McGaughan. Always in line for the ladies." He winked at the waitress as she refilled his tea glass. "Thanks, sweetheart. So do you live around here?"

chapter 21

Cole felt like he was in a Pepto-Bismol commercial.

Pink leotards, pink tights, pink walls and ceiling, with mirrors reflecting it all from every direction. At least the floor was a warm, honeyed wood, worn from years of ballet slippers and toe shoes sliding across it. The prosaic color grounded him, made him less ... bilious.

The only male in the room, he stood in a corner like a coat rack. Gilly assured him there were male dancers in the other class. Not that he would have felt more comfortable with men around. He carried a certain skepticism when it came to ... What the heck did you call male ballerinas? Anyway, he was sort of relieved to see only girls here. They were all beautiful like an array of rosebuds in a florist's display. Drooping and bending and pointing and stretching with toned, graceful muscles.

Gilly had asked him to meet her here at the studio because she only had a short lunch break between her Saturday classes. Her audition with the American School of Ballet was coming up this week, and she was dead set on getting in.

Laurel still wasn't gung-ho about her baby sister moving off to the Big Apple, but then Laurel had better get used to the idea that she couldn't control everything.

Funny how most of his thoughts these days came back to Laurel—what she thought, what made her laugh, what moved her closer to God. All that stuff a mystery because of the schism between them. He thought of it as a great body of water, like an ocean with tides that rolled two islands closer to one another on occasion and separated them again just when it seemed an isthmus might form.

Leaning against the wall, arms folded, he watched Gilly twirl on the toe of one shoe, the other leg lifted to the front, poised with uncanny balance. His mom had had a music box dancer just like that when he was a little kid. It had tinkled out a waltz every time he opened it—until he'd cranked the little brass key too hard one time.

He had always been breaking things—something Teri reminded him of often. She'd always been warning him not to get too close to baby Tucker. Which was why Cole loved the wrestling team. He could pound people's heads and not get in trouble. Miserable to be nearly six feet tall in the eighth grade, but when he got to high school and they found out he was strong as an ox, things got better.

The music from the boom box on the floor—a string quartet playing something classical—soared to a crescendo and then dwindled to silence. The cluster of ballerinas in the center of the room folded to the floor as well, heads bowed, arms posed in graceful arcs.

Gilly burst up from the center like a geranium bloom and leaped over the other girls. "Cole! You came!" She flung an arm around his waist and gave him a brief hug. "Sorry I'm so sweaty. Ugh! Let me throw on some shorts and we'll run next door for a snow cone."

She towed him toward the entrance to the studio, grabbing a duffle bag out of a locker along the way. Stopping only to step into the blue nylon shorts she'd worn for the Enterprise tour, she continued to chatter as she led Cole outside.

"So what did you think about the dance? That was the group number for our recital. I have a solo too — Boy, I wish you could've seen it, I choreographed it myself. Maybe you can come to the recital — never mind, you'd have to sit through all the baby dancers and they take like a million years, even though they're so cute you could just eat 'em up with a spoon. Madison's dancing this year, you should see her costume."

Brows raised, Cole held open the door to the snow cone shop, letting Gilly pass through. "I wondered if you were going to keep talking until you passed out from lack of air."

She laughed. "I just missed you," she said frankly. "I haven't seen you all week."

They ordered snow cones — rainbow for Gilly and watermelon for Cole — and took them outside onto the patio to eat. Cole relished the idea of being missed, even by a teenager with the attention span of a hummingbird — which she resembled, with the flaming red hair confined in a purple bandanna and her pink leotard covered in the slippery blue shorts.

Gilly sat down, pulling her feet onto the concrete bench. She had replaced her toe shoes with red cloth China-doll slippers. "What are you smirking at?" she demanded, slurping syrup out of her cup.

"I was just thinking I should wear my sunglasses when I go anywhere with you."

She poked out her blue tongue. "So I like variety. Life's too short to be satisfied with boring."

He leaned back with one elbow on the table, savoring the sweetness of the icy treat. "There's a certain amount of truth in that, but when you're my age you learn a little caution with it. In fact—" he hesitated—"if I'd had even a grain of caution when I first met your sister, I wouldn't be in such a pickle with her now. She told you I was the one she ran off with, right?"

Gilly regarded him with bright eyes for a moment. "Yeah, and you know what? If you'd had any caution, she never would've paid any attention to you at all. Laurel doesn't like to admit it, but she admires guys with—let's just say, a strong sense of self-confidence."

Cole stared at her. "Is that right." He wasn't asking a question, because the statement rang with absolute truth. "Then why were we so obviously bad for one another?"

"Maybe the timing wasn't right." Gilly lifted her slender shoulders. "You weren't a believer then, were you? Laurel was, but even she'd tell you she was pretty immature." Gilly's delicate, piquant features grew serious. "You know about my brother Michael, don't you? What happened to him, what he did, affected the whole family."

"Laurel told me a couple of weeks ago. First I knew about it. You were, what—about eight then?"

Gilly nodded. "It sounds awful to say this, but I didn't know him well. He left home just about the time I was born, and he only came home when he was so broke he didn't have anyplace else to go. But Laurel loved him, and it ate her up that he wouldn't even try to get off the drugs."

Cole sat there with the ice and red syrup melting unnoticed in his paper cup. *Timing.*

What about now? Was it a new season? Did he and Laurel have a chance to do something about the passion that was still between them? Was it a holy thing, an attraction planted and stirred by God, or was it something the enemy wanted to use against him and her both?

He looked at Laurel's brilliantly clad little sister, whose soft expression made his throat tighten. "Gilly, will you pray for us?"

"You know I will. I have been for some time." Her black lashes swept down as her cheeks pinkened. "I've been praying for your brother too. He seems kinda lost."

"Kinda." Cole snorted. "The kid's been wandering around in la-la-land so long, he's lost the map. Keep praying. Which reminds me—I have a favor to ask, that's why I came by today."

"Whatever you want." Gilly's bright smile flashed.

"Tucker's finals are over, and I thought I'd invite him down to hang out for a week or so before he goes home. He seemed to like you ... maybe you could find a little time to spend with him?"

"I gave him my email address, but I haven't heard from him." Her lips tightened. "I don't chase boys."

"Good for you." Cole tugged on the purple bandanna, pulling it teasingly over her eyes. "You don't need to. They'll be chasing *you*, soon as you slow down long enough to get caught."

"Well"—Gilly straightened her headgear—"I personally think Laurel's all messed up. If you weren't such an *old guy*, I'd slow down for you."

He smiled. "So can I tell Tucker you'll be around?"

She shrugged. "I guess so. But he'll have to call me. Like I said, I—"

"—don't chase boys," he finished for her. "Spoken like a true southern belle. I'll tell him." He tossed the remains of his melted snow cone into a trash can. "I think your break time's over. Let me know how your audition goes."

"I will." She slurped down the rest of the syrup in her cup, which was now a nasty shade of brown, and danced back to the studio. With a wave, she disappeared through the glass door.

Timing, he said to himself. *Well, Lord, what about that?*

"'From Dauphin Island to Veto ... I love Alabama.'" Laurel grabbed the script to keep the ocean breeze from snatching it from her hand. "I don't know, Renata, it sounds like I'd vote to chuck half the state into the Gulf."

Renata rolled her eyes. "Everybody's a critic. Dauphin Island's as far south as you can go without falling in the ocean; Veto's up on the Tennessee state line—don't you get it?"

The two women stood on the public beach watching Noah Campany check lighting through his camera lens. The young sound tech/videographer had arranged to meet them here to take advantage of the soft morning light on a beautiful Gulf Shores beach.

Laurel would like to have taken advantage of a couple more hours of sleep.

She yawned. "I get it. But I can't help wondering if Derrick's releasing some of his hostility at you by writing lame copy for my TV spots." She eyed the tense figure of the PR manager, who watched the camera setup with an eagle eye. Feet planted wide, arms folded over his broad chest, Derrick wore his power sunglasses despite the still-dim light.

Renata bit her lip. "That possibility crossed my mind. I wish we had another good writer available."

"Hey, guys! We heard there was a beach party!"

Laurel looked around to find Gilly, wearing a jungle-print sarong over a modest black swimsuit, bounding toward them. Behind her, Cole and Tucker trudged through the dry white sand, each carrying a lumpy canvas bag. Cole's younger brother had hit town on Wednesday, the same day Gilly flew back from a victorious ballet school audition.

Laurel caught her sister in a hug. "How's the future brightest star in New York ballet?" She'd missed the family's welcome-home celebration due to a speaking engagement.

"A little jet-lagged, but other than that—flying high." Gilly backed away, flung out her arms, and pirouetted with more enthusiasm than grace. She kicked off her flip-flops and ran down to the water. "Wow! Look at those colors—reminds me of melted Skittles."

Tucker followed Gilly, and the two of them splashed into the foaming surf up to their knees, laughing and pushing one another like preschoolers.

Sensing Cole behind her, Laurel closed her eyes against the smear of purple-orange-and-red horizon. Was she going to feel like this the rest of her life? Longing for him but fearing what would happen if she gave in again?

Without touching her, he stood quietly at her back. The canvas bags hit the sand with a soft thud. "Thanks for letting me bring Tucker to hang out."

"He's a good kid. I don't mind." She turned her head. "Gilly's got a fairly large crush."

"Ha. She informed me if I wasn't so *old*, she'd be tripping after me."

She sighed at the smile in his voice. "Why are you doing this, Cole? Gilly doesn't understand why we don't—why I can't—" She made herself face him. "It's just going to hurt her when you go back to New York."

He looked down at her, his strong face pensive. The wind blew a tress of her hair across his mouth, and he pulled it away, rubbing it between his fingers. "What if I don't go back?"

Panic struck her. He had to leave eventually. His job was in New York. "I don't know what you're thinking. Why would you not …" She looked up into his eyes, fascinated by details of his face. The way the waking sun pulled bronze and golden flecks from his gray irises. The white scar standing out like a check mark across his tanned cheek. The gentleness in the curve of his mouth.

Oh, Father, what if I'm wrong about him? How do I know what the truth is?

Instead of answering her, he dropped her hair, the backs of his fingers brushing the lace at her neckline. "Pretty," he murmured.

"What?" She felt like a kid who'd gotten lost in a carnival fun house.

"Your outfit. Looks good on you." His eyes skimmed the sheer billowy sleeves of her white blouse and the gauzy seafoam-colored skirt that fell nearly to her bare feet. "That'll translate well to film."

She put her hands to her suddenly hot cheeks. "I hope so." Sucking in a breath, she looked around for Renata, who had wandered over to argue with Derrick. "We're supposed to be ready to film, but I hate the script."

"Let me see." He took the paper from her and scanned it. "Good night. Who wrote this? Never mind," he muttered, squatting to root through one of the bags. "I'll fix it." He found a pen, sat down on the sand, and scribbled on the back of the original script. "Here. Try this."

She read it and smiled. "Oh, Cole, this is good."

"Just don't tell anybody I wrote it, okay? I could get in trouble."

"Why? Oh. Impartiality of the press, right?"

He looked at her. "I'm having a really hard time being impartial, okay?"

She wetted her lips and swooshed a foot through the sand. "Thank you."

"You're welcome. Go film your spot, then we'll have breakfast. Gilly packed it, so it's probably chocolate cake and gummy worms. But I'll take you for pancakes later if you want."

Something in her heart took a flying leap, and her tongue fastened itself to the roof of her mouth. So she nodded and backed toward Renata, who had apparently been trying to get her attention for a couple of minutes.

"What's the matter with you, girl? Noah's standing on his head because the light's changing, and there you are lollygagging with your boyfriend. Don't tell me you're not in love with the man, it's all over your red face. Come on, stand here and look wise and judge-ly so we can take your picture, then we'll go to the studio for the voice-over—" Renata put her hands on her hips. "*What?*"

"Look at this revised script." Laurel handed it over.

As Renata perused the text, a slow smile dawned. Her narrowed eyes cut to Cole, taking pictures of Gilly and Tucker with a small digital camera. "I could ask, but I don't want to know. This'll work." She folded the paper and tucked it into her pocket. "I'll take care of the changes. Now get over there and pose before Derrick has a stroke."

Cole settled in to load photos from Matt's camera onto his computer. Pictures of Gilly riding into the water on the shoulders of his musically intense younger brother made him shake his head in amazement. After spending the day goofing off at the beach, the two of them had decided to ride go-karts at a track on the southwest side of Mobile. They had invited the "old guy" to come along, but Cole elected to spend the time ostensibly polishing a couple of articles for the *Journal*.

What he really had in mind was pulling out a set of chalk pastels he'd found on sale at an art store this week.

After making his living writing so long, he was afraid he might have forgotten the techniques of form, space, and depth. But when he began to sketch with a pink chalk stick, looking at a photo of Laurel enlarged to fit the computer screen, the image of her three-quarter profile emerged on the paper in three or four quick strokes. Pleased, he added a few lines for the curve of brow and ear. Shading in deeper colors, smearing and blending with his fingers, he became engrossed, and when his cell phone rang, he looked at the digital clock on the nightstand. Almost ten o'clock.

Stretching his cramped shoulders, he put the paper and chalks aside and flipped open the phone.

"McGaughan, what are you doing?"

It was Hogan. Cole glanced at the portrait, glowing with shades of mahogany and sienna and lustrous pinks against a brilliant Gulf sunrise. "Just killing time. What's up?"

"I need to talk to you. Come up to my room, all right?" Tension laced the usually laid-back voice.

"Sure. I'll be right there." Frowning, Cole shoved the phone in his jeans pocket and picked up his wallet. Hogan sounded jumpy as a chicken in a KFC.

He rode the elevator down and knocked on Hogan's door.

Opening it, his friend swept a pile of clothes off the chair onto the floor. "Sit down. I want you to listen to something."

Cole stayed beside the door. "If you've been bugging Laurel, I don't want to know. The thing with her old roommate was bad enough—"

Hogan, jimmying with a small cassette recorder, looked irritated. "What kind of moron do you think I am? Never mind, don't answer that." He mashed the "play" button with his thumb. "All right, don't sit, then. Just listen."

Cole instantly recognized Matt's voice, then Wallace Field's. He decided to sit down.

When the recording stopped, he stared open-mouthed at Hogan, who had moved to the curtain, twitched it open, shut it again, and started to pace the small room.

"The guy's a criminal." Cole got up and rewound the tape. "When did you record this?"

"Friday a week ago."

"And you're just now telling me about it? Man, we could've already blown this guy out of the water. What's the matter with you?"

"It took me a while to decide to do it. I'm not naturally righteous like you, McGaughan. I've got bills to pay, and this guy is gonna be one of the power-brokers. At least he could've been, until he went off the deep end. Besides, you heard him. He's crazy enough to be dangerous. He could take me out if I turn him in. *When* I turn him in." Hogan grabbed the curtain again and stared out into the parking lot as if he were Bruce Willis expecting a hit man to shoot through the window. "Maybe it's easy for you to do the right thing, but I had to think it through."

"What are you going to do with this?"

"Nothing yet. I wanted you to take it to the police. Then you'll get the exclusive story."

"Why would you do that?" Cole pinched the bridge of his nose. Field wasn't the only one to dive off the high board without his water wings.

"I've been doing a lot of thinking this week. For months I've been watching you and listening to you and testing you to see if you meant what you said. You know, about the religious stuff. And I've come to the conclusion that you really do. You're not a professional like my dad, and you don't preach at me, but it never leaves you. There's something genuine and—and—different, and I'm going after it too. My dad's gonna spaz, so don't tell him, until I figure out how it's gonna work in my sorry messed-up life, okay?"

Cole decided not to point out that he didn't even know Matt's father's name. "Okay." He could follow up on the spiritual discussion later. It was critical to get this tape to the police. "I'm assuming you've got a paper trail too. You know you'll have to be a witness, right?"

"Yeah." Matt sighed. "And I know I'll make zero *dinero* after the months of work I've put in for this ..." After a few choice words, he caught himself and grinned sheepishly. "I mean, this wretched dirtbag."

"That may be the least of your problems. You're right that Field is going to be mighty unhappy with the people responsible for ending his career. Are you ready for that?"

Matt just shrugged. "I don't know what I'm ready for, man. This is all new territory. I'm even thinking a change in career might be in order." He folded his arms, looking Cole square in the eye. "One thing I gotta say. I'm sorry for what I did to you—getting into your computer, sending that file without your permission. Those were not the acts of a friend, no matter who was paying me. I owe you more than an exclusive story, and if there was any way I could make it up to you—"

"It's already forgiven." Cole stuck out his hand.

Matt shook hands and whacked him on the arm. "If she ever forgives you, I want to be best man at the wedding."

"You got it. Now let's do some more investigation and see if we can slam Field's rear in jail."

"Mr. Goldman! How nice to see you." Laurel stood at the open front door of an upscale home in west Mobile, trying to hide her shock. The last person she would have expected to request one of her campaign yard signs was the complainant in young Marty Welch's arson hearing. She hadn't seen Mr. Goldman since a rather unsatisfactory conversation regarding Marty's fascination with fire.

She glanced at Renata, waiting in an SUV loaded with red-white-and-blue "Kincade for Chief Justice" yard signs. A team of enthusiastic volunteers was delivering them all over the city and surrounding county on this warm Sunday afternoon, as were teams in other areas of the state.

Renata gave her a thumbs-up.

Laurel hoisted the sign. "I'm sorry if I disturbed you. I may have the wrong address ..."

"No, no." Mr. Goldman, who had made his first million a few years ago selling prosthetic hips and knees, grabbed the sign, smiling. "I asked for someone to bring it by, but I wasn't expecting the judge herself. I'm a big supporter of yours, Judge Kincade."

"You are?"

"Yes, ma'am. After we talked about the kid who burned the Dumpster back of my office, I decided to see what I could do about volunteering at that group home where he stays. Took him fishing a time or two. Don't know if he'll ever straighten out, but I can sleep at night knowing I've done a little bit to solve the problem."

"Wow. That's — that's amazing. Thank you, Mr. Goldman."

"Good luck with the election. I'll be voting for you."

Laurel walked back to the SUV, mentally scratching her head. She relayed the conversation with Mr. Goldman to Renata, who laughed. "I think that's what you call turning the other cheek."

"Can you believe the way my poll numbers have taken off in the last couple of weeks? Even Brandy the Wicked has had little to say lately." Laurel relaxed in the seat. "It's such a relief, after the hits we took early on." She smiled at Renata. "You did a great job helping me recover from all that. I know good and well it wasn't Derrick or the consulting firm."

"No, it certainly wasn't." Smirking, Renata pulled over. "Let's put a few here in this corner lot." She got out of the vehicle and charged around to the back, where she began to unload signs.

Laurel got out with her hammer. "Renata, if there's something you're not telling me, I should remind you of our conversation about transparency."

"Oo-hoo. Lean on me, why don't you. Sorry, I'm not break-ing a confidence." Renata walked off and whacked one of Laurel's signs into the ground in front of a "Field for Chief Justice" sign.

"Now that's just not right! You're telling me you can't tell me ... Oh, you know what I mean." Laurel reached down to scratch a mosquito bite on her calf. "You didn't get illegal information about George Field somehow, did you? Because if you did, I'd have to turn you in, and that would be very bad—"

"Of course I didn't do anything illegal." Renata laughed. "Good grief. I'm just *protecting my source.*" She winked broadly.

"Protecting your source. You mean like a ... reporter ..." Lau-rel's stomach flipped. "*He's* been coaching you?" She clutched the sign, nearly clocking herself with it. "I should've known, after he rewrote that commercial."

"You should have known a lot of other things, Laurel." Renata took the sign from her and jammed it into the ground. "I know reporters are supposed to stay neutral, but the man is on your side. He's crazy-bonkers in love with you—you just don't want to see it. Here, give me that thing before you hurt yourself."

Laurel handed over the hammer, watched Renata drive two more signs into the weedy empty lot, then followed her like a sleep-walker back to the car. They rode back to the campaign headquar-ters in silence. Renata hummed tunelessly along with the radio, while Laurel tried to corral her spinning thoughts.

If Cole loved her, she would have to love him back.

chapter 22

Cole parked across the square from Yazoo City's white stuc-
coed courthouse, in front of a century-old storefront with
crumbling brick and dusty, gilt-lettered plate-glass windows. The
old man had summoned him. So, after sending Tucker back to Tupelo, he'd loaded his gear in the truck and prayed all the way from
Mobile to Yazoo City. For Laurel, her family, and for himself—
God, not my will but yours.

As a college wrestler he'd learned to study his opponent's
strengths and weaknesses, develop an offensive strategy going
into the match, and rely on technique to win over strength. As a
journalist he practiced the virtues of research and preparation.

As a lover he was flying on instinct.

He didn't know when it occurred to him that dead, rust-cov-
ered secrets held them all hostage. Maybe last night as he sat
alone in his hotel room, flipping through channels, missing Laurel, missing his family, missing the noisy chaos of Manhattan. The
commercial with the Gulf Shores spot breezed across the screen.
Its voiceover in Laurel's rich soft cadence almost made a song
out of the words he'd scribbled for her. He would have closed his

eyes to listen, except he couldn't take his eyes off Laurel. Kneeling against a jeweled backdrop of ocean-sky-sun, she wrote the word *justice* in the sand with her finger. The camera tightened as a wave washed the word away; then in a technical trick rolled backward to leave *Kincade* in its place.

It was a beautiful, elegant spot, and it would give her massive name recognition in the last week before the primary.

It would also take her away from him for good. Success would bring a whole new level of responsibility, because in Alabama the conservative candidate stood every chance of winning. If she won the primary, she was going to Montgomery.

He was going back to New York either way, having failed to breach the walls of her distrust and fear. He couldn't imagine what she was afraid of. Frustration nearly suffocated him.

Flicking off the TV at the end of the commercial, he'd closed his eyes. Maybe most people did that with God's love every day— flinging it back in His face, preferring the safety of the familiar over the beautiful risk of extravagant devotion. Cole had done it himself for so many years that he'd buried himself in corrosion. The sandblasting process had nearly killed him.

At least he had no pride left. Scraped and bloody, but free.

The hardest part was watching Laurel continue to protect her family's reputation, letting their shame bind her like Sleeping Beauty in an airless spiritual closet.

He crossed the street and stopped on the sidewalk, head tipped back to stare at the octagonal cupola on the courthouse's red-tile hip roof. The tower clock bonged 3:00 p.m. Cole wondered if Beowulf's stomach had knotted this way at the entrance to Grendel's lair. Shaking his head at his own nonsense, he entered an ancient lobby smelling of lemon wax and mildew and climbed a set of worn mahogany stairs to the third floor. What was the old man going to do, anyway? Pull out a dueling pistol like some Faulknerian patriarch and dispatch the enemy?

At the top he walked along the circular gallery until he came to a series of doors with gold-engraved name plates. The third one, Judge Gillian's, was propped open with a cast iron doorstop in the shape of a cat. Cole rapped on the door once with his knuckles as he entered.

A diminutive middle-aged lady with gray-streaked black hair and a set of sharp maroon fingernails was typing a document into the computer with mind-numbing speed and deafening noise. A network of crow's feet radiated from her eyes as she looked up and smiled. "Afternoon. What can I do for you, sugar?"

"I'd like to see Judge Gillian, please."

"Do you have an appointment?"

"Yes, ma'am. My name's Cole McGaughan."

The woman's mouth dropped open. "The one that—" She lowered her voice to a whisper. "—married Miss Laurel?"

Cole frowned. So the old man had blabbed. He said politely, "I prefer to discuss my business with the judge himself."

"Oh—oh, certainly. I'm sorry, I'll just ... " She picked up the phone and pushed an intercom button. "Judge, your three o'clock appointment's here." After listening for a moment, she replaced the receiver and looked up at Cole wide-eyed. "You can go in. Oh my." She patted her flat chest.

Cole thought about assuring her that he'd survived 9/11 in Manhattan and probably could handle a conversation with an eighty-year-old Mississippi judge. Instead he winked at the wide-eyed gatekeeper and knocked on Laurel's grandfather's office door.

His epitaph was going to read: "What I did for love ..."

Matt had no clear idea what his return to God was going to mean for the big picture of his life. He knew one thing, though. Somehow he had to right the damage he'd done to McGaughan.

On Wednesday afternoon he finally tracked down Laurel Kincade in her office—not an easy task, considering the fact her staff protected her as if she were Julia Roberts on vacation.

He knocked and, at her clear "Come in," stuck his head inside the sanctum. "*Hola*, Your Honor."

She looked up from a stack of files on her desk and smiled— faintly, with obvious patience. "Hello, Matt. What can I do for you?" She glanced at the paper in her hand, letting him know she was busy. He was clearly still on sufferance.

Lord save him from brilliant women. McGaughan was going to have his work cut out for him. Matt swaggered in and grabbed the only straight-back chair in the room, turning it around to straddle it backward. *Own the room, baby.*

"Okay, Laurel, here's the deal." He ignored her blink of surprise at being addressed in such a familiar way, right inside her holy of holies. "It's time you and I had a little confab, and you're going to listen to me this time. Actually, I'm going to make a phone call, and you're gonna listen while I talk to somebody else. I want you to keep quiet. Not a word. When I get done, we'll discuss options." He reached in his pocket for his cell phone. Then he pulled out an earpiece wire, which he tossed onto Laurel's desk. "Stick that in your ear."

Her mouth opened as if she wanted to argue. But after a moment she nodded and put the earpiece in.

Matt found Derrick Edes's number and dialed it.

Edes picked up after two rings. "Edes here. What's up, Hogan?"

"Field told me to check in with you today and get an update. Anything from the Castleberry woman that would be helpful?"

Laurel's eyes widened, and Matt laid a finger over his lips to caution her.

"She's quit talking to me," said Edes, disgust in his thick voice. "Won't see me anymore socially. You'll have to figure out another angle."

"I've got a perfect angle. The whole bunch hangs out in church, so I've been following them there. You should try it sometime." Matt pressed the cancel button as Laurel pulled the earpiece from her ear. "Now do you believe me?"

The attic was stuffy, dusty, and smelled of cedar and moth balls. She came up here twice a year to switch out the seasonal items in her wardrobe. Currently the sealed boxes contained fifteen or twenty sweaters in colors suitable for a fair-skinned, dark-eyed redhead; a couple of wool blazers in black and gray; and an ankle-length cashmere coat that saw duty only during the month of February.

On this rainy Wednesday afternoon, fashion storage was the last thing on Laurel's mind. She sat cross-legged on the rough attic floor, elbows on the knees of her jeans and a computer print-out pressed to her face. For three days she'd been wrestling with the realization that she had been wrong. Not just wrong—she'd been monumentally off, on so many levels she might never find her way back.

Even by rearranging her docket to accommodate campaign functions, her schedule in the past few weeks had been so crazy she'd had to sneak off in the middle of the day just to grab thirty minutes alone. Maybe she had a chance to attain a lifetime career goal, and maybe she had a great family and a good church and a truckload of friends. But Matt Hogan and the FTD florist website had confirmed it: Laurel Kincade sucked eggs in the wisdom department.

She let herself look at the list again.

Pink rose … Please believe me.

Gladiola, flower of the Gladiators (*how appropriate*) … Give me a break, I'm really sincere.

Purple gilly flower … You'll always be beautiful to me.

Bluebell … Humility, everlasting love.

Purple Hyacinth … Please forgive me.

Blue forget-me-not … Faithful love, undying hope.

Oh, Cole. She'd held a bouquet of First Corinthians Thirteen in her hand and opted to give it away. Weren't you noble, Laurel Josephine—blessing the nursing home with your lover's gift, out of anger?

At least she'd kept the card, though heaven only knew why. At the time she'd been so upset, so hurt, she'd felt like setting it up for target practice and having at it with the slingshot Fafa gave her for her third birthday. But something made her stick the card in the drawer of her silverware hutch.

She looked again at Cole's gentle words. *Please call me.*

Maybe she would find the courage to do that. But first she had to confront the past. Acknowledge that her pride and arrogance and lying had been every bit as sinful as Cole's profligacy. That grief was no excuse for running away from God and flinging herself into self-indulgent forgetfulness.

She laid the card on the floor with the floral list and opened the shoebox she'd removed from Grandma Kincade's cedar chest—her hope chest.

As a little girl she'd played in the chest, begging Grandma to let her try on the old-fashioned calico sunbonnets passed down through generations of Kincade women, to handle the antique China-head doll and the miniature flatiron. As the eldest granddaughter on that side of the family, the chest had come into her possession when she graduated from high school. It had seemed the only safe place for the shoebox, after Fafa took care of the details of the annulment.

Hope chest. Could there be hope for her life, with or without Cole? Because of the way she'd repeatedly pushed him away, nothing was certain. The sundering of their relationship had been as violently passionate and sudden as their coming together. Even now she could hardly bear to think about the look on Cole's face when she'd yanked on her clothes and slammed out of that hotel room in New Orleans.

Blinking against tears, she unlocked the chest and lifted the lid. She had to dig under a pile of quilts and heirloom dresses to get to the box. Her mother's bridal veil, sealed in plastic, nearly undid her. She was to have worn it. The French Quarter wedding to Cole had been a mockery. She pushed the veil aside and removed the memorabilia of her one night with Cole. Her husband, her first and only lover.

The rubber band holding the lid on crumbled when she touched it. She laid it on the floor, cradling the box in her lap. The red roses were on top, dried to wrinkled black crepe paper, their spicy odor still fresh. Swallowing against the tightness of her throat, she took them out, then lifted out a dusty Pat O'Brien's hurricane glass. Inside the glass was a crushed napkin and a cigar band, pleated and taped to fit her finger.

Why in the world she'd kept this stuff . . . Almost involuntarily the ring went on her finger. Left hand, ring finger.

Oh, Lord, how could something I did in such rage against you mean so much to me now?

She began to cry, hot tears turning into hard sobs that shook her body.

I'm so sorry, sorry, sorry. I've told you this so many times, Lord, and I know you forgave me, but I don't feel forgiven.

Are you going to let Cole go?

The thought shocked her, as if she'd plugged a wet finger into an outlet.

"What do you mean, Lord?" she whispered into her knees. "How can I let him go when he's not mine anymore? Never really was?"

Pray for him, but let me deal with him, as I deal with you. He's mine. Stop expecting him to be perfect. Stop expecting yourself to be perfect. You're both jars of clay. My power is made perfect in weakness.

Familiar phrases lay upon her mind like cool compresses, soothing the frustration and guilt. Gradually she relaxed until her cheek rested on one knee, hands clasped loosely at her ankles. The tears became damp sniffles and then a long sigh. She could feel the paper band on her finger, slick and stiff with age. She didn't have the right to wear it. She'd pushed Cole away.

Feeling about a hundred and two years old, she sat up and smeared the wetness off her face with the hem of her T-shirt. She couldn't help smiling a little at the uncharacteristic gesture. *Cole, how you've changed me in so many ways.*

Sighing, she started to remove the cigar band. Then stopped and looked at it, rubbing the back of it with her thumb.

Cheap as it was, it represented the mystery of marriage. Cole was still free, and so was she. Once upon a time they had given themselves to one another; therefore, according to God's Word they were still one flesh. Or should be. The thought made her warm to the core.

She picked up the card and touched the dried ink of Cole's signature. *Please call me.*

Smiling, she repacked the cedar chest, refolding the clothes and bonnets, tucking the doll and flatiron under the veil with haphazard haste.

In ten minutes she was in the car headed toward the Holiday Inn.

Judge Pete Gillian got up from his desk to shake Cole's hand. Awkward history floated like dust motes in the room, reminding Cole that he was on enemy turf. This was the man who had ended his marriage before it had a chance to get started.

"How are you, sir?" Cole took the upholstered chair in front of the desk. He made himself relax, crossing an ankle over the opposite knee.

"Better than I deserve." Laurel's grandfather speared Cole with an eagle stare perfected during the course of more than forty years on the bench. "Appreciate you coming all the way up here to see me. Can't easily get away. The wife keeps telling me to retire, but what would I do sitting home with her, twiddling my thumbs all day?"

That, Cole presumed, was a rhetorical question. "No problem. I had a couple of things I wanted to ask you too, and they wouldn't play well over the phone."

The judge raised his white brows. "That right? Well, ask away. Let's clear the air."

Cole nodded. "All right. To start with, I'd like to know if you really didn't recognize me or my name when we met back in November. Or was that some kind of game you were playing with Laurel and me?"

The old gentleman's face flushed. "I do not play games, young man. Of course I knew the name, but clearly Laurel hadn't told anyone else. She wanted that insane marriage annulled, so I filed the papers for her. I was ready to come after you with the proverbial shotgun, but she didn't want you harassed in any way. In fact, she asked me not to delve into your background or your family, and would have kept your name from me if she could have." The judge picked up a heavy Mont Blanc pen lying on his blotter and pointed it at Cole. "Do you have any idea what was going on in our family at the time?"

"Yes, sir." Cole kept his voice even. He didn't appreciate the feeling of being hauled into the principal's office—a scenario with which he was all too familiar—but respect for age was all but bred into his DNA. "I know now Laurel had just found out her brother's death was a suicide. If I'd known that at the time, I wouldn't have—" He stopped, looking down. Would the twenty-one-year-old Cole really have done anything different? "I knew Laurel wasn't acting herself, but she never told me what was going on at home."

"And you didn't have the decency to *ask* her what was the matter?" Judge Gillian's face was splotchy with outrage.

Cole felt his own face heat. Man, he was getting tired of apologizing for his BC behavior. "Of course I asked her. She just said she'd had a really bad day and wanted to forget about it for a while. So I set out to show her a good time. A bunch of us were in New Orleans for Mardi Gras, and I'd run into Laurel at Pat O'Brien's. There was a huge crowd there, people dancing and drinking and cutting up, and, well, we both got pretty well soused. I'd never seen Laurel drunk before. She was so funny, and I could tell she liked me, but she'd never let herself—well, let's just say this was the first time she let me get within—" Cole broke off again. He couldn't have said why he was blurting all this out to an old man who had every reason to hate his guts. Private stuff he'd never told anybody. He grabbed the back of his neck and looked away. "I'd been in love with her for a long time, sir. As much as I was capable of loving anybody but myself. That wedding would never have happened if we hadn't both been drunk. But when I woke up the next morning sober, I was really happy to see Laurel there."

"She told me you took a call from a girlfriend that morning." Judge Gillian glowered.

Cole shook his head. "Girlfriend? I didn't talk to any—" Memory surfaced. There had been a phone call at the crack of dawn, waking both him and Laurel. He'd been so startled he'd stumbled out of bed, found his cell phone in his pants pocket, and answered it. "It was my stepmother. She'd had a fight with my dad, and she wanted me to talk to him about giving her some more money."

The old man glared at him. "I believe you're telling the truth. But your subsequent behavior was inexcusable. I kept an eye on you, boy. I helped your father wash that DUI clean. I didn't want any smear connected to Laurel, if your relationship to her became known."

Cole felt his mouth drop open. "*You* did that?"

"I most certainly did," the judge snapped. "And it's a good thing I did, given the discovery I made not two weeks ago."

Apprehension, cold and hard, clutched Cole's stomach. "Discovery?"

"Yes. But first—" Judge Gillian rolled the pen between his palms, an uncharacteristically agitated gesture. "I want to know if you still love my granddaughter."

Cole had a strong inclination to tell the old man to take a hike. He'd had enough of being interrogated like some juvenile offender. Something in the judge's eagle stare, however, kept him in his seat. "I love her more than life," he said steadily.

Judge Gillian tossed the pen onto the desk and pulled at his lower lip. "Then you've got your work cut out for you, boy. The order for the annulment papers was filed without my signature. You and Laurel are still married."

"I have no idea where he went."

Laurel stared at Matt Hogan in dismay. "Are you sure? Think, Matt. He wouldn't leave town without telling you, would he?"

They were seated in the hotel lobby, Matt restlessly bouncing a leg as he shook his head. "Don't know, Laurel. All he said was he had an appointment in Mississippi and he'd be back in a day or two. Took Tucker with him." Hogan shrugged. "I'm sorry. Wish I could tell you what you want to know." He brightened. "You want to see my kitten before you go?"

A thrill not unlike winning a wrestling tournament with a desperation takedown move in the last seconds of a match shot through Cole as he stood in line at Delta gate A-3, waiting to hand over his boarding pass. The Jackson International Airport on Wednesday night hummed like a dirt-dobber nest, but he hardly noticed. His last article for the *Journal* was in the can and on its way to Aaron Zorick. He'd polished it while he waited for his flight to be called, and emailed it with utter satisfaction in a job well done.

Field was going to be toast, thanks to the paper trail Hogan had handed over. Edes would go down with him.

But his elation had nothing to do with a certain career homerun.

The judge had informed him he'd looked up the annulment and contract when Cole showed up in March; otherwise nobody would ever have known the signature was missing on the annulment. Cole would never have known Laurel belonged to him—at least in the eyes of God and Louisiana law.

All he had to do was get her to leave it that way. This time he wasn't going to push or shove or demand his rights. He was going to leave the whole situation in the hands of his Father, who loved Laurel more than Cole himself did. Which he could hardly comprehend, but there it was.

Therefore he handed his boarding pass to a lady in a blue uniform, watched her zip it through the card reader, and walked down the jetway headed to Church Street, NYC. Hogan would say he was crazy. But Matt didn't know the Lord well enough yet to understand that peace came from taking your hands off a situation and resting.

God had more than once demanded Cole give his love for Laurel back to Him. He wasn't about to disobey—even when it looked like time to snatch and run.

chapter 23

Laurel got up at five, brain blurred with the cobwebby residue of a sleepless night. Shooing Charles Wallace back inside, she went out, still dressed in her gown and robe, to get the newspaper. She sat down on the front step with the plastic-wrapped bundle in her hand. No flowers this time. Just a misty late-spring morning, birds singing in the bushes and the rising sun waking sparkles of dew on the grass. Mrs. Dolmier across the street opened the door to let her dachshund out, and he went sniffing around the side of the house. A couple of streets over, a car passed with a quiet shooshing sound.

Normal, everyday sights and sounds, when nothing in her life would be normal again.

Cole was gone. Matt Hogan didn't know where he was. So she had ultimately pushed him away, so hard and so often that he took her at her word. It wasn't like him to leave without saying good-bye. Cole had always been a man of action and a man of words. Whatever he wanted, he went for with the drive of a bulldozer.

Ergo, he did not want Laurel anymore.

She'd thought about calling him last night, but every time her thumb rested on the "dial" button, an imaginary conversation took place in her head. *Hi, Cole, this is Laurel. Hey, I've changed my mind. I'd like you to choose me again.*

Her skin crawled. Apologizing in person was one thing, but stumbling out words through a cellular connection, when he might be anywhere ... where people could overhear ... It didn't bear thinking about.

Maybe he'd come back. Maybe he'd gone home to Mississippi, like Matt suggested. Maybe she had lost him forever.

Until she knew for sure, she had to go on with her life.

She opened the paper to scan the headlines before heading inside for some peanut butter toast. On the front page, Cole's byline jumped out at her under a screaming two-inch head-line: "Mobile DA Wallace Field Caught in Underhanded Political Maneuverings."

Heartbeat speeding, she read the article through, then read it again with her hand over her mouth. "Cole ..." she whispered.

Well, he'd done it. Cole sat at his little kitchen table with the newspaper open as he slugged down a glass of milk with a couple of Twinkies. The article ought to send Field's poll numbers into the basement, simultaneously boosting Laurel's through the roof.

Truth. Killer or healer, depending on where your heart was.

He tried to picture Laurel waking up and reading his words. He hoped she was pleased. Maybe it would make up for the damage done by the other article. Although it had been truth as well, the timing had sure stunk.

Wadding up the wrapper from his breakfast, he left the newspaper open on the table and got up to feed the fish. Mrs. Lee had taken good care of them, even Bilbo, who drifted fat and sassy around the rocks at the bottom of the tank. He couldn't help thinking wistfully of Rebel, bounding into the Theissens' pond with an almighty splash, barking playfully at the children.

One pet's as good as another, he told himself, whacking the punching bag as he went to the bedroom to get dressed for work.

He had to remember to go by and see Mr. Zorick first thing. Wanting to keep his options open, he hadn't bothered to let the editor know he was back in town. The assignment being what it was, he could've written from home today. But the idea of being stuck in this apartment all day was about as appealing as eating paste. No, much better to go on to the office, where there'd be distractions to keep him from thinking about Laurel, wishing he could hear her laugh, wondering what she was doing ...

He stood in the open closet door, drifting for a minute, picturing her in a sober black robe. It would cover up one of those feminine, gauzy blouses she loved, and that over something lacy, which would in turn cover up—

He slapped the door with the flat of his hand and looked up. "Lord, this ain't gonna do," he said aloud. "You've got to redirect me."

His gaze snagged on the stack of shoeboxes on the top shelf. They were full of letters and photos from high school and college. Mom always laughed at what a sentimental packrat he was about stuff like that. The one on the bottom ... He reached up and yanked it out, carrying it over to the bed. He sank down and pulled off the lid.

The marriage license was on top. His signature and Laurel's, both of them shaky because they'd been laughing so hard, kissing every few seconds, drunk more with desire than alcohol. But, God, he wondered, what made a marriage? Was it this piece of paper, or was it the vows themselves, or was it the consummation that followed? Maybe it was none of those things. Maybe it was the blessing of commitment before friends and family and God himself—all of which he and Laurel had deprived themselves.

He laid the license on the bed and took out the tall hurricane glass. At some point he'd stuffed it with balled-up plastic K-Mart bags to keep it from breaking. It was marked with fingerprints around the base, and a faint lipstick print was still on the rim. Blinking rapidly, he set the glass on the floor and found the brown-and-gold paper ring. She'd put it on his finger, giggling because it was so ugly, yet exactly like hers. They'd actually smoked the cigars in the middle of the night, sitting up in bed like a couple of morons—only Laurel's had made her violently ill, and he'd had to hold her hair while she leaned over the toilet. Then he'd watched her brush her teeth and kissed her until she forgot she was sick.

Now he *was* crying, and he couldn't stop because he wanted so badly to go back and undo every stupid selfish choice that took him away from Laurel.

"Father, what am I going to do? You've got to help me."

Peace. Be still. He heard the words as if they'd been spoken aloud. Dragging in a breath, he pressed the heels of his hands to his eyes. *Peace. Be still.*

Okay, so he had a choice. Trust or doubt. He'd faced this decision when it came to the Twelve Steps that unbound him from alcoholism. Delivered then, delivered daily, he could be set free now too.

He got on his knees, pressed his face into the mattress, and poured out his needy heart. Gradually rest came.

On the last Saturday of May, hundreds of supporters of Kincade for Chief Justice turned out for a barbeque rally in Eight Mile, Alabama's Chickasabogue Park. Marshmallow clouds drifted in a brilliant blue sky above emerald-green grass, and victory, as sweet as the breeze off the river, floated in the air.

The guest of honor was playing horseshoes with a gaggle of children when her campaign manager blew into the microphone set up on the covered platform for the speeches.

"Excuse me, folks! I have an important announcement." Renata tapped on the mike, making it squeal. "Yo! Y'all listen up!"

Gradually the noise of conversation and children's shrieks and laughter died down. Every gaze focused on Renata. Her beaming white smile eclipsed even her eye-catching white crop pants, red-striped shirt, and high-heeled jeweled sandals.

"Yeah, thanks." Renata nodded, setting her large, flashing earrings to swaying. "I'd like for Judge Kincade to come to the platform for a minute."

Laurel shook her head. Her speech was scheduled for later, after the meal.

Renata laughed. "Quit giving me the evil eye, Judge. I know this is out of order, but I just found out some awfully good news, and I need you up here."

Bewildered, Laurel mounted the shallow steps at the end of the platform. "What's going on?" she whispered, putting a hand over the mike.

Renata moved her hand. "I want everybody to plan to be home Monday night at seven, with your TV tuned to MSNBC. Our very own Judge Laurel's gonna be interviewed on *Hardball*!"

After a collective gasp from the crowd, wild whoops and cheers erupted, enveloping Laurel, adding to her shock. "That's national television," she said stupidly, gaping at Renata. "How'd you do that?"

Renata backed away from the mike. "I didn't do anything. Apparently Chris Matthews has been following the articles in the

Journal. He thinks you're smart and gorgeous, and he wants to meet you."

"Oh my goodness, that's in two days. How am I going to get ready that fast?"

"Worry about that later," Renata muttered. "Right now you need to say something inspiring to your people here."

"Oh, yeah." Laurel shook her head and focused. She brought the microphone to her mouth. "I'm so honored by your encouragement and support ..."

Thirty minutes later she was enveloped by her family in a group hug. "Way to go, Lolly!" Gilly squealed. "Can I go to New York with you?"

"I don't know, Gil, I think these interviews are done from a local affiliate station—"

"No, you weren't listening." Hands in the air, Renata did a little shimmy. "They want you to come there. You get an all-expenses paid trip for two."

"Oh, please, me me me!" Gilly pogo-ed on her toes.

"We'll see." Dazed, Laurel met her father's smiling eyes. "Daddy, I'm going to New York."

Cole was sitting in a sports bistro, having lunch with a couple of buddies from the paper, when an MSNBC commercial flashed on the TV screen across the room. His burger went down the wrong way.

"McGaughan, are you all right?" Gleeson pounded him on the back, nearly dislodging Cole's lungs as he tried to cough up the bite of burger.

"I'm—okay," he gasped, wiping his streaming eyes, "except I'm having hallucinations." He found his water glass, drank it all, and cleared his throat. "Did anybody hear who Chris Matthews's guest is tonight?"

Gleeson squinted at him. "Some lady judge from Alabama. Kendall or Kincade or something like that. Running for state supreme court chief justice. Why?"

Cole didn't answer. His heart was racing like a Corvette with a full tank of gas. Laurel was in New York. Laurel. In New York. Tonight. He could almost hear the Lord saying *green light*.

He looked at Gleeson. "You guys know anybody who works on the *Hardball* set?"

Laurel had been to New York with her family a couple of times on vacation, but this was different. Nerve-racking for more reasons than one. The anticipation of national television exposure shook her to the core for sure. But awareness that somewhere in the city Cole McGaughan would be breathing the same air sent her into a state of permanent gooseflesh.

She wound up taking Gilly along because her little sister loved the city and already knew it like the back of her hand. They flew into LaGuardia on Sunday, and the show put them up in a Hilton close to its Manhattan studio. Laurel and Gilly got up early Monday morning, dressed for shopping, and found breakfast in a bakery on the corner down from the hotel.

"So what are you going to wear on the show tonight?" Gilly wiped a chocolate milk mustache off her upper lip.

Laurel grinned. "I'm thinking we'd better check out Nordstrom for the answer to that question."

"You are a woman after my own heart."

So they shopped to their hearts' content, and came back to the hotel around two that afternoon loaded with packages.

Hands on hips, Gilly surveyed the outfit lying on the bed in splendor. "You are gonna be so hot in this."

Laurel laughed. "You mean mature and respectable and election-worthy."

"No. I mean hot." Gilly dusted her hands in satisfaction. "He should see you in this."

Laurel didn't have to ask who she meant. Her sister had a terminal case of hero-worship for Cole McGaughan. "Gilly."

"I mean it. I'm going to call him and tell him we're here. He'd take us to dinner—"

"You pick up that phone and I'm locking you in a closet." Laurel leveled a stern look at Gilly. "*I* mean it."

"Oh, all right. But I think you're taking this whole 'girls don't call boys' thing way too seriously."

Laurel let the makeup artist give her a coat of sheer bronzer that diminished the glare of the lights on her fair skin. When she looked at her reflection in the dressing room mirror she hardly recognized herself. Good grief, she almost looked like a movie starlet. She tugged at the scoop neckline of the blouse she'd let Gilly talk her into buying, wondering if it was just a tad risqué. Nothing inappropriate showed, but maybe she should have gone for a turtleneck.

Too late now. A production assistant had stuck her head in the door and told her she had five minutes and somebody would come to get her. Gilly had a seat in the studio booth, and she knew all her family, friends, and supporters in Alabama would be watching. Fafa and Gran too. *Oh, help.* Her heart was about to drum out of her chest, and she could see red splotches start to work their way up her throat. Definitely should have bought a turtleneck.

She took a breath and had the presence of mind to begin praying. She thought of Jamika flinging out an arm and proclaiming, "What time I am *afraid*, I will trust in *thee*." A smile crept into her heart and across her lips. She repeated the verse aloud and felt better. "Thanks, God," she added.

Then she remembered standing in the Port City Productions studio hallway with Cole. The way he'd touched her shoulder, calming her, telling her to explain in a couple of sentences why she wanted the job. *Go get 'em, princess*, he'd said with that crooked smile, leaving her feeling protected and encouraged.

Lord, why couldn't I see him the way he was? All I could see was my embarrassment and shame.

That was the whole problem, she saw now. Focusing on herself.

So don't do that anymore. Think about how you're going to share, think about the needs of others.

"Judge Kincade?" The assistant was back in the doorway. "We're ready for you, if you'll follow me."

She followed the young woman through a maze of hallways into a small studio. The studio crew was talking quietly, cameras moving, lights being raised and lowered, directors giving instructions over headsets. It reminded her very much of opening night at the Playhouse.

Relaxing, she followed the assistant to an oddly ugly desk where she instantly recognized Chris Matthews being fitted with a wireless microphone and earpiece. He smiled and shook hands. "Welcome to New York, Judge Kincade. Thank you for coming."

"I'm honored to be invited."

"Please sit there, and take it easy. Okay?"

Laurel nodded.

"I'll ask the questions, and you be prepared for me to take off on your answers. The appeal of this show is my digging into topics not necessarily covered elsewhere."

Laurel nodded again. "I understand." She smiled. "You don't scare me."

Matthews laughed. "I figured. That's why I invited you." Apparently someone spoke into his earpiece; his eyebrows rose, and he winked at Laurel. "Showtime."

The familiar theme music cued, the crew quieted, and lights glared in Laurel's face. A red-eyed camera zoomed in on her as she was introduced. She pretended to be comfortable, when she inwardly felt like jumping out of her skin. *Lord, Lord, rescue me. I'm out of my depth.*

Go get 'em, princess, she heard in her ear, and this time it wasn't Cole. She felt the Lord's presence in a more powerful way than she'd ever experienced.

Chris Matthews addressed her with his trademark boyish grin, and she responded with a heartfelt smile of her own. The Lord was on her side. Who could be against her?

Ten minutes later she found out.

"So, Judge Kincade, I've been following your campaign, and you're running on a strong Christian family values platform. But according to an article published this spring in the *New York Daily Journal*, you had to come clean about some indiscretions of your own. What was that all about?"

Laurel clenched her hands but kept her shoulders and face relaxed. "It was about exactly what you said—youthful mistakes. I never claimed to be perfect."

"So all that about the trip to Mardi Gras and a three-day marriage was true?"

"Of course it's true. I never denied it."

"Your response to it has been late in the game." Matthews's challenging expression held a hint of curiosity. "Like you were forced into owning up."

Laurel bit her lip. "I realize how it sounds," she said quietly. "I've thought about it a lot over the last few weeks. This won't be particularly good television," she smiled faintly, "but I actually agree with you."

Matthews laughed, caught off guard. "What do you mean?"

"I want to go on record as admitting that keeping the facts about my elopement and annulment from my family was the wrong thing to do. My motive for doing so was shame and embarrassment, which I avoided for a time ... but I've paid for it in spades. I never healed from the emotional scars of that whole catastrophe, because I had to hide them. The only one who knew was my grandfather, and he lives too far away to be the counselor I needed." She tilted her head. "Mr. Matthews, are you familiar with a verse in the Bible that says 'The truth will make you free'?"

Matthews nodded his white-blond head. "I'm a good Catholic. I'm familiar."

"Then you know what it means. Since that story released, I've had opportunities to counsel young people in danger of falling into the same emotional trap I did. And believe me when I say, a pedestal is a rickety place to sit. It's a lot safer on the ground."

"I have to say I admire your candor."

"Thank you. I want to make it clear that when I sit on a judicial bench, it's not with the idea that I've never failed or made mistakes or had embarrassments of my own. It's with a keen awareness that but for the grace of God, there go I. Each of us is bound by the laws of our own country and state. If I step outside the law, I'm subject to its penalties, like anyone else. What qualifies me for the bench is not personal perfection, but training in the law, God-given perceptive abilities and wisdom, and willingness to sacrifice my time and resources for others."

Matthews looked like he would interrupt, but Laurel was on a roll. She held up a hand.

"There's one more thing I want to say. At first I was extremely angry with the reporter who broke that story, but I've lately come to see that he did me a great favor in forcing me to face my weaknesses. Pride is a terrible fault, Mr. Matthews, a deadly sin if you will. As is lying. Those two things cost me a relationship that was very dear to me." She cleared her throat against a wad of tears that had collected. "I'd do some things very differently if I had the chance."

The host held Laurel's eyes for a moment, then looked into the camera. "We have to go to commercial break right now, but when we come back, I have some more questions for this lovely and surprisingly humble southern judge, Laurel Kincade from Mobile, Alabama. Stay tuned, we'll be right back."

Cole had to get to Laurel. Had to let her know he was there, rooting for her, praying for her. He had no idea what he'd say to her beyond that. No idea either if the "relationship that was dear to me" meant him or someone else. Frankly he didn't care. But he couldn't let her face another barrage of questions without telling her how much he loved her, how sorry he was to have left her alone the last two weeks. It had obviously been hard on her. Something about her was different.

He spotted Gilly up in the control booth, watched her eyes widen. She put a hand over her open mouth. She waved wildly, and he gave her a wink and a thumbs up as he strode toward a female production assistant.

The young woman turned to block the passage of this crazy guy who seemed prepared to jump over her to get to Chris Matthews. "I'm sorry, sir, but you're not allowed on the set."

"I know. I need to get a note to Mr. Matthews."

She frowned. "I don't think—"

"He'll want to see this. Look." He handed her the note he'd scribbled on the back of a subway ticket he'd had in his pocket.

The young woman's eyebrows disappeared into her bangs. "Holy—Is this for real?"

"Yes, ma'am. Here's proof." He showed her another note he'd been carrying around in his wallet for five long days, waiting for the okay to use it. *Green light.*

The assistant deliberated for all of two seconds before she took Cole's subway note and bolted for her producer. Unnoticed, Cole followed.

He got close enough to the set that he could see Laurel check her face in a little mirror in her skirt pocket. She looked beautiful as always, though they'd put too much makeup on her. She looked like a beach bunny. He smiled, wishing he could take her hand and tell her everything would be okay. He'd never heard such beautiful words as that confession in front of millions of people. If she'd been lovely before, the new inner layer of humility gave her a look that could only be described as luminous.

He edged closer to the lighted stage area. And then she saw him, recognized him. She froze, wide-eyed, looking as if she might get up.

But just then, the producer handed Cole's note to Chris Matthews, and he watched the two men confer. Reading lips, he saw Matthews ask if it was verified. The producer nodded. With a quick glance at Laurel, Matthews said something like, "Let's go with it."

The lights came back up and cameras started rolling.

"Welcome back to *Hardball.* I'm Chris Matthews and we have as our guest tonight conservative candidate for the Alabama Supreme Court, Judge Laurel Kincade. Judge Kincade, if elected you would be the first woman to serve as chief justice of your state's highest court. I'm interested in your take on how women affect the direction of our appellate courts. Do you think you'll have more influence over issues like abortion rights than a male justice would?"

Cole watched Laurel relax. She was used to this line of questioning, and had developed a series of answers that neither undermined her personal morals nor pigeonholed her where she didn't want to go. Matthews probed and pushed her, but she didn't back down.

But she did keep an eye on the shadow where Cole stood, behind a camera. He enjoyed watching her fence with the hardnosed TV journalist. She was doing great, and he almost thought Matthews would ignore the opportunity presented by the note in his hand.

One minute left to the end of the segment, and Matthews pulled the trigger. "Judge Kincade, you've been such a good sport about answering my questions, but I have just one more, if you don't mind, before we go."

Laurel, patently off-guard, cast a quizzical look in Cole's direction, though there was no way she could see him. "Sure, I guess so."

"Thanks." Matthews gave her an insouciant, disarming grin. "What would you say if you found out there was a technical flaw in your annulment, and you're actually still married?"

Why? Why did you do that in front of all those people?" Laurel pulled the earpiece out of her ear and dropped it with the microphone onto Chris Matthews's desk. Giving the smirking host a stunned glare, she walked toward the stage-left camera. "How could you, Cole McGaughan? And stop laughing. It's not funny!"

Thank God that awful show was over. She'd actually begun to enjoy herself until she spotted Cole, lurking behind the camera like a dinosaur trying to hide behind an ostrich. She was going to kill him.

But first she was going to kiss his brains out. She flung herself at him, standing on tiptoe to haul his head down, and caught his mouth with hers, open and desperate. He picked her up so that she could reach him more easily, accommodating her, pressing her close with his arms tight around her waist. She kissed him until her lips started to hurt, then pulled away with a loud smack that would have been embarrassing if he hadn't started in on her neck, making her forget everything except how much she loved him and had missed him.

"Would you two get a room?" Gilly's voice came from somewhere below, and Laurel grabbed enough composure to peer down at her little sister through a fog of passion.

Cole dropped Laurel instantly, and she staggered against him. "Sorry, squirt," Cole said in a blurry tone of voice. "Got carried away there."

"Is it true?" Gilly demanded. "Are you still married? Because if you are, I protest, because I wanted to wear a bridesmaid dress with one of those flower tiara thingies and have Tucker for an escort, and it would totally be unfair not to have a wedding."

"We are," Cole said, cupping Laurel's face and looking at her with an expression that turned her knees to Jell-O. "But we're going to renew our vows in front of every Kincade and Gillian and McGaughan in Alabama and Mississippi." He tore his gaze away long enough to glance at Gilly. "You can wear a flower tiara if you want to, but I doubt you're going to get Tucker in a tux."

Gilly folded her arms and looked smug. "You leave him to me."

"Gilly said we should get a room," said Cole, planting a line of kisses along Laurel's nose. "I think that's not a bad idea."

Laurel sucked in the breath which her husband had managed to knock out of her repeatedly over the course of the last hour. It was midnight, and Gilly was in the bedroom of the suite asleep. Cole had stayed for, as he put it, "denouement." Denouement had rapidly turned into seduction. Not that Laurel was entirely opposed. But she felt some explanation was in order.

"We'll get a room after we're married in a church in front of our friends and family. I want to wear my mother's bridal veil."

"You Kincade women and your headgear," Cole grumbled. But he stroked her face with the backs of his fingers, smiling. "I love you, Laurel."

"Oh, Cole." She took his fingers and kissed them, eyes blurred with tears. "How could I have treated you so badly? How could I not have believed you didn't send that article?"

"Don't go too easy on me. I did write it, after all, with the intention of sending it."

"I know, but ..." Laurel looked up at him, trying to show him with her eyes how much she regretted the damage they'd done one another. "We're going to have to start over, aren't we?"

"Well, it's more a matter of taking up where we left off. We were beginning to get along pretty well before my friend Matt decided to 'help.'"

"Cole, listen to me. No, I mean it," she added when he seemed inclined to explore the curve of her ear with his lips. She took his face in her hands. "I meant what I said when I told Chris Matthews I was glad the article came out with the truth. It forced me to be honest with myself, and it made me listen to God about some things I was trying to hide from him too."

"What? The fact that you're the most gorgeous human being he ever created, and that I'm going to have a very hard time keeping my hands off you until you've got that veil on your head?"

She sighed and let him kiss her. "You're impossible."

"No, I'm in love, and I had to wait five whole days to get the green light. It was the longest five days of my life."

"What are you talking about?"

"Never mind. But hearing you say you'd lost a relationship that was very dear to you was music to my ears."

"Speaking of music, will you play your banjo for me in the wedding?"

"I'll play the kazoo if it'll make it happen faster."

She laughed and kissed him.

On the first Tuesday of November, Cole whisked Judge Laurel Kincade McGaughan out a back door of the Battlehouse Hotel Ballroom and into a waiting limousine. In the company of family, friends, and supporters, they had spent the last three hours celebrating her election as the new Alabama Supreme Court chief justice. Now it was after midnight, and they were headed home to Charles Wallace and an orphaned mixed-breed puppy named Colonel.

"Well, Justice McGaughan, are you ready to move to Montgomery?" He settled Laurel close, and she wrapped her arms around his waist.

"Yes, but I'm glad we're keeping the house here. I'll want to come home a lot." She rubbed her cheek against the lapel of his suit. "It's a good thing you have a flexible job that you can take with you wherever you go."

"As if I'd let my wife go off without me." His *wife*. That was still peculiar, even after three months.

He looked down at the thick gold band on his ring finger. She'd tried for sentimentality and asked if he wanted to use the cigar bands for the ceremony. Laughing, he told her he wanted something a little more permanent. So the paper bands stayed in Laurel's hope chest, and they visited a friend of the family who happened to be a jeweler.

Cole touched Laurel's engagement ring, a one-carat diamond solitaire with a matching wedding band like his. He still couldn't get over the fact that it told the world she belonged to him.

The renewal of their vows had taken place on the first Saturday of September. Wade officiated over the sweet, simple ceremony, with Tucker playing guitar as Laurel came down the aisle. Gilly and Mary Layne served as maid and matron of honor, Hogan as best man, and Madison as flower girl. Neither kazoo nor banjo made an appearnance that day, but Cole later gave Laurel a private honeymoon concert that had her crying with laughter.

She was smiling now. "Was it weird not being in the press corps tonight?"

"A little. But standing next to you, watching you shine, made up for it."

He brushed a thumb across her cheek and smiled. Yeah, it was hard being married to such a brilliant, beautiful, godly woman, but he'd suck it up and survive somehow.

Read the first chapter of Elizabeth White's next book: *Controlling Interest*

Coming in 2008!

Natalie Tubberville had one thing on her mind as she whipped her ice-blue Miata up the ramp to the Memphis International Airport terminal. Well, three things. A Big Mac, supersize fries, and a chocolate shake. Chasing down details for Dad's oil-rich Pakistani clients since five a.m., she hadn't stopped to breathe, much less satisfy her howling stomach.

Screeching into a parking space, she shoved the gear shift into park and hopped out of the car. She glanced at her Swatch watch. Tweetie Bird pointed to ten minutes of five. Yasmine Patel, a mail-order bride for some Pakistani computer guru, deserved a warm welcome, and Natalie hated to make her wait. Wasn't Yasmine's fault her dad had put a twist on Eddie Tubberville's arm, thereby hijacking a good chunk of Natalie's vacation.

Wonder what a Pakistani girl would look like. Did they wear the hookahs you always saw in the movies? Wait, *hookah* didn't sound right. Come to think of it, that was a pipe. The caterpillar in *Alice in Wonderland* smoked a hookah. Bookah, then. No, *burka*. Something like that. She should have asked Daddy for a picture. Yasmine would be dark-haired, no doubt, and small. Maybe with one of those red paint splotches between her eyes. If more than one Middle Eastern young woman had arrived on this flight, Natalie was going to be in big trouble.

Natalie hauled it across the lobby toward baggage claim. Her platform clogs made it hard to run, but she couldn't stand to leave them in the closet this morning. When you got new shoes, you were supposed to wear them. It was a rule somewhere. Besides, at five-foot-four she needed the extra inches.

Should have made a sign. Wait. Good idea. She dug in her purse—a little red-beaded wrist bag, barely big enough to carry a lipstick and a credit card—until she found a folded-up program from *Annie*, which she'd attended at the Orpheum last night. Clinique Crimson Tide lip pencil came next.

By the time she reached baggage claim, she had the program covered in crooked red letters: YASMINE P. Smiling and holding the program above her head, she took up a station facing the hallway where deplaning passengers entered the baggage claim area. A stream of tourists and home folks trickled by.

She caught the eye of a businessman in a tired-looking suit. "Excuse me. Were you on Flight 57 from Amsterdam?"

"Huh?" The man glanced at her over his shoulder. "Yeah. First one off the plane."

Considering the Patel fortune, Yasmine had probably flown first class, too, and shouldn't be far behind. Natalie could spring for a late lunch at Mickey-D's. Or maybe Ruby Tuesday. Daddy wouldn't mind paying.

A couple of old women in polyester pants outfits shuffled by. Then a cluster of teenagers, apparently home for spring break. Natalie waited, dancing with impatience—and aching insoles— on her cork platforms. Maybe she'd take them off and pretend she was a model some other time.

One clog in hand, she spied a dark young woman hesitating behind a middle-aged couple in matching "I Love Holland" T-shirts. The girl wore a long, silky apple-green tunic over loose-fitting matching leggings. Shiny black hair peeked out from under a diaphanous embroidered shawl, and intricate beaded earrings swung against her fragile jawline. A series of thin gold bangles jingled on one wrist, and a diamond pendant sparkled at her throat. Wow. Exquisite.

But the big black eyes were shadowed with fatigue, the full mouth turned down at the corners. The twelve-hour flight must've been a killer.

"Yasmine!" Natalie waved the program. She dropped her shoe and tried to shove her foot in it before Yasmine disappeared. "Yasmine Patel!"

The young woman stopped, passengers swarming around her like bees around a particularly exotic orchid. She stood on her toes and caught Natalie's gaze. Her eyes flicked up to the improvised sign, then widened. She looked over her shoulder and bolted around the Holland tourists—away from Natalie.

Natalie got her shoe on without twisting her ankle. "Yasmine! Hey, it's me, Natalie Tubberville. I'm your ride!" She dodged a mom pushing a baby stroller and caught up to her passenger. "Aren't you Yasmine?" She swung around in front of the Pakistani girl, forcing her to stop. Good grief, she was a little thing. Natalie felt positively gargantuan.

Yasmine's shoulders slumped. "I am Yasmine Patel." She smiled reluctantly, showing small, perfect white teeth. "You are sent for me?"

"Sure am." Natalie held out a hand.

Yasmine offered her slim, elegant fingers. "So happy. Thank you for coming." Extravagant black lashes swept downward. "I am feeling ... some lost."

Natalie tried to peg the accent. A bit sing-song, infused with a British twang. Sophisticated, compared to her own Tennessee drawl, but definitely wobbly. Natalie's heart softened. Maybe the girl was acting weird because she'd expected her fiancé to meet her.

"Well, come on, let's snag your luggage, and I'll buy you some lunch. You hungry?" She took off toward baggage claim.

Yasmine tip-tapped along beside Natalie on jeweled sandals. "Thank you, I am not hungry, just—please, could you slow down?"

"Good grief, I'm sorry." Natalie slowed, looking down at her diminutive companion, who was panting like a Pekeapoo on a leash. "Wasn't thinking."

"It is no worry. But I would like a drink of ..." Yasmine took a deep breath, as if coming to a monumental decision. "Starbucks. Yes, caramel vanilla macchiato, if you please. Whole milk with a packet of Splenda. Whipped cream on top."

Natalie blinked. Yasmine hadn't seemed to be the demanding type. "Starbucks?" That was going to add fifteen minutes onto her wait for lunch. She switched the mental list around and decided on Carrabba's for lunch. Big juicy steak with Caesar salad on the side. Daddy owed her big-time for this.

Yasmine looked up at her with huge, limpid near-black eyes. "I did not see a Starbucks sign somewhere? I thought all American airports—"

"Of course there's a Starbucks. No problem. This way." Natalie made a U-turn.

"No, no. Please." Yasmine clutched Natalie's arm. "You get it while I find my luggage. We shall save time." She linked her fingers under her chin. There was a solitaire rock the size of Baghdad on her engagement finger. "Please? I am anxious to see my—my fiancé, but I am sooo thirsty."

Okay, kinda different, but what do I know? Natalie sighed. "All right. You go on to baggage claim, get a skycap to help you, and I'll be right back." Natalie backed toward the refreshment center. "No problem."

"Whipped cream," she muttered as she limped into Starbucks and stood in line for what seemed like an hour. Tweetie was pointing to five-thirty by the time she'd ordered, recklessly adding a double mocha espresso for herself. She'd be awake all night, but then half the time she was anyway. Life was too interesting to waste it sleeping. *Carpe diem.*

She sat down at a little round table to contemplate her guest's odd behavior. Maybe she'd been raised in a harem. No, that was Mesopotamia.

Ten minutes later, she had laid a trail of Splenda packets in the form of a giant yellow *N* when she noticed the counter clerk craning his neck. "Caramel vanilla macchiato and a double mocha espresso?"

Natalie jumped up and snatched the drinks along with a handful of the yellow packets. Surely Yasmine had her luggage in hand by now. Coming from that far away, planning to stay and get married, the Pakistani girl probably had a ton of clothes. Unless she planned to do some serious trousseau shopping. Natalie brightened. She could offer to help with the shopping.

She walked fast, sipping the espresso and wincing at the pain in her feet. The clogs were staying in the closet tomorrow, new or not. There was the carousel for Yasmine's flight, a few pieces of luggage still going round and round. She scanned the crowd. No bright-green tunic and shawl. Just plain everyday American T-shirts, suits, and baseball caps.

Natalie could've sworn she'd told Yasmine to wait in baggage claim, but maybe she'd gone outside.

She circled the area one more time, then, sipping espresso for fortitude, stomped toward the exit. Chasing the girl all over the airport hadn't been part of the agreement. Daddy owed her dinner at the country club and a movie. Nothing less.

A line of taxis waited outside. People were stowing luggage in trunks, paying off drivers. "Yasmine?" Natalie called uncertainly.

Her eye caught a flash of apple-green disappearing into a white van parked at the Northwest Airlines entrance. The van's side door slammed from the inside, the end of a gauzy scarf catching in the crack.

Holy schmoly. Yasmine had gotten into a complete stranger's van. What was she thinking? Panic shot from the soles of Natalie's feet straight into her chest.

"Yasmine!" She took off running, heedless of whipped cream and hot coffee sloshing out of the tops of the two cups. "Ow!" Her purse dangled on her wrist, swaying wildly. Her feet screamed with pain. If she fell and broke her neck it would serve her right. She should've worn jeans and sneakers today. A denim miniskirt was completely inappropriate apparel for chasing heiresses.

The van pulled out into the drive, headed for the exit. Natalie chugged faster, beginning to pray. *Oh, Lord, what's going on?* She kicked off the shoes, tossed aside the coffee, and bore down. Her final Little League baseball all-star game flashed through her brain.

Pitcher Natalie Tubberville rounds third and heads for home. The centerfielder makes the throw. She slides to avoid the catcher's mitt. Her hand swipes at the corner of the plate and misses. She's out!

The van wheeled out of sight, pouring diesel smoke into the sweet Memphis-in-May air.

When Daddy found out she'd misplaced the heiress-bride, he was going to disinherit her.

Lovely.

Matt Hogan was giving fasting a whirl. Test-drive it around the block, see what happened.

Dad would probably say he was being sacrilegious at worst, flippant at best, but a guy couldn't be too careful. Even with God.

After all, he reasoned as he loitered by the hostess station at the Rendezvous, there was some verse or other about trying God and proving him faithful. Not a clue where that was, or what it actually said, but Dad had drummed enough Scripture into him by the time he'd gotten out of high school, that he'd headed straight for the closest pigpen—metaphorically speaking. Now that he was out, the Word stuck, marching through his mind at random times. He was finally learning to apply it.

The wood smoke smell of the place made him glad he hadn't chosen to swear off food. Eddie Tubberville had offered to feed him today, and Matt was looking forward to tucking into some ribs. But he wished he'd decided to forego something besides women. The blonde seated across from his new business partner wasn't bad.

Tubberville was a piece of work all right. Granted, the guy was single—divorced, to be precise—but the girl looked young enough to be his daughter. Cute, in a clean-scrubbed kind of way. Not at all the type Matt would've picked for a highroller like Tubberville. The cornsilk hair was chopped off chin length, tucked behind one ear. Little black glasses perched on a button nose, and a dimple flashed beside her mouth when she talked. Which was a lot.

Not Matt's type either, come to that. Fasting from women was no sweat. At the moment, anyway.

He checked the hang of his old blue sport coat, worn with khakis and a faded yellow polo. He needed to impress Tubberville, his new partner in River City Investigations. Bankruptcy had sat on the horizon, ready to sail into port, and Tubberville had interceded with the guns of big money.

Deep breath, Hogan. Swagger over like you own the place.

As he approached Tubberville's table, the blonde's hands circled. "Daddy, I'm telling you, she just disappeared! The van was gone before I could take a breath. What was I supposed to do?"

Daddy? So Tubberville wasn't such a sleazeball as he'd thought.

Tubberville's back was to Matt, so he took advantage of the distance to listen in.

"I'll tell you what you were supposed to do," Tubberville barked. "You were supposed to go to the airport, hold up a sign, and take her to her hotel. How can you possibly lose a woman in a lime-green harem costume?"

"She wanted coffee, and I was trying to be hospitable! How would I guess she'd abscond with a couple of yahoos in an electrical van?"

Matt cleared his throat.

Tubberville turned around. "Hogan! There you are." He stood up and offered a handshake. "I'm afraid you've walked in on a situation here. Meet my daughter Natalie. Natalie, this is Matthew Hogan. He runs the PI agency I was telling you about."

Matt nodded.

Natalie sort of grimaced, as if she wasn't sure whether she should smile or not, then gave her attention back to her dad. "Anyway, she *knew* I was there to pick her up. I mean, there was the Orpheum playbill and everything!"

Matt had no idea what a theater program had to do with a missing harem princess. He was more interested in the fact that this girl had ignored him. Women did not ignore him. He stuck his hand in front of her face. "Pleased to meet you, Miss Trouble — uh, Tubberville."

She looked down at his hand, then up at his face. Behind the glasses, her eyes were a pale, black-shot green, with black lashes and eyebrows. Cat eyes. Reluctantly she shook his hand, a glint of humor tugging the corner of her mouth. "Me too. Have a seat and join the fray."

"You don't know how true that is," Tubberville growled. "The trouble part, I mean. This girl's been making chaos out of order since she rode her bicycle into the school building in kindergarten."

"Daddy!" Natalie's bottom lip stuck out.

Matt grinned. "Catch me up. Who's gone missing?"

"Daughter of a business client of mine, Abez Patel. The girl's name is Yasmine. She was set to marry a young man she's been engaged to since birth. Guy named Vinay Kumar."

"I take it these people are Middle Eastern." Matt looked up as a waitress brought him a glass of water and a menu. "Thanks."

"No problem," said the waitress, giving him a gratifying once-over. "I'll give you a few minutes to look at the menu."

"Just bring me the ribs special with a Coke." He looked at Tubberville. "You guys order yet?"

"We were about to. Triple that order, little lady." Tubberville dismissed the waitress with a wave.

Natalie bristled. "But, Daddy—"

"You know you always order ribs, so don't get all snotty on me." Tubberville glanced at Matt, a twinkle lurking in his eyes. "Girl eats like a football team and still has to run around in the shower to get wet. Burns up a thousand calories a day flapping her mouth."

Natalie's face flamed. "If I could get a word in edgewise, I'd remind you I haven't had a bite since dawn. I was going to take Yasmine to dinner."

Matt, who considered himself a connoisseur, could see little to complain about in Natalie's figure, even if she was a little on the skinny side. She had on a modest red knit top that complemented her pale, shiny hair and clear English-rose complexion. For some reason he felt like coming to her defense.

"Everybody loses a bride occasionally," he said mildly. "What's the big deal?"

"The big deal is Abez Patel's honor, not to mention a three-million-dollar oil account." Tubberville glowered. "We don't find her, we're all going to be on the skids. Including you, Hogan."

"Me? What's it got to do with me?"

"If I take a hit on this thing, I'll have to fold the agency. Can't afford a losing investment." Tubberville folded his arms.

"Huh? Tubberville, you can't fold my agency!"

"Since I own 55 percent of the company, I certainly can."

"Whoa. Just hold the bus right now!" Matt's stomach did a three-sixty flip. He glanced at Natalie, who was staring at her dad open-mouthed. "I let you buy in to help me get back on my feet—not to blow me down like a tornado."

"Daddy! You own a detective agency?" Natalie's voice rose on an excited squeak. "I didn't know that!"

"That's because it's none of your business," Matt said, raising his eyebrows. "It's my company. I started it, and I run it. Your dad's just the—the CFO."

"I have legal controlling interest, which means I hold the purse strings. And here's what you're going to do if you want River City Investigations to stay in the Yellow Pages. You're going to find Yasmine Patel and bring her back for her wedding."

Matt considered himself a fairly phlegmatic sort of guy. Took quite a jolt to upset his apple cart. Plus, he'd recently surrendered his life to God. So he gripped the edge of the table. "You're not my boss, Tubberville," he said quietly. "You can't tell me what to do."

Tubberville leaned back, flicking his napkin open as the waitress appeared with a loaded tray. "I just did."

"Daddy, let me!"

Both men looked at Natalie, whose eyes were wide, hands clasped under her chin.

"Let you what?" Tubberville's gaze slid to Matt. The tension in the atmosphere was as thick as the odor of barbecue pork and onion rings.

"Let me find her. I'm a trained detective. For goodness' sake, I have a degree!"

Matt snorted. "In what? Cosmetology?"

Natalie's translucent skin flushed from her collarbone to her hairline. "I'll have you know," she said through gritted teeth, "I graduated magna cum laude from the University of Memphis with a degree in criminal justice. I've been working for the sheriff's department down in Tunica for the past two years, and I passed the detective's exam last week."

"Is that right?" Matt grinned. "Well, maybe you *should* go looking for the sultan's daughter—especially since you're the one who lost her!"

"Now wait just a minute—"

"Hold on, you two." Tubberville grabbed his daughter's wrist. "Take a deep breath, honey."

Matt looked from one to the other. He had signed a contract which gave a major portion of his agency to Tubberville. It had seemed like a good idea at the time. Now—not so much.

He tried to regroup. "Suppose I do go looking for this girl. Are you going to pay my expenses?"

"I won't have to. Abez Patel will pay a chunk of change to get his daughter back. From what Natalie says, we don't know if Yasmine left on her own or if she was kidnapped."

"Kidnapped?" Matt frowned. "Why don't you just bring in the police?"

"Because it's a touchy situation. Abez has enemies and allies all over the Middle East. We alert the authorities, and we risk getting the feds involved with what could be just a family scandal.

Until we know why Yasmine left, Abez wants to keep it a private search."

"You mean the guy already knows his daughter's missing?" Matt shook his head. This ball of yarn just kept getting more snarled.

Tubberville nodded grimly. "He knows. And he's not happy."

Natalie shook off her father's grip on her wrist. "It *is* my fault. I'm going to find her."

Matt looked at her impatiently. She had set her chin, and the soft lips quivered. Playing the femininity card. His sympathy for her dissolved. "This is a professional investigation. I don't think the Tunica sheriff's department is going to want to let go of their secretary."

"You are an insufferable pig." Her eyes blazed like peridots under a jeweler's lamp. "But I'm going to assume you're upset and ignore you." She turned to her father. "Dad, look, I know I can find her. I'm a woman, and I can figure out how she'll think. Besides—" she glared at Matt—"I actually care."

Tubberville rubbed his chin, then absently picked up a rib. "Maybe you're right. It might be effective to have a woman working on the case, too. What do you think, Hogan?"

"I think—what—what do you mean, what do I think? I think you're crazy." Matt wanted to howl with laughter. He was supposed to work with a little girl who looked like Gidget and—magna cum laude or not—seemed to have the attention span of an ADHD flea?

Tubberville dropped the rib bone onto his plate and wiped his mouth. "Well, it doesn't matter what you think after all. It's my company. Or rather, mine and Natalie's. I bought it with the intention of setting her up to be your partner and giving her 25 percent if she decides she likes it. So work with her or take your agency into bankruptcy—and I'll hire another PI to find Yasmine."

Fireworks

Elizabeth White

Susannah is out to prove that pyrotechnics genius Quinn Baldwin is responsible for a million-dollar fireworks catastrophe during a Mardi Gras ball.

With her faithful black Lab Monty, she moves to the charming backwater city of Mobile, Alabama, to uncover the truth. But this world-traveled military brat with a string of letters behind her name finds herself wholly unprepared to navigate the cultural quagmires of the Deep South.

Captivated by the warmth and joy of her new circle of friends, Susannah struggles to keep from falling for a subject who refuses to be anything but a man of integrity, compassion, and lethal southern charm. *Fireworks* offers a glimpse into the heart of the South and a cynical young woman's first encounter with Christlike love.

Softcover: 0-310-26224-0

Pick up a copy today at your favorite bookstore!

Fair Game

Elizabeth White

Jana Cutrere's homecoming to Vancleave, Mississippi, is anything but dull. Before she's even reached town, the beautiful young widow hits a stray cow, loses her son in the woods, rescues an injured fawn, and comes face to face with Grant Gonzales, her first high school crush.

Grant recently returned to town himself amid hushed controversy. His only plan: leave the corporate world behind and open a hunting reserve. Seeing Jana again ignites old memories ... and a painful past. Tensions boil over when he learns exactly why she returned. Jana plans to convince her grandfather to develop a wildlife rescue center – dead center on the prime hunting property he promised to sell to Grant!

With deadlines drawing near for the sale of the property and no decision from her grandfather, can Jana trust God with her and Grant's future, or will explosive emotions and diametrically opposing views tear them apart?

Softcover: 0-310-26225-9

Pick up a copy today at your favorite bookstore!

ZONDERVAN®
.com

Three ways to keep up on your favorite
Zondervan books and authors

Sign up for our *Fiction E-Newsletter*. Every month you'll receive sample excerpts from our books, sneak peeks at upcoming books, and chances to win free books autographed by the author.

You can also sign up for our *Breakfast Club*. Every morning in your email, you'll receive a five-minute snippet from a fiction or nonfiction book. A new book will be featured each week, and by the end of the week you will have sampled two to three chapters of the book.

Zondervan *Author Tracker* is the best way to be notified whenever your favorite Zondervan authors write new books, go on tour, or want to tell you about what's happening in their lives.

Visit *www.zondervan.com* and sign up today!